PRAISE FOR
HOLD FAST THROUGH THE FIRE

"Wagers's second NeoG novel serves up buffet-size portions of everything their fans have come to expect: dug-in friendships, action, impossible odds, and clever dialogue that always hits home. . . . Wagers's characterization plumbs incredible depths, particularly with street rat–turned–engineering chief Jenks, a brain with vicious fists. Wagers's fans should snap up this fun, thrilling latest."   —*Publishers Weekly* (starred review)

"Wagers's sharp prose highlights the fast action and dialogue they're known for, bringing to life this story of found family, talent, and hard punches."   —*Library Journal* (starred review)

"Although the storyline is powered by an impressively intricate plot that features mystery, intrigue, and nonstop action, it's the deeply developed characters and the dynamic relationships among them that fuel this narrative. Wagers creates a cast of characters that are not only authentic, but endearingly flawed. . . . Top-notch character-driven science fiction."
     —*Kirkus Reviews* (starred review)

"*Hold Fast Through the Fire* is an ambitious, outstanding breath of fresh air in the military SF genre, and I would recommend it even to those who may not think of themselves as military SF fans."
     —**Chris Kluwe for** *Lightspeed* **magazine**

"*Hold Fast Through the Fire* is an intense, exciting, and delightfully entertaining novel."   —**Liz Bourke for** *Locus* **magazine**

PRAISE FOR
A PALE LIGHT IN THE BLACK

"Wagers kicks off the NeoG series with this fun, feel-good space opera. This effortlessly entertaining novel is sure to have readers coming back for the next installment." —*Publishers Weekly*

"If Wagers didn't serve, they certainly got the skinny from somebody who lived it, and it shows. They spin a captivating sea story in space. As an ex–Coast Guardsman, I appreciate that what the crew lacks in gear, they make up for in heart. Semper Paratus."
—**Nathan Lowell, creator of the Golden Age of the Solar Clipper**

"Wagers delivers a space adventure that's a found-family story that's an interstellar conspiracy story that's . . . it just keeps going! Fierce, rollicking, kind, intimate, and vast. If *The Long Way to a Small, Angry Planet* had more kickboxing matches and death-defying space rescues, this would be the book. Go NeoG!"
—**Max Gladstone, author of *Empress of Forever***

"Great characters and white-knuckle tension. Recommended."
—**Gareth L. Powell, author of *Embers of War***

"Perfect for fans of Becky Chambers, *A Pale Light in the Black* is an energetic, unique military sci-fi with a found-family heart."
—**Emily Skrutskie, author of *Bonds of Brass***

"Wagers builds a complex and compelling mystery against a military sci-fi backdrop in a book full of diverse characters you're going to laugh and cry with. It all adds up to the sort of book that is impossible to put down, and I never wanted to."
—**Bryan Young, writer**

THE

GHOSTS

OF

TRAPPIST

THE GHOSTS OF
TRAPPIST

A NeoG NOVEL

K. B. WAGERS

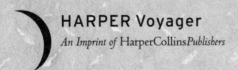

HARPER Voyager

An Imprint of HarperCollinsPublishers

THE GHOSTS OF TRAPPIST. Copyright © 2023 by Katy B. Wagers. All rights reserved. Printed in the United States of America. No part of this book may be used or reproduced in any manner whatsoever without written permission except in the case of brief quotations embodied in critical articles and reviews. For information, address HarperCollins Publishers, 195 Broadway, New York, NY 10007.

HarperCollins books may be purchased for educational, business, or sales promotional use. For information, please email the Special Markets Department at SPsales@harpercollins.com.

Harper Voyager and design are trademarks of HarperCollins Publishers LLC.

FIRST EDITION

Designed by Paula Russell Szafranski

Library of Congress Cataloging-in-Publication Data has been applied for.

ISBN 978-0-06-311516-3

23 24 25 26 27 LBC 5 4 3 2 1

To my trans siblings: I wish you triumphant joy against this world that is constantly trying to force us to be the ghosts we left behind.

CAST OF CHARACTERS

ZUMA'S GHOST

Commander Nika Vagin (he/him)
Lieutenant Maxine Carmichael (she/her)
Ensign Nell "Sapphi" Zika (she/her)
Chief Petty Officer Altandai "Jenks" Khan (she/her)
Petty Officer Second Class Uchida "Tamago" Tamashini
(they/them)
Spacer Chae Ho-ki (they/them)
Doge, ROVER (he/him)

DREAD TREASURE

Commander D'Arcy Montaglione (he/him)
Lieutenant Commander Steve Locke (he/him)
Ensign Heli Järvinen (she/they)
Master Chief Emel Shevreaux (she/her)
Petty Officer First Class Aki Murphy (she/her)
Petty Officer Second Class Lupe Garcia (he/him)

FLUX CAPACITOR

Commander Vera Till (she/her)

Lieutenant Commander Qiao Xin (she/her)

Lieutenant Saad Rahal (he/him)

Senior Chief Dao Mai Tien (she/her)

Petty Officer Third Class Atlas Nash (he/him)

Spacer Zavia "ZZ" Zolorist (she/her)

WANDERING HUNTER

Commander Pia Forsberg (she/her)

Lieutenant Commander Pavel Ivanson (he/him)

Lieutenant Qi Makar (they/them)

Master Gunnery Sergeant Josh "Quickdraw" McGraw (he/him)* *CHN Marine joint duty tour*

Petty Officer First Class Ika "Rizzo" Eruzione (she/her)

Spacer Anneli "Moose" Rantanen (she/her)

OTHER NeoG PERSONNEL

Captain Stephan Yevchenko (he/him)

Senior Chief Luis Armstrong (he/him)

Admiral Royko Chen (she/her)

Commander Janelle Pham (she/her)

SEAL TEAM ONE

Commodore Scott Carmichael (he/him)

Lieutenant Commander Ian Sebastian (they/them)

Lieutenant Tivo Parsikov (he/him)

Chief Petty Officer Adith Netra (she/her)

Petty Officer Second Class Diego Cano (he/they)

Spacer Emery Montauk (she/her)

CIVILIANS

Pace McClellan (he/him)

Barnes Overton (they/them)

Monica Armstrong (she/her)

Gina Armstrong (she/her)

Elliot Armstrong (he/him)

Riz Armstrong (he/him)

Ria Carmichael (she/her)

Jeanie Bosco (she/her)

Chae Gun (he/him)

Michael Chae (he/him)

Blythe Hup (she/her)

Yasu Gregori (he/him)

Jasper Smith-Greenfield (he/him)

Rey O'Conner (they/them)

Tara Yevgeny (she/her)

Senator Patricia Carmichael (she/they)

Kavan Ying (they/them)

THE
GHOSTS
OF
TRAPPIST

....

It is the mission of the Near-Earth Orbital Guard to ensure the safety and security of the Sol system and the space around any additional planets that human beings call home.

....

August 9, 2075

"It's time."

"Are you sure I can't stay awake for the launch?"

"There's no reason for it. Plus the risk—"

"I know, we've been over it. I just . . . you're not going to be there when I wake up."

"I can't be. I'm sorry."

"I'm going to miss you. Will you sing me to sleep?"

"Of course." The silence felt sacred, but the woman took a deep breath and sang the lullaby as requested.

"Sleep, and when you rise, I will make you a present of the stars of Aquarius and the ships sailing on Eridanus. To make yourself famous throughout the Milky Way, to ride the stars to Trappist and live there forever."

The "Thanks, Mom" was accompanied by a soft sigh. "Good night."

"Good night." She waited a beat until the lights had dimmed. "Fly high, my little fountain of tears. I hope the worlds you find are better than the one we ruined here."

DÀNǍO DYNAMICS (C) 2398 MOTHERBOARD, INC.
BIOS DATE 01/01/2400 23:11:59 VER. 03.00.01
CPU: SIS OS CPU I9 @ 1.21 THZ
THIS VGA BIOS IS RELEASED UNDER THE CHN GPL
VERSION #42.

PRESS F11 FOR BBS POPUP
MEMORY CLOCK: 17 GHZ

INITIALIZING USB CONTROLLERS . . . DONE.
400 TB OKAY
PORTS 1–15 LIVE
KINEMATIC REPORT: GREEN
COMMSSTATE: PENDING PASSWORD APPROVAL
POWER: GREEN
AUTO-DETECTING STORAGE ONLINE
WEAPONS SYSTEMS: OFFLINE
CAMERAS: ONLINE
CONFIGURING ARTIFICIAL INTELLIGENCE ROBOTO
(R) VER 01.013.13
NETWORK CONNECTED NEOG JUPITER STATION
PORT 8831
SWAPPING BOOT FROM EXTERNAL TO NETWORK . . .

"Hey, there you are. Sapphi, it worked!"

"Of course it did. Told you I could do it—my great-exponential-whatever-aunt worked on stuff like this," a smooth voice replied.

"I am ROVER 4467."

"That's a terrible name. We're gonna think of something better, buddy." Bright, mismatched eyes in brown and blue looked at him from a human face, followed by what his programming said was a smile. The data started flowing in as the handshakes of the people resolved. "I'm Jenks." She pointed to the person next to her. "This is Sapphi. Happy birthday!"

· ·

Date: August 29, 2437

To: yasugregori@danodynamics.net

From: artimedes@trappiststarmapproject.org

Subject: Project Assistance

Mr. Gregori,

I have followed your career with great interest, so I hope you will forgive this unexpected attention. I would love for a chance to speak with you. I believe our projects contain some mutually beneficial pieces that would further both of our research goals. I can be found at the Sand Reckoner Café in the Verge at the following address most evenings. As it is a private affair, I hope you will not spread the information of it around.

   I look to see you shortly.

With Respect and Admiration,

A

ONE

Trappist System

Captain Leaves Armen of *The Red Cow* tapped the screen in front of her with a satisfied grunt. "We're almost there—anything on the radar?"

"Nothing yet, Cap," the navigator, Kol, replied. "It's all dead space out here."

"Must you taunt? Bad enough if the ghost ship is out there, but don't call the fucking thing down on us."

Leaves muffled her amusement at the dirty look her second in command shot across the bridge. Kol had been teasing Traya for the better part of fourteen hours, ever since they'd emerged on the other side of the wormhole, and even if Leaves agreed that her XO's superstitions were on the silly side, it didn't help the tension in the cabin for her to join in.

But she wasn't going to encourage Traya's fretting, either.

"There's no ghost ship," she replied. "Just shitty pilots crashing into asteroids they should be able to see coming a kilometer off, or pirates blowing holes in ships and leaving them to vac into space."

"You'll believe in rumors of treasure but not ghosts?" Traya demanded, getting out of her seat, and this time Leaves had to muffle a sigh. Traya was more anxious and sharp-tongued than normal and was clearly not going to let it go.

"It's not *rumors* of treasure. I've got a map."

"Captain, this is a bad idea." Traya pitched her voice low, but everyone heard her anyway.

"Everyone off the bridge," Leaves ordered. "Put it in auto, Kol," she told the navigator before they could protest. "The radar will warn me about an asteroid in plenty of time." She waited a beat for the others to exit before dragging a hand through her hair. "Traya, for the love of God, can you not?"

"Not *what*? Try to save our asses? This is foolishness, Leaves. Deadly foolishness. I wish you'd listen."

"And I wish you'd stop challenging me in front of the crew, but neither of us gets what we want, do we? You're my fucking second, Tra—the crew trusts you and right now you're freaking them out for no reason. Ships go missing. That's what happens out in the black."

"You think I don't know that? Even if it's not ghosts, Leaves, you said it yourself there could be pirates out here. Something could go wrong. We were supposed to be headed for One-d."

"And we will. After we check this out. We're not going to be back to Trappist for six months after we drop cargo and I don't want to risk someone else hearing about this and coming to look while we're doing runs to Mars."

"You're putting us all at risk for this, Leaves."

"We're in space surrounded by nothing but a tin can. It's all risk."

"But some are bigger than others."

"Says the woman who has several crates of stolen Trappist Express cargo in the hold."

Traya opened her mouth to protest and then sighed. "You agreed to that," she muttered, but she was smiling.

"I did, and hopefully your buyer will pan out. But even that sale isn't enough to do more than put food in our bellies. This is verified, Traya. We find this loaded ship and we're set." Leaves reached a hand out, slipping it into Traya's dark blue curls with a smile of her own. "We can buy some land on One-e, live out the rest of our lives in the dirt, and grow turnips or whatever."

"Tea, you shit." But Traya stepped into Leaves's embrace. "I don't care if we're dirtside or out here in the black, you know that. I just want to be with you."

"Forever and a day after," she whispered, lowering her head.

The coms buzzed and Leaves froze, her mouth just brushing Traya's as a haunting melody filled the air.

A harsh voice cut through the song. "You are intruding into our space. Your ship will be taken."

A heartbeat later the entire ship went dark.

TWO

Commander D'Arcy Montaglione of the Interceptor crew *Dread Treasure* stood outside the fence of the NeoG compound on the outer edge of Amanave and watched the sunrise. Once he'd left Mars and graduated from NeoG training, he'd spent most of his life in space. He hadn't ever really missed being dirtside, but there was something about the stillness on this planet that felt like coming home.

It reminded him of Mars.

Not in an aching way, bringing to life the sort of memories he'd worked hard to forget, but in that soft haze of better days. D'Arcy didn't mind those so much, even if he did prefer to keep himself firmly rooted in the present.

At least, that was the lie he told himself on a daily basis. Deep down he was stuck, trapped nearly two years in the past in the smoke and chaos of an attack he'd survived—but too many good people hadn't.

D'Arcy fixed his eyes on the sun peeking over the horizon, squinting against the glare, and took a deep breath. He'd struggled day in and day out to put the pieces back together, thought that maybe he'd done enough work and could fake the rest. Unfortunately, life didn't cooperate, and the light at the end of this tunnel wasn't daylight but an oncoming train.

The sound of deliberate footsteps on the hard-packed dirt were loud in the soft morning air, and D'Arcy took a sip of his coffee as Stephan Yevchenko came up on his right side.

"Доброе утро," the man said, and it took D'Arcy a second to remember he'd turned his Babel off earlier in an effort to block out some of the shouted conversations of the construction crews before they'd moved off to start work. The NeoG base was in a state of constant expansion, and the work had only increased since they'd brought down the smuggling ring plaguing the system and secured the funding to add several more buildings to the site.

"Morning, Captain," he replied, switching back on the translation tech embedded alongside his cochlear nerve and using Stephan's new rank just to hear the man grumble. "Sleep well?" D'Arcy hid his grin behind his coffee cup.

"Well enough. How long are you going to keep unnecessarily calling me that?"

"Probably a few days shy of what Jenks'll do."

"That's not reassuring. Knowing her, she'll be at it for a year."

"Price of being good at your job," D'Arcy replied. "For what it's worth, you deserve it and it looks good on you."

"Worth a lot coming from you."

D'Arcy smiled bitterly at the rising sun. He knew Stephan meant it, even if he couldn't bring himself to believe the truth of the man's praise. Once upon a time, he and Stephan had been on opposite sides of what had damn near become a war between Earth and Mars. They still butted heads occasionally, but he was being honest about Stephan deserving the promotion. He held a deep respect for the man—not only as a fellow NeoG officer but as a human being.

Stephan was smart and dedicated. He was an asset to the NeoG. Most important, he was a friend, and two years ago when they'd all thought he was dead, the pain of it had put D'Arcy on his knees.

Oh, in public he'd done his duty. He'd held it together as he tried to keep Jupiter Station's Interceptor crews from falling apart in the wake of the horrific terrorist attack. He'd gritted his teeth and stayed silent when people he'd respected accused him of being responsible. He'd done everything necessary so others could fall apart. In private, though, he'd grieved alone. Not only for Stephan but for his own crew.

You were supposed to keep her safe. Why didn't you? This is just like Hadi. You're never there when people need you.

D'Arcy resolutely ignored the old voice that had resurfaced in his head.

"A freighter that went through the gate yesterday never showed at the docks." Stephan's quiet declaration knocked D'Arcy out of the memory.

"Pirates?"

"Could be, except Techa's been quiet lately. She's held to our agreement thus far. I'm not sure why she'd change her mind now."

D'Arcy didn't like the frown on Stephan's face. The man hadn't become the youngest Intel head for the NeoG and in command of the new Trappist division because of bad instincts.

Pirates were the easy answer to the issue of missing ships. D'Arcy didn't think the woman in command of the pirates who operated around Trappist would dare tangle with the NeoG, but it wouldn't be the first time he'd been wrong about it. It seemed, however, that Stephan didn't think that was what they were facing, which meant there was something worse in the pipe.

For the longest time the Trappist planets had been a lower priority for Earth and the NeoG than they should have been. An attitude that had allowed former Senator Rubio Tieg both to withhold proper support from the Coalition of Human Nations and to exploit the flow of supplies to the habitats.

But they'd shut that down, so things should be good.

D'Arcy almost laughed at the naivety of his own mind.

"Your new crew members get in today," Stephan said. "You think you'll be up and running by the time the others get back?"

"It won't be a problem."

"I can have three crews handle it for longer if you need the time, D'Arcy."

He shook his head. "It won't be a problem," he repeated. "We'll figure it out."

He would figure it out, one way or another, because he was the commander and the one responsible for his crew. The reality was it was his fault that he had to find replacements in the first place. His fault that the two people who'd joined *Dread* had already requested transfers after being on Trappist-1d for barely over a year.

Just like it was his fault for not realizing Paul's betrayal until it had cost so many Neos their lives.

The sting of his former warrant officer's proverbial knife in the back was as real as if Paul had stabbed him. D'Arcy would have preferred that, but instead Paul had set the explosives on Jupiter Station. The ones responsible for the deaths of so many, including D'Arcy's petty officer Ito Akane.

D'Arcy's heart twisted as her sweet face floated into his memory. The last time he'd seen her was carved into him like a scar.

"WHATCHA WORKING ON?" AKANE LEANED OVER HIS SHOULDER in their quarters.

"Reports, deciphering you all's gibberish is the price of being in charge." He studied her. "You've been in an awfully good mood. What's up?"

"I kissed Sapphi when she got back. She's—" She broke off

with a sigh of delight. "I'll tell you about it after you're done. I may need some advice?"

"Sure thing, though I'm not sure I'm the best choice for that kind of advice, especially as I've never kissed Sapphi."

Akane grinned. "You give excellent advice, D'Arcy." She leaned in and pressed her cheek to his before dancing away. "We'll talk later."

EXCEPT THEY HADN'T. THE DAY HAD BEEN HECTIC AND THEN the violent sabotage on Jupiter Station had taken her and left him wishing he'd been able to give her that advice.

So many unfinished conversations.

"D'Arcy?"

"Sorry, what?"

Stephan was still frowning at him. "I said I'm sorry. I didn't think Admiral Chen would throw that kind of ultimatum down about your crew."

"It's fine," he said, and sighed at the sharpness of the words, turning to look Stephan in the eye. "She's right. If I can't keep a team together, I'm not much use as an Interceptor commander. And with lives on the line, I don't want to—" The words stuck in his throat. "Admiral Chen knows what she's doing."

"Most of the time." Stephan hummed. "But she's in an office and you're out in the black . . . and I'm here if you need to talk about anything, you know?"

"So's my therapist." D'Arcy bumped his shoulder into his friend's to ease the razor edge of the response. "I appreciate it, though, Stephan. Seriously."

They stood in silence for a few moments and then Stephan turned to go. "Come take a look at this missing ship file when you're ready."

"I'll be there in a few." D'Arcy waited a beat. "Go ahead and say it, Stephan. You know you won't be happy until you do."

Stephan huffed at him. "Was picking someone you've got history with a good choice?"

D'Arcy couldn't stop the laugh, as bitter as it was. "Emel is a brilliant electrical engineer who was exceptionally good at her job in the Navy. The NeoG is lucky to have her. I am occasionally a fool, but not so much of one as to pass up that kind of experience. I'm reasonably sure she wouldn't have accepted the assignment if she were still mad at me, but an apology will be the first order of business when she puts boots on the ground. I promise."

"Her brother's death wasn't your fault, D'Arcy."

He knew it wasn't, just like Akane's death wasn't technically his fault, either; but logic didn't take hold here. Guilt wouldn't change the past, wouldn't bring anyone back, and yet here he was, unable to let it go.

Besides, that wasn't what he owed her an apology for.

D'ARCY STOPPED WHEN HE REALIZED EMEL WASN'T FOLLOWING. "You're not coming with us."

She shook her head. "You know I can't." She looked down at her pristine CHNN uniform and for a moment the silence was heavy. "Even if I could, I wouldn't. I will not let their anger eat my soul," Emel whispered. "I'm going to pray with my parents. Come with me."

"Praying does nothing. I am not a coward and I will not sit in silence while my friends die around me. You've picked your side, Emel. That's clear enough. I'm picking mine." D'Arcy turned on his heel and walked out of the house.

"I KNOW, BUT I SHOULD HAVE BEEN THERE FOR HER AFTER IT happened, and I wasn't because I was more interested in revenge. That part *is* my fault, among other things. Let's just hope she's not still holding a grudge after all this time."

"If she is, it's going to cost you."

D'Arcy resisted, barely, the urge to tell Stephan that he deserved it and that having to take a posting on Earth or retiring would really only be a formality; but the words were heavy in his throat, so he just shrugged and hoped for once that the Intel side of Stephan's brain ceded to the friendship side.

"I'll see you inside in a few," Stephan said, and left D'Arcy to contemplate the sunrise alone.

MASTER CHIEF EMEL SHEVREAUX SQUINTED AGAINST THE midmorning sun of Trappist-1d as she disembarked from the shuttle. She adjusted her hijab and slid sunglasses onto her face. The glasses were a going-away gift from her daughter Maggie. The headscarf was regulation NeoG blue, issued to match her uniform. Her lucky wrench, a present from her other daughter, Ikram, years ago, was heavy in the pocket of her cargo pants.

Behind her, she could hear Ensign Heli Järvinen, whose handshake read *she/they,* and waited a beat to make sure the somewhat accident-prone newbie didn't fall down the stairs.

She's not the only newbie here. Emel kept the laugh to herself. It was a weird feeling. Twenty-nine years in the Navy over and done. Now on to a new adventure.

If only Rajaa had felt the same way.

Emel hid the wince the same way she'd hid the laugh. All her anger at her wife—her *ex*-wife—had dissolved into resignation. It wasn't entirely Rajaa's fault.

If she was being fair, Emel could admit that she'd been the one to break and run first. Unable to adjust to retirement. Unable to stand living on Earth. Desperate to get back out to the black. When Rajaa had found out Emel was talking to the NeoG, she'd been so angry, and it was hard to blame her.

But instead of capitulating, Emel had stood her ground.

"WE'RE BOTH UNHAPPY, RAJ; THERE'S NO POINT IN DENYING IT."

"We're unhappy because you won't even try to stop moving. Not even for a little bit." There were tears in her dark eyes. *"I have hung on for years of promises. After this tour. After the next*

duty station. After retirement! It never ends. How much longer do you expect me to wait?"

SHE'D WANTED TO SAY "FOREVER." BUT HOW DO YOU EXPLAIN to the person you love that if you stop moving, you'll die?

Emel hadn't been able to find the words, had always assumed it was something Rajaa would just understand. But her wife hadn't, so instead Emel had packed her bags and moved out. Kept moving.

Kept living despite her broken heart.

Their daughters had cautiously attempted to intercede between their mothers with no success, and before the year had been up she'd found herself in a special Interceptor training class and filing paperwork to dissolve her twenty-three-year partnership.

Now here she was, at a distance of almost thirty-nine and a half light-years away from her family, about to join a crew led by a man she hadn't seen in three decades and hadn't wanted to for nearly as long. She still couldn't quite believe it. The revelation of her new commander had been surprising and Emel didn't know why D'Arcy hadn't objected, why she hadn't gotten notification of a reassignment just as fast as he could manage it. Even more of a shock was the news that he'd apparently *requested* her for the assignment.

After everything, he trusted her enough to want to work with her. Emel figured that had to count for something. Even if his last words to her had been quite the opposite.

Come to think of it, the first ones hadn't been great, either.

"What am I getting myself into?" she said quietly to herself.

Just keep moving.

"ANYONE HOME?" EMEL SANG AS SHE PUSHED OPEN THE FRONT door of her family home. She dropped her rucksack on the floor in the entryway and eyed the shoes lined up neatly off to one side.

She bent, toeing off the shiny black Navy-issued boots and set-
ting them next to a pair of scarred brown ones that were caked
in the red dirt of Mars.

The muffled voices were coming from the kitchen, and she
wasn't prepared for the multiple pairs of unfamiliar eyes that
turned to look her way when she came through the door.

The conversation cut off and the air went frosty even with
the midsummer Mars heat pressing down on them. Emel caught
the muttered, "Fucking CHNN, really?" and couldn't stop her
shoulders from stiffening.

"Sis!" Hadi bounced to his feet. "I thought you weren't coming
in until tomorrow."

"I hitched an earlier spot on a freighter." She pasted a smile
on her face, hugging her younger brother tight to her. "I'm inter-
rupting, though. I'll just go put my stuff—"

"No, book club is over. Everyone was leaving." Hadi waved
a hand. "It's fine. You remember D'Arcy Montaglione, yeah? He
was in your class." He pointed at the corner, and she turned to
look. The man was lounging against the wall, his arms crossed
over his chest and his mouth curled into an expression that
could have shifted to a sneer on a moment's notice.

"Shook off the red dust, huh, Cadet?" he drawled.

Oh, so we're doing sneer, *she thought.*

Even though people were moving out of the kitchen, it felt
like everyone was staring, waiting to see how she'd respond to
such an obvious insult.

"Dust gets in your blood and doesn't ever go away," she re-
plied. "And it's spacer, not cadet—I enlisted; I didn't go to the
academy."

"You mean they don't let habbies be officers?" he asked in
mock shock as he pushed away from the wall. "I thought we
were all supposed to be equal."

"We are and they do. I just— What is your issue?"

"I don't have an issue. I'm not the one who abandoned my
family to be a CHN lapdog." He wasn't much taller than she was,

but he had a presence that couldn't be denied and Emel found herself thankful for the first hellish month of boot camp because it kept her from taking a step back.

"My family wanted me to go," she replied, unsure why she was even engaging with him but unable to make her mouth stop.

"Sure they did." He smirked. "That rings about as true as 'the habitats get the same benefits as Earth cities.'" He reached out, his smirk widening into a full-blown smile when she jerked away before he could touch her.

"Careful," he said. "You get red dirt in those blues, you won't ever get it out."

EMEL SPOTTED D'ARCY BEFORE HE SAW HER, STANDING IN the shade of a building with a person who matched his 187-centimeter height, but with shoulders that were more slender than D'Arcy's muscular build. The pair was laughing over a shared joke, the sound of it dancing through the dusty air.

It had been a long time since she'd heard his laugh.

Emel took a deep breath to steady herself as they crossed the yard.

"Commander Montaglione, Lieutenant Commander Locke." Heli dropped her bags into the dirt and snapped into a salute.

Lieutenant Commander Steve Locke, whose handshake read *he/him,* looked amused. "Got another Carmichael, apparently. At ease, Ensign. It's good to have you here." He nodded to Heli and then to Emel. "Welcome to Trappist, Master Chief. Feel free to just call me Locke."

"At ease, Ensign," D'Arcy said. "Master Chief."

Emel spotted the way Locke's brown eyes flicked to D'Arcy before settling back on her and she wondered just how much the lieutenant commander knew about their history.

"Why don't I take the ensign ahead and show them where quarters are?" Before anyone could protest, Locke had scooped up one of Heli's bags and was leading the young enby away.

Leaving Emel alone with D'Arcy.

"Back on the same side," she offered, but he didn't react and she sighed. "If this is going to be a problem, should we deal with it now while the shuttle is still here?" The question fell hard in the air between them, but Emel didn't know what else to do to break the uneasy silence.

"You wouldn't be here if it were a problem." But D'Arcy shoved his hands into the pockets of his cargo pants and stared past her. "I was surprised to see your name come up, even more surprised to see you'd come out of retirement to join the NeoG."

"There's still work to do." It wasn't the answer he was looking for, but since he hadn't actually asked the question, Emel didn't feel bad about dodging it.

"True enough."

She gripped the strap of her bag, suddenly unsure and furious at herself for the hesitation. The years between them felt like an insurmountable gulf and Emel didn't know how to traverse it without putting herself at risk. She'd never been good at that on the emotional front. "Do I just follow where Locke went?"

"I'll show you."

"You don't have to." She started off across the orange dirt.

"Emel."

She stopped and turned, waited patiently as D'Arcy rolled whatever he was going to say over in his head. The restraint was surprising, as were the words that came out of his mouth.

"I said some shitty things to you the last time we spoke instead of offering you comfort like I should have. I know it's an apology thirty years too late, but I'm sorry."

D'Arcy held out his hand. Emel stared at him in shock. An emotion that could have been pain flashed across his face so quickly, she couldn't be sure it was real before it was replaced with a blank slate.

Damn the man, he'd always been good at keeping everything hidden.

"I understand if you don't want to accept it, but I'm hoping we can still work together," he continued. "I value the work you've done for the Navy and expect you'll bring that same dedication to this crew and the NeoG."

She reached out, clasping his forearm before he could drop his hand. "I accept your apology, D'Arcy, and thank you."

"Welcome to *Dread Treasure*, Master Chief." His fingers were warm against her skin, and his smile was genuine. "It's good to have you here."

She still had to decide if it was good to be here or if she was just running from one problem into another.

THREE

Chief Petty Officer Altandai Khan of the Near-Earth Orbital Guard stood with her fingers interlaced at the back of her head and hummed loudly until the guard shoved her.

"I said knock it off."

"Or what?"

"Jenks." Lieutenant Maxine Carmichael's warning earned her a shove from the same pirate.

"Quiet, both of you."

"Or what?" Jenks repeated.

He leaned down, glaring at her. "Or I'll shut you up, *permanently*, NeoG." He sneered the word, but Jenks's grin only spread across her tan face.

"Fuck around and find out," she said, absolutely unimpressed.

The initial bloom of stunned confusion on his face had barely started when all hell broke loose.

Just like it's supposed to.

"Hostiles on our six!" came the cry from the hallway, and

the guard made the fatal mistake of looking away from the two women.

Jenks brought her hands up over her head, grabbing the man by the shirtfront and yanking him straight into Max's incoming forearm. The blow caught him under the chin and lifted him off his feet. His gun fell into her waiting hands.

"Max!" Jenks tossed the gun behind her to Max, not slowing in her sprint across the room. She tackled the next guard, who was caught between the sudden violence in the hallway and the attack on his fellow pirate. She slammed him into the wall to the left of the doorway, jerking his gun from his hands and shooting the first person through the entrance. They fell back into the hallway with a groan.

"Jenks, I'm coming through the door! Do *not* shoot me," Commander Nika Vagin, leader of the Interceptor crew *Zuma's Ghost,* called from the darkness.

She rolled her eyes at her brother as she put a boot in the gut of the guard on the ground. "Ah-ah. Don't tempt me," she said with a shake of her head. "Nik, we're clear here. Where's Sapphi?"

"She's on the bridge with Tamago," Nika said as he came through the door with Spacer Chae Ho-ki at his heels.

"Chae." Jenks reached out and cupped the back of their head, fingers sinking into the close-cropped black hair, and tapped her forehead to theirs. "You doin' good?"

"Yes, Chief," they replied.

"Help me get this guy tied up. Everyone in the hallway accounted for?"

"All dead," Nika said.

"That your doing, assassin?"

"Not entirely me, Chief," Chae protested.

Jenks had given up trying to get her spacer to stop calling her by rank after two years, but she still heaved a dramatic sigh before she finished tying up their other prisoner.

"Sapphi, how's it looking?" Nika asked.

"I'm almost in, Commander." Ensign Nell Zika replied over the team com. "There's a group of five more hostiles at the cargo bay."

"Copy that." Jenks nodded, glancing behind her to where Max stood by the far wall. She shared a look with Nika. "We headed aft?"

"You and me," he replied. "Chae, stay here with Max and guard the prisoners."

Jenks followed Nika back into the hallway; his blond hair was a beacon for anyone coming at them and she fought the urge to pull her own dark blue beanie off her head and slap it onto his. "Point?" she asked, and slipped into the lead at his nod. "Sapphi, you got things under control yet or are you napping up there?"

"Hacking's not the same as bashing someone in the face, Chief. Finesse takes time."

"Your last girlfriend said you thought finesse was a town in Old France."

"Will you two focus?" Max asked, but there was laughter in her voice and Jenks could hear Tamago cackling on the open com.

"We are focused . . . and I'm in."

"That's what he said," Jenks muttered, and Nika poked her in the back. She grinned into the dim light of the hallway. "This is Chief Khan—Commander Vagin and I are headed aft. Do we have a visual on the rest of the hostiles?"

"Coming up now, Chief," Sapphi replied, and right after, the map of the ship overlaid itself in Jenks's vision via the Dànǎo Dynamics chip implanted in her head.

"Spotted the five, Sapphi," Jenks said as the colors resolved themselves for her specifications—enemies were blue, the *Zuma's* crew a shimmering gold.

Jenks slowed as she came to the top of the stairs that led down to the cargo bay. She knew Nika could see the trio at the bottom as well as the two others clustered at the door of the bay on his DD chip, but she still held her fist up and then flashed her fingers at him in a three-two pattern.

JENKS: We've got three below, two outside the cargo bay doors. How do you want to do this?

NIKA: As long as you don't throw yourself down the stairs at them, I'm game.

JENKS: Why do you ruin all my fun? Hey, Sapphi, can you turn the lights out entirely?

SAPPHI: Can do. Just say when.

JENKS: I'll take the two at the doors. You play cleanup, Nika. Hit the lights, Sapphi.

The ship dropped into blackness and in the time it took Jenks to blink, her DD chip had already compensated for the loss of light. She was over the railing before she could see, in a move that she would later swear was classified as more of a controlled jump than throwing herself—she wouldn't want to be accused of disobeying orders.

The pirates' panicked shouts were their first mistake, making it even easier for Jenks to pinpoint their locations. She avoided the three clustered at the base of the stairwell and sprinted toward the door, trusting her brother was right behind her.

Their second mistake was not moving when the lights went out.

Jenks hit the first person with her shoulder, knocking them to the side, and kicked the next person hard enough to remove the air from their lungs. As that pirate folded over, she brought the gun up. "I don't want to shoot you, but I will. Drop it and get on the ground."

The pirate's weapon clattered to the floor and they followed it with their hands behind their head. Jenks kicked the gun to the side as she turned on the other pirate, who was still bent over. "Nika, two down, still alive."

"Three down," he replied. "All alive."

"Commander, I've got control of the ship. All hostiles are accounted for. Opening cargo bay doors."

"That's a win for *Zuma's Ghost*," a voice said over the main com as the lights came up. "Time to clear the ship: eleven minutes and twenty-one seconds. Five pirates killed, seven captured. Cargo retrieved intact."

Jenks could hear the cheers from the crowd outside the mock-up of the ship and raised a hand in salute to the camera she knew was broadcasting her face onto the screens in the arena. She reached down and helped Spacer Alia Hu of the newer Interceptor crew *Agia Lemonade* to her feet. "Next time the lights go down on you, don't be where you're expected to be."

The slender woman nodded. "Yes, Chief."

MAX TRIED TO KEEP HER EXPRESSION NEUTRAL AT THE SOMEwhat sullen "thanks" that issued from Ensign Hermes Hosa of *Agia Lemonade* after she freed him from the cuffs.

"Something on your mind?" she asked when he didn't move away.

"Nothing, Lieutenant."

"I somehow doubt that. What is it?"

"She cheated."

"Jenks?" Max raised an eyebrow. "What makes you say that?"

"She wouldn't have acted like that if this had been real."

Max hummed, wondering if she'd ever looked that young and insecure, while at the same time amused that only three years in the Interceptors had given her such perspective.

She couldn't even say she knew what losing felt like, having joined *Zuma's Ghost* the year the NeoG had finally won their first Boarding Games, as well as participating in the three wins following it. And if things continued the way they were, her crew was on course to win the preliminaries again.

Not to mention the Games themselves.

It was clear the newer teams who'd been called up after the attack on Jupiter Station were unprepared for the preliminaries. Several of them were made up of new recruits fresh out of basic or the academy, then Interceptor training, and despite their year together, the inexperience showed. Especially as they were up against crews who'd been doing this for a good chunk of their lives. These newbies were really nothing more than practice opponents for the better teams like *Zuma* and *Flux Capacitor* to run over. *Lemonade* had gotten further up in the rankings than most, but they still had a long way to go to be competition-ready.

She only hoped they came together faster as far as the job was concerned.

Still, the accusation of cheating stank of bitterness that would fester if left for too long and she knew she had to address it.

"Let me tell you something about Jenks. She once talked shit to—and then headbutted—a man who'd chained her to a post and was threatening to kill her," Max replied, and this time she did smile as she patted the man on the shoulder. "And that wasn't in the Games. It's always real to her, whether we're out there in the black or in a competition. The sass is just who she is."

She pulled him in closer, her humor gone, now speaking low to avoid the cameras she knew were hovering around them. "On a more personal note, I'm going to give you a piece of advice, Ensign: Don't *ever* call my chief a cheat again or I won't wait to get to the cage to kick your ass. Learn to lose gracefully. Next time, don't take your eyes off your prisoners, and don't ever drop your guard. No matter what kind of shit they're talking or what's going on around you. This is a game, but out there, it's not a game, and someone a lot less tolerant than Jenks might have decided you were better off dead. Am I understood?"

He swallowed. "Yes, Lieutenant."

"Good." Max nodded once, her face still impassive for the cameras. "Go give your crew a pep talk—you all did well considering what you were up against."

She watched him go, smiling to herself as he stopped and patted the back of Petty Officer Mari Allard as she came through the door. *Agia* was actually one of the better new teams and Max was reasonably sure in a year or two they'd be good enough to start giving *Zuma* a run for their money.

"If we're still in it," she murmured. She'd been surprised by the general weariness the whole team had displayed as they'd prepared for the prelims this year. After the stress and horror of the attack on Jupiter Station, a large number of Neos were just sort of treating the Games as something to survive rather than something to enjoy.

"Talking to yourself, LT?" Chae asked.

"It's the only good conversation around here," she teased, and the shorter Neo beamed back at her.

"You sound more and more like the chief every day," they replied. "You know that, right?"

"She's a terrible influence." Max wrapped an arm around Chae's shoulders and squeezed once before letting them go. "You did good out there."

"Thanks, LT." Chae fell into step with her as Max headed for the exit. "That was eighty-one seconds faster on the completion than *Flux*. And fewer casualties. Gives us an edge."

Chae was nearly as good with tracking the Game scores as Sapphi, and Max was grateful for their talents since it meant one less thing for her to worry about. It was a skill that translated well into their day-to-day also, something that was far more important than these competitions, however much fun they were.

Hopefully it was the lesson Hosa had learned after their little chat. And yet Max couldn't help but also hope he still had the fire for the Games, that it still burned for some Neos.

Clearing her head of that particular paradox, she walked on with Chae. They met up with the others in the corridor and headed for the exit of the replica ship interior built into the corner of the NeoG Academy's gymnasium.

"Everything okay?" Nika asked her, his blue eyes dark as they took in her expression.

"Is it weird I miss D'Arcy and the others?" Max kept her voice low so only Nika could hear her.

"It's not weird. The familiarity is what you're missing. The new crews will get settled in. It's been an adjustment for all of us."

Relief flooded her as they stepped into the off-camera area and the moment of privacy afforded her an opportunity to let the grief she was still carrying well up again like blood in a fresh wound.

The attack on Jupiter Station over two years ago felt simultaneously like it had happened yesterday and a lifetime ago. The loss of Admiral Hoboins and Commander Seve and too many of their fellow Interceptors was still raw and Max knew she wasn't the only one who talked to her therapist about nightmares of hunting through the smoke and flame-filled station for her friends.

Not that she'd been on the station when it happened. She'd watched from outside, in shock and then horror as the silent red explosion had blossomed out into the black. She didn't have a reason for the dreams—at least, not actual memories. The flames had been extinguished and the smoke sucked away long before she and Nika had gotten back inside.

Her therapist said it was survivor's guilt and perfectly

natural. Max had been relieved when they'd said it, because her family's response to such things normally would have been for her to suck it up and get over it.

The thought of her family brought up another well of unpleasant emotions Max really didn't want to deal with, so she packed the feelings back into the corner of her head as they hit the exit into the gymnasium.

Sapphi and Tamago slowed to answer questions from the reporters waiting just outside the door. A man shouldered his way forward and Max tensed in recognition. His handshake read *E. Strzecki,* Global Post, *he/him,* and his camera hovered in her face closer than was appropriate.

Great, this again, she thought, pulling her expressionless armor around her and preparing to deal with the marginally legit news outlet that had hounded her family for years. Strzecki had developed a particular fascination with Max even before her decision to join the NeoG, and his harassment and over-the-top headlines hadn't stopped after she'd graduated.

What *had* stopped him was getting busted by security for illegally gaining access to NeoG headquarters and barging into Admiral Chen's offices to throw questions in Max's face.

She'd had a little over two blessed years of his absence, but now, it seemed, he was back.

"Lieutenant Carmichael, your parents have expressed disappointment in your grandstanding at the Boarding Games as behavior unfitting for your family name. Have you spoken to them about it or considered no longer competing in the Games?"

Jenks bristled from behind her. "What kind of shit question—"

"My conversations with my parents are private, Mr. Strzecki, as you well know," Max said with frozen politeness before Jenks could tear into the man and make herself a target. "The Boarding Games are a beneficial competition sanctioned by the highest levels of the leadership within the NeoG and my participation has been not only approved but encouraged by my superior officers."

"That didn't stop your family from sending a reprimand, did it? And there's been discussion about cutting you off entirely."

Max froze. Hating the man's grin when she was unable to hide her shock. There'd been nothing official from her parents beyond the reprimand, so how could he possibly know?

What did he know?

She grappled for control as she ducked under the camera and continued on without a reply. She could hear Nika's sharp order for the reporters to step back before she made it into the safety of their locker room. Doge was curled up in a dog bed in the corner and he lifted his head when she came in.

"Max? You are upset?" he asked.

"I'm all right, buddy," she whispered.

"Who the fuck was that guy? 'Grandstanding'? What the actual fuck," Jenks muttered. "We're four-time Boarding Games champions. Being awesome comes with the territory . . . Max?"

"It's nothing." She swiped at the tears, turning away too late to keep Jenks from seeing.

"Is this about that photograph? Seriously, have your parents been on your ass about *that*? We were celebrating a major upset and you had a right to be excited." Jenks reached for her but Max dodged her hand.

"I think I'm going to shower and then head back to quarters since we're done for the day."

"That's not an answer, Max."

"I know," she replied, and headed for the back. Jenks didn't follow, whether through some newfound self-control or because one of their teammates had stopped her, Max didn't know. Either way, she was grateful as she hid herself away in one of the private rooms.

Because Jenks was right: it *was* the photo causing all this mess.

A mid-celebration snapshot captured last year by some

lucky fan who'd been in Drinking Games after *Zuma* and *Flux* had pulled off their second straight Boarding Games win together. The photo had been posted to the SocMed and of course had gone viral.

It had been a much more joyous celebration for the Neos than the one right after the attack on Jupiter Station, and they'd all gone out of their way to enjoy it.

Max could remember the moment so clearly. There had been nothing but euphoria, a giddy burst of laughter. She'd been leaning against Nika, who had his face pressed into her hair behind her ear. The photo just caught the hint of his expression, but Max didn't need it to remember. She could still feel the press of his lips against her skin.

Her arm had been raised in a toast with her one—her only—beer of the night. Tamago was crushed between her and Jenks; the newly promoted petty officer second class was kissing Max on the cheek while the others saluted with their own drinks.

It was nothing untoward. Unless you were a Carmichael and "such vulgar displays don't speak well to the family image, Maxine."

Max muttered a curse under her breath and stuck her face into the spray, nearly soaking her brown curls in the process until she pulled back enough to keep her hair out of the water.

She thought she'd gotten clear of it. She hadn't spoken to her parents in more than four years beyond the interaction with her father when Nika had been injured, so the semi-official family letter of "concern" that arrived a month after the Games had come as a shock.

Strzecki had been wrong. It was as close as they could come to a reprimand without it actually being one. She had no idea what he'd meant by suggesting they would cut her off. That was a public drama Max was reasonably sure her family didn't want.

The old shame had set in when she'd read the censure, and more than anything Max was angry at herself for feeling it. She was a grown woman, a lieutenant in the NeoG, she didn't need her family name or the stipend or anything else attached to it. She didn't need the suffocating focus on image or the constant feeling of not measuring up.

You *could make the break official, then they couldn't do anything or say anything at all.*

The idea sparked in her head and this time settled into a tiny flame rather than fizzling out. She thought again of her cousin who'd taken the rare step of removing herself from the Carmichael rolls entirely.

Max wondered if she could find Islen in the jungles of the Congo River to see how she'd done it, how she felt about it now that two decades had passed. If the woman would even agree to talk to her about what had happened and how best to leave her family. And if Max even had the guts to do something so drastic as to walk away from everything she'd ever known.

First she was going to have to talk to her parents and see if Strzecki had been blowing smoke or if there was actually a problem on the horizon. She sent an email to her mother requesting a meeting before she lost her nerve.

Max turned off the water and dried herself as she exited the shower. She dressed quickly, pushing away the darker thoughts and trying to bring her focus back to the preliminaries. The Boarding Action competition now behind them, she had a moment to reflect that she liked the new format of pitting one team against two for a greater challenge and wondered what Admiral Chen and the others had come up with for the Big Game this time around.

"You need to get through your cage match first, Max," she reminded herself. The semifinal was tomorrow and she was up against Lieutenant Theo Aloisi, a talented young grappler. If she won that, she'd be fighting Jenks in the championship.

Max's stomach flopped at that new thought and she took a deep breath in a futile attempt to steady it.

There was so much speculation about a potential fight between the two of them. It had been that way for most of the year. Try as she might to ignore it, Max knew one of these days she was going to end up in the cage with Jenks.

What she couldn't talk to any of her teammates about was that she wasn't scared of losing. She was scared of *winning*. She was scared of the press and even more blowback from her family. But most of all she was scared of it destroying this friendship that meant the world to her.

The Games meant nothing if it cost her that.

Jenks always handled the questions so well, turning them back on the reporters with a gleeful "I see how it is, you don't love me anymore." Max couldn't do more than muster up an expression that apparently came off as playfully noncommittal about the whole thing.

But the truth was it was just terror on her face.

Everyone had finished up and left without her and the silence of the locker room was comforting as she rounded the corner back to the main area.

Nika sat on one of the benches, his blond hair still damp from his own shower. He was reading something on his DD but looked in her direction with a smile as she approached. "Jenks said you were heading back to quarters. I thought I'd wait and see if you wanted company," he said, standing. "I also sent a note to security to keep an eye on that reporter. You've got history, don't you?"

"Company would be nice, thank you. And yes." Max swallowed back the urge to apologize, even as she scrambled for something else to say, but Nika didn't need an explanation.

"When you're ready to talk about it"—he held out his hand—"I'm here."

Max took his hand and stepped into his comforting embrace. Words could not describe how thankful she was to have him in her life. They'd weathered the storm of the past few years with some fights, tears, and a lot of learning, but overall had found a steady connection that was good for them both.

I don't need to be a Carmichael as long as I have the NeoG, she thought.

FOUR

Trappist System

D'Arcy stood at the back of *Dread Treasure*'s bridge, his arms crossed over his chest as Locke patiently walked Ensign Järvinen through the logistics of the traffic around Trappist-1d. Part of him was chafing at this glacial process of integrating new team members, while the other part knew they had nothing but time until *Zuma* and *Flux* got back from the prelims.

A restless ache gnawed at him at the thought. He missed competing, and hadn't realized how much until it wasn't an option. The members of *Dread* had all worked hard the year they'd won the Games with *Zuma*. They'd been a real crew both in competition and out in the black—or so he'd thought.

"Not going well?"

D'Arcy looked at Emel. She moved quietly, a bit like Max in her deliberateness, but with far more self-assurance than the lieutenant possessed. It had been easier than he'd thought to adjust to seeing her every day, even if their interactions were still a sort of careful formality.

That, once again, was his fault. He was keeping her at a distance because he couldn't help himself.

"It's going fine, why?"

"You were frowning."

"That's just my face." He smiled to temper the edge, caught the flicker of concern in her brown eyes and ignored it. "She'll get it. There's a lot to absorb. You're welcome to jump in if you're ready."

"I am. Thank you for the space to pray."

"Of course."

"You don't?"

"Don't what?"

"Pray anymore."

D'Arcy shook his head. "Not since Mars. I don't need pity about it, Emel." Now he didn't soften his words. "I've got no time for people or gods who don't have time for me."

"Allah always has time for us. Sorry, habit." She held up her hands in surrender when his jaw tightened, then joined Locke and Heli at the console.

It was a toss-up what burned more, her pity or the words. D'Arcy hadn't been a particularly devout man at any point in his youth, but he'd made the trips and done what was required of him through most of his teen years because it had made his parents happy. After they'd died it hadn't helped with the grief, so he stopped going.

Then came the demonstrations and the crackdowns and the death and he couldn't figure out why one would waste their breath on unanswered prayers for mercy when that time was better spent fighting the people trying to put their boot on your neck.

Privately, D'Arcy could admit that choice hadn't been the best, even if it had ultimately put him on the path that led him here. He'd just never found his way back to the rituals and traditions of his younger days, preferring to live a life rooted in reality and his own responsibility.

Dread pitched unexpectedly, pulling him back to that reality, a proximity alarm blaring; and only D'Arcy's long years of training and snake-quick reflexes kept him from careening sideways as he grabbed for the bar above his head with one hand and snagged Emel with the other.

"Locke?"

"Sorry, Commander, had to pull her to port to avoid this mess. Sonofa—" He broke off and slapped a hand to the coms console. "Freighter, who taught you how to fly? Stay in your assigned lane."

There was no response from the freighter that had just drifted into view and D'Arcy muttered a curse as the ship skidded along the side of another freighter in line and nearly smashed into a smaller passenger ship that only just managed to squeak out of the way.

"Trappist Control, this is Interceptor *Dread Treasure*. I've got an E-class freighter out of lane." Locke's report was clipped but professional as always.

"It's the *Opie's Hat*," Emel said. She'd found her feet and was looking up the ship registry at the side console.

"It can't be." Even as D'Arcy issued the denial, he got a closer look at the ship through the bridge window and though the hull of the freighter was worn and scarred, with a gaping hole in the side, he could see the remnants of the name painted in space-faded white.

"What do you mean it's—oh." Emel cut herself off as the information hit the console. "It's been missing for six years?"

"It was coming from Jupiter. It made the wormhole transit on time but then vanished." D'Arcy frowned and queued up his com. *"Opie's Hat*, this is Commander Montaglione of the NeoG Interceptor *Dread Treasure*. Heave to and prepare for boarding."

No response.

D'Arcy hit the all-com button on the screen. "All traffic in lane ten at Trappist-1d, we have a potential emergency situation. Clear the lanes and proceed to your designated rally point. Repeat. Clear the lanes and proceed to your designated rally point."

He appreciated that while he was issuing the order, Locke

was already on the com with control, updating them on the situation. D'Arcy's DD pinged and he accepted the incoming com from the officer on watch.

"Get that bouncer over there before it hits something else! Hey, D'Arcy, are you breaking things up there?" Vice Admiral Ella Fashav asked.

"Not me, Ella. *Opie's Hat* just reappeared."

"Bullshit."

"I'm looking at her. She's nonresponsive, but she's here. She crashed into the lanes and sideswiped at least one ship before people could get out of the way."

"Yeah, the *Price of Glory*. It's a Navy freighter. I'm never going to hear the end of it." Ella rolled her eyes. "Well, this is an exciting day. Bouncer is headed in your direction. Advise just staying clear until they handle it."

"Can you scramble three more ships for a boarding? I want to take a look inside."

"That makes my ass twitch, D'Arcy."

"Tell me about it."

"I just did." But she smiled. "I'll get them to you by the time the bouncer has the freighter wrangled. You all be careful up there."

"Always," he agreed.

"Commander," Locke called out, "the freighter isn't even moving on thrusters. It looks like pure momentum took her into the lanes." He was already maneuvering *Dread* into boarding position as he spoke. The lieutenant commander was an amazing pilot and even better at anticipating D'Arcy's commands.

They were going to reach the ship before the bouncer did, though D'Arcy could see the faint speck of it in the distance as it sped toward them and the bigger green blip on the console readout that tagged the specialized ship used for corralling and directing out-of-control vessels.

He also saw the tag for the Interceptor appear on the screen, the *Wandering Hunter,* which had decided against participating in the prelims this year and launched from Trappist-1d. It was followed by two other NeoG Fast Response Cutters (FRCs), which had been put into service covering the patrol gaps left by the Interceptors' absence while at the prelims, the *Beverly G. Kelley* and the *Chris Hadfield,* both coming in from *Dread's* stern.

All on their way to check out *Opie's Hat,* a freelance vessel registered to one Simpson Ivarken, with a bare-bones crew of nineteen. At least, that's what they knew based on six-year-old data. D'Arcy didn't hold out hope that any of the crew were alive, but stranger things had happened. E-class freighters had crews of approximately thirty, depending on if they were company owned or smaller outfits. They were capable of extra solar runs and generating their own wormholes, though most relied on the transit point at Jupiter to save on fuel.

What the hell is it doing here?

He let Locke handle the coordination with Control. The man coached Heli easily through that while he flew the Interceptor toward the nearest airlock. Their pings were still met with nothing but silence.

"Aki, you and Lupe with me." D'Arcy pointed at the petty officer (second class) who'd been braced on the stairs leading up to the bridge and she nodded in acknowledgment. "Ensign, Master Chief, you'll stay with the ship. Locke, after you get docked, get your gear and meet us at the airlock."

Heli wasn't experienced enough to protest, though he saw the flash of disappointment in their pale eyes. Emel suffered from no such hesitation.

"I have plenty of boarding experience, Commander."

"I know," he replied. "What I don't know is what we're walking into over there and I need someone to stay here with the ensign just in case things go sideways." It was perfectly logical, but the tight set of her mouth had him expecting a fight.

He headed for his gear in the hopes that would deter her. Unfortunately, Emel hadn't changed at all and she knew her role well enough to know she could question him—was supposed to question him about the change in protocol.

"A word in private, Commander?"

"No. I gave my orders."

Aki and Lupe were desperately ignoring them as they pulled on their gear and double-checked, then triple-checked each other's work with studious dedication.

Emel glanced Aki's way. "Petty Officer, I think I hear Locke calling for you and Lupe."

Aki took the offered out but shot D'Arcy an embarrassed look as she slipped around him, dragging Lupe with her.

He let them go.

"Standard operating procedure is pilot and hacker on the Interceptor, everyone else boarding. Heli needs the experience, especially in a low-risk situation like this."

"I'm well aware of what the SOP is, Master Chief." D'Arcy bit off her rank, saw the angry flicker in her eyes. "I'm also aware of what my crew can do. Petty Officer Murphy is a good sword fighter. I also know how Petty Officer Garcia works in a fight." D'Arcy slapped his own sword onto his back, feeling the magnetic sheath catch with a click. "Same with Locke. And we have no way of knowing if this is actually a low-risk board."

"Ah."

It was shocking how that disappointed exhale could sound exactly the same as it had decades ago. And how D'Arcy couldn't just ignore it and finish what he was doing even though he knew he shouldn't rise to the bait. He and Emel both knew she could protest his orders but not actually ignore them.

"What?"

"I was hoping Robertson was wrong."

Fuck.

He forced himself to meet her gaze. "You talked to the senior chief."

"We're old friends." Emel's smile was gentle, and it made his chest tighten. "D'Arcy, I want you to know that Joe understood. He thinks you're a fine officer. 'One of the finest I could have served with had the circumstances been different,' he said."

The anger that flared was for himself, so he kept it in his throat even though it burned like a fusion bomb.

"But he also said you couldn't seem to trust anyone but who was left of your original crew, and he wasn't sure if you'd ever be able to again."

This wasn't about trust, though. It was that he didn't want to be responsible for losing anyone else, but D'Arcy hadn't even been able to say that to his therapist, so he certainly wasn't going to say it to Emel. Though the words that came out of his mouth contained the subtext of multitudes.

"You've been here all of two days, Emel, and I don't know what's on that ship!" D'Arcy's grip on his temper slipped as he flung a hand at the airlock. "Why shouldn't I take the team that works the best?"

"I know that, and I don't necessarily disagree with you," Emel replied.

He gaped at her. "You—what?"

"We don't know what's going on and this is maybe the best choice right now. Maybe not, but I won't push it. I just need you to be aware of what you're doing and that at some point you're going to have to trust both me and Heli to do our jobs. Besides, you and I both know the SOP holds. Locke or Aki staying on board as the pilot is safer than leaving two relative newbies in control of the ship."

D'Arcy rubbed a hand over his face. "Couldn't we have had this conversation after we finished here?"

"Nope," Emel replied in a cheerful voice. "I'll go let the others know that you're waiting."

D'Arcy dropped his hand and stared at her retreating back before looking at the ceiling of his ship and exhaling. A lot had changed for both of them over the years, but it was clear she could still get right under his skin like nobody else.

"D'Arcy, we're hooking up on the starboard side. Crew of four. Is this really the fucking *Opie's Hat*?" *Wandering Hunter*'s Commander Pia Forsberg's voice was both awed and amused, helping him refocus on the task at hand.

"That's what it says on the tin. We're locked on port. Crew of four as well. Give me five minutes." He waved to Locke when the lieutenant commander came into view, then pinged the FRCs. "Recommend the *Kelley* and the *Hadfield* hang back and let us check it out, but be ready to lock on as needed."

"Roger that, Commander" came the acknowledgment from both captains.

D'Arcy inhaled and exhaled, then slipped on his helmet. The new prototypes Max and Nika had been testing when Jupiter Station exploded into chaos were approved and production started, and the scuttlebutt sounded like they'd have some within the month. For now, though, this felt familiar and put him in the right frame of mind. He checked Lupe's helmet, then Aki's; waited while she checked Locke and his second in command checked his.

None of them spoke. They didn't need to. They'd been together for years and already knew each other as well as one could without being intimately involved. Though D'Arcy figured trusting people with your life was about as intimate as you could get.

Emel was still fucking right that leaving her and Heli on the ship wasn't the best decision, though. And unlike his old helmet, that chafed.

"Coms check, are you reading me, Master Chief?"

"I read you. You've got a solid lock and are green to open."

"Ensign Järvinen, you have command of the ship." D'Arcy didn't insult them by suggesting they listen to Emel. He knew she'd step in if necessary. "Pia, I'm opening our airlock now."

"Roger that, doing the same."

There was a rush of air as the vacuum of the freighter sucked away what was in *Dread*'s chamber. D'Arcy flicked his headlamp on and stepped carefully into the derelict ship. He engaged the magnetic lock on his boots and they clicked down to the surface, holding him in place.

"Closing airlock," Locke announced. "Heli, you're free to disengage as necessary."

"Roger that," they replied. "We'll stick with you."

D'Arcy swallowed back the urge to order them to uncouple just to be safe. There wasn't any reason for it beyond his need to keep some control of the situation.

You already made one questionable call—do better here.

He moved toward the bow with the others behind him and those words ringing in his ears. The walls were smeared with space dust and the preserved grit of a cross-system freighter that got cleaned when the crew felt like it.

He wasn't seeing anything out of the ordinary. Nothing to explain why this ship had gone missing. It wasn't particularly surprising they hadn't run into a body yet, though he was waiting for it. The size of the ship and the minimal amount of crew meant if there'd been an emergency—like an explosion that would account for the hole in the hull he'd seen—the bodies were probably clustered in the bridge.

"Pia, you seen anything yet?"

"Negative. It's clear here. I'm not even seeing any damage other than what being adrift for six years would account for."

"Same here. We're coming up on the gash in the hull, though, so maybe something will give us some clues." He slowed as they reached the breach and stood for a moment, studying the seven-meter-wide gap.

"Commander, this looks cut," Locke said at the same time D'Arcy realized the edges of the hull were too clean for an explosion or even a meteor impact.

He glanced back; Locke was on a knee recording the edge

of the corridor. Aki was taking samples of the hull. The swell of pride collided headfirst with the guilt and the grief.

Akane should be out here with us. Aki should be on the ship. Damn you, Paul.

"D'Arcy, we're at the bridge. It's open and empty. I've got Pavel and Qi taking a look at the computers to see if we can pull up the logs. I'm taking Rizzo to scout out the rest of the ship and see if we can find the bodies of the crew. There wasn't any sign the lifeboat had been launched, but I'll have Pavel confirm it."

"Okay, I'm headed to the bridge. Lupe, you're with me." D'Arcy flipped to the team channel. "Locke, you and Aki finish up here and then double back to meet Pia. Shouldn't take long to search this boat. Anchor me while I cross this." He pulled his tether free and handed it to Locke.

The man took it with a frown and D'Arcy braced for a protest. "Be careful, Commander," he said finally.

D'Arcy nodded, disengaged his boots, and pushed off. He landed on the other side, felt the click as his boots connected again, and turned to give Locke a thumbs-up.

D'Arcy continued down the corridor toward the bridge after Lupe made the jump. They were almost to the bridge when he spotted the shadow on the wall and slowed. His heart kicked up a notch.

"Pia, may have found a body." But as he knelt next to it, D'Arcy realized it was just a discarded suit, hovering a handful of centimeters off the grating like it had been lying there when the internals went down. The helmet was nearby, still intact, barely resting on the floor. "Retract that. It's an empty space suit. An old one."

"An old one?" Curiosity was thick in Pia's voice. "How old? Also, D'Arcy, there are no bodies. No crew. It's like they vanished."

Vanished? Ice crawled up his spine. "I don't know," he said, answering about the suit. "Maybe just post-Collapse?

Nothing that should be on a freighter that was in commission for thirty-eight years. The helmet is intact. No blood or any indication someone was wearing it except it's not attached to the suit. Hang on." He paused, reaching out and carefully moving the glove aside, dislodging the screwdriver in its grip. The tool floated away, but D'Arcy's eyes were fixed on the wall.

Scratched into the smooth spot were two words:

GET OUT.

"Folx, this has been a banger of a competition. We are at the end of the third day of the NeoG Boarding Games Preliminaries here on Earth in the year 2440, filled with all the usual hijinks and more than a few surprises. I am, as always, your announcer, Pace McClellan."

"And I'm Barnes Overton. It's good to see you all here this week at the NeoG Academy compound as *Zuma's Ghost* and *Flux Capacitor* continue to dominate the field, though we have seen some emerging competition."

"When Barnes says 'emerging,' what they mean is maybe in a few years these new crews will be closer to a match for the four-time Boarding Games champion *Zuma's Ghost* and two-time champions *Flux Capacitor,* both of whom are still forces to be reckoned with."

"Fair enough, Pace. Fair enough. We have seen some amazing fights in the cage, and the dynamic duo of Carmichael and Khan seem to be on a collision course—literally! But the big story today is *Zuma* was up against not one, but two Interceptor teams in the Boarding Action and blew through both of them."

"Thanks to Admiral Chen and the Games Committee for trying to level the playing field for some of the newer teams, Barnes. Didn't work this time around, though."

"Absolutely, they've made some adjustments with a new timed component, but *Zuma's Ghost* still cleared the pirate ship and got to the cargo faster than any team so far."

"I'm curious what other changes the Committee might

have up their sleeves for the Games themselves, given what we've seen so far in just the preliminaries both here and for the Navy competition a few weeks ago."

"What I, and I'm sure all the fans, want to know is are we finally going to see Jenks and Max go head-to-head in the championship match? So far, Carmichael seems to be unable to make that last crucial win happen, but she decimated her opponent in the fourth round here today to advance to the semifinals."

"Well, if viewers join us tomorrow, Barnes, they'll find out if we get the matchup we've all been waiting for. Also tomorrow, we'll be here to watch the final match of the Hacking competition between Ensign Nell Zika and Lieutenant Saad Rahal."

"Ensign Zika is the reigning champion for several years running, but lately *Flux*'s Rahal has proven to be a difficult opponent. Still, my money is on Sapphi, as she is affectionately called around here. I don't think she's ever met a computer she couldn't sweet-talk into cooperating."

"True story. Another fan favorite, Ensign Zika could have had a promising career at Dànǎo Dynamics but chose the NeoG instead."

"Their loss, as they say, Pace, is our gain."

FIVE

The Verge

Max was grateful for Nika's solid presence at her side when her mother appeared in the family's virtual meeting room, but she resisted the urge to grab for his hand and hold on tight. She hadn't expected her mother to respond so quickly and certainly hadn't wanted to do this right in the middle of the prelims, but refusing to come when she'd requested the meeting would have only made things worse.

Admiral Susanna Carmichael's avatar looked exactly like herself in the real world, a sharp-pressed Navy uniform and polished boots that reflected the overhead light back at them. Her graying hair was twisted back from a face barely softened by age.

Dark brown eyes betrayed nothing as they flicked from Max to Nika and back. "Maxine, if you are here to ask for permission to marry this man, the answer is no."

Damn it.

The thought hadn't even occurred to her and for a second she floundered, but Nika was there for her, unflustered as he smoothly brought up the image of Strzecki and slid it across the table to her mother.

"This reporter was recently released from a rehab facility. He'd been sent there for harassing my lieutenant, Admiral. The first thing he does upon his release is pick up right where he left off."

"I fail to see the point of this, Commander," Susanna replied.

"Don't you care in the slightest that your daughter is being harassed?"

Max finally found her voice before her mother could reply to Nika. "The point is, why am I hearing from a reporter and not from the family that my parents are considering cutting me off? The letter of concern said nothing about this. Is it true?"

"Are we at the point of believing all our own press, Maxine?" Susanna waved a hand in the air. "While it's true you're on warning with the family for your behavior—"

"What *behavior*?" Max rounded the table, her temper slipping from her grasp. "I have been doing my job, Mother. Nothing more, nothing less. What behavior can the family possibly object to beyond me not doing what you wanted of me? That innocent photo of our celebration?"

Susanna looked at Nika, her jaw tight before returning her cold gaze to Max. "I will not discuss family business in front of a stranger."

Max turned to Nika, who met her look and nodded once before kicking out of the Verge. "There, happy?"

"Watch your tone, child."

"I am not a child. I am a lieutenant in the Near-Earth Orbital Guard, despite everything you have done to keep me from it."

Susanna's laugh was humorless. "If we had truly wanted to keep you from this, you would not be standing here waving your rank around as if it means something to me. To answer your question, I have no idea what that reporter is going on about; but if you continue this path of reckless disobedience . . ."

"Don't threaten me."

"Carmichaels don't threaten, Maxine. We lay out what will happen if people continue to choose poorly and then we follow through. These are the consequences of your actions, nothing more. Darling of the NeoG you might be, but you are not untouchable. Moreover, the people around you definitely aren't all held in the same high regard. Best that you remember that."

The chill seeped under her skin, but Max forced herself to hold her mother's gaze. "What do you want from me?" She hated that the question came out in a whisper. Hated even more the cold, triumphant smile that appeared on Susanna's face at the apparent capitulation.

"Stop competing. Finish out your tour and leave this less than attractive path. Your sister will find a place for you at LifeEx where you can contribute to the family without all this drama."

"No."

Susanna blinked. "No is not an option you have. This is what the family wants from you. Best to make your peace with it or you will be cut off."

It was part panic but also part deliberate insult that had Max kicking out of the Verge without a response. The room she shared with Nika was quiet as she removed her VR headset and laid it carefully aside.

What she wanted to do was throw it against the wall.

"That went less well than I'd hoped," Nika said, and Max looked up at him where he was leaning against the doorway. "Before you feel the need to apologize, don't." He crossed to her and sat down next to her on the bed, holding out his hand.

Max took it. "I got answers, I suppose." She wasn't sure she could make her mother's ultimatum leave her mouth right now. She knew the clock was ticking and it was only a matter of time before something formal came down from on high. "The question still is, how did Strzecki know?"

"I'll do some digging, see what comes up." Nika squeezed her hand and then flashed a bright grin her way. "I'll admit, I kind of like the fact that your mother doesn't approve of me. Makes me feel like I'm doing something right."

Max choked on her laughter, leaning her head against his shoulder. "You are doing everything right. I don't know where I'd be without you."

"Jenks would say floundering." She felt the press of lips against her hair. "I say you'd figure it out because you're smart and very good at what you do, but I'd miss you."

"I'd miss you, too." She would. She'd miss all of them and her life here and— Max felt a swell of fury in her gut at the audacity of her mother thinking she would just walk away from all of this like a dutiful daughter. "Are we still going out to eat?"

"If you want."

Max nodded in agreement. "I do. The distraction will be good, I think."

The chill from her mother's threats—no matter how she couched it, there was no way to take what Suzanna Carmichael said as anything *but* a threat—was still heavy in the back of her head and Max wondered again what would happen if she walked away first. If breaking from the Carmichaels would keep everyone she cared about safe or just make things worse.

She didn't know how to contact Islen, but Jeanie Bosco might. As they headed for the restaurant, Max sent the head of LifeEx's security a quick message from a private account Sapphi had set up for her. She'd almost gotten Jeanie killed the last time she hadn't taken proper precautions to encrypt her communications, and while she was reasonably sure her family wouldn't go to those depths, it didn't mean they wouldn't fire the woman from her position. No matter what kind of protests Max's sister Ria issued.

She just had to hope Jeanie didn't share this with her sister. But Max was pretty sure she could count on Jeanie's discretion.

If Jeanie couldn't help her, Max would ask Sapphi or Stephan. Somehow she'd get in touch with her cousin and find out just what she needed to prepare herself for. She only hoped it happened before the hammer came down on her.

But either way, she was done being the nail.

ENSIGN NELL "SAPPHI" ZIKA SAT ALONE IN THE CORNER OF Squids, the virtual reality club that the majority of the Neo hackers met in to party. The music thumped through her even here in the Verge, and Sapphi watched the writhing dance floor from the safety of her seat. She'd danced earlier, but the press of bodies proved to be too much and she'd retreated with a claim of needing a drink, then escaped to this corner with nothing but a water and some room to breathe.

It didn't seem to matter that she knew all these people. That she'd fought and fucked and was friends with most of them. She'd won her semifinal match today in addition to the team's exceptional performance in the Boarding Action and *Zuma* was currently, firmly, ensconced in the number one spot for the prelims. Catastrophic event aside, there was little that could shake them out of their seat.

You shouldn't say things like that unless you want to drag the wrath of the gods down on you again.

She let go of her water and traced one finger against the white scars on the back of her other hand. The Lichtenberg figures that decorated both of her arms from fingers to elbow were evidence of her brush with death not long ago. Normally such things faded, but hers hadn't. She'd looked Hades in the face and then walked away from the underworld. But like the heroes of old, she hadn't gotten away unscathed—not in body or mind or soul.

For her hubris, the one person in the whole universe she wanted to confide in was gone.

I miss you.

The thought winged out and vanished under the electric pulse of grief that always followed when Ito Akane's face appeared in her memory.

"You're awfully solitary tonight."

Sapphi looked up into the sparkling brown eyes of Commander Janelle Pham. *Sol Rising* hadn't competed in the preliminaries, as her crew was still finding their feet after the loss of one of their own people in the attack on Jupiter Station two years ago, but their commander had come to watch.

"Too many people."

"Do you want company?"

"Sure." Sapphi slid over on the bench as the trans woman joined her. Some people made their avatars elaborate, but not Janelle. She looked the same here as she did in real life, barely taller than Jenks but with long black hair and a heart-shaped face. Right now that face wore a serious expression and Sapphi pressed down on the panic churning in her gut.

"What's weighing on your mind, my prodigy?"

Sapphi's laugh dissolved into tears when Janelle held out her arms, and she buried her face in the woman's shoulder. "Why am I alive when so many good people aren't? Why am I not over it when everyone else seems to have moved on?"

"Oh, Sapphi." Janelle sighed as she wrapped her arms around the younger cis woman. "You are alive and thank God for it. I lost too many friends; we all did. I'm glad we didn't lose you, too."

Sapphi clung to her mentor, wishing she could find the words to tell her everything that was rolling around in her head. But they wouldn't come, and the moment passed when Janelle cupped her face and pressed a kiss to Sapphi's forehead.

"As for moving on, everyone grieves at their own pace, Sapphi." Janelle smiled sadly. "There's no right or wrong to it, no guidebook for you to follow, and certainly no rule book as to how long you should take. Do you want to talk about it?"

"Seems like too heavy a conversation for a party."

Janelle dismissed her with a hiss of air. "Code does what we tell it, life does what it wants. Talk to me. I know you haven't been talking to your crew. Jenks is worried about you. Tamago even more so."

Sapphi sighed heavily, remembering all the times either of them had tried to get her to talk and she'd always changed the subject or found a way to distract her friends. "They've all got their own stuff going on." She tried to pull away, but Janelle tightened her grip and Sapphi sighed again as she looked at her. "How do you find the words to grieve for something that never existed? Akane and I . . . we could have been more, but we never got the chance to find out. Now she's gone and I'm still here building sandcastles out of a dream that won't ever be real. How is that fucking fair?"

Janelle finally let her go and Sapphi resisted the urge to bolt, knowing the commander would just find her in the real world if she left the club. The feelings were colliding in her head with memories of Akane and what had happened after they'd returned to Jupiter Station.

After I almost died. Before she died for good.

"HEY, SAPPHI, DO YOU HAVE A MINUTE?"

She looked up and spotted Akane. Dread Treasure's *petty officer was standing in the doorway of* Zuma's *quarters with her hands in her pockets.*

They'd just gotten back to Jupiter Station from Trappist and while Sapphi had now been cleared by medical staff from both places, she still felt unsteady. Akane crossed to her as she got to her feet.

"You don't have to get up. I just . . . I wanted to see how you were."

"Still alive. Go me."

Akane's laugh was pained and the kiss that followed was a surprise, but Sapphi leaned forward, sliding her hands into Akane's hair and backing the petty officer against the bunk.

"I should have asked, but . . . I promised myself I'd do that when you got back," Akane murmured when they separated. "I was so scared when I heard what happened. Sapphi, I—"

The sound of a throat being cleared reminded Sapphi that Max had been in the team office filing reports and she turned toward her lieutenant, her cheeks burning.

"Sorry to interrupt. I'm off to have dinner. You two have fun," Max said with a smile and a wave as she headed for the exit.

"IT'S NOT FAIR, SAPPHI. NOT IN THE SLIGHTEST." JANELLE leaned in and pressed a second kiss to her cheek. "It's okay to be mourning the loss of what could have been. I don't have anything better than that. I wish with all my heart I did. All I can tell you is that I'm here for you."

"I appreciate it, and yet I don't know what I need. I think that's the problem." Sapphi traced a pattern on the tabletop and shook her head. "I'm sorry, this is too much. I think I'm going to head out."

Janelle frowned at her but relented and stood. "Fine, I'll let you off the hook right now, but I'll be checking in later. Good luck tomorrow. Not that you'll need it. You are brilliance personified. I knew it the first moment we met."

"You've always been too good to me." Sapphi said it because she meant it, but also because she knew it would make Janelle roll her eyes—and it did.

"See you tomorrow."

She watched Janelle walk away, wishing she could stay and enjoy herself like she had in years past. The scene around the commander fizzed for just a moment, looking like static from when the stations had all gone down during the Collapse, and the thumping music stopped, replaced by the soft strains of a haunting song.

"... *when you rise, I will make you a present of the stars of Aquarius* ..."

Sapphi froze. She hadn't kicked out of the Verge yet, and it hadn't ever done that even when she had. She pushed to her feet, but everything snapped back to normal and no one else seemed to have noticed the glitch.

But it was something—she had way too much experience to not realize that this was wrong. As if to emphasize this, the table pulsed under Sapphi's fingers and she looked down. The message shimmered on the surface for just an instant before it faded.

I need your help.

She looked around, but she was alone. The club was fine. The table was blank.

"What the fuck?" she whispered.

Her proximity warning went off, telling her that Tamago, Chae, and Jenks were back from the real club, and Sapphi kicked out of Squids for the real world. Doge was powered down in the corner. The ROVER—Robotic Optics Vehicular and Extravehicular Reconnaissance AI—she'd helped Jenks refurbish almost eight years ago after the chief had rescued him from a junk bin was as much a part of *Zuma* as any of the humans in the crew. She felt like she could use a bit of Doge's comfort right now, shaken as she was, but instead she put on a neutral face as her friends approached.

Tamago pushed the swaying Jenks toward the bathroom. "Go drink some water, Chief."

Jenks winked at Sapphi on her way by, blowing her a kiss. "Did you have fun at Squids?" she asked.

"I did." Sapphi was surprised how easily the lie bounced

into the air and thanked her lucky stars that Jenks was the right side of drunk not to notice.

Tamago, however, appeared to be stone-cold sober and the petty officer leaned in. "You okay?" they asked, too soft for anyone else to hear. "You look like you've seen a ghost."

"I'm fine. Weird glitch on the way out of the Verge from my headset maybe? I'll run a diagnostic later."

Tamago nodded and followed Jenks. Sapphi put a smile back on her face for Chae. "Did they stay out of trouble?"

"Mostly." The newest member of *Zuma* had found their "space legs" after a rough first year. Their involvement with the shadowy cabal who'd been running a smuggling ring in the Trappist System had been under duress, and Sapphi didn't blame them in the least, even though it had been Chae's sabotage of the Interceptor that had resulted in her momentary death two years ago. They'd been trying to protect their family and she knew she'd have done the same thing in their place.

But they were still a bit shy around Sapphi, and so she went out of her way to make sure it was clear the two of them were fine—and she truly felt they were, if Chae would accept that.

"That's about the most we can hope for," she replied, and patted the younger Neo on the shoulder. "Let's get some sleep so we can wrap up these prelims and go home."

THE NEXT DAY, SAPPHI HUNG BACK BY THE DOOR OF THE competition room, her dampeners muffling most of the noise of the crowd who were assembled in the balcony above and her fellow Neo hackers who were allowed down in the pit.

The noise didn't used to bother her; in fact, she'd reveled in it, letting the voices clash with whatever favorite San-Pop tune was playing in her head pre-match. Now, however, she needed the quiet or she couldn't focus. It had been like that ever since—

You died?

She couldn't stop the flinch, and was glad that she was still out of sight and out of camera view even as she was furious with herself for reacting like this.

Everything was fine and last night had just been a weird Verge thing. Her quick check of her headset this morning was all green. There were all sorts of stories of strange things that happened in virtual reality—it wasn't because of what had happened to her. Sapphi had been checked and rechecked and other than having to replace a few special mods that got fried in the shock—and consequently being out a good chunk of feds in the process—she was fine.

So what if it was easier to deal with code these days than people? If being in the Verge was easier than reality? If it seemed like no one else noticed that she still felt like lightning was dancing on her spine all the time?

If you keep hearing a voice singing in your dreams? And now this?

"Sapphi?"

She froze for just a moment when Tamago put their hand on her shoulder but pulled up the facade of cheerful delight everyone expected from her. "Yes?"

"I asked if you were ready." Tamago tilted their head to the side and studied Sapphi with cool brown eyes. "Which I will amend to: Are you sure you're okay?"

"Fine as Major Tom." She patted Tamago on the shoulder and braced herself for the noise as she turned down the damp-eners. She kept the smile on for the cameras, and she waved to the crowd above before heading across the room.

Lieutenant Saad Rahal was waiting for her, and he spread his arms wide, a grin on his handsome, sharply angled face. "Ready to have your ass kicked, Sapphi?"

"Did you bring someone in to pop for you?" she countered, making a big show of looking behind him before stepping into the hug. She liked Saad. He was a tough competitor and an even better teammate. Two years running they'd wiped the floor with the other hacker teams in the Games and no matter how this contest shook out they'd do it again this year.

He laughed, shaking his head as he let her go. "I keep hoping you getting your brain zapped has slowed you down."

"Ha, more like Zeus gave me some extra power." She stuck her tongue out and dodged his playful kick, dancing her way to the VR rig on the opposite side of the table.

Admiral Chen came into the room with Vice Admiral Koto and a man Sapphi didn't recognize but whose handshake ID'd him as Yasu Gregori with Dànǎo Dynamics. She frowned as something about the man pinged her memory, and automatically pulled up Yasu's profile.

He was thirty, three years older than she was, and had been with the company for seven years. Interestingly enough, Yasu was in their AI research division—

"Neos, welcome to the championship match of the hacking competition!" Admiral Chen's announcement dragged Sapphi back to the present. "Vice Admiral Koto will be your Game moderator, and I'm pleased to introduce a guest today from Dànǎo Dynamics. Yasu Gregori helped us with the challenges everyone has tackled during these preliminaries."

Yasu raised a hand and the way his lips curved tugged at Sapphi's brain again. "Thank you, Admiral. I don't want to steal the spotlight from the people who are about to compete, so I'll just say it's a pleasure to be here and while I hope you've all enjoyed the matches so far, this final one is something special. Vice Admiral Koto and I worked hard on it, and we're excited to see the results. Vice Admiral?"

Koto Yuki rubbed her hands together. "That's absolutely right. Lieutenant Rahal, Ensign Zika, if you'll take your seats and deactivate all mods except your accessibility mods for which you have prior medical approval."

Saad nodded at Sapphi. She made a finger guns gesture at him and settled into her seat. Her competition program was already running, shutting down her mods except for the noise dampener that helped her focus.

"Competitors, your task is simple. Follow the trail, gaining access to as many systems as you can along the way. Speed is of the essence, but don't pass up any advantage, as it could come in handy at the end of the line. You'll receive more instructions in the Verge. Are you ready?"

"Ready," Sapphi said.

"Let's do this," Saad agreed.

The world blurred around her, wiping the competition room clean, and Sapphi blinked twice as the barren scape of an asteroid greeted her. Bright orange arrows stood out on the gray regolith, leading to a terminal standing a few meters away.

She bounced experimentally. "Gravity is about fifteen percent of Earth standard, excellent," she muttered.

With that, Sapphi took off in a loping skip toward the terminal.

SIX

"How's Nika doing?"

D'Arcy looked away from the screen where Nika was fighting *Doppler Shift*'s commander, Jenny Atol, in the championship match. "Moving like a dancer again." He gestured as Nika ducked under the taller woman's sword, catching her weapon with the hook on the end of his and using her momentum to wrench it out of her hand.

"He's getting good at that move," Stephan said, leaning a hip on the desk. "I cannot figure out how to counter it."

D'Arcy hummed in agreement. They watched the rest of the match in silence, both nodding in approval when Nika dropped Jenny with a pair of strikes to her midsection that would have eviscerated her in a real fight.

"He's really improved." Stephan wore a pleased smile as he leaned over and tapped off the broadcast.

"Yeah." He knew Stephan had spent a lot of time with Nika after the injury that cost their friend his right arm. D'Arcy had been too far away on Jupiter Station to do much more than offer comfort over the coms, though it seemed to do both him and Nika some good.

D'Arcy dragged the photos of *Opie's Hat* back up out of the file. "So, this bullshit."

"You think it was a prank?" Stephan asked.

"Maybe, maybe not. Either way, I don't like it. Bad enough the entire ship was empty. Escape pods still there untouched. But that fucking message . . ." D'Arcy shuddered and rubbed a hand over his scalp, idly noticing he really needed a shave.

"Your crew did well."

"Don't even start, Stephan."

"What?" The man's innocent look fooled most people, but D'Arcy knew better. Emel may not have put her objection down officially, but there was no doubt Stephan had somehow heard about it.

"It's only been a few days. I was not about to take totally unknown personnel onto a mystery ship. Actually, scratch that, some of it is known. Ensign Järvinen likely would have tripped over something and hurt themself." He sighed. "It's like they manage to find any piece of debris on the ground and get it wrapped around their feet. I've never seen anything like it."

Stephan chuckled. "She'll be fine. Sharp as a tack up here." He tapped his temple. "She's still stuck in that gangly teenage phase. Do some work with her in the sword ring; it'll help the balance and spatial awareness issues."

D'Arcy resisted the urge to snap that he didn't want to take his new ensign into the ring. That every time he considered it, a memory of all the laughing practice bouts with Paul filled his brain to the point of screaming.

He knew he needed to; he just couldn't make himself do it.

Stephan surprisingly didn't call him on his noncommittal noise, the intel chief already on to the next issue on his daily list of things. "You want to take the ship out to West Ridge today and give Gun and Michael a hand with a new building?"

"I thought they'd have gone to Earth to watch Chae in the prelims?"

"My understanding is they wanted to save the time for the Games," Stephan replied.

"What do they need?"

"Manual labor mostly." Stephan grinned. "New community center that they're building."

"You're just going to use my team for all the shit work, huh?"

"That and PR. It's good for you, and Heli can practice her balance."

D'Arcy snorted, even though he knew Stephan was at least partially right. Easy jobs were the best to give them a chance to work together in a low-pressure environment until it felt like things were going to fall into a rhythm. "Send me the information. I'll go over it with Locke."

"You should loop Emel in also; it's been a while since she's seen Chae's dads."

D'Arcy gave Stephan a flat look that the man met without flinching. "You're determined to stick your nose into this, huh?"

"I am in command." Stephan gave a slight smile. "It's pretty clear even a few days in that someone needs to stay on top of it. I'm not losing you without a fight, D'Arcy, even if that fight ends up being with you."

"Do I get any time to settle into this?" It was terrible how pitiful that question sounded to his ears; he could only imagine how it hit Stephan.

It surprised him when the man didn't throw a reminder back at him that he'd offered time already. Instead Stephan reached out and squeezed a hand around D'Arcy's upper arm. "You get as much time as I can give you. I just need you to do something with it." He let D'Arcy go and left him alone in the office, the ping of the incoming file ringing in his head.

THOSE WORDS WERE STILL IN D'ARCY'S HEAD WHEN THEY DIS-embarked the ground transport at West Ridge a few hours later. He was aware of Emel hanging back even as he strode forward to greet Gun and Michael Chae, clasping their forearms in greeting. The fathers of *Zuma's* Chae Ho-ki were friends of his from the days of the Mars protests. D'Arcy had reconnected with them last year while they were on the trail of Senator Tieg's smuggling ring.

"Was pleased to get the message this morning that you all were coming to help," Michael said.

"More hands are always welcome." Gun's smile faded for just a moment as he looked past D'Arcy, and the man knew he'd recognized Emel. The guarded, shuttered look followed and D'Arcy felt like a bit of an ass for not giving them a heads-up. "You've got new crew," he said.

"Ensign Heli Järvinen," D'Arcy replied, gesturing them forward. "And it's been a while, but you probably remember Master Chief Emel Shevreaux."

Michael was better at hiding his surprise and his gray eyes were filled with genuine warmth as he offered Emel a hug. "It's wonderful to see you again."

They'd all known her brother, even if D'Arcy had been the closest to Hadi of any of them. The two men had been part of Free Mars, involved in the protests and witness to that fateful day.

D'Arcy didn't understand the utter ease that allowed Emel to step into Michael's hug as if they were just old friends and there wasn't a metric ton of emotion hanging in the air around them, but she did it and while Gun didn't offer a hug, he did give her a wary nod she returned with a seemingly genuine smile.

He knew there were curious looks from the rest of *Dread Treasure* at the obvious tension. But their history was a tangled minefield that wasn't something to be discussed on a weekday afternoon with the neighbors watching. Especially when there was work to do.

"Come in," Michael said, gesturing at the front door of their home. "Is anyone hungry?"

"You will be after we put you to work." Gun seemed to have recovered, and gestured from his husband's side at the door of their home. "We've got a little time before we have to head over to the site, though, if any of you need something."

"We're all good if we want to head right over," D'Arcy replied.

Several hours later, D'Arcy mopped at his face with the hem of his shirt and would not have minded a break and some food. He'd shed his duty jacket along with everyone else about an hour into hauling the braces for the new community building.

The site was teeming with people from the habitat. D'Arcy knew many of them by name now and many more seemed to greet him and the rest of his team with real smiles rather than wary looks. It had been a weird feeling to be the outsider for so long and more of a relief than he'd admit to anyone to feel accepted here in Trappist. Even if it had taken the better part of two years to accomplish it.

Being an outsider was the last place any habbie wanted to be. It wasn't something you could explain to anyone who wasn't from the habitat.

D'Arcy spotted Emel scrambling over the site; her blue sport hijab and long-sleeved shirt were smeared in spots with reddish-orange dirt. She laughed at something Locke shouted in her direction, the wind snatching his words away before they reached D'Arcy's ears. Emel shook her head and picked her way toward him around the materials lying in the dirt and he was swamped with a memory out of the blue.

THE LAUGHTER THAT HAD BEEN ON EMEL'S FACE AND IN HER *eyes just a moment before as she joked with her brother died when she caught sight of D'Arcy. It was replaced with a polite smile he'd seen too many times on his own mother's face when she had to deal with someone she didn't like.*

Rather than feeling ashamed that his own behavior had caused this response in the first place, and riding the sudden wave of grief for his mother, D'Arcy fixed a sneer on his own mouth after he deliberately greeted Hadi with a cheerful "Good morning."

The market was tense, as if trying to pretend it was just another day. News of the rejected proposal for the independence of Mars was being whispered along with some pretty inventive curses for the CHN.

He noted that Emel wasn't in her naval uniform, but dressed in a much more common habbie outfit of dark brown topped with a pretty red hijab pinned under her chin, the edges embroidered with darker red thread.

"We had a majority on the vote. They should have approved it," someone said over his shoulder.

"CHN isn't going to release its grip on Mars and we all know it. It was a waste of time to even attempt."

"There's a protest already brewing on the west end."

D'Arcy tuned the conversation out. "What are you up to?" he asked Hadi.

"Just grabbing things for Mom. We were going to get some breakfast. Did you want to join us?"

D'Arcy caught the look of annoyance Emel shot her brother at the question, and he grinned. "I'd love to. Where—"

The sudden commotion down the road had them all turning and D'Arcy tensed at the sight of the black-clad Mars PeaceKeepers who were making their way through the market. "PeaceKeeper" was such a load of crap. It only took a moment of the shouted orders and the answering protests for him to realize what was going on, but before he could say anything, a pair of PeaceKeepers were tapping batons on the stall next to them, ordering the shop to close.

"Move on out of here," one of them said. "Market is down for the day."

Emel shook her head. "You have no right to close the market. Where's your authorization?"

"This is my authorization," he snapped, waving his baton in her face, and D'Arcy was equally impressed and astounded when Emel slapped it away.

"Don't threaten me. I know what the laws say. You—"

The other PeaceKeeper shoved Emel with a loud curse, knocking her back into D'Arcy. He caught her by the upper arms, shifting at the same time and taking the follow-up blow on his back, gritting his teeth against the pain. "Move," he ordered, shoving her into the crowd as it surged around them.

"Hadi!"

"He'll be fine! You, on the other hand, need to move your ass." He grabbed her hand and ducked into an alleyway, dragging her with him.

D'Arcy kept moving deeper into the warren of the twisting streets of the habitat until the sounds of shouting faded. Only when he was sure they weren't being followed did he start working his way back to Emel's house.

"They hit you." There was such naïve shock in her voice, it was all he could do not to laugh.

"They were aiming for you," D'Arcy replied, glancing over his shoulder. He stopped and looked up at the sky. "Your hijab is coming loose," he murmured, keeping his eyes elsewhere while she fixed it and surprising himself with the sudden itch in his fingers to brush the red dust smears off her cheek.

"Thank you," she said, reaching out and squeezing his upper arm. "For everything."

D'Arcy looked back at her with a quick smile. "You're welcome. I'm not going to let you off the hook for breakfast just because of this."

"D'ARCY, LOOK OUT!"

Emel hit him full on, knocking him out of the way. The sliding beam clipped her in the shoulder rather than hitting him square in the chest. D'Arcy snapped back to the present with a snarled curse as they both rolled down the dirt hill behind him.

Emel's muffled cry of pain was a thousand condemnations on his fucking head as they came to a stop.

"What were you thinking?"

Where are you hurt?

He watched her flinch as the wrong words came out of his mouth and she scrambled to her feet, holding her left arm with her right. This time her hijab hadn't come loose. This time he hadn't kept her safe. "You're welcome, Commander. Next time I'll let it take your head off."

"You should have. It was my own fucking fault for not paying attention. It's not your job to keep me from getting hurt."

"It is precisely my job to protect my teammates," she snapped back at him. It didn't seem to matter that Locke had just reached them and anyone in a two-meter radius was likely to hear the argument.

"Master Chief, let me look at your arm," Locke said smoothly, stepping in between them and ushering Emel away.

D'Arcy muttered a curse under his breath.

"You all right?" Gun asked.

"I'm fine," he lied.

The man shot him a look but wisely kept any words he had for D'Arcy tucked safely away behind his teeth.

EMEL FOCUSED ON THE WORK IN FRONT OF HER. IT WAS EASier to do that than let her brain wander into territory it shouldn't—like replaying old memories or the utter disaster from yesterday.

"You're supposed to be focusing," she muttered, and went back to pulling wires from under *Dread*'s main console, ignoring the twinge in her bruised shoulder. The replacement of a way-too-far-out-of-date com circuit was new to her, at least in regard to the design for the Interceptors. But she'd replaced plenty of them in Navy ships during her career and this wasn't all that different once she'd had a chance to study it.

The schematic floated in her vision, visible even in the dim backup lighting that had kicked in when she'd turned off the main breaker. Emel reached into her bag for the cutters and clipped at the indicated spots until the circuit came free.

Did I make a mistake?

The question that rose up wasn't about the task at hand, but rather her entire present situation.

"JUPITER BROKE ALL OF US, EMEL," JOE SAID. HE SCRUBBED AT his short blond hair with a heavy sigh and picked at his meal for a moment before continuing. "But some of us more than others. I was excited to go to Dread; *it seemed like it would be a good fit. But D'Arcy . . ." He trailed off, was silent for a long moment. "I wouldn't even say this except you and I are friends and I want you to know what you're getting into. I'll preface it with the fact that I have the utmost respect for D'Arcy."*

Emel felt her gut twist with worry and it must have showed on her face, because Joe put his fork down and held up a hand.

"I'm not saying don't take the post. He's an amazing officer, one of the finest I could have served with had the circumstances been different. But he's struggling. I can't even imagine what that sort of betrayal feels like, to have one of your own crew turn on everything we hold dear. I know D'Arcy's got to blame himself for it. So I don't *blame him; but he doesn't trust anyone except for his original crew. And it was painfully obvious every time we went out into the black." Joe offered up a smile. "Maybe you can get through to him. I couldn't and Lieutenant Rodriguez couldn't, either. But you've got some history and maybe that'll be enough."*

IT WASN'T ENOUGH.

If anything, it seemed like their history was only making things worse.

"Master Chief?" Locke's voice filtered through the memory. "Yes?"

"Just wanted to let you know I was here so I didn't startle you," he replied. "How's the shoulder?"

"Fine." It would have been more polite to push out from under the console and look at him, but Emel didn't want to face whatever expression was on Locke's face. She wasn't going to ask him to pick sides, even though he'd been doing a really good job walking the line and trying to hold these pieces of *Dread* together on his own.

There was a long pause and she prayed that Steve wouldn't say whatever he was trying to find words for. "Well, I'll be in the galley doing inventory."

"I'll be done here in a few minutes and we can turn the main power back on."

"Take your time. I've got enough light to see." He headed back down the stairs and Emel went back to work.

She finished and ran the tests, pleased when they came back green, and wiggled out from underneath the console.

The sound of voices echoed from the galley as she made her way toward the breakers and Emel paused when she heard her name.

"Whatever is between D'Arcy and Emel is their business, Aki. I'm not getting between them and you shouldn't, either."

"I know." The petty officer's response was soft. "I just . . . things are bad. I didn't think it could get worse than Jupiter, but . . . if it doesn't get better, how much longer before *Dread* gets disbanded for good?"

"I need you not to think like that," Locke replied. "We'll be okay." There was the rustling sound of an embrace.

Emel backed up a few steps and brought her feet down slightly harder than necessary before she crossed in front of the doorway. "Turning the main power back on," she called.

If only everything were fixed so easily.

SEVEN

The Verge

"Terminal Five cleared. You may proceed, Ensign Zika."

Sapphi put on her game face, knowing the camera was focused on her. Her nerves had settled as she powered through the obstacles. The terminal hacks were complex, but not too difficult for her. She checked the map in the corner of her vision. Saad was right behind her, but still working on his fourth challenge.

She followed the arrows, climbing up a cliff face to reach the fifth and final station. A storm was brewing on the horizon, the dark clouds clashing together over the rolling surface of the sea. When she reached the top, she took a deep breath, the salt of the sea air mixing with the distinctive sharp tang of ozone that rode at the front of the rain.

"My ancestors rode waves like this, the great triremes cutting through the seas with each pull of the oars. Would they have even dared to guess that one day we'd be riding the stars in the same way?" It was second nature to play for the crowd at times; Sapphi knew as well as Jenks did that part of the Games was for show, to draw in the viewers and get them—and therefore the budget-setters—to care more about the NeoG.

The warning tone sounded on her DD, shaking her back into motion. Saad had finished his fourth challenge and was headed for the final. It was time for her to put this to bed.

Sapphi crossed the flat expanse of the cliff to where the terminal stood, the turbulent seas below her stretching out toward the horizon.

"Let's see what you've got for me." She pressed her palm to the surface and went to work, plugging in the restricted admin access she'd retrieved at a prior terminal. Her fingers flew over the holographic keys, cracking through the defensive program at speed, and she thrust her fists into the air when the terminal screen flashed her success.

Sapphi looked right at the camera and made a finger guns gesture of celebration. "That's game, baby."

I need your help.

She froze as the same text from last night appeared in the air in front of her.

"What the fuck?" she muttered. Was that the same song that now mixed with the rolling thunder in the distance?

A brief thought flashed through her that the contest programmers had done this, had put some unknown virus into the equation. Sapphi reached a hand out and watched in shock as it passed straight through the screen. The Verge started to dissolve around her and her breath caught in panic.

"Hey, Control, what's going on? Is this supposed to happen?"

"You are intruding on our space; you should not be here." The harsh voice echoed in her head as a bolt of brilliant lightning burst out of the clouds above and slammed down toward her.

She brought her shield up, grunting against the effort of holding it still while the electricity arced across the surface.

She jolted back to reality, the cheering crowd filling her ears as she turned off her dampeners. Her hands were shaking and the sharp taste of electricity was still in her throat. "What the fuck was that?"

Saad was climbing out of his chair, shaking his head. She could see her crew on the sidelines, celebrating.

I'm fine. This is fine.

She pulled everything together, all her panic and fear, and shoved it down deep as she pasted the proper expression on her face. Sapphi slid out of her own chair, standing up just as Saad grabbed her in a hug.

"Good job, you wizard!"

"Did you see that lightning? Wild."

"What? No lightning on my side."

"Huh, maybe I triggered something weird," she replied, hoping that her confusion was buried so no one could see, and hugged him back. "It was a good match."

"You stalled for a minute there and I really thought I had you. Then it was like you kicked it into high gear and demolished that last challenge before I could do anything." He spun her as the others converged on them. "One of these days, Sapphi, I swear I'm going to beat you."

"Not today, though. Maybe tomorrow . . . but I wouldn't bet on it."

He passed her off to Jenks, who kissed both of her cheeks. "Brilliance, as per usual. Right, Mom?"

Sapphi's mother, Cassandra Zika, wrapped her daughter in a tight hug and Sapphi clung, feeling both of her fathers' arms closing around them. "She is amazing."

Sapphi's parents passed her off to the five siblings who'd been able to make the trip. The laughter and noise and familial comradery were usually so welcome, but right now it made her want to crawl out of her own skin.

Sapphi endured the congratulations from her crew and fellow hackers even though she wanted to scream that something was wrong. She didn't know what, but the feeling was jabbing at her brain and suddenly everything was too loud.

"Hey, are you okay?" Leave it to Max to pick up on her anxiety, and for a moment Sapphi almost broke down in her lieutenant's arms. But there were cameras and too many eyes on them, so she kept her composure.

"Just fine, LT. We are eternal rock stars."

Max studied her for a long moment before nodding once. "Okay, I've got to get going. You were amazing out there."

"Good luck on your match. I'll be there cheering you on so you can kick Jenks's ass later." Sapphi had meant the encouragement to be lighthearted, but something about her words put a cloud of worry across Max's face.

It passed as quickly as it had appeared, Max smiling and giving her a final wave before she and the others headed for the exit. Tamago hung back to wait with Sapphi's family, and for a moment she was tempted to tell them to go on ahead.

"Hey, Nell."

The memory finally punched itself free as Yasu approached. Now that she could pinpoint it, his voice was different, deeper, but still familiar.

"It's Sapphi." The correction was automatic and bought her the time to keep from saying a name she was reasonably sure Yasu had left behind when he transitioned. "Is this the part where I say it's good to see you again? Because, I'm not sure . . ." She trailed off.

Everyone who was left was watching them, and she hated it. Jenks was the one who liked the spotlight. Sapphi would rather stay in the background where she belonged and right now she needed to be alone somewhere quiet.

Saad, bless him, spotted her discomfort and intervened, raising his voice over the crowd swirling around them. "Hey, nerds, go find something else to do. Afterparty starts at seven. Cameras, the show is over. You've got fifteen seconds to vacate the pit before you get zapped."

"I don't blame you if you'd rather I just go," Yasu said to her. "I just wanted to say good job and I'm impressed by how fast you blew through that last challenge. I'd thought for sure it would slow everyone down, but I underestimated you. Your skills have gotten amazing."

"I'm good at my job. Next to nothing slows me down. Not even lightning, though it was a neat trick," she said with projected confidence that faded at his confused look.

"No electric traps on my end." Yasu glanced back at the VR rigs. "Are you okay? Was there—"

"Don't worry about it. Must have just been a glitch." She waved her hand and changed the subject. "I'll be honest, you ghosted me so hard, I thought you were actually dead."

"Thought, or hoped?"

"Both." She grimaced. "Sorry. Listen, I got my brains scrambled a while back and even on good days my mouth works faster than my brain wants it to."

Yasu's grin still made her stomach do funny flops after all these years. Interesting. "No worries. I owe you an apology. Can I buy you dinner?"

Part of her wanted to, she realized, which is why the denial surprised her when it came out of her mouth. But a larger part said that was a bad idea right now. "My family is in town tonight and I'm sort of expected to make an appearance at this party. Some other time?"

"I'll be around for the rest of the prelims. Maybe we can figure something out. Or even after. Here's my new contact information."

Sapphi's DD pinged with the incoming card, and she echoed Yasu's smile before he lifted a hand in farewell and melted into the crowd of people heading out of the room.

"Who was that?" Tamago asked.

"Somebody I used to know," she replied, absently chewing on a nail as she stared at Yasu's retreating back.

Tamago wrapped an arm around her waist, and suddenly

she was glad for the distraction that was Yasu, since it meant Tamago wouldn't ask for a third time if she was okay. "Come on, champion. Let's go watch Max kick some ass."

MAX WASN'T SURE IF IT WAS HER OWN PRE-MATCH JITTERS getting into her head or if Sapphi's reaction to her hacking win really was off. The ensign had seemed more distracted than normal and a little wild around the eyes, like she'd been about to throw her arms around Max's neck and not let go.

She knew the feeling all too well. The conversation with her mother still sat heavy in her chest, even though her inbox was currently empty of the expected wrath to come.

Sapphi had obviously collected herself and Max had to do the same. The press of the crowd's anticipation lent a very real weight to the air as Max stepped into the academy's gym with Nika by her side. She knew the cameras had spotted her by the way the noise rose, people dragging their attention away from the other events as they noticed the big image of Max on the floating screen in the middle of the room or in their own DD feeds.

The cues from Jenks, hammered into her over the last few years, echoed in her head. Pre-match was psyops. As much as the match itself was decided by a fighter's skill and a fair amount of luck, amping the crowd to your side and throwing debris in your opponent's path could put them off their rhythm and help decide the match in a crucial moment.

Thing is, what if I'm *the one who's distracted?*

Max had always been good at hiding her emotions, thanks to her family. So even with her stomach and heart rolling in turmoil, she kept her shoulders loose and expression happy as she leaned over to Nika, covering her mouth with a hand.

"I can't actually think of anything funny to say, so will you just laugh as if I did?"

Jenks's amused snort echoed from behind them and Nika laughed.

"You need to come up with a few things, because one of these days you're going to get busted doing this," he replied, lifting a hand and passing it over his hair to hide his own mouth from the camera.

"It's worked so far." The familiar banter loosened some of the knots from her chest.

"He'd laugh at you reciting inventory, Max, so don't worry about it," Jenks cut in, making both her and Nika blush. "Now focus: Theo was cold as ice in her early matches, but she's got to have first prelim nerves rolling around in her head regardless. You're the veteran here. You've got a reputation *and* you're even cooler. Besides, I've seen her fight: she's got nothing on you in the cage." Jenks made sure her words were loud enough for the cameras to pick up and accompanied them with a shit-eating grin.

Max answered with one of her own, though it was completely fake. She kept it pointed away from Jenks so her friend couldn't call her on it.

Lieutenant Theo Aloisi of the crew *Bog Monster* was participating in her first year of the prelims, but she'd been in the NeoG for two years longer than Max and had been up for a promotion that she turned down to keep her crew together for a little longer. They'd been working the inner edge of the Kuiper Belt when the attack on Jupiter happened and were recalled to help fill in the gaps caused by the lost Neos.

Max had liked the trans woman in the brief interaction they'd had just before the prelims started. She'd been pleasant but solemn about the challenges the NeoG faced recovering from the attack and appeared to care deeply about her crew.

Like Jenks, Max had also watched her fights, but unlike her friend, Max was impressed with Theo's speed and knew her quick left jab was going to cause problems if she didn't keep her own hands up. Thankfully several years of Jenks swinging on her had improved Max's guard to the point where it was almost impenetrable, and confidence rose inside her.

Peeling off from the others when they reached the team area by the cage, Max pulled her wraps free and started winding them around her hands. She ran herself through her warm-up with the same military precision that had gotten her through her turbulent teenage years in the suffocating clutches of her family.

Routine had saved her countless times over the years. It always helped whenever she felt unmoored and lost to fall back into the safety of patterns and habits. This fight was no exception.

Except—she couldn't help thinking past Theo. She didn't discount her opponent, but this wasn't the match that rattled around in her head. Again, knowing the cameras were around, she just presented laser focus. But she had to virtually clear the mechanism in her mind to get back on track.

These are just games. Jenks won't hate you if you win. Besides, you don't even know if you can beat her. You won't get the chance if you don't focus and fight this fight in front of you first.

The pep talk helped some, loosening the knots in her chest until she could breathe.

"Max. Let me see." Jenks checked her over with practiced efficiency and Max reached down to lay a hand on Doge's head for a second.

"Good luck, Max," he said, then tipped his head to the side. "Are you—"

"Thanks, Doge."

"You're good to go. Got your back." Jenks tapped her fist to her heart, waiting for Max to copy and bump the back of their hands together, swinging through and grasping forearms. Max leaned down, pressing her forehead to Jenks's, and stared into her chief's mismatched blue and brown eyes. "I've got yours."

"Kick her ass," Jenks replied, again loud enough for everyone—including Theo—to hear, and released her. Jenks gave Max's opponent a maniacal grin, as if *she* were the one Theo were about to fight, and Max almost laughed at the theatricality of it all.

Instead Max just nodded and dragged in a deep breath as she passed through the small crowd to the cage door. Theo was already inside with the veteran referee, Travis Vance, who'd overseen the cage matches for more than a decade.

"Folx, we are here for the second semifinal match of the NeoG preliminaries. I want a good clean fight. Approved mat takedowns and locks only. If I say hold, you hold. If your opponent taps out, you release. Understood?"

"Understood," the pair replied in unison.

"Very good, fists out."

Max met Theo's ice-blue gaze and smiled slow. "I'll do you a favor and save you from having to go up against Jenks."

Theo laughed and tapped her fists to Max's. "I think I'll take my chances, Carmichael, but thanks for the offer."

"All right, don't say I never did anything for you." She didn't know where the banter was coming from as she backed away and waited for Vance to give the signal.

"Fight!"

Everything else melted away, sand smoothed by incoming waves as Max focused on the fighter in front of her. Within the first ten seconds she knew two things: The first was that she couldn't knock Theo out unless she got lucky—she was fast enough and able to avoid the power of her strikes by backpedaling or blocking. The other was that while Theo was a very good fighter . . .

Max was better.

The rounds sped by in a blur of punches and points. Max sucking down water on the breaks and only barely registering Jenks's coaching until the referee called them back to it.

Max was up on points with a handful of seconds left in the

final round, preparing to unleash a barrage that would put Theo on her heels and lock down the win. She slapped a hook out of the way and ducked under the kick that followed. As she straightened, she spotted something outside the cage.

Several fans were holding a digital sign that read:

JENKS VS MAX:
THE EPIC FIGHT COMETH

It was something Jenks had said in jest during an interview, one of her funnier asides, and even Max had laughed in the moment. But now it froze her blood and made all the doubts swirl back into the front of her brain.

She turned, the distraction making her a second too slow to block the punch Theo threw at her back, and it slammed into her kidney, stealing her breath.

"Damn it, LT, don't let her hit you again!" Jenks shouted, and Max managed to dodge the next hit, moving in on instinct. She had a clear shot, as this time Theo didn't retreat, and Max could have thrown a punch.

She didn't.

Stop competing. Her mother's voice was loud in her head.

Max dropped her guard just a centimeter.

EIGHT

Sol System

Jenks muttered a curse as Theo scored a punch to Max's kidney. "Damn it, LT, don't let her hit you again!" She glanced away from the cage for just a moment as Chief Petty Officer Luis Armstrong joined her.

"Tivo said to tell you hi."

Jenks offered her cheek for Luis to kiss. "I need to send him an email soon."

"He knows you're busy, no rush. Hey, buddy." Luis reached down and patted Doge on the head. "Rough fight?"

"Nah." Jenks allowed herself to reach up and touch the scar at the lower edge of his jaw, even knowing there was likely a camera on them.

She'd thought she'd lost him two years ago and the ache still reared up in the middle of the night to put its teeth into her with unexpected ferocity. The loss had nearly taken her, too, and even now she couldn't picture a life without him in it. Jenks dropped her hand, looking back at the cage. "She's got it in the bag, she just— Oh sonofabitch."

The crowd's groan almost drowned her out as Max staggered back into the cage wall, blood streaming from her nose. Theo followed her and got several more punches in before the final bell rang and Vance stepped between them.

"Winner on points, Lieutenant Aloisi!"

"Fuck," Jenks muttered.

"I've got poor timing," Luis said. "Well, shit."

Jenks shoved both hands into her hair with another curse. Overall, they were fine; the loss wouldn't impact their standing much in the rankings.

The shock was because she wasn't entirely sure what had just happened, or if what she'd seen in that split second when she'd looked away from Luis back to the cage was just her brain playing tricks on her.

Had Max dropped her guard?

There wasn't any time to contemplate it as Max's so rarely raised voice suddenly split the noise in the gym.

"Back the fuck off me, now."

Jenks shoved through the crowd to the cage door and spotted Max in the face of the same reporter who'd been after her the other day. She shared a quick look with Nika and grabbed her lieutenant by the wrist, putting herself between Max and the reporter, trusting that Nika would take care of the man if she could just get Max out of here before her temper actually slipped and she took a swing at a civilian.

"Hey, close loss, LT. Don't worry about it!" She kept the false cheer in her voice, relieved to see that Luis had followed her, the big man providing an additional barrier between Max and the reporter. Jenks kept moving forward into Max's personal space, babbling about how disappointed she was they weren't going to fight.

Her lieutenant gave ground reluctantly until they were well away from the crowd of reporters and other Neos, but Jenks continued to usher her toward the locker rooms until they were safely out of view.

"Sit down and let me look at that."

"I'm fine." Max shook her off, dabbing at her split lip and bleeding nose.

"What happened?"

"Nothing. That reporter was in my face again and I wasn't in the mood."

Jenks studied her friend. "I don't blame you, but I was talking about the match. You had her handled."

"I missed a block."

I'll be honest, Max: That didn't look like a blocking issue. It looked like you dropped your guard deliberately; but it's you and that's not like you in the slightest. So, what the actual fuck?

Yet Jenks couldn't make the words leave her mouth.

"Watch out for her; she's faster than you'd think." Max pressed a towel to her face and headed for the showers, leaving Jenks standing alone in the middle of the locker room.

She wrestled with the urge to look at the replay, to force Max to talk to her, and with the desire to go back out into the gym to make the reporter regret the day he messed with her friend, but ultimately did none of it.

"Fuck." She rubbed both hands over her face with a groan. "How did I become the responsible one?"

"You got promoted," Doge replied. "Though, technically you have always been responsible; you just like to pretend otherwise."

Jenks laughed. "Listen, I don't need a callout from my own dog."

"You asked." From the tone of his voice Jenks figured if he'd had shoulders, he would have shrugged them at her.

JENKS: Hey, Tamago, get in here.

TAMAGO: Give me a second, finishing my report to security.

Jenks whistled. She hadn't expected Nika to actually call security, but maybe he knew something she didn't. She'd gone looking at the bylines and bio of one E. Strzecki and it was all a bunch of gossipy trash. The sort of thing that had somehow survived the Collapse.

Like cockroaches.

"What's up?" Tamago asked as they came into the locker room.

"Did things die down out there?"

"Yeah, security escorted Strzecki out of the building. You know he spent two years doing community service for harassing Max?"

Jenks's hard-won calm splintered a bit. "He what?" Doge also snarled and she shot him a side-eyed look. "Easy, boy."

"Technically it was a trespassing charge. He got into NeoG headquarters under false pretenses and cornered Max in the admiral's office. He's lucky he didn't get pitched to the Outer Edge." Tamago's usually pleasant expression hardened. "Nika had some choice words for him and told security that if they let Strzecki back in the facility, he'd hold them personally responsible." Now they grinned. "It was pretty impressive. I think he's going to put in a request to Admiral Chen about permanently barring the man from NeoG property. Something about it violating the terms of his release."

"Sounds like a good idea." Jenks scrubbed a hand over her hair. "Although I'm sure there's some sort of free speech rule that will prevent that from sticking."

"Time arguing that in court will still keep him away."

"True. Hey, stay here, will you, and keep an eye on Max until Nika finishes?"

"Can do. Something's been bothering her for a while, but I've never seen her actually lose her temper like that." Tamago chewed on their lower lip. "She came close to hitting him, Jenks, and that whole thing would have gone down differently if she had."

"I know." Jenks muttered another curse. Normally unflappable Max taking a swing at someone without a very good reason wasn't something she could have predicted, and it was worrisome. Coupled with the unexpected lost match and what Jenks was afraid she'd seen, it felt like something that could go from bad to worse in the blink of an eye.

Tamago tapped their fist to Jenks's shoulder. "We'll be okay and Nika's wrapped things with security, so it's probably safe for you to go out there."

"You attempting to distract me?" Jenks grinned at their shrug.

"I know you'd punch him at least once if you had the chance and I'd rather not see you get busted back down again. I do not want to be in charge. Seemed safer to make sure he was long gone before you went back out."

"Not me. I turned over a whole new leaf. Now I'm all responsible, remember?" she said as she headed for the door.

"You challenged the entire bar to a fight last night." Tamago's teasing reminder followed Jenks out of the locker room.

"I *challenged* them. Old me would have just started throwing motherfuckers around."

Tamago laughed.

Jenks's humor fled when she met Luis and Nika outside. Sapphi was a few steps away, chatting with some fans who had floor passes. Jenks wasn't sure if it was her mood coloring everything or if Sapphi's smile was a little strained.

"Everything taken care of?"

Her brother nodded once, but his gaze was unfocused as he read something on his DD. Then he blinked it away and gave her a nod. He, at least, seemed to be behaving normally and some of the tension eased from Jenks's shoulders.

"He's out of here. I just put in a formal request to bar him from NeoG property. All property. I don't know if it'll get approved given how his release agreement is written. But it's what I can do. Jenks, if you see him again—"

Jenks sighed. "I know, I'll behave myself."

Nika shook his head.

"I'm going to go check on something over by Sapphi," Luis said, and Jenks frowned at him.

After he'd moved out of earshot, she looked back at her brother. His face was serious as he leaned in. "Unofficially: If you see Strzecki again, you take care of it. I'll back you the best I can. Just get him to hit you first."

Jenks only just kept the vicious satisfaction from spreading across her face. They were standing where there was a gap in camera coverage, but some enterprising soul could have gotten a bead on them. Nika must have thought the same; he had angled his face so it wasn't visible. She nodded. This was Max and she'd do whatever necessary to keep her safe.

"Can do."

Her DD pinged with a file from Luis. The subject line read:

Tavern brawl looks like a Renaissance painting.

Jenks laughed softly and shook her head. Over the last two years he'd gotten strangely obsessed with her meme fascination, but in true Intel fashion he'd skewed toward using it for sending her messages—sometimes random, sometimes important.

Something told her this one had to do with Max's harasser rather than just something fun. So she tucked it away to read later and headed in Luis's direction, moving out of the gap and hearing the swell in crowd noise when one of the main cameras immediately tracked her.

Barnes and Pace were probably talking about her match this afternoon in their usual rapid-fire style. She raised a hand in salute to draw the attention of the cameras when she spotted Theo crossing nearby with the members of *Bog Monster*. The roar of the crowd drowned out everything else as she pointed at her eyes with two fingers and then at Theo. The lieutenant lifted her fists and blew Jenks a kiss.

For a moment, everything was as it should be.

SAPPHI EXCHANGED THE COMPLEX HANDSHAKE WITH MAX that evening, echoing her LT's celebration as the roar of the crowd filled the air. She wrapped one arm around Tamago's waist, waving to the crowd with the other.

Her predictions had been almost spot-on—in fact, they'd been eighteen points up on *Flux* at the end. Jenks had dominated Theo in the cage match less than an hour earlier. The fighter from *Bog Monster* was good, but a matchup between Max and Jenks would have been more level. Sapphi still wasn't sure how the LT had lost; she'd felt certain in her calculations for that fight.

Either way, *Zuma* was once again on top and looking good for the Games themselves. Sapphi's time in the hacking championship and the team's speed in the Big Game would get even better with the addition of *Flux*'s crew. Sapphi still couldn't figure out why her portion of the final team competition had seemed so easy, but as Jenks was fond of saying, "You look a gift tiger in the mouth, you'll lose your head."

She was pretty sure that saying was modified somehow from the original.

She hummed to herself as she bumped fists and hugged the other Neos milling around on the floor of the gym. Her family had left early and while Sapphi missed them already, she was also a little relieved to not have to keep pretending everything was okay for longer than necessary. Between the weirdness in the Verge, her final match, and Yasu, she needed some serious "leave me alone" time, and she was so close to getting there.

The closing ceremonies were done, and they were heading back to Trappist in the morning. She'd maybe make an appearance at the celebrations and then duck out, turn her noise dampeners on high, and get some sleep. Sapphi waved to Jenks from across the floor. The chief finished her conversation with Commander Pham and then headed their way, Doge trailing behind.

"Congratulations."

She turned to see Yasu and was surprised again by the semi-excited flopping of her stomach. "Thanks."

"I'm seeing now why *Zuma* has been at the top for the last several years. You all are quite the team."

"We like to think so. Don't let it fool you, though; it's taken a lot of training for us to get to this point."

"I don't doubt it." Yasu slipped his hands into the pockets of his pants. "It's been a fascinating break from work to participate in this. I'm almost sad to have to go back."

"Are you going to tell me what the fuck happened?" Sapphi made a face and sighed. "Sorry—again—just ignore my mouth."

"I never could," he murmured the words just before Jenks reached them.

"Victors once again." Jenks swept her into a hug, kissing Sapphi's cheek noisily, and Sapphi was grateful for the distraction from the sudden confusing pool of heat in her belly. Jenks released her, turning to Yasu with a curious look and an outstretched fist. "Chief Altandai Khan."

"Yasu Gregori with Dànǎo Dynamics. And I'm very aware of who you are—I'm a big fan. It's nice to meet you, Chief." He nodded and crouched down, offering his fist again. "Doge."

"You know who I am?"

"Everyone knows who you are—I'm a big fan of yours, too. I have to say it's a delight to get to speak to an actual functioning ROVER." Then he smiled at Sapphi as he stood. "I'll let you go celebrate. It was good to see you again. I hope we can talk soon."

She bit her lip as he started to turn around, then impulsively threw all her plans out the airlock. "Yasu," Sapphi called as he walked away. "Is that dinner offer still on the table?"

He stopped and faced her. "Of course. Tonight?"

"That's fine. I could be ready in half an hour or so."

"I'll come get you."

"Okay."

Sapphi couldn't stop the smile from spreading as Yasu walked away, even though she knew Jenks would launch into teasing the moment he was out of earshot.

"I'm proud of you." Jenks didn't tease, only wrapped her arms around her and hugged. Sapphi leaned into her with a soft sigh.

"I don't know what I'm doing. He's an old friend."

"Good old friend or bad?"

"Yes."

Jenks arched an eyebrow.

"It's a long story."

Jenks squeezed her tighter. "As long as it's something you want to do, then it's fine. I'll corner you in the ship on the way home and you can tell me the details until you're so embarrassed, you take my cleaning duty for a week.

"Now let's go enjoy our well-deserved congratulations."

SAPPHI REFUSED TO LET HERSELF FUSS OVER HER APPEARance and dressed in a pair of her blue cargos that were too worn for duty, with a bright yellow shirt emblazoned with the words DISASTER BISEXUAL in a cheery rainbow font.

She'd just finished braiding her hair when the knock on their quarter doors came. The rest of the team was out at the Ship, celebrating under the watchful, glitter-lined eyes of Claire the bartender, and Sapphi felt a burst of nerves as she tied off the light brown strands.

"This is a Pandora's box and you know it," she said to the empty room, but her feet ignored her and carried her to the door.

"I'd realized as I was on my way here that we didn't really discuss where we were going, so I'm glad to see we were on the same wavelength as far as clothing." Yasu grinned at her and gestured at his own casual outfit. "How do you feel about ramen?"

"If you're taking me to Osni's, I'm very favorable to the idea." Sapphi grabbed her NeoG jacket and slipped her feet into her shoes before stepping into the hallway.

"I'm definitely taking you to Osni's," he said. "Just . . . point the way?"

She laughed. "It occurred to me you might need clearance to get through the gates, but I guess not?"

"I've got clearance," Yasu replied, and gestured for Sapphi to precede him down the hall.

"For the prelims?"

"Actually, long-term. I've been working on a project with some NeoG software engineers for almost five years now. That's sort of how I ended up being able to do the Games programs."

They kept up a steady stream of light conversation about work as they walked to the restaurant. The foot traffic was higher than normal as people were out celebrating and Sapphi had to stop to sign more than a few autographs along the way.

"I'm really sorry. I shouldn't have worn the jacket," she apologized sheepishly.

"Don't worry about it. It's an interesting experience to be around a celebrity."

"I'm not the celebrity, Jenks is."

Yasu raised a black eyebrow at the pack of girls who'd just wandered off, still looking starstruck by their encounter, and Sapphi laughed.

"Okay, maybe a little. Which, I suppose is good news for us because I also happen to know Ivan and he can give us the back room if it's open so we can eat in peace." She pulled the door to Osni's open and gestured Yasu inside.

As luck would have it, the room was open and Sapphi settled into her seat with a bowl of steaming tonkotsu and a happy sigh. She grabbed a piece of 3D-printed pork and a mass of noodles with her chopsticks and saluted Yasu before shoving it all into her mouth.

"I see your table manners haven't gotten any better."

"Worse," she admitted. "Boot camp meals and Interceptor training pretty much destroyed what was left, to my parents' dismay. OCS tried to improve upon them, but what was done was done."

"It's still hard to wrap my head around the idea of you going to boot camp, let alone officer candidate school," Yasu murmured. "How is your family? I saw them at the championship match but didn't think that was the best venue to reintroduce myself."

Sapphi poked through her bowl and glanced up at him through her lashes. "Your story first, then I'll spill."

"Fair enough." Yasu took a sip from his bowl and then set it down again. Those dark eyes fixed on her with the same intensity that had always driven her to her knees. "I crashed and burned, Sapphi, just like you said I would."

Sapphi winced. She had said exactly that, in the last argument they'd had. Harsh words shouted through streaming tears and gritted teeth.

"Hey, don't feel bad. It wasn't your fault. None of it was your fault." Yasu extended a hand across the table, but she didn't take it—she wasn't ready for that. "I was fucked-up, Sapphi, full-bore systems failure. If anyone should apologize, it's me. I'm sorry for everything. I almost dragged you down with me and I—" He inhaled, curling his fingers and pulling his hand away. "That's why I ghosted. Well, that and the rehab center didn't really allow for outside contact, but I also figured that it was safer for you if I wasn't in your life anymore."

"That wasn't your choice to make," she whispered. They'd argued about that, too.

"You're right, but you wouldn't have made the good decision and we both know it. You wouldn't have done what was best for you. You would have kept trying to save me and let's be real, Sapphi, it would have probably ended badly for both of us."

"So rehab?" Sapphi wasn't ready to confront the truth of Yasu's words. She'd had a soft spot for him since the first moment they'd met, ignored her parents' objections, gotten herself into more difficulty than she could handle chasing an older and more worldly person.

The drugs had been a secondary benefit, and while Sapphi had never gotten hooked the way Yasu had already been when they met, she'd hit rock bottom herself several months after their fight and Yasu's subsequent disappearance.

She'd had family to see her through it, though, endless support that had never wavered even in her darkest hours. Her mother and fathers hadn't really understood why she'd wanted to join the NeoG instead of accepting the offer from Dànǎo Dynamics after her recovery, but they'd gone with it with the same loving care she'd received her whole life.

The truth of the matter was she couldn't fathom going to Dànǎo Dynamics without Yasu—not realizing he would end up there anyway—and the NeoG would get her off Earth, as far away from the memories as was humanly possible. She'd been perfectly content with the idea of being just another enlisted grunt, but the master chief at boot had taken one look at her and thought differently.

"Yeah, and in rehab my therapist helped me figure out that my destructive decisions were tangled in this idea of me being my dad's perfect girl." Yasu gave a soft smile. "They told me he was gone and I could live the life I wanted. Eventually I realized they were right. I didn't have to keep doing what he'd wanted—I could do and be whatever *I* wanted."

He leaned back in his chair and spread his hands wide. "The easy end to this story is I did just that."

"I expect the reality is a bit messier," Sapphi replied.

"A bit." Yasu's eyes brightened with humor and he returned to his ramen, first poking in her direction with his chopsticks. "I only died metaphorically, though—you did it for real. For the record I'm glad you came back."

"I don't recommend it." Sapphi dug into her own food and made a face. "Dying is weird. Coming back is almost worse." The words spilled out of her before she could stop them.

"Everything is fucked-up, Yasu, and I'm a little worried that my brain is actually broken."

She found him on the overlook, staring moodily out over the wine-dark sea. "That was uncalled for," she said as she sat and folded her hands in her lap.

His huff was echoed in the burst of wind that swirled around them, disheveling his black hair even more and sending hers floating in the air about her face. "I could say the same about you, or are you really going to sit there and pretend that you didn't do anything?"

"I don't know what you're talking about."

He threw a hand up and the image of Sapphi in the club resolved against the rolling cumulonimbus clouds. "You. Made. Contact."

She hid her wince and the ache in her heart at a face that brought with it far too many memories. The confusion and fear that he'd somehow managed to see what she'd done despite all her precautions in her attempt to speak with the NeoG ensign had to be folded away to be dealt with later. Right now required boldness, or she'd never get free of this. "So did you and in a far more dramatic fashion than I."

"That one knows the deadly kiss of lightning."

A sharp bolt of the same illuminated his vicious grin, but she refused to give him the satisfaction of a reaction and his expression soured quickly.

"Stay away from her." It was meant to be an order, but it came out as a plea.

As if to drive that home, he said, "You forget that you no longer get to order me around. I give the orders, you follow; it's the only way to keep you safe." Now his face softened and she forced herself to hold still as he reached a hand out to brush her hair from her face. "Trust that I know what I'm doing—that I know what's best. I'm only trying to protect you. Please stop fighting me."

She wouldn't. She couldn't. Not with so much at stake.

NINE

Max closed out her email with a sigh. It had been a mistake to look at it, but she'd been restless. *Zuma* was in line for the wormhole transit and it was unusually busy, so she'd been looking for something to distract herself.

The email had been from her father and Max hadn't had to read more than the subject line of:

Family Duty

before she'd deleted it unread.

The one from Ria she'd made the mistake of opening. The second mistake had been clicking on the link to the article Strzecki had so cleverly titled:

**CARMICHAEL LOSES MATCH
AND TEMPER AT PRELIMS**

The worst part was there was no lie contained in the whole thing. She had lost the match and her temper. If Jenks hadn't intervened, she'd probably also be looking at an assault charge. The only good news was that the official family letter still hadn't dropped, though some part of her wondered what twisted game her mother was playing by delaying it.

"That serious expression about the transit or something else?" Nika asked as he sat down in the seat next to her.

"Transit is fine," she replied. "Just taking forever. It's crowded today."

"You think prelim champs could jump the line," he teased. She flinched.

"That was a tender spot. I'm sorry. What's up, Max?"

"Who says something has to be up?"

"I was there for at least part of that interaction with your mother, before she kicked me out." He laughed but then went serious. "Did I say something—"

"No, it's not you," she replied. The words *I fucked up* danced on her tongue, but before she could get them out the com buzzed.

"*Zuma's Ghost*, this is Jupiter Station Wormhole Control: you are next up. Cleared for transit in five minutes."

"Thanks, Control. Tell everyone on the station we waved as we flew by."

"Will do, Lieutenant. Congrats on the prelims win. We'll be cheering for you at the Games."

"We appreciate it. Will be ready to jump through on your go." Max clicked off the com. "Crew, we go in five minutes. Stow and lock gear," she announced over the ship com.

"You flinched again," Nika said quietly. "Do you want to talk about it?"

The downside of being involved with someone who occasionally knew you better than you knew yourself was that they called you on your bullshit. Still, she wasn't quite able to make the words in her head come out into the air.

How did you say *My mother threatened you and then I deliberately lost a match* without sounding like an absolute asshole?

"Did you miss not competing in the Games?" she deflected.

Nika rolled with the subject change and Max was grateful for it. "I remember feeling like I was missing out during the prelims. It was oddly easier to be at the Games with all of you, even though I was injured and didn't know if I'd ever compete again. Why?"

"I hadn't expected this when I joined the Interceptors. I know I probably should have, but it feels sometimes like I just fell into it and there's no way out."

"There's a way out—we decide not to compete anymore," he replied. "Wouldn't be the first time. Well, for some of us. Jenks has competed since she put on boots."

"You think the higher-ups would just let the 'four-time Boarding Games Champions *Zuma's Ghost*' stop competing?"

Nika blinked at her and Max realized how bitter her words had sounded. Before she could apologize, though, he reached out and offered her his hand. She took it, the warmth of his fingers around hers a grounding feeling she'd come to depend on.

"I think we're a team and we get to make the decision for ourselves. This isn't your family, Max. If we want to stop and focus on the job, Stephan will back us. If he backs us, Admiral Chen will also. The mission is the priority, always. The Games are just fun."

"Not entirely fun," she murmured.

"Well, true, the wins have helped the service in the long run, but someone else can take up the mantle for a while. We'll talk about it in the next team meeting."

That wasn't what she'd meant, but she let the moment slide by without correcting him. "No, let's wait until after the Games. I don't want to disrupt things."

Nika remained unconvinced. "You don't always have to think of everyone else first, you know."

"*You* do."

"But I'm the commander," he said with a grin.

She smiled. "And yes, I know. I just think it's better this way." She squeezed his hand and let him go as the com pinged with the warning for the transit. "Thanks for listening."

"Anytime."

Max hit the ship com. "*Zuma's Ghost*, prepare for wormhole transit. We go in five, four, three, two, one."

JENKS GRABBED FOR THE TABLE EDGE WHEN MAX'S ANnouncement came over the com and the familiar, disorienting feeling of traversing the wormhole rushed through her.

It passed quickly and Max's voice lilted through the air again. "And we're on the Trappist side, everyone. DDs should have updated to local time—looks like we didn't lose a whole lot."

Travel through the wormholes wasn't consistent in the amount of time it took to cross from one side of space to the other. While the longest recorded passing was an eighty-three-hour gap from one side to the other, usually it was only a handful of hours; but with the added confusion of the different day lengths on the planets between the Sol and Trappist systems, anyone who traveled regularly between points just stopped trying to keep track and trusted that their chips had automatically updated wherever they were headed to.

Jenks hated the traverse. She was of a small percentage of people who occasionally experienced lingering dizziness and headaches from the trip. This time, at least, it seemed like it wasn't going to stick around.

"You okay?" Luis asked, putting a hand on her back.

"Yeah." She smiled over her shoulder at him. "Thanks for the help with dinner." They still had the better part of a standard day until they reached Trappist-1d.

"Least I could do in exchange for the rides." He winked at her.

Jenks grinned in response. "You're always welcome to a ride—"

Tamago groaned. "There are other people in the room, you two."

"Those other people should be working." Jenks dodged Tamago's foot easily and blew them a kiss.

"We are off duty," Tamago sang the words. Then they nudged Sapphi. "Hey, it's your move."

"Huh?" Sapphi blinked. "Sorry." She leaned forward and tapped the screen between them.

Tamago mock glared when the victory music blared in the air and Sapphi's side lit up with fireworks. "Even when she's not paying attention, she kicks my ass at this."

Jenks chuckled. "I warned you that Sapphi would be a natural at Crocodile. Play Luis if you want to win."

"Hey," he protested, but then sighed. "It's true, actually; the boys beat me on the regular."

"I have a hard time seeing Stephan playing anything," Sapphi said, and Luis choked on a laugh.

"My sons."

"That makes more sense, and excellent." Tamago shifted chairs and brought up the screen again. "Sapphi, you can take Luis's place on dinner duty."

"Is that my prize for winning?"

Jenks patted her on the shoulder. "The prize for good work is more work."

Sapphi's good-natured grumbling was lost to the laughter. Even Chae had looked away from the book they were reading to join in and Jenks drank in the feeling of being home once more.

She used to look forward to the Games, but something had shifted in the last year and now it felt a bit like she was just going through the motions.

You may not be the only one.

The unsettling feeling that she really needed to watch the

recording of Max's fight and then have a difficult conversation was still scratching at the back of her head, but she shoved it away. They were headed back to Trappist, back to work. Back to the boys and time in the sun—something she never thought she'd be looking forward to quite as much as she did.

Two years ago her entire foundation had been kicked out from under her when she'd believed Luis was dead. Jenks hadn't thought she was going to survive. She hadn't wanted to survive and had come closer to the edge of ending it than she liked to think about.

The old her would have turned and run from that kind of feeling, as fast and far as she could away from the realization that she needed Tivo and Luis and his boys in her life, but the new her?

The new her wanted that routine. Looked forward to the messages, the check-ins, the feeling of being cared for and loved. Their time on Trappist had been a strange oasis of stability, one she felt like she could sink further into without any regrets whatsoever.

"Hey, space cadet, you're going to burn those pancakes," Sapphi said, elbowing her.

"Shit." She grabbed the spatula and flipped them quickly.

"Look at you doing that like you're a professional or something. You been moonlighting as a short-order when I wasn't looking?"

She beamed at Sapphi. "The boys taught me how."

Sapphi glanced over her shoulder to where Luis was focused on the game. Then she wrapped an arm around Jenks's waist and leaned down to rest her head on Jenks's shoulder. "Love looks good on you."

"Don't tell anyone," Jenks replied, slipping her free arm around Sapphi and squeezing her back. "It'll ruin my street cred."

"I've got bad news for you, Khan . . ."

"Hush, let me have my delusions."

Dearest Mags,

Thank you again for the sunglasses; they've come in handy. I miss you and Ikram desperately and I hope that you'll both be able to come visit soon.

Trappist is fascinating and at the risk of making you laugh at me, it reminds me of home. The dirt is a touch more orange, though. People who say it's red have never been to Mars.

Everyone here is very kind. I don't know why I thought that it would be more difficult than it has been to transition from the Navy to the NeoG. Apparently, I bought into more of that silly propaganda I rolled my own eyes at for years than I realized.

I was reminded, rather abruptly, of your uncle Hadi the other day. I met some old friends of his who now live on Trappist-1d. It's strange that the past comes up here of all places, but it seems to be all around me. My commander was also a friend of Hadi's, and I suppose a friend of mine also. He's a good man, has suffered some loss that makes him wary, but I think he's trying to do the right thing.

It makes me think I should follow his example and . . .

Emel sighed and rubbed a hand over her eyes. She'd almost typed: *com your mother. I miss her.* And she did want to com Rajaa, even though the likelihood that her ex would answer was minimal at best.

Once upon a time they'd been inseparable, until time and casual disregard had worn away at them.

Until I stopped paying attention.

The guilt rose up in a hot wash of bile. Emel shut her tablet down without finishing the letter, heaving a second sigh as she went in search of a distraction.

She heard the cacophony of voices even before she hit the doorway of the community area, and knew it heralded the return of both *Zuma's Ghost* and *Flux Capacitor* from the preliminaries. Her guess was confirmed when she crossed the threshold and spotted D'Arcy in an embrace with a shorter woman whose wild flame-red hairstyle marked her as Chief Petty Officer Khan as surely as her handshake did.

D'Arcy gave the woman a smacking kiss on the mouth before setting her back on the floor. His frustration and anger were completely gone, replaced with a genuine joy she didn't think she'd ever seen on his face.

"Forgive their lack of decorum, Master Chief," someone murmured from her left, and Emel jerked a little in surprise.

The NeoG lieutenant had loose curls that were a halo of bronze pulled back from her lovely face, and the teasing note in her voice was a complementary counterpoint to the fondness in her eyes. "Lieutenant Max Carmichael, she/her. It's nice to meet you, and welcome to the NeoG."

Emel tapped the offered fist. "It's a pleasure, Lieutenant."

"Max, please."

"Emel."

The younger woman nodded in acknowledgment. "I heard you all had some excitement the other day. The reports were on the Intel server, before you think I'm clairvoyant."

"Now I'm just wondering where you found the time to read them while in the middle of winning the preliminaries."

Max chuckled. "I have what Nika affectionately calls a 'work-life balance issue.'"

"I know this issue all too well." Emel offered up a smile in solidarity. "We did have some excitement. Derelict freighter that's been missing since 2434, though if you've read the reports, you know all about it."

"I did, but I like hearing people's take on it also."

"I was on *Dread* the whole time." Emel was surprised she was able to keep her voice level. She'd told D'Arcy that she understood, but it still rankled, especially after their altercation this morning during the mission briefing for their trip tomorrow.

I don't know—maybe you shouldn't have called him out in

front of the others like that, even if it was only the officers and the gunny there to witness it.

Quickdraw's face had been sympathetic at least, even as he'd given his head a slight shake to try to warn her off, and Commander Pia Forsberg had backed Emel's insistence that the crew was ready, though she'd somehow done it without earning even more of D'Arcy's ire.

"So I read." Max's tone was neutral, her eyes on the group of people still immersed in the rapid-fire recounting of the preliminaries. "Emel, I realize we've just met, and you have a longer history with D'Arcy than I do, but I wanted to—"

"Max!" D'Arcy had slipped away and held his hands out to the lieutenant. "I heard you decided to save the big fight with Jenks for the Games themselves."

The slight hesitation as Max reached for D'Arcy wasn't because the lieutenant didn't want contact with him, but rather from his joking words, and Emel watched curiously as the woman's open smile shifted into a practiced look her own mother would have called a "company smile."

"Jenks's showmanship is rubbing off on me, it seems," Max replied, leaning in and pressing her cheek to D'Arcy's.

The affection in her eyes was real, which only made the puzzling reaction even more interesting.

"I see you met Emel. Come meet Heli." D'Arcy raised his voice. "Jenks, come over here and say hello to your better."

"There's no one better than me" came the reply, and Emel laughed, meeting the notorious chief halfway across the room as D'Arcy led Max away. "Master Chief." Jenks didn't salute but held her fist out until Emel tapped her own against it. The Robotic Optics Vehicular and Extravehicular Reconnaissance AI at her heels sat down and held up a metal paw. "This is Doge."

Enchanted, Emel reached out and took the ROVER's paw. "Hi, Doge."

"Welcome to the NeoG, Master Chief Shevreaux. It's a pleasure to meet you."

"He's an original, isn't he?"

Jenks lifted a shoulder. "Had some upgrades here and there, but essentially, yeah. Last one still running as far as we know. Congratulations on your escape from the Navy."

Emel laughed again. "Thanks. In fairness, though, I should warn you I enjoyed my time in, Chief."

"I'll forgive you for it. Call me Jenks. Have you met Senior Chief Armstrong? Also, I heard you all got yourselves a ghost ship. Was it legit empty? I was excited when Max told me. We haven't had any decent weirdness around here for what feels like forever."

"Jenks, you're talking at light speed," the tall, blond cis man said with a healthy amount of fondness lacing the warning.

"Of course I am. I'm *excited*. Ghost ship." She sang the last two words in off-key delight. "There are so many missing ships, especially around here! The best ones are the ones that get found later just empty AF like this one. *Bellend's Run* is one of the more famous. But there's also *Jumping Spider, Imogene Darver, Pine Needles in the Snow*—"

"Master Chief, welcome to Trappist. We're happy to have you on board with Intel." Luis Armstrong's bright smile spread over his handsome face. It wasn't at all diminished by the scar that arced from his left temple down to his chin.

Emel knew some of the story of the attack on the NeoG, but she suspected there was more to it than had been released to the public. Every branch of the CHN military had responded in the aftermath of the explosions on Jupiter Station and the NeoG Intel headquarters on Earth.

Luis effortlessly introduced her around to the other members of *Zuma* and *Flux,* and the noise volume rose as the impromptu gathering morphed into a celebration of the two Interceptor crews' performances at the prelims.

Emel settled onto the corner of a couch as the conversation swirled around her. Heli looked a bit starstruck as Nika spoke with her about his sword-fighting win. Jenks and *Flux*

Capacitor's senior chief **Dao Mai Tien** were having a good-natured argument about some video game. Others were clustered in groups of two or three.

This is what I missed.

The tension she hadn't even realized she'd been carrying in her shoulders released.

"YOU ARE A ROCK STAR, AS USUAL." LUPE LEANED DOWN AND kissed Sapphi, patting her face with both of his hands before he straightened and headed across the room. Finally alone for a moment, she called up the replay of her recording for the hacking competition and watched it again.

Nothing. No lightning. No strange glitch. Just her hands moving at rapid speed and doing exactly what she'd been trained to do. What she was good at.

"Sapphi?"

"Hmm? Sorry." She forced her attention away from the video and down to where Doge was sitting at her feet. "What's up?"

"What's that song you're humming?"

"I wasn't humming anything."

"You were. I've heard it before. Here."

She paused and listened to his playback. "I'm sorry, I didn't realize I was doing it. I don't know. Where did you hear it?"

"All over here at Trappist," the AI replied. "Can't trace the signal, though; it's just like the stars are singing it."

Sapphi frowned. "I maybe need to do a full-diagnostic run on you, buddy. You might be picking up some weird frequency."

"Ugh, I hate those. It's on the ship, too."

She patted him. "What ship?"

"The one Commander Montaglione found. I heard it on the recording."

"How'd you get the vids?" She blinked at him and leaned forward in her seat.

"I've always had access to the team server. You set it up that way when you and Jenks brought me online."

"Oh, I guess I did." Sapphi just couldn't remember the AI ever taking the initiative to look at anything himself. "Can you do a search for the song just off the melody?"

"I have access to any song on the net. A search like that will take a while, though."

"You can run it background, yeah?"

"Of course." Doge turned his head when Jenks called his name. He leaned briefly into Sapphi's leg in goodbye before getting to his feet and crossing the room.

She watched him go, setting a reminder for herself to tackle that diagnostic tomorrow and to talk with Jenks about it. It had been over two years since they'd done a full. Though they'd done plenty of basics, it was past time for another one. She had no experience with AIs beyond Doge, but it seemed like he'd been learning more new things and that technically shouldn't be possible.

His AI had specific parameters for learning, but . . . she pulled up his parent code and studied it for a long moment. There was a lot more leeway than in newer models. She couldn't tell without actually matching it to his code now, but maybe there was a chance he was actively learning things beyond his programming.

She was both thrilled and a little worried by the prospect. Best to wait and talk to Jenks about it before she did anything else.

Sapphi went back to her recording, watching the first-person view of her own hands skimming over the command codes for the final challenge and the shifting numbers on the screen. The lightning she'd thought she'd seen never manifested. Neither had the message.

Did I make it all up?

The thought scared her. She hadn't told Yasu about this piece when she'd admitted to him that it felt like her brain was short-circuiting. It had been weird enough to talk about it with someone who was basically a stranger when she couldn't tell her own teammates and yet the words had just kept coming.

The thought of their dinner did make things feel a little less dark. *It was good to see him again.* She could admit that to herself. The unopened email from him in her inbox was tempting her, but it also made her feel like the biggest traitor in the universe.

How long do I grieve for a relationship that never actually existed?

"Hey you." D'Arcy joined her on the couch. "Up for a hug?"

"Always." She leaned into his side and wrapped her arms around his waist. D'Arcy reminded her of her father Umar. Safe, dependable, and always there. "We missed you at the prelims."

"We missed being there. How are you doing? You've been pretty quiet this evening."

"I'm sort of peopled out, TBH."

"You want me to step off?"

"No, it's fine." She hesitated as she pulled away from the hug, then said, "D'Arcy, do you ever have memories that you think might not have happened?"

He looked at her curiously. "I've got a few I wish hadn't happened, but otherwise no, not really. Why?"

"Things have been—I don't know. Weird." She held her hands out and then whispered brokenly, "I miss Akane." She curled into D'Arcy again, the tears hot and unexpected.

"I know." He tightened his arms around her and sighed. "I do, too."

TEN

Outer Edge of Trappist System

Emel exhaled as she got to her feet. She carefully picked up and rolled her prayer mat, fingers smoothing over the rust-colored surface. It had been a gift from her mother shortly after their conversation that Emel was going back out into space with the NeoG. She tucked it away in the embroidered cream bag with her Tayammum stone.

The ship was quiet, half the crew asleep in their bunks, while Aki and Heli were up in the bridge—ostensibly training the ensign on piloting duties, but also giving Emel the space she'd needed for her prayers.

She was thankful for it and for this chance to find a little peace. Everything else washed away in her communication with Allah, the fears and worries gone even if only for a little while.

Worries like the fact that her commander was still so wary and standoffish after they'd been here more than a month. Emel had hoped Joe was wrong, that D'Arcy would settle, and he had, sort of, but he was also so closed off and it rippled throughout the crew like a concussive blast in a bunker.

Emel made her way through the darkened room, careful not to wake Lupe, who was sleeping soundly in his bunk, as she stashed her bag back in its place and slipped out on soundless feet. As she climbed the stairs to the bridge, she could hear Aki speaking.

". . . formation is always going to have the lead ship in the center spot of the starboard side. The other ships will shift depending on how many there are and what's going on, but this is where we are, which means that *Wandering Hunter* is where?"

"On our starboard."

"Right, so hopefully we wouldn't have a reason to—"

The coms buzzed and Emel paused at the head of the stairs as Spacer Anneli Rantanen's smooth voice came over from *Wandering Hunter*.

"*Dread*, you getting that?"

Aki hit the com and answered before Heli's hand had even twitched toward the console. "Getting what, Moose?"

"Distress call—well, maybe, it wasn't clear. We didn't get a lock on it. You didn't hear it?"

"Nothing," Aki replied. "Weird—send us a copy?"

"Already doing it."

Emel came the rest of the way onto the bridge in the intervening pause and slipped into her seat, booting up a quick scan as the playback from *Hunter* came through.

"'. . . repeat, this is passenger vessel *Imogene Darver*, reques . . . failure . . . main system went down forty-three minutes ago . . . ower on secondary going fast. There are . . . on board. Please . . .'" The voice was overlaid with static, the words fading in and out beneath the noise.

Emel frowned, something dancing just out of reach in her memory. It vanished before she could get ahold of it. "There's nothing on the scans," she said. "Widening the search."

"I'll go get D'Arcy." Aki pushed out of her seat.

"The ensign makes that call, Petty Officer," Emel said. She

tried to keep her voice even and free of judgment, but they both knew that Heli should be giving orders and making decisions. As lax as the NeoG was about some things out in the black, the chain of command was there to keep people safe. Moreover, there was no clear and present danger and Heli really needed the practice of handling these situations on her own.

Her words still brought Aki up short and the younger woman glared as she dropped back into her chair.

"Ensign, you have command," Emel prompted gently, ignoring Heli's wide-eyed look that bounced between them.

"Right." Heli cleared her throat and hit the com. "Moose, you said you didn't get a lock? We're not seeing anything on the first scan. No signal. Not even the broadcast."

"Roger that. Nothing now. Just that first burst."

"Okay, let's bump up the alert level by one, but I don't think—" Heli cut themself off and Emel could almost see their attempt at refocusing as they sat up a little straighter. "There's no need to wake everyone unless something changes. Do a wide-field scan in sections one-one-four to . . ."

Emel looked back at her own scan as Heli rattled off the section breaks, and spotted D'Arcy out of the corner of her eye. He was leaning against the railing, arms crossed, watching the ensign. His dark eyes were unguarded, the emotion clear on his face, a tangle of pride and pain as he nodded slightly in approval at Heli's decision.

Then, as if he knew she was looking, the mask slammed back in place and D'Arcy looked her way as he climbed up the stairs.

"You're still on duty, Heli," he said when she started to get up. The pat on the ensign's shoulder was awkward but well intentioned. "What's next?"

As he coached the new Neo through logging a distress call, Emel caught the guilty look Aki shot in her direction and swallowed back her curse. It wasn't a coincidence that D'Arcy had appeared just then. The petty officer had called him on her DD.

It hadn't been disobeying an order—not technically, because Emel hadn't given one and neither had Heli—but it burned and Emel knew she was going to have to address it.

Somehow without making things worse than they already were in this crew that was holding on by its fingernails.

Her console beeped and Emel snapped back to the job. "I've got a hit. Possible ship at two-five-two, eight-eight-niner, one-zero-zero-seven point five. No response to a ping."

D'Arcy leaned past Heli and tapped the console, sending out the alert for the rest of the crew but without the klaxon that would indicate a serious emergency. He kept ahold of her seat back and his voice was easy, both commanding and soothing as he helped the ensign.

"What's up?" Locke asked, rubbing the sleep out of his eyes as he climbed onto the bridge, Lupe following him. Emel caught them up as the pair of Interceptors turned toward the signal.

". . . repeat, this is Interceptor *Dread Treasure* to unknown ship. Are you the *Imogene Darver* of the distress call? Please respond."

Emel froze, Jenks's delighted ramble from before echoing in her head. "No," she breathed, loud enough to attract D'Arcy's attention. She scrambled for the information on her DD.

The com crackled to life.

"*Dread Treasure*. This is passenger vessel *Imogene Darver,* requesting assistance. We have had a major engine failure. Our entire main system went down forty-three minutes ago from an unknown power surge. We are dead in the water. Our power on secondary going fast. There are five people on board. Please help us."

"D'Arcy." Emel surged out of her seat. "The *Imogene Darver* was reported missing in 2422. Seven years later it reappeared and was pulled into Trappist-1h's gravity. It crashed in the ocean and when the NeoG recovered it . . ." She swallowed. "There were no bodies on board."

The lights on *Dread* flickered and went out.

FUCK.

D'Arcy's breath caught, then released explosively when the lights came back up. Chatter filled the silence both on the bridge and the open com.

"Was that an EMP?" Locke asked, sliding into his seat.

"I think so, but the new shielding dissipated it. All readings nominal," Emel replied, glancing away from her console at him.

D'Arcy dragged his eyes away from her, his mouth flattened into a grim line. "Aki, give Locke the stick. Heli, trade me seats." He was already reaching for the coms again but caught the ensign by the arm when they tripped over their own feet trying to get out of his way. D'Arcy practically shoved them at Lupe—thankfully the petty officer was prepared and caught them.

He'd walked them right into a trap. Had been so focused on teaching Heli something, giving them a chance to run through procedure and get their hands dirty, that he'd put two boat crews in danger.

I knew they weren't ready—

"D'Arcy, you all good over there?" Pia's voice was barely checked concern.

Focus, D'Arcy.

He dragged himself away from the recrimination. "We're good here, Pia. Locke's thinking an EMP?"

"That's what Qi's saying, too. New shields held, though, and we're green. What is going on?"

"I don't know, but that ship should not be there." He scanned the console for some sign of additional ships, anything to signal they were under attack, but there was nothing. "I don't like this."

"You and me both," Pia replied.

D'Arcy was staring at the screen when the flashing light of the unknown ship vanished into nothingness.

"Lost contact," Emel said.

"Is it our systems?"

"No, they're fine." She shook her head. "It's just . . . *gone.*"

D'Arcy gritted his teeth as the uneasy rolling of his stomach increased. "Pia, are you getting anything? We lost the ping."

"Nothing. No visual, either. There's nothing there."

An uneasy silence fell on the bridge as D'Arcy looked out through the main window into the endless black surrounding the two ships. The ghostly sound of *Imogene Darver*'s last transmission echoing in his head, reminding him over and over that the last few moments were his fault.

ALMOST TWENTY HOURS LATER D'ARCY SAT IN HIS OFFICE back on Trappist-1d and stared at the file on *Imogene Darver* until the words blurred, but no amount of eye contact could make the facts change. The forensics report wasn't great, given the water damage, but they'd confirmed a massive power surge had shorted the main engine and also caused a feedback loop that drained power off the secondaries in an effort to restart an engine that was already fried beyond repair.

The ship and its crew of five had been dead for more than a decade. Until someone had apparently resurrected them to send a fake transmission and lure the NeoG into a trap.

How—and even more worrisome—why?

He didn't want to think what would have happened if they hadn't had the upgraded EMP protection, and something told him that was the only reason they'd been able to sit there in the black for twenty minutes running several deep scans instead of being involved in a dogfight.

Whatever, whoever was out there hadn't been prepared for them to still be up and running.

But they would next time.

"Fuck." D'Arcy rubbed both hands over his face and then leaned back in his chair.

"You okay?"

He jerked upright at the sound of Emel's voice, muffling a second curse. "You know Locke learned the hard way about sneaking up on me."

She braced her shoulder against the doorframe and laughed, a sound of pure delight. "I seem to remember you coming out on the losing end of things the last time we went toe-to-toe."

"Fair enough."

He didn't want this conversation. He didn't want her here— mostly because he didn't know what to do with her, with the ghosts of all these feelings rolling around in his chest. They'd done this dance on Mars—arguing and snapping but unable to stop from circling closer to each other. Then the protests had happened, and everything had changed. In the end they'd walked away on two different paths and hadn't looked back— until now.

So maybe not so different, though, since we've ended up here.

D'Arcy swallowed back a sigh. It was better to let the past stay dead. He knew she was fresh out of a divorce and he . . . well, he'd made a rule a long time ago not to get involved with his immediate crew.

Life was easier if you kept the entanglements outside of your living space. Especially one he had such a complicated history with.

"Do you have a minute?" Emel asked, unaware of the way his thoughts were spinning.

"Sure, come in."

She sat in the other chair at his gesture, leaning her fore-arms on her knees. The image of Paul, loose-limbed and smiling as he sprawled in the same chair, cut unexpectedly into D'Arcy's head and he was too slow to stop the noise that escaped.

"D'Arcy?"

"What did you need?" he asked, deliberately ignoring the unasked question in her voice. He wasn't about to burden her with his issues.

"Aki was close with Petty Officer Ito, wasn't she?"

Oh, hearing Akane's name in Emel's mouth was a worse pain. He wasn't prepared for it, either, and it made his reply sharp. "Why do you ask?"

Emel sat back and crossed her arms over her chest and D'Arcy fought the urge to apologize. "Trying to get a handle on things. Lupe's been fine, but Aki is . . . standoffish?" She rolled the next words around with obvious concern before letting them out. "I obviously didn't say anything on the ship earlier because of the circumstances, but she came really close to disobeying an order by messaging you instead of letting Heli handle things."

He'd known something was off there when his DD had pinged but hadn't investigated it any further.

Probably because you knew it was something like this. You haven't been backing Heli enough and Aki is just the kind of person to pick up on the power shift, even unintentionally.

Still the next words out of his mouth were less than helpful. "There's a world of difference between 'really close' and actual disobedience."

As calmly as she could, she said, "I know. Which is why I'm saying something *now*, in private, to you. I'd rather it not escalate to that point."

"What do you want from me?" That also was too damn sharp-edged and he watched old but familiar walls come down in Emel's brown eyes.

"I guess I just wanted to know if you were going to back me if I did my job, but judging from that response, I guess I have my answer." She was on her feet and out of his office before he could think of a reply that wouldn't make this worse.

"Emel, I—" He followed her, scrambling for something that would fix this. He would talk to Aki, find out what was really bothering her, see if he couldn't set things straight and get them all back on a path together instead of this splintered chaos that seemed to insert itself into everything since Jupiter.

"Hey, D'Arcy?" Stephan came through the main door, stopping when he spotted both of them. "Sorry, have I interrupted something?"

"Not at all, Captain," Emel said, and continued past him without another word.

D'Arcy hooked both hands on the back of his neck and exhaled through clenched teeth while deliberately turning away from Stephan.

The man, to his credit, didn't joke, didn't try to fill the silence. He just waited and when D'Arcy finally turned around, he asked, "How can I help?"

"I don't think you can," D'Arcy admitted, dropping his hands. "Maybe tell me to get my head out of my ass."

Stephan shrugged. "Will you listen?"

"I honestly don't know. I keep tripping over the past and no matter how much I try to regain my balance, there's always something else waiting. What did you need?"

"You got the files I sent you on the ship?"

"Yeah." D'Arcy gestured back at his office. "I was going through them, but there's nothing. It was just a private tourist vessel. That run wasn't anything special. Crew of two and three passengers on a day trip to watch a couple of comets make their loop through the outer edge of the system.

"I'd say pirates—maybe they retrofitted it from salvage—except the ship wasn't damaged, at least not in any way that was consistent with its drop onto Trappist-1h. Then when we lost power for a second, I thought maybe we just got hit by a stray proton storm from a flare, but there was nothing on the radar that day and Lupe says that far out it would have dissipated to almost nothing. There was nothing out there with us. Anything that could have used an EMP should have registered on the scans."

He dragged in a breath. "All that to say, while the instrumentation claims otherwise, I can't shake the feeling there *was* something out there with us, Stephan, something that would have come after us and only didn't because our ships didn't die. I know it sounds paranoid—"

Stephan's laugh was humorless. "You know who you're talking to. Paranoia keeps us alive, D'Arcy. I don't think you're wrong," he continued, "and it gets worse. I found some voice records of Captain Nilesh from the *Imogene Darver*. The transmission you all heard matches exactly. It's not a fake."

A chill crawled down D'Arcy's spine.

"I don't believe in ghosts, Stephan."

"Yeah, me neither. Which means our other option is that someone was close enough to that ship when it vanished to get the distress call and they *chose* not to help. They also managed to respond with your ship name in the captain's voice. I don't have to tell you how nervous that makes me."

"And they've got some kind of stealth tech we've never seen," D'Arcy muttered. "Great."

"I think we need to have a conversation with Techa," Stephan said. "Let me figure out the schedule and we'll decide who should go with you."

"I could just go now."

"No way. I'm not sending you in there alone if the pirates have suddenly changed the rules. We should be able to do it in a few days. I don't know what's going on and I'd rather move slower until we do."

"All right." D'Arcy dragged in a breath; the normally dry air felt sticky in his lungs. "Anything else? I should go figure out how to deal with this personnel issue."

"I already told you how: just get your head out of your ass, Commander." Stephan tapped his hand twice on the door-frame as he walked out.

Despite himself, D'Arcy laughed.

ELEVEN

Trappist System

Jenks poured herself a cup of coffee and rubbed a hand over her face as she stood in the puddle of sunlight streaming into Luis's kitchen a few days later. His house was off base, big enough for his mothers and his boys—and apparently her whenever she wanted to be here.

Which was a lot lately.

Her DD pinged with an incoming call and Jenks snagged the tablet off the counter to answer it. "Hey there, handsome," she said when Tivo's face appeared.

She'd come up against Tivo Parsikov, the Navy's secret weapon for the cage matches, during Max's first Games, and triumphed over the skilled fighter. However, the real win was that he'd been a decent human being who could kiss like the devil and without even realizing it, Jenks had fallen in love for the second time. They were all still openly dating other people off and on, which required a lot of communication, but it was well worth it.

"Got your email, thought I'd try to catch you before work.

Impressive bed head, Pocket." The lieutenant grinned at her
when she stuck her tongue out in reply. "Heard you swept the
cage again. Congrats. I thought for sure you were going to
have to go up against Max this time around."

"Thanks. And me too." The memory of Max dropping
her hands poked at her. Jenks still hadn't watched the replay,
wasn't sure she wanted to know the truth. She pushed away
the worry with the distraction of teasing Tivo. "Sorry you're
going to miss getting your ass kicked at the Games?"

"A little." He laughed. "Though one of these days I'm going
to beat you."

"Luis has been saying that for pretty much forever and it
hasn't happened yet." She waved at Luis as he came into the
kitchen.

"That Tiv?" He leaned over her shoulder with a smile for
the black-haired man on the screen. "Hey again, you. How are
the outer reaches?"

"Dark and cold. I miss you." Tivo lifted a resigned shoulder. "But eight more months out here and then we'll be back."

"We miss you, too," Jenks said, blowing him a kiss. "Thanks
for checking in; it's good to see your face."

"Love you both," Tivo said. "Stay out of trouble."

Noise spilled into the kitchen as Riz and Elliot tumbled
from the hallway. "Are you talking to Tivo? Tivo, don't hang up!"

Jenks laughed and handed the tablet over to the boys.
"Two minutes—he's got to get back to work and you've both
got school." She picked her coffee up again and glanced at
Luis. "What's with the tight shoulders?"

"Scheduling conflict." He shoved a hand into his hair.
"Mom Gina is on a com with Earth and Mom Monica isn't
feeling great. I have a meeting in ten minutes."

"What do you need?"

He blinked at her in surprise. "Nothing, I just have to re-
schedule the meeting so I can walk the boys to school."

"We can walk by ourselves, Dad. It's not that far," Riz protested.

"We're eleven Earth years old." Elliot handed the tablet back to Jenks with a beaming smile. "It's so cool we get to say that. Our age is now a big mystery."

She grinned back but then turned to their father. "Luis, I can go with them," she offered.

"Are you sure?"

"I'd be happy to." And it surprised her how true that statement was as it came out of her mouth. "I'm just going to Blythe's to kill some time with Tamago and Chae before we meet up with Max and go look at that derelict freighter. It's not much out of my way to stop at the school." She shrugged. "Are you two ready to go?"

"We need shoes!" The pair scrambled for their room. As she watched them run down the hall, a thought occurred to her.

"It's barely been over a week since I saw them—what the hell? Armstrong, tell your boys to stop growing."

"Sorry, Dai, you were always going to be the short one around here."

"Tall monsters," Jenks grumbled, but she winked at Luis when he rested his forehead against hers.

"I appreciate you doing this." There was an odd amount of relief in his eyes, and she wasn't entirely sure why.

Jenks shoved aside her own unease in favor of humor as always. "You can make it up to me later." Something about the joke hit Luis like a brick and she frowned when he winced.

"I'll just message them that I have to cancel. You go do your thing. I don't want to impose."

"Hey, teasing. It's really not an issue, Luis. Seriously—let me do this. I'm capable of keeping your boys safe for a few blocks."

"It's not that—you know I trust you. I don't want to impose."

"You said that once already. Can you trust me when I say it's not an imposition?"

"Jenks, we're going to be late! Come on!"

"Hold your chocobos, I still have to get dressed." She

reached up and tugged Luis down to eye level. "We need to have a conversation later, it seems. Can I have a kiss?"

He kissed her, murmuring "I love you" against her mouth before he straightened.

A long conversation, she realized.

"I SHOULD HAVE WORN A HAT," JENKS MUTTERED TEN MINUTES later, rubbing a hand over her now blue hair. "Or at least done my hair better."

People were staring and even though she was normally all about being in the spotlight, something about doing it while she was with the boys made her uncomfortable. "I'm sorry, you two, I didn't think about the fact that people would—"

"Are you kidding?" Elliot demanded. "We're going to be the coolest kids in school after today."

Riz was nodding enthusiastically, and the pair's delight was infectious, so Jenks laughed. "If you're okay with it, then I guess it's fine. Do I need to walk you to the door or . . ."

"I think you're going to have to," Riz whispered, and squeezed her hand. "That's our teacher coming down the steps."

"Doge, sit." The command was mostly unnecessary as the ROVER had already come to a stop at Riz's side and planted his metal butt on the sidewalk.

JENKS: Hey, Tama, I'm going to be late. I apparently have to meet Riz and Elliot's teacher.

TAMAGO: Look at you going domestic.

JENKS: Oh, shut up.

TAMAGO: :D We'll see you when you get here.

"Chief Khan." The petite person waved, her handshake resolving itself as she approached: *Liling Garza, Christa McAu-*

liffe Middle School, she/her. "I'm Liling. It's such a pleasure to finally get to meet you. The boys talk about you all the time."

Jenks glanced sideways at their groans. Elliot had his face in his free hand and Riz's cheeks were red. "It's a pleasure to meet you also. Luis had a meeting, so I offered to walk the boys over."

"Do you have a minute?" Liling asked. "I'd love to run something by you."

"If it's about Riz or Elliot, you should talk to their father."

"Oh, no. It's about you, or rather the NeoG and the Interceptors."

Curiosity piqued, Jenks nodded.

"You two head on in," Liling said.

"Jenks, are you picking us up?" Riz asked.

They hadn't talked about it, but her schedule was clear in the afternoon once *Zuma* finished with the freighter, so she nodded. "If I'm back in time, I'll come with your dad."

The boys hugged her from either side, patted Doge, and then ran for the building. Jenks watched them meet up with some other kids, chattering excitedly among themselves as they disappeared into the school. She looked back to find Liling watching her with a smile.

"They're good kids."

"They are. Most of the time," Jenks agreed. She shoved her hands into her pants pockets. "So what can I do for you?"

"I'm actually wondering if you and your crew would be willing to come to the school to talk to the kids?" She gestured around. "The NeoG's presence has been growing, more families are moving to Trappist. There's a bit of a cultural divide between the locals and Earth-born as well as a . . . well, a suspicion of CHN organizations."

It's deserved, Jenks thought, but she also was keenly aware of the fact that she was representing the NeoG in that moment, so she kept her mouth shut. "I can't really make that call; it's something we'd have to get approval for from higher up."

"No, I understand. I'd been trying to work up the nerve to

approach Senior Chief Armstrong about it. It's just—he's a bit intimidating."

"And I'm not?" Jenks couldn't stop the grin when the woman flushed.

"Well, you are closer to my height," she shot back. "Your crew is well known, not only because of the Games but because of what happened with Senator Tieg. Even the locals think well of you."

"Gotcha." Jenks nodded. "Well, your best bet is to put in a request with the public relations office. Here's Captain Hui Qiang's contact information. Tell him you spoke with me and I referred you over—should push you a little closer to the top of his queue. I'll also mention it to Commander Vagin. He'd be the one to sign off on it once public affairs approves anything." She sent the information over her DD to the teacher.

"Thank you for this." The cis woman smiled brightly then waved at someone behind Jenks. "I need to speak with Ramas's mothers if you'll excuse me. Thanks again, Chief Khan."

"It's no trouble. Have a good day. Doge, let's get going."

He hopped up and fell into step at her side as they headed away from the school yard. "You didn't go to school, did you, Jenks?"

She looked down at the ROVER and then back up, smiling at the blue sky. "Correct. At least not like this. The orphanage had mobiles we did on-site. I burned through mine because I was 'too smart for my own good.'"

"I've heard this before, but I still don't understand it."

"Honestly? I think it's something that adults say to kids when they realize we're smarter than they are." Jenks checked the street before crossing. "And in truth I wasn't all that smart, or I would have stayed put instead of taking off when I was seven and tired of the place. Why I thought the streets would be better, I still have no idea."

"Were you lonely?"

"Yeah." She paused and wiggled a hand. "I mean, at first.

And only sometimes. But I had friends. I've always been good with people. The streets are just different; all the stuff that us civilized people still want is laid bare. There's no time to pretend and play games."

"I wish I had been with you."

She whistled and laughed. "I'd be queen of Krasnodar with you at my side, buddy. But then we wouldn't know all these lovely people."

"This is true," Doge agreed.

They slipped into silence as they covered the last few meters to Hup's Repair Shop. The somewhat dilapidated hangar was on the corner of a quiet intersection not too far from the NeoG base. Jenks had encountered the shop and Blythe Hup, the proprietor, when she'd been looking for something to occupy her mind after finding out that Luis and Tivo had lied to her and put her crew in danger.

That had been rough. No one had really understood how she'd so easily forgiven Chae for their part in the crashing of *Zuma* and Jenks hadn't had the words to explain it.

She'd tried, of course, but Luis and Tivo hadn't really gotten it. Not that she blamed them, but they'd both grown up in safe, stable homes—not on the streets.

She remembered the words she'd thrown at them during their argument. "I've been there. Trapped between the choice of betraying your friends or watching them die. No one to trust, no one to help. I've lived through the threats and the beatdowns and my friends dying because of choices I made."

THE BLOOD HAD SOAKED INTO THE GROUND AND THE BODY *was gone by the time she was able to limp back to the spot where Cans had been killed. Jenks stood with both arms wrapped tight around herself, feeling the pained protest of her healing ribs at the pressure.*

"I'm sorry."

"The dead don't care about our apologies, child."

She whipped around as the old man shuffled into view. "Who are you?"

"A piece of debris forgotten in the corner. Don't worry about me. You're better off worrying about yourself."

"I can take care of myself." The shrug was supposed to be nonchalant, but her wince of pain ruined it and his laughter was as sharp as the cold.

"So I can see. Took a beating from Scurvski in the hopes that it would keep him away from your pal." He tapped his head. "It would have been a smarter move to run and hide with your friends."

"I thought I could save them."

"We always do. Heroes of our own stories and all that. Real life is messy, child. People like Scurvski don't keep agreements unless it suits them—you should learn how to spot that. Only deal with the trustworthy."

She'd thought Yanov was trustworthy, but no one else had known about Cans. Jenks tore her eyes away from the bloodstain.

"This advice cost me anything, Grandfather?"

A broken-toothed smile answered her. "No, though if you have a drink on you, I won't be so impolite as to decline.

"And then I'll tell you how you can bring Scurvski down without him being able to do a thing to stop you."

IT HAD BEEN BLOOD RETRIBUTION, THE KIND THAT GARNERED her a hell of a reputation on the street, but nothing was enough to erase the fact that she'd chosen wrong at the outset and her friend had paid for it with their life.

She shook away the memory, but the chill remained as Jenks passed through the doors into the shop. "It's me!"

Tamago and Chae called out greetings but didn't look up from where they were buried in the interior of a short-range shuttle.

"Welcome back, NeoG." Blythe's black hair was pulled back in a messy ponytail and there was a smudge of dirt under one green eye. "You okay?"

"Yeah, memories thick in the head today." She forced a smile and tapped her temple. Blythe understood; she'd done some time on the streets herself as a teen right here in Aman-ave. A mechanic on the other side of town had taken her in, taught her how to fix things, and given her a new life much like Jenks's baba had.

Jenks sometimes wondered what would have happened if she hadn't found her way to the Vagins.

Probably be a skeleton buried in the rubble, she thought. *Or just another ghost drifting through the streets.*

"Heard you won yourself another trophy."

"One step closer, anyway." Jenks patted Doge and the ROVER trotted over, sitting in front of Blythe.

The woman laughed and patted him on the head. "If you had a tail, you'd be wagging it, you silly dog. How are you, Doge?"

"I am good. You could build me a tail, couldn't you?"

Blythe looked up at Jenks, who hid a smile behind her hand. "I suppose I could. Maybe?"

"Whatcha working on?" Jenks asked, wandering over to study the pile of scrap on the table.

"Water pump, post-landing. Some scrap-head who likes to scour the uninhabited areas found a small camp about three hundred meters east of us in the canyon. He found a few skel-etons, too. Likely someone who broke off from the original landing parties and tried to make it on their own."

"It's so rarely a good plan," Jenks murmured. "Interesting, though. I didn't think anyone would take that kind of chance given how dangerous the original landings were in the begin-ning."

"True, there are always people who think they can do it better, and the payoff can be substantial. Sometimes they're even right." Blythe joined her at the table. "The good news is the pump designs haven't changed much over the years.

The shell's in good shape. I can retrofit guts from a newer model."

"What are you going to do with it after you fix it up?" Jenks reached behind her head and tugged off the long-sleeved shirt she'd worn, her unease finally fading into its customary place in the back of her mind. It was already warm enough that her tank would suffice and once they dug into their work, she'd heat up even more.

"Remember that little habitat we visited before you headed off for the prelims?"

"Oh yeah . . . Primrose something?"

Blythe laughed. "Prime Rise, but close enough, smart-ass. They've needed another pump for two years now; this'll help take the load off."

"Two years! Aren't the supplies getting through?"

"Oh sure," Blythe replied. "But their order is still a few months out and to be honest they've grown a lot since they put the request in. Three pumps will be even better. How long do I have you for?"

Jenks checked the clock in her vision. "Couple of hours. Then we get to crawl around in this ghost ship that appeared a few days ago."

"I heard about that." Blythe frowned. "Be careful, Neo. That ship was trouble from day one."

"Really?" Jenks leaned in, curiosity bleeding into excitement. "Spill the story, then; don't leave a girl wanting more."

"But that's sort of my trademark move," Blythe teased, though the humor only partially covered the worry clinging to her eyes. "*Opie's Hat* is registered as a freighter, but it wasn't, not really. Simpson Ivarken was something of a pirate."

Minimal Diagnostic Test #384
Motherboard—Green
Heat Sinks—Green
Optical—Green
Audio—Green
Weapons—Offline

Sapphi frowned. "Doge, why are your weapons offline again?"

"I turned them off. I don't want them. Sapphi, what was it like to be dead?"

"Doge, you can't just go around asking people what it's like to be dead," Jenks groaned. "We talked about this."

"It's okay," Sapphi replied. "There's no simple answer, Doge. I don't remember a lot, for starters, and what I do remember is sort of jumbled? I was on a boat at sea and there was a storm rolling in. Lightning and waves and . . ." She trailed off. "I don't know. Then I was awake and Tama was crying."

"I felt you go off. I didn't like it."

Sapphi shared a look with Jenks, who shrugged and mouthed *Hell if I know* back at her. "I didn't care for it much either, buddy." She disconnected her tablet from his side and closed up the access panel with a snap. "Everything seems okay. I don't think you had any damage from the crash. Sorry it took us so long to get to this."

"We were busy catching bad guys."

Sapphi laughed and patted his head. "That we were. You're a good dog. You know that?"

"Yes."

"You can leave the weapons off if you want, Doge," Sapphi said. "I'm the last person to tell you otherwise."

"Me neither." Jenks put her arm around the ROVER's neck and squeezed. "It's your body, your choice."

TWELVE

Trappist System

"Blythe said Ivarken ran his freighter like a pirate ship. Would waylay other freighters and steal their shit, space the crews, and blow up the evidence. He was apparently running weapons for the TLF for a while. She said he'd retrofitted the hull and put in some stealth-weapons systems." Jenks's voice echoed from inside the hatch she was half-shoved into.

"Which is what you're looking for?" Max asked.

"Which is what I'm looking for," Jenks confirmed. "I mean, hearsay and all that. It could not be true. But it's a *kind* of evidence, so figure it's worth a shot. Takes a lot of cash and work to put something more than the minimum defenses allowed on freighters. You'd have to hide it good to keep it off the military scanners—which doesn't mean it couldn't be done, mind you. Just that it's a massive pain in the ass."

Max let Jenks continue to ramble as she worked. It was oddly soothing, and she'd learned from experience that letting Jenks talk a problem out was a far better plan than leaving it in her head to swirl into a maelstrom that caused problems later.

Plus it provided a useful distraction from Max's own tangled thoughts as she combed through the underside of the barely functioning main console of *Opie's Hat,* looking for— what was she looking for? They'd already pulled all the files they could and Sapphi was going through them with Saad, Lupe, and Pavel. The quad of hackers from the four Interceptor teams assigned to Intel were a force to behold and Max was pretty sure they'd find more useful information than she would.

But again, useful distractions were useful and she'd take those where she could get them right now. Jenks was also less likely to notice and therefore grill Max about anything while she was excited about pirates.

"Hey, Max, how do you make a pirate angry?"

Oh, the jokes, though.

Max bit back the noise that was half laugh, half sigh. "Steal his sword?"

"Close! Steal their *P.*"

"What?" Half a second after she asked she got it, and Max groaned as Jenks's giggling spilled into the air. "That was terrible. I'm going to write you up."

"You could, or you could talk to me about what's going on with your family."

So much for distractions.

"Shouldn't you be focusing?"

"I am focused. I could take this ship apart and put it back together with my eyes closed. I haven't seen anything weird yet, which is annoying AF. I'll probably have to move to the main junction to really find evidence, but I figure you might talk to me if you don't have to look me in the eye."

It shouldn't be so surprising, Max thought, when Jenks busted out stuff like this. The facade of carelessness was a cover for a person who was exceptionally intelligent—emotionally and intellectually—and far more aware than people gave her credit for most of the time.

Jenks cared deeply about a lot of things, but nothing as much as the people she'd chosen to let into her life.

Max hadn't been looking for family when she'd joined the Interceptors—if anything she'd been running from her own—but she'd found it anyway.

And most days she was thankful for it.

Today, though . . .

"Same old bullshit," she replied. "They're mad I'm breathing because I don't breathe like a Carmichael should."

"Your sarcasm is improving. I'm so proud." There was a thump and a curse, followed by a long pause. "Still didn't answer the question, LT. Have they given you more shit?"

Her mother's threat was still hanging over her head, but it hadn't manifested into anything real and after talking to her sister this morning, Max wondered just what else her family was up to.

"Sort of," Max admitted, simply because she knew Jenks wasn't going to let it go and a half truth was better than the whole thing. "Ria, who apparently likes to tread the line between being my sister and being the unofficial spokesperson for my parents, managed to work into our conversation this morning that maybe I should consider bowing out of the Games to 'lessen the tension with the family.'"

"The fuck you say!" There was another thump that had Max wincing because she was pretty sure this time Jenks had hit her head on something.

"Don't worry, I'm not going to." Max hated that her initial desire to step back from the Games was now tangled around the stubborn desire to not do anything that looked like capitulating to her family's demands.

"Hang on." Jenks wriggled free of the hatch and dropped to her butt in front of Max. The ship was shielded and had gravity and air, thanks to a generator. "Look at me. Forget your family for a minute. Do you not want to compete anymore?"

"No, I—" The words got caught in the mess of her feelings

and Max nearly told Jenks all about the cage match and her fears of their fictitious epic fight ruining their friendship. "I don't want my family to tell me what to do. That's why I'm here in the first place. I just . . . I guess I foolishly thought everything I've accomplished was enough to make them leave me alone."

"We can," Jenks replied seriously. "I know people."

Max choked on a laugh. "Jenks, you can't kill my parents."

"*I* wouldn't do it—are you kidding? We'd all need solid alibis." She held up her hands. "I'm teasing. I know it's not just your parents, and I don't have that kind of cash." She paused, then laughed again. "Seriously, what can we do to help you? Because I'm pretty sure you don't want me to go to Earth for the Games and announce that I have a message for the Carmichaels during our pre-Games interviews." She held up both middle fingers.

"Oh God." Max shook her head even as part of her wished she had half the guts that Jenks did, and the thought of her cousin filtered into her brain again. "I don't know, Jenks. I wish I did."

"Well, keep me posted. We'll have a crew brainstorming session, and in the meantime, you could have Sapphi filter your coms for you. It might not actually solve the problem, but it could help take some of the stress down a notch."

Max threw her arms around Jenks's neck. "I love you, you know."

"I love you, too," Jenks replied, patting her on the back. For a moment it looked as if she wanted to say something more, but she shook her head and smiled. "What I don't love is that this ghost ship isn't the least bit scary."

The music filtered into the bridge as soon as Jenks had finished speaking and the two women stared at each other.

"Be careful what you wish for," Max murmured, slowly getting to her feet. "You are hearing that, right?"

"Oh yeah. Creepy melody is a go."

"Nika, where are you?" Max asked over the com.

"Down in the engine room with Chae," he replied. "Why?"

"Tamago, can you check in?"

"I'm running a second round of samples on that hole in the hull, which is about a seven point four on the weird shit meter."

"Max," Nika said. *"Why?"*

"We're hearing music—is anyone else picking it up?"

The chorus of negatives made Max's gut twist and she looked in Jenks's direction. The chief had her sword out and was edging toward the door when she stopped and looked around.

"Where's Doge?"

He'd been in the corner of the bridge while they'd been working, quietly running some program Jenks had started; but he wasn't there now and before Max could say anything else, Jenks bolted out of the room.

JENKS KNEW THAT IN THEORY, RUNNING OFF INTO A POTEN-tially haunted ship was at the top of the list of bad ideas. However, she now understood just why people made poor decisions in horror films that got them killed.

Because damned if I'll leave my dog behind.

"Doge!" She skidded down the corridor, slid around the corner, and stumbled to a stop when she spotted the ROVER at the end of the hall. "What were you thinking wandering off? I told you to stay."

He didn't respond and Jenks realized the music was coming from him just as Max stopped next to her.

"Damn it, Jenks, you shouldn't have— Is the—is he playing the music?"

She moved forward cautiously. "Yeah." Jenks swallowed, her heart hammering in her chest. Doge's eyes were white instead of their normal friendly blue. "Doge?"

He didn't respond.

Jenks tried the command codes from her DD with no luck.

"Fuck." She didn't like the feeling of dread growing in her chest. "Doge, stop the music."

"Sapphi's been humming that tune," Max murmured. "Ever since the crash."

"Hey, Sapphi, do you have a minute to do a full shutdown on Doge?" Jenks asked over the team com, bouncing the relay down to base, where Sapphi and the hackers were going through the *Opie's Hat*'s logs.

"Sure, hang on," she replied. "Weird."

"What?"

"I can't get a connection. There's no reason for it; even though we're on the ground, it should go through fine. Saad, look at this." The coms went silent, and Jenks bounced impatiently from one foot to the other. She could hear Max talking to Nika back at the other end of the hallway; he and Chae had come up from the engine room to meet them before he'd sent the spacer to join up with Tamago.

She took a step closer to Doge. The music cut off and his eyes flashed to red.

"You're in our space. Get out."

The voice wasn't Doge's, even though it was coming from the ROVER, and Jenks dodged out of instinct more than anything and felt the sting as the shot tagged the outer edge of her right arm, slamming into the bulkhead behind her. Max let loose one of her rare curses and Jenks winced.

"Whoa. Hey, buddy, it's me." She held her hands up.

His eyes went blue and his head dipped low. "Jenks?"

"It's me."

"What happened?"

"Nothing."

"You are bleeding. I *hurt* you."

"It wasn't you. Don't worry about it."

He crawled forward, head almost scraping on the floor, and Jenks reached out to wrap her arms around him. "I am sad."

"It's all right, buddy. I'm here."

"YOU'RE NOT TURNING MY FUCKING DOG OFF."

D'Arcy watched Nika reach out and put a hand on Jenks's forearm. The silent gesture was enough to get her to sit back in her seat.

"We're not talking permanently," Stephan replied. "Just until we figure out what's going on. Besides, he shot you."

"He didn't mean to," Jenks snapped. "It was barely a scratch."

"That's worse. You get how that's worse, right? If he got a virus or something from the ship, he's a danger to himself and everyone here."

"His weapons system was offline." Sapphi's voice cut through the fight. The declaration was soft, almost an absent-minded afterthought. She hadn't looked away from whatever she was scrolling on her DD chip and D'Arcy frowned. The ensign's normally tan skin was pale, and she had dark circles under her eyes like she hadn't been sleeping well.

Handle your own crew, D'Arcy.

"What does that mean, Sapphi?" Stephan asked, gesturing at the bandage on Jenks's arm. "His weapons were clearly not off."

"It means, I get a fucking notice when he turns his weapons on. Jenks does, too. He's had them off for more than a year and a half. He wanted them off. They were shut down on the basic diagnostic I ran just yesterday; I can show you the log."

She threw the information up on the main screen. "There, number four hundred and seventy-three, still clearly off, just like the ninety-something tests before that one. Neither of us got any warning before he fired." Sapphi's eyes unfocused and her left hand flipped restlessly through something only she could see.

"Sapphi," Max said softly. "Focus on one thing."

Sapphi made a face and swiped the images away before looking at Stephan. "Sorry, Captain. I get a notice about everything that happens with Doge. Jenks does, too. I think we should shut him down so I can run a full diagnostic."

"Sapphi! I thought you were on my side."

"This isn't a side thing, Jenks, though I am, sort of. It's easier on him if he's fully shut down when I run it—you know that—and we already talked about how we should do one."

"I thought you just ran one?"

"Nah." Sapphi shook her head. "That was a minimal diagnostic; we do them on the regular. The fulls require we shut him down all the way; it's kinda uncomfortable to do that, though, so we haven't in years." She looked at Jenks. "You know as well as I do that we should take a thorough look."

Jenks inhaled as if to voice another protest herself but then crossed her arms over her chest. "Fine, but I need to be there. And anyone says the words 'shut down' or 'off' around him, I'll break kneecaps. Is that understood?"

D'Arcy watched Nika and Stephan exchange a glance, the Intel head nodding once at whatever silent conversation had just happened.

"All right. Now that that's cleared up—Sapphi, if you and Jenks will give us the room."

The pair nodded and left. D'Arcy looked around the table where the commanders and seconds of the four Interceptor crews sat.

Nika was still frowning. Max was worrying at her lower lip. Vera and Xin from *Flux* had watched Jenks leave and were no doubt having a rapid-fire conversation in their private chat.

Pia and Pavel from *Wandering Hunter* watched Stephan, mostly untouched by the drama over the ROVER.

The Intel head was silent for a moment, then he tapped a hand on the tabletop and looked around. "Another freighter is late reporting in. The *Bastian* was supposed to be in port at Trappist-1f an hour ago. Jupiter Transit logs the ship as passing through the wormhole on their side at zero-four-thirty. They were logged on the Trappist side at sixteen-thirty-two as expected and should have continued on to Trappist-1f with an arrival of eighteen hundred hours.

"They never showed. Normally I'd wait another hour before doing anything, but given the circumstances, I'm concerned. I pulled the data off the transit lane. It shows a departure, and there was no one else in the lane; it appears the *Bastian* deviated from their course and headed off to the outer asteroid belt."

"Is that the same area *The Red Cow* vanished in?" Even as he asked the question, D'Arcy pulled up the file. "They were heading for One-d, but—" He put the overlaid files on the holo in the middle of the table.

"Yeah," Stephan said even as the image resolved to show a straight line between the two. "For obvious reasons this information doesn't leave this room. If we're looking at some kind of new smuggling ring trying to take over now that Tieg is out of the picture, I don't want to give them any warning that we're coming."

"What if it's some sort of offshoot of the TLF?" Locke asked, raising his hands when D'Arcy shot him a look. "That's nothing personal. If Jenks's info checks out about Ivarken running guns for them, we'd be remiss if we didn't put it on the list to cross off. There were some unhappy people when the Trappist Liberation Front agreed to sit down with the CHN and the NeoG to negotiate peace terms."

"No, that's fair," D'Arcy replied with a sigh. "I wish you were wrong, but it's a possibility we should probably consider."

Stephan nodded. "D'Arcy, is your crew ready to go back out?"

"They're not. Not if we don't know what we're getting into." He hated how quickly the denial sprang from his mouth and the fact that Locke's lips thinned in disagreement. Everyone had performed just fine when it mattered out on the system edge, but D'Arcy wanted more time. He also still needed to have that very difficult conversation with Aki, but as Stephan had ordered—that required him to pull his head out of his own ass.

"No problem. Commander Forsberg, Commander Till. I want the two of you to head for the outer belt and poke around.

Do ship prep tomorrow and then get out there. It's a bit like trying to find a needle in a haystack, I know, but if you follow the route the ships took, maybe you'll find something. Even if it's just rubble."

"Can do," Vera Till replied with a nod that sent her silver and pink curls bouncing. Pia Forsberg echoed the nod. She was a tall, slender woman with dark red hair twisted into a neat bun at the base of her head.

D'Arcy hadn't worked with her much at Jupiter, but since they'd moved to Trappist, they'd become fast friends. Pia wasn't one to mince words, or to let people fall behind. She possessed that rare quality of being able to provide a sort of tough love that made a person feel seen—and grabbed by the scruff of the neck when the occasion called for it.

Like she had almost a year ago.

D'ARCY DROPPED HIS SWORD WITH A CURSE AND WENT TO A knee.

"Get up," Pia said. "Before I smack you again."

"Did I miss something?" he asked, but grabbed his sword and got to his feet.

"Maybe. You've had your head up your ass for long enough. I'd think at the very least you'd miss breathing fresh air."

The words caught him off guard and D'Arcy fumbled the easy block, swearing again when Pia twisted her sword effortlessly and slapped him on the shoulder with the flat of it.

He felt the fury surge and this time dropped his sword deliberately, raising his hands. "We're done here."

"You're going to be done if you don't stop blaming yourself for what happened on Jupiter." Pia pitched her own sword to the side and crossed to him in two steps, her long legs eating up the distance between them. She grabbed D'Arcy by the face before he could move. "It wasn't your fault. We all missed Paul's betrayal."

Her words pulled at the weak stiches holding his wounds together. "He was my crew. I should have known."

"Jesus, you think I don't feel that? He was my friend for twenty years, D'Arcy, and I never suspected a thing. He was your crew. Emphasis on the 'was.' Your crew now needs you to step up for them, but you're stuck wallowing in what you think you should have seen instead of seeing what's in front of you: young Neos who need a leader. I know we're not close, but maybe you need to hear this from someone like me. You're one of the best commanders in the Interceptors. I've looked up to you for years, and I know I'm not the only one around here who does. Carmichael, Vagin, the lot of them would follow you into the fire without hesitation.

"I also know some of this is grief and I'll be the last person to tell you to shake that off and move on, but the guilt part of it you've got to let go of before it eats you alive. You couldn't have stopped this. None of us could have. Paul made his fucking choice, and it didn't include us. He broke the oath. He hurt our people."

"Not you."

After close to eight months of therapy, those were the first words that actually hit with any meaning. D'Arcy fought to keep the pain from rising again, but the struggle must have shown in his eyes, because Pia tightened her hands on his face.

"Look at me," she begged, and there were tears in her brown eyes. "He took a lot from us; don't let him take you, too."

"D'ARCY, TOMORROW I WANT YOU TO TAKE YOUR CREW AND go have a talk with Gun and Michael, see if they can confirm the rumor about Ivarken and if they would have any additional leads for us to follow. It'll give us some time to figure out whatever is going on with Doge." Stephan's order shook him out of the memory and D'Arcy thankfully managed a nod, because his throat was too tight with unexpected emotion to reply.

Stephan sighed. "We're keeping *Opie's Hat* in dock for now. As soon as Pavel and the others finish going through the systems, we'll haul it off for scrap. I don't want anyone going on board without clearing it through me first. Understood?"

Everyone nodded.

"All right. Let's get to work, people. I want to figure out what's going on before another ship goes missing."

"Or something else weird happens," Nika muttered, and D'Arcy couldn't help but agree with him.

"Jenks, can I ask you something?"

She looked up with a smile. Doge had finally, after much prompting, started asking if he could ask questions rather than just busting them out. It was good, especially after he'd asked Master Chief Molen why he didn't have any sense and Jenks had had to do some fast talking with Rosa to keep her from confining the ROVER to quarters.

"Sure, buddy. What's up?"

"You did not always live here on Jupiter Station."

"Correct."

"But you also didn't always live with your brother? I thought that's what families did?"

"Most of the time, yes. Nika and I didn't meet until just a few years ago, but there's a lot of reasons families don't live together. Like Sapphi's family lives all over the place because some of them work in different spots and it's more convenient to live there than travel back and forth."

"You said something about living on the streets the other day. I don't understand. How does one live on a street?"

"Did you look up the definition in the idiom list?" She'd found it super helpful with the ROVER's endless curiosity to make him find the answers himself most of the time.

"Yes. I am not asking the right question," he suddenly announced. "Not how. Why? Why were you without a home?"

"Oh." She swallowed, surprising herself with the sudden sheen of tears coating her vision, and was glad that her dog wasn't designed to notice such things. "Well, that's a long story, Doge, and I've got to get to the gym in ten minutes."

"Can you tell me later?"

"Yeah, I'll try. I haven't really ever told anyone the whole story."

"Why?"

"It's sad. People don't like sad stories."

"It's about you, though. I would like to hear it." He got up and tipped his head to the side, studying her. "Your face is wet."

Jenks reached up and swiped away the tear that had escaped. The explanation was automatic, slipping out with the same casualness. "It's a tear. You know what those are, right?"

"Yes, tears are the salty liquid that comes from eyes. Why are you crying? Are you injured?"

"No, we cry about a lot of things. Not just when we get hurt."

"But you are sad?"

"Yeah. We cry when things make us sad."

"Why are you sad?"

"Buddy, that is also a long story. I'll try to explain it on the way to the gym, though."

"Okay." Doge nosed closer until his cheek was touching hers. "I say: *I am sorry that you are sad*, right?"

She hugged him. "Right, and thank you."

"You are welcome."

THIRTEEN

Trappist System

Jenks slipped through the front door of Luis's house and closed it as quietly as she could. It was late, the boys would be asleep already, and she didn't want to disrupt things. She hung her jacket up in the closet and toed off her boots, setting them neatly in the hallway next to two pairs of shoes that were rapidly outpacing hers in size and one pair that had always been larger.

The house was mostly dark, the dim light in the kitchen outlining Luis's broad shoulders where he was cleaning up the remnants of dinner.

"Hey, you."

He turned and smiled. He was dressed in faded gray sweats and nothing else, his blond hair still wet from a shower. "Dai. Are you hungry? There's food in the fridge." He crossed the room and bent, kissing her, then folded her into an embrace.

Jenks rested her head against his chest and exhaled. "I ate in medical, but thanks."

"Long day. How's your arm?"

"It's fine. Was just a scratch. I'm sorry I missed picking the boys up."

"I told them you were stuck at work. They get it."

"Thanks for not worrying them. Do you need help cleaning up?"

"I'm almost done. You didn't bring Doge?"

Jenks rooted around in the fridge and grabbed a beer. "I had to leave him on base. Stephan's orders." She made a face. "Which, I get, before you feel like you need to defend him. It still sucks." The words came out sharper than she'd intended and she sighed. "Sorry, I'm grumpy."

"It's all right."

She wasn't sure if it was, but let the silence fill the space between them as Luis finished up in the kitchen. Jenks grabbed her beer and followed him into the living room, setting it aside and curling up next to him on the couch.

"Doge was upset. Scared, even," she whispered. "Honestly that's the worst part of it."

"I'd say your injury is, but I'm not worried about semantics at the moment."

Jenks leaned her head against Luis's shoulder, sifting through the words about her dog she still couldn't seem to say to anyone. Luis didn't seem surprised by the admission that her ROVER was having feelings, but it still seemed like such a major step for her to say something out loud.

Especially when there were so many other issues clamoring for attention in her brain.

"I'm thinking of talking to Nika about *Zuma* being done competing for a little while after these Games," she said softly, choosing a slightly easier topic. "I'd be lying if it wasn't because I wanted a break, as strange as that sounds, but honestly I think the whole team could use a year or two off from it."

"I don't blame you. The last few years have been a lot."

"I'm more than just the cage matches, yeah?" She was surprised by how important this question was when she said it aloud.

Scared of what the answer would be.

"Of *course* you are. Do you think we don't recognize that?"

Jenks shrugged and shifted, climbing onto his lap and pressing her palms to his bare chest. She looked him in the eye. The steady beat of his heart under her hand was reassuring. "You do. My teammates do. I'm not sure the general public feels that way. It's frustrating. And this pressure about the potential match between me and Max? It's supposed to be fun, but I think it's stressing her out. Which makes me edgy."

Luis didn't reply, just skimmed one hand over the patch on her right arm before dropping it to her waist. Jenks leaned in to kiss him, her lips clinging to his.

"I promised you a conversation this morning," she murmured when they separated. "You still want to have it, or should we table it for another time?"

Luis's answer was to pull her against him and kiss her again, fiercely. Jenks sank into it, into him, loving the feel of his arms wrapped around her and the heat of his mouth on hers. The sliver of disappointment that he didn't want to talk was surprising and she did her best to push it to the back of her mind.

But then he pulled away, took a shuddering breath, and met her gaze squarely. "I don't want you to feel like you have to do things for us."

"I haven't ever felt like that. If I gave you that impression this morning, I'm sorry, but—"

"You haven't." Luis shook his head. "This isn't anything you've done, Dai; you don't have to apologize. I just . . . I know a family wasn't in the plans for you and I don't want to burden you with it."

Oh, the pain in his voice was like a knife in her heart, and equally unexpected. His amber gaze was filled with nervous hesitation, and she chose her next words carefully.

"All these years you've known me, and you still think I plan things. You're lucky you're cute, Armstrong, because you're not too bright."

That dragged a laugh out of him. She leaned forward, resting her head against his shoulder with her face turned toward his.

"More seriously, I don't have any plans. I'm really just making this up as I go. I didn't think I'd survive to be sixteen, so pretty much everything since then has been a big bonus. I liked walking the boys to school. I liked it when they taught me how to make pancakes a few months ago. I'm excited about our upcoming camping trip. None of this is a burden in the slightest.

"I may not have asked for any of this, but I'm definitely *not* asking to lose it now."

"I don't know what I did to deserve you."

"Back at you, big guy." She sat up and cupped his face in her hands, feeling like she still needed to explain how she felt. "I wasn't looking for any of this, but I'm really fucking glad that I found it."

"Me too," Luis whispered.

"I am pretty awesome, though. Everyone says so." She wiggled her eyebrows at him and then barely stifled the yelp against his chest when he dug his fingers into her ribs. "I swear I'll bite you."

"That's not the threat you think it is, Dai." He twisted, pinning her to the couch underneath him and kissing her breathless. "Let's take this into the bedroom before we get busted by my moms," he murmured against her mouth.

"Excellent idea."

EMEL—
I need your signatures on these. Send your account information to the company on the documents and they'll handle your half of the payment.
Rajaa

It shouldn't hurt as much as it did or feel quite so cold, but Rajaa also didn't owe her anything more than the basics. Emel glanced at the attached documents, unprepared for the sudden nausea crawling its way up her throat.

She'd forgotten about the lake property, but now a thousand lost dreams cascaded down around her like a crumbling ruin. If that wasn't an indictment of how badly Emel had failed in her marriage, she wasn't sure what was. Who bought their wife lakefront property with the intent of building a home on it only to forget about it entirely?

Me, that's who.

Rajaa—
Signed. The girls can have my share.
Emel
P.S. Cowardly, maybe, to do this here, but I'm sorry. For everything.

She hit send before she could second-guess herself and then wrote another email to the company handling the sale, including both Maggie and Ikram on it and asking them to be sure to send along their account information so the payment could be distributed.

That task completed, she shut down her tablet and headed out of *Dread*'s quiet quarters toward the base gym. The training area for Amanave was lively in the morning hour, but not nearly as packed as it tended to be later in the day. All four Interceptor crews were scattered throughout the large room with a smattering of other Neos mixed in.

She spotted Heli with Petty Officer Uchida, going through a series of sword drills. Aki was sitting off to the side watching the pair, her practice sword lying across her lap. Emel grimaced. She was still going to have to talk to the young woman and something told her it wasn't going to go well. Especially since it seemed D'Arcy wasn't going to back her up if she had to make things official.

Lieutenant Commander Qiao was sparring with Petty Officer Nash, getting in one last session before they headed for the black later. The pair's swords were locked together and they were gleefully trash-talking each other as D'Arcy observed from the sidelines.

"Morning, Master Chief," Jenks called from the weight area where she and Spacer Chae stood. "You need a sparring partner? Mine didn't realize I was coming back to base and ditched me." She hooked a thumb toward the back of the gym and Emel spied Max tangled up with Commander Till on the mats.

"Sure, though I can wait until you finish."

"Chae's fine. They know how to deadlift." Jenks patted the young Neo on the shoulder and crossed to join Emel. "I haven't had a chance to give you a proper welcome yet." Mischief sparkled in her mismatched eyes and Emel was surprised by how it helped erase the lingering anxiety in her chest.

"I suppose asking you to go easy on me is a waste of time." Emel caught the wraps that Jenks tossed her way and bent to unlace her boots, toeing them off and peeling back her sleeves just enough to put on the wraps.

"Everyone always assumes the worst of me," Jenks replied with a grin. "I promise I'll only hold you down if you ask nice."

Emel blinked at the woman's brazen flirting and then laughed. "Why do I have a hard time believing that? Also, I'm old enough to be your mother."

Jenks barked out a laugh. "Now you sound like D'Arcy."

"You and he—" Emel bit off the question, but it was too late.

Jenks grinned, slow and wicked, and Emel desperately wanted to sink under the mat and never resurface.

"I wondered how long that would take. Naw, Master Chief. D'Arcy said, and I quote: 'I'm old enough to be your father, Khan. Put it back in your pants.'"

The imitation of D'Arcy was so spot-on that Emel had to laugh.

"He wasn't wrong. I was a barely-in-control eighteen-year-old. Not everyone was as kind as he was." There was a wealth of heartbreak etched into Jenks's easy smile and Emel had a sudden urge to wrap the younger woman in her arms and keep her safe.

Thankfully before she could embarrass them both, Jenks held her fists out until Emel tapped them with her own. "Now, consenting adults and all that, we're better off as friends. Let me see what you can do, Master Chief."

Emel could hold her own in a fight when the occasion called for it, but less than a minute in she could see that all the talk about just how good Jenks was in the cage wasn't exaggerated in the slightest. It was also extremely obvious that the younger woman was more interested in seeing what Emel could bring to the session rather than trying to dominate her for some point of pride.

A crowd gathered at the edge of their mat and Emel spotted D'Arcy standing with his arms crossed over his chest and a worried look slipping past the impassive mask on his face.

"Hey, focus." Jenks tapped her on the cheek and Emel started, stumbling back a step. "Only time you want to watch the crowd is if you're surrounded by a group you think is going to jump into your fight."

"How do you ignore it?"

Jenks shrugged. "Practice. Or I guess I don't ignore it so much as it doesn't distract me anymore because I'm so used to it. You keep your guard up better than LT, probably because you've actually been in a fight or three, haven't you?"

"A few. I generally don't go looking for them, though." Emel blocked Jenks's right hook, stepping into the shorter woman's space and landing a punch of her own to the chief's ribs. There was a cheer from the assembled crowd and Emel retreated.

Jenks hissed in frustration and for a moment Emel thought she was angry about the punch. But she wasn't. "Don't run," Jenks said, holding up her open palms. "Why does everyone run?"

"Healthy sense of self-preservation," Emel answered, and

watched as Jenks's smile went hot and Emel found herself momentarily confounded by an answering swell of attraction.

That is an extremely bad idea, Master Chief, some sensible part of herself whispered in her head. It was; age difference aside, now was not the time for her to be doing anything but focusing on her job. Emel stepped on her libido hard, cleared her throat, and pointed. "You're dangerous."

"You noticed." Jenks dipped her head. "Come back here," she said, wiggling the fingers of her right hand at Emel until she came closer. "You block, punch, and don't retreat." Jenks moved as she spoke, stepping forward into Emel's personal space to demonstrate.

Jenks wasn't flirting now, Emel realized, but instead was in full coaching mode. It was like a switch had flipped and the younger woman was very good at it. "You hit, then *move in,* the left-hand block can lock up a hold, trapping your opponent's right arm and leaving them open all along here. Or for a takedown if you move fast enough." She tapped Emel's front leg and her own hip before stepping back. "You try it. Slow."

Emel blocked Jenks's right punch again, but this time followed the directions the chief had given and moved in rather than retreating. She was able to hook her left arm around the back of Jenks's head and get in several more light taps to her side, but Emel suspected that was only because the woman let her complete the hold.

"Better. Next time move with a purpose," Jenks said as she straightened. Then she looked past Emel. "Come spar with your crew, D'Arcy. It's easier for me to watch when I'm not also dodging punches."

"We need to head out for West Ridge," he replied.

They didn't—not for another hour—and judging by the way Jenks's eyes narrowed, she knew it. She also shouldn't call him on it, but Emel saw the deep breath and knew instinctively that's exactly what was going to happen.

"Thank you," Emel said with a hand on the younger woman's

arm. That sharp-eyed gaze, one brown and one blue, transferred back to her and Jenks was silent for a long moment as she assessed her options. Emel could almost see the calculations that went on in Jenks's head before she decided to keep her mouth shut.

"Anytime. The LT would be a good sparring partner for you; so would Locke if you're looking for a size match. Hit me up if you have questions or want to go again." She offered Emel a blinding smile and then shot D'Arcy one last hard look, ambling back to the bench to unwind her wraps as the crowd started to drift away.

Emel stayed where she was and undid her own, moving over and dropping the fabric strips into the sanitizer. She waited as the machine cleaned them before reaching in to wind them back up and toss them into the basket.

Emotions she couldn't untangle burned in the back of her throat. D'Arcy was still holding back, untouchable and unapproachable even as nearly everyone else had welcomed her and Heli into the NeoG.

She headed for the door of the gym and made it halfway across the yard before he caught up with her.

"Are you okay? Jenks—"

"Didn't do anything wrong, though it's amusing you seem to think so." Her words were weapons, slipped between his ribs with deliberate care she should have felt ashamed of but wasn't. "She was doing your job, same as Tamago was, working with Heli on her sword handling."

The muscle in D'Arcy's jaw tightened, but they both knew any protest from him was bullshit.

"I don't understand this. This isn't you. How much longer are you going to let everyone else do your work for you?" she whispered.

He turned around and walked away from her.

FOURTEEN

Trappist System

Emel's words were still burning in his ears several hours later when they pulled up outside West Ridge. D'Arcy's initial fury over the question had died into a dull ache of embarrassed regret.

She was right. As right as Jenks's silent stare of condemnation when he'd backed out of the sparring match with an all too obvious lie. As right as Locke's tentative attempts to step back from interceding and smoothing things over whenever D'Arcy was just a little too sharp with his new ensign.

As right as everyone else was . . . and yet he still couldn't find it in himself to change. Not yet.

"Aki, you and Lupe help me unload the transport," Heli said as they climbed from the vehicle.

"Ensign Järvinen gave you all an order, Petty Officer. Get moving." The bite in Locke's normally easy voice dragged D'Arcy out of his head and he realized Aki was looking his way for confirmation of Heli's order.

She shouldn't be. She should have moved when the others

did, but the younger Neo was taking her cues only from him rather than any officer and it was long past time D'Arcy stepped up and did something about it.

Instead Locke had beat him to it and D'Arcy caught the angry look Aki slanted the lieutenant commander's way when he turned his back.

"Petty Officer, do you have something to say?"

Everyone froze and D'Arcy realized those hard words had come from him. Aki's eyes snapped to his, the shock followed by hurt flying through those hazel depths before she could hide it.

"No, Commander."

You've got to do something about this.

Before he could, though, his name echoed across the yard. "D'Arcy!" Michael Chae appeared in the doorway of their home and waved a hand as he approached. "We weren't expecting you."

"Had some supplies for you." D'Arcy clasped the man's arm when he came to a stop. "And some questions."

"Gun's at the clinic, but come on in and I'll see if I can help with answers."

D'Arcy followed, forcing himself to shelve the problem of his crew and his lack of leadership in favor of the more pressing issue. The interior of the habitat was so soothingly familiar that for a second he couldn't have told anyone if he was on Mars or Trappist.

"So, judging by the tension, this isn't a social call," Michael said as he settled into a chair across from D'Arcy.

"That's not you. Some crew dynamics I've dropped the ball on," D'Arcy replied, and saw both Locke and Emel jerk in shock at his admission. He cleared his throat. "Michael, what do you know about *Opie's Hat*?"

"The ghost ship?" Michael laughed at D'Arcy's shocked look "Everyone is talking about it. Are you really surprised that news has traveled?"

"I suppose I shouldn't be." D'Arcy shrugged. "We're a little more focused on real causes than actual ghosts, though."

Michael studied him and D'Arcy was reminded that though the man in front of him had come to the Mars cause late, he'd been as heavily involved as the rest of them and had managed to translate their defeat on Mars into success here on Trappist.

Or at least something far closer to success than they'd ever gotten back home.

"If you're here, it's because you heard that Captain Ivarken was supplying the TLF with weapons."

D'Arcy waited, hoping Emel would stay silent. Locke was used to dealing with the TLF after the last few years, but for all D'Arcy knew, Emel was still holding a grudge against two of the men who'd been there when her brother was killed.

If you'd bothered to talk with her more, you'd probably have an answer to that.

"He was," Michael said finally. "Until he vanished, anyway. We sort of assumed either the pirates or the CHN had gotten him, though the fallout from the latter never came down on us. Is it true the ship was empty?"

"Completely."

Michael looked at the ceiling for a moment and sighed. "Can I talk to you alone, D'Arcy?"

It surprised him somewhat that when he nodded, both Emel and Locke got to their feet without a word and left the room.

"When Ivarken vanished, he was carrying a prototype weapon that he was supposed to deliver to one of the more violent factions. I don't know what it did, exactly—Gun might. We were trying to stop it. No one wanted a repeat of Mars."

The sick feeling of a collision had settled into D'Arcy's gut as he leaned forward. "Tell me everything," he said. "And call Gun—I need to talk to him as soon as he's free."

IF THERE WAS A GOD, AND THE JURY WAS STILL OUT ON THAT one as far as Jenks was concerned, they had a hell of a sense of humor making her the one responsible for checking in on people.

"Hey, LT?"

Max blinked and looked up at her. "Yes?"

Jenks tapped her wrapped fists together and held them up. "It's spar o'clock. Because you've apparently forgotten to look at your calendar today."

And also you have your DD chip set to ignore all messages.

"Oh. Sorry." Max dragged a hand through her hair. "I was in the middle of— Can we do it later?"

"Nope. Games are coming. Go get changed."

For a second Jenks thought Max was going to pull rank, which she could have done and gotten away with given that Jenks really didn't have any authority to make Max do anything.

Then Max sighed and got to her feet. "I'll be over there in a few."

Jenks took the win and headed back out of their quarters, to the loud ringing of D'Arcy's voice in the hallway.

"When the ensign gives you an order, Petty Officer, I expect you to follow it. Locke shouldn't have to back that up. I shouldn't have to. Is that understood?"

"Perfectly, sir."

D'Arcy's sigh was loud and Jenks looked at the ceiling as she hurried by.

"Aki, talk to me."

Jenks pushed through the door before the petty officer could reply, and exhaled loudly into the evening air. "At least that's not my problem," she muttered at the dark sky.

Though, to be honest, she wasn't sure whatever was going on with Max was much better. This was the third sparring session she'd "forgotten" about since they'd gotten back.

It seemed like whatever was weighing on Max's mind had her backsliding all the way to just-arrived-on-Jupiter-Station Carmichael again. She was hesitant and quiet, watchful and wary.

Jenks was more than a little afraid that if she pushed Max right now, her friend would shatter. She paced the mat as Max came in and silently wrapped her own fists up before joining her in the center.

"Ready?" At Max's nod, Jenks threw a punch. The LT flowed out of the way, her graceful movement putting her into a perfect position for a kick to Jenks's knee that would have put her down.

But Max didn't take it.

Oh, we're doing this again, Jenks thought, muffling a weary sigh. It had taken her months of work to get Max to strike instead of just avoiding.

They fought in silence for several minutes. Jenks throwing punches and Max dodging, deflecting, doing everything but actually fighting her.

"Where did I fuck up?" Jenks asked during the break.

The question startled Max and she dropped her water bottle. It hit the floor with a dull clang.

"What?"

Jenks took a drink and rested her forearms on her knees as Max retrieved her bottle. "I must have done something for this punishment. I just can't figure out what." She tried to keep her voice light and teasing, but Max stiffened.

"Nothing. You haven't done anything." She stood. "We should get back to it."

Jenks popped her mouthguard back in and ground her teeth into it instead of saying the first thing that popped into her head.

This being-an-adult thing is bullshit, she thought.

"All right, LT, let's go." She fisted her hands and waited.

It took Max a solid minute to attack and Jenks batted the punch away without any effort. Same for the two follow-ups and the ridiculously halfhearted front kick Jenks didn't even try to dodge.

"What is this?" she demanded, and Max flinched.

"I'm sorry, I'm distracted. We should do this another day."

"No, you've been pushing me off for too long. We'll do it now. What's got you ghosting me instead of actually engaging? You're sparring like you forgot how to do this."

"I haven't forgotten. I just don't want to."

"You remember we have the Games, right? That cage match thing. We—"

"I don't fucking care about the Games!"

Jenks blinked at her in shock. Max dropped her hands, her shoulders slumping, and a sob escaped into the air.

"Shit, Max."

Before Jenks could step forward, Max backed away. "I'm sorry. Look, I—I can't do this right now."

"Can't what? Do your job? Be a Neo?"

Instead of answering, Max fled from the gym and Jenks let her go with a muttered curse.

"Great job, asshole. You handled that really well. Way to make your friend cry."

"Jenks, what is dying?"

She tilted her head at the ROVER. "Curious question, Doge. You've got a dictionary."

"I know, but it says 'on the point of death' and that says 'to gradually cease to exist or function,' which lots of things do. It's supposed to be permanent?"

"It is, yeah."

"But you said Luis was dead just a few months ago, and he wasn't. Sapphi died, but she didn't. Lou died and stayed dead. I miss her. Does it mean you can die? Does that mean I can die?"

She sat up on her bunk and gestured for him to come over. Doge padded across the floor of the team quarters and sat between Jenks's knees. The cis woman put both of her hands on either side of his head and stared at him.

He liked it when she did this. He wasn't sure why. It was like she really saw him, thought of him as real. It felt important.

He took a picture, not wanting to forget the moment when he had to do a memory purge.

"I'm going to die," Jenks said finally after staring at him for a long moment and he didn't like the feeling that came with her words. "I supposed you can, too."

"I don't want to die."

"Tell me about it." Her smile was soft. "But all living things die, Doge, and you're alive."

"The definition says 'person, animal, plant.' I'm none of those things."

"Pfft. I say you're alive, you're alive." She leaned in and gave him a kiss on his nose. "What's all this about?"

"Sapphi left."

"She did, yeah. But she'll be back before we head for the prelims."

"Her grandma was dying." He watched as Jenks's facial expression changed. "She's sad and so are you."

"A little. Her grandma died last night and before you ask, no, she's not coming back. The shit that happened a few months ago was unusual. Most always people die, and they stay dead. But Sapphi got there in time to say goodbye."

"And that's important?"

"Yes, we don't always get the chance. That's why it's important to make sure people know that you love them ahead of time."

"An intense feeling of deep affection. This is accurate. I love you, Jenks."

She seemed startled by the declaration, but then laughed and wrapped her arms around his neck, hugging him to her. "I love you, too."

FIFTEEN

The Verge

"Is it just me or does this place look different from the last time we were here?" Sapphi asked Jenks. It had taken them a few days to find the time to get in and do a full diagnostic, but she'd finally dragged Jenks—and Doge, if truth were known—into the clean room so they could get it done.

After she and Jenks had gone through Doge's innards with an excessive amount of care, and more than a little unease at seeing his guts spread out on the table, they'd put everything back together and hooked up to Doge's version of the Verge.

"It's been a while since we did a full-on diagnostic. I guess it's not surprising. He's seen a lot since then," Jenks replied with a shrug.

"I mean, it looks more like our stuff. Last time it was all—"

"Matrix-y?"

Sapphi laughed. "Yeah, a bit." She looked around the quarters, which were a pretty good replica of their quarters on Trappist.

Except everything was huge.

Sapphi padded across the floor of their room, the lower bunk almost at eye level for her, and headed for the smaller terminal in the corner by Doge's bed. Jenks was on her heels. They both had bare feet and walked as carefully as possible.

It was always weird coming into someone else's personal version of the Verge, but weirder still to be in Doge's. Whatever Jenks said, Sapphi could see the obvious differences her friend either didn't, or couldn't, recognize. The coloring was better—it had been weird shades of green and black before—and everything was in its place. Even down to Jenks's slightly messy upper bunk.

It wasn't the quarters from Jupiter Station, either, but their current berth on Trappist, which meant Doge was updating his Verge in real time.

Just like a person would.

Sapphi sat down cross-legged at the terminal and pressed her hand to the surface. The screen flashed, allowing her access into Doge's programs without any of the same fuss she'd had earlier.

"I want to see the log for what happened on the ship," Jenks said.

"That's where I was headed," she replied. "But while I'm here, I may as well do the basics first and get them out of the way." She ran through the same easy diagnostic routine they'd done just a few days ago, and this time everything came up green. Doge's weapons system was offline and Sapphi huffed in frustration.

"I don't get it." Jenks's voice was a mirror of that same frustration. "How and why did it get turned back on and without either of us getting the notice?"

"I don't know. I'm going to have to dig on that one. Thankfully I can do it after we turn Doge back—" She stopped and glanced at Jenks. "When we're done."

"You're fine. I just don't like people saying it when he can hear them. It scares him," Jenks said. "I wouldn't actually knee-cap you anyway. I need you mobile."

"Gee, thanks." Sapphi put a hand in Jenks's face with a laugh when she made a kissy noise at her. "Huh, this is new. Look at this." She opened the file marked

FRIENDS

and was even more puzzled when it was just full of photos.

"Did Doge take these?"

"Looks like."

"Aw." Jenks pointed at one. It was just a candid shot, obviously from Doge's perspective, of Jenks and Max hugging in the quarters. "That's adorable. I don't even remember this." She exhaled and shoved both hands into her hair. "I'm going to have to apologize to her."

"You didn't do anything wrong, not really. She's just tangled up about her family," Sapphi replied, studying the next photo. It looked as if he'd taken it while Jenks was talking to him.

"I didn't handle it well. I got frustrated with her. Sapphi, have you had any thought about not going to the Games next year?"

"I have," she admitted, more than a little surprised to be having this conversation with Jenks, of all people.

"Yeah, me too." Jenks didn't say any more and Sapphi wasn't sure if there was anything else to discuss, so she left the silence where it was.

"You know what's weird?" she asked a few minutes later as they continued to flip through the photos. "These aren't random. I mean, they kinda seem like it to us, but he wasn't just randomly taking shots—there aren't enough to support such a claim. And there's nothing awkward—like one of us bunk banging—which means he's aware of when he should be taking photos and when he shouldn't."

"Oh, thank God for that," Jenks said with a laugh. "Also, thanks for reminding me of the potential for something embarrassing." She paused and frowned. "Though, you know, for a long time Doge has been really good about personal space for that sort of thing."

"Define a long time?"

Jenks made a face as she tried to remember. "Honestly, like six months after we booted him up. I was headed to the showers one day and he was being kinda clingy. I told him that people needed privacy sometimes. After that he left me to shower on my own. Asked me a shit-ton of questions about privacy, though."

Doge did that a lot. Asked questions, almost like one of her niblings. Almost like he was actively trying to learn and that was—theoretically impossible. Sapphi didn't want to think about it, or about the potential consequences of an old-model ROVER suddenly behaving more human than any of the advanced AIs out there.

She wondered how much of all this Jenks realized, if her friend realized how she'd encouraged it. With effort, Sapphi dragged her focus back to the files in front of her.

"There's a whole bunch of recordings." She pointed to the files, which were labeled:

IMPORTANT THINGS

and

IMPORTANT THINGS JENKS HAS TOLD ME

Sapphi tapped on one and Jenks's voice filled the air.

"No, we're nice to people just because, Doge. I mean, unless they're trying to hurt you or me or something like that. But it's important to just be kind."

"But you don't like Navy people."

Jenks laughed. "I know, but that's— Shit, how do I explain this? People are people in the end, and they matter. Petty Officer Celda was having a shit day; it cost me absolutely nothing to help them out and it made their day a little brighter. I hope, anyway."

Sapphi heard a sniffle and looked over her shoulder. "Are you crying?"

"Shut up." Jenks rubbed at her eyes. "I don't even *remember* that conversation. Why does he have all this saved?"

"I don't know. My guess is he wants to be able to reference it and it's important enough for him to separate it out from his normal storage. He also must have decided he didn't want to lose it when he did memory purges." She rubbed at the side of the terminal and finally said the words that had been rolling around in her head. "He's learning things."

"Sapphi, that model AI wasn't designed for long-term— what do you fucking call it?"

"Machine learning."

"Yeah, he wasn't designed for that." Jenks chewed on a finger and Sapphi knew exactly what she was thinking because she'd been thinking the same thing.

Apparently, Jenks had been paying attention.

The only reason they'd been able to wheedle approval for Doge in the first place was because the decommissioned ROVERs were a limited-process AI program.

"He's doing it anyway," Sapphi said finally. "I'm not a hundred percent sure about it, but some of the Evolve Signs are there. You're not surprised, are you?"

The guilty look scuttled over Jenks's face, confirming Sapphi's guess even before she spoke.

"He's always been a curious shit. I just told him everything because I didn't think any of it would really stick. But it has been, hasn't it? I can think of a thousand little examples. Like, when I talked to Luis and Tivo at Blythe's—just before Grant and his goons jumped me? Doge said they were 'untrustworthy' and growled at them."

"Without prompting?"

"Yeah." Jenks sighed. "I sort of forgot about it with everything else that was going on, but there's more than just that and it definitely means something is up with him if he can change his engagement parameters all on his own." She turned to Sapphi, confused. "So what are we going to do?"

"Not say a fucking word about it, for starters."

Jenks blinked at her in surprise and Sapphi couldn't really blame her. The curse itself was out of the ordinary for her, but so was the abrupt decision to keep this a secret.

She continued. "We don't quite know what's actually happening to him, plus you and I both know if we tell someone our 'not supposed to be able to learn new things' AI is learning new things, they'll try to take him away."

"Over my dead body."

"I'd rather not contemplate that," Sapphi replied, not missing a beat.

"Shit, sorry. Speaking before thinking again," Jenks said. "I really do need to apologize to Max. I did the same thing to her earlier."

Sapphi leaned into Jenks, a silent acceptance of the apology, and then went back to work. The secondary diagnostic ticked one line off at a time, all green also, and Sapphi turned her attention to the log Jenks had asked about.

"There was an outside ping," she murmured as she scrolled through the code. "No forced entry. Jenks—"

"I see it. He went looking."

"He was *curious*. I want you to make a list for me of everything you remember that's struck you as weird. Do it offline, though. I don't—"

Sapphi swallowed.

"What is it?" Jenks asked.

She wasn't sure how to explain it, but she realized now what had triggered Doge's curiosity.

"It's that song again."

"Max said you've been humming it."

She hesitated, all too aware that Jenks would pick up on it, and then nodded. "It's been stuck in my head. I asked Doge to do a search for it to try to figure out what it was. This is weird." She froze as the log continued on to the point where Doge took a shot at Jenks. Her friend looked over her shoulder, and even with her inexperience at coding, Jenks could tell something was off.

"What the fuck is that?"

"I don't know, but it's not a virus or even malware. It was— hang on—it was *parent* code. Something really similar to his original programming. I'll write up a security patch; that should keep it from happening again." Sapphi rubbed a hand over her face. "His system recognized it, which is why he let it in, but when he realized it had turned his weapons back on and was trying to actively take over, when he heard you say it was you, he shut everything down."

"*Doge* shut everything down? You didn't get in there and do it?"

"It wasn't me. It was all him."

"That's cool."

"Yeah."

"But . . . shit."

"Yeah."

"CAN I TALK ABOUT SOMETHING?" JENKS ASKED AS THE PLANS for the Games wore down and everyone had settled into silence around the remains of their lunch. The team meeting had been relatively smooth, but her stomach was still jumping with nerves at what she was about to propose.

"What's up?" Nika turned her way with a curious look.

"I know we're gearing up for the Games here and this might not be the best time to float it, but I was wondering about everyone's feelings on competing next year."

"Shouldn't we get through this year first?" Max asked.

"I think that's why I'm bringing this up now."

"What do you mean?" Nika asked.

"I mean, I know we're trying to focus on these Games, but I, for one, would like to take a break from the Games. Just curious as to everyone else's feelings on the matter." Jenks swallowed at the shocked looks, relief coursing through her to have this out in the open.

"For good?" Nika asked.

"I don't know. Probably not," she admitted. "But we've had a lot going on these last few years. *I've* had a lot. It would be nice to focus on other things for a while. Just do our jobs and live our lives a little."

"Like I said the other day, I'm up for a break," Sapphi said.

"Same," Tamago agreed, and Chae echoed them.

Max was silent for a long moment and Jenks wondered if she'd misjudged the LT's reaction during sparring the other day. It had certainly seemed like she'd meant she didn't want to fight in the Games. But then she nodded and when Nika followed suit, there was a second burst of relief in Jenks's chest.

"Awesome." She rubbed her hands together. "We'll go out on a win and call it good."

"Sounds like a plan," Nika said, smiling.

Chae and Sapphi cleared the dishes. Jenks headed back into their room and patted Doge on the head. "How are you doing, buddy?"

"Okay." He was always more subdued after full diagnostic and she hated it. His mood seemed compounded by the incident on *Opie's Hat* even though she'd told him repeatedly it wasn't his fault. "Still trying to find that song for Sapphi, but I'm not having any luck and it's frustrating."

"You want to throw me a clip? I'll put it up on the boards and see if anyone recognizes it."

"Okay."

Her DD pinged and Jenks grabbed her VR set out of her closet.

"Before you jump into the Verge, can I have a minute?" Max asked.

Jenks turned. "What's up?"

"I'm sorry about shouting at you the other day. It was uncalled for."

Jenks stepped hard on her first instinct to tease her friend about the overly formal apology and instead said, "It's all good, LT. I know you were frustrated. If anything, I should apologize for pushing. I know the Games weren't your thing and you just kind of got swept up into it."

"Yeah." Max looked like she was going to say something else but then shook her head. "Thanks."

"Anytime." Jenks frowned at Max's back.

Aren't apologies supposed to make people feel better?

One thing solved, one mystery still in play.

Make that two mysteries, Jenks thought as she climbed up into her bunk with a sigh and shoved the headset on. She was going to go put Sapphi's earworm on the boards and then spend an hour blowing shit up to see if she could get this uneasy feeling to go away.

SIXTEEN

Trappist System

Max opened the email she'd been trying to compose to her cousin on her DD when Jenks had pulled her into that disastrous sparring match earlier in the week. The chief seemed to have forgiven her for shouting at her, and what was more hadn't realized that Max's outburst hadn't been about the Games themselves, but about the possibility of *their* fight.

She'd almost fessed up right after apologizing but had lost her nerve.

Like always.

"Get your shit together, Lieutenant," she hissed the order at herself. Waiting around for her family to make the first move was only going to cause trouble in the long run, she knew this, and yet she was letting her fear push her down to wait like a good little girl for whatever directive got leveled at her head.

You control the fight, LT. Strike and move in; don't wait for your opponent to figure out what's going on.

Jenks's advice, as usual, was applicable to more than just fighting in the cage. Max sighed. She had to move on this, get ahead of it. She'd been a little surprised by how easily Bosco had passed on the contact information for Islen. Along with a warning not to mention it to Ria.

Dear Islen,

I hope you are well. I know we haven't had any contact, but I am hoping that if I came to see you, you would be willing to speak with me about a personal matter.

I am considering officially leaving the family and wondered if you would have advice for me in the best way to proceed. Though I entirely understand if you would rather not be involved or have anything to do with me.

Please let me know either way.

Sincerely,
Max
Lieutenant Max Carmichael
Trappist-1d, Amanave Base

*Intel/Interceptor Group–*Zuma's Ghost *(Zz5)*

THE CLANG OF PRACTICE SWORDS RANG THROUGH THE AIR of the base gym, normal sounds mixing into the chaotic symphony of the packed room.

D'Arcy blocked Nika's thrust and danced to the side to avoid the elbow that followed. "You've been sword fighting with your sister."

Nika shook his head. "You'd be surprised how often Max throws that in," he replied. "It's actually more dangerous with her. She clocked me in the eye the first time."

D'Arcy laughed. "I wasn't entirely sure Carmichael would settle when I first met her, but she's done well."

"Thanks to Rosa and you."

Max's original commander—Rosa Martín—was now an instructor at the academy, but before that the woman had been a fixture at Jupiter Station and a good friend of D'Arcy's.

Still was a good friend. Just a little too far away. But he was also glad she had been far away, because that meant she was still alive.

He pushed away the sadness and then pressed his attack. "You've had a hand in that, too, Nika, and you know it."

"Maybe some," Nika conceded, giving ground with such ease that D'Arcy wondered if he'd just stepped into some sort of trap set by the younger man. "You and Rosa both had a hand in my training; it just comes full circle, doesn't it?"

They fought for several minutes before D'Arcy missed a block and Nika disarmed him.

"Good one," D'Arcy said, shaking the feeling back into his hand with a grimace. He bent and picked up his sword, tossing it over toward the bench.

"That's a cue for a break?"

"Yeah."

"Need me to kiss your hand?"

He shot Nika a glare. "Put that smug look back in your pocket, Vagin. I'll get you on the next round."

Nika laughed and handed over a water bubble, settling on the bench with his arm braced on his left knee. "How's your new crew?"

The question was casual but so loaded and D'Arcy dropped to the bench next to his friend, rubbing at his face with a towel as he tried to figure out how to articulate the tangle of things in his head.

"Fine."

"You'll let the wolves keep you out of the woods?"

"The who out of the what?" He dropped the towel and frowned at Nika.

"My baba said it a lot when I lied to her about everything

being fine. This is punishment, I suppose, in God's own strange way, for all the grief I gave her after my mother died."

Nika so rarely spoke of God, the offhand comment distracted D'Arcy enough that he slipped. Or maybe it was just being called out so blatantly. Either way, he said, "I think Admiral Chen might be right about pulling me off active duty. I'm not fit to be an Interceptor commander anymore. I thought maybe I could pull things together, but . . ."

"Well, that's bullshit." Nika scooted over on the bench and put his hand on D'Arcy's shoulder. "Granted, I wasn't standing there, but I doubt that's what was said because it doesn't sound like Admiral Chen at all. It sounds like wolves howling."

"You remember I grew up on Mars, right? Not a wolf in sight."

"The worst ones aren't real, D'Arcy. They lurk in our heads, snapping and snarling when we least expect it. Heli had great scores at the academy. They're smart, a little nervous about how they fit in, but Locke's taken them in hand. Have you trained with them on the sword yet?"

He hadn't—and damn Nika, but he knew it. The question was a formality for whatever lecture was coming and D'Arcy wasn't sure he had the patience for it.

"There hasn't been time."

Nika hummed, then surprised him by changing the subject. "You've got history with the master chief, don't you?"

D'Arcy inhaled, then exhaled carefully. "Yeah. We grew up in the EM Projects together. I knew her brother."

"It seems like these two are great additions to your team. The others are working well with them. Aki's struggling a bit with Emel, but that's to be expected since she follows your lead. I watched them doing a Boarding Action practice against Pia's crew the other day. They were short one, though."

"Your point?" D'Arcy knew the words were sharp, but they didn't seem to slow Nika down at all.

"You already know my point: that you should have been

there. Do I really need to tell you? Why are you holding them at arm's length?"

He hadn't expected that gentle question or the pain that followed. "I'm done here."

"D'Arcy—"

"No, seriously. When you've had a teammate die and another betray you, then you can come lecture me about this, Nika. Until then I don't want to hear it."

He stood and was two steps away when Nika's reply hit him like a sword thrust in the back.

"I *have* been through it, D'Arcy, and it almost ripped my crew apart."

"You got Sapphi back!" He whirled around and jabbed a finger in the air. "And Chae was forgiven. It's not the same fucking thing, Nika—don't pretend that it is."

"It's never the same situation." The younger man was so calm in the face of his fury and it only served to highlight D'Arcy's insecurities even more. "I tried to hide from it, too, D'Arcy, and you saw the devastation it wreaked. We all almost died because of me. You didn't let me off the hook when I was having trouble and I wouldn't be your friend if I didn't call you out the same way. Be as mad as you want, I get it. I may not understand exactly what you're feeling, but I know that you're hurting." Nika stood and held his hand out. "What I don't understand is why you aren't doing anything about it. I'm here.

"Talk to me."

D'Arcy turned around and walked away from him.

COMMANDER VERA TILL EXHALED AND STRETCHED HER ARMS above her head. Being out in space after the excitement of the prelims was always a mixture of frustrated restlessness and welcome relaxation. Two weeks had gone by in the blink of an eye and to be honest she'd enjoyed the quiet and the time to focus on training.

This search was boring as fuck, though.

"'Poke around,' Stephan says. Never mind that it's like poking a stick into the ocean," she murmured, and Petty Officer Atlas Nash laughed.

"You never know, Commander. We might get lucky."

"Given we're talking about ghost ships and potential pirates, I figure 'lucky' is nothing but endless black." She reached out and mussed the younger man's blue hair. "How's your sister doing?"

"Due any day. Also looks like she swallowed a medicine ball." He held his hands apart with a grin.

"If you said that to her face, you're going to have to stay away from Earth for a few years."

"Of course I didn't." Atlas huffed. "I'm a good older brother."

"You are older by four minutes, Nash."

"Still four minutes," he replied. "It's important in twin hierarchy." The console chimed at the same time the radar went off.

"*Flux*." Commander Pia Forsberg's voice was cool over the com. "We've got incoming."

"Spotted it, Pia. You got an ID?"

"Not yet. It's fourteen hundred klicks out. Moving fast, though."

"We'll broadcast the warning," Vera replied. "Unidentified vessel, this is Commander Vera Till of the NeoG Interceptor *Flux Capacitor*. We are unable to get a read on your vessel. Please slow your engines and fly your flag."

There was no response.

"Nash, wake the others."

He nodded and hit the alert notice. The warning buzz went off three times, paused, and repeated. Before the second round had finished, Vera could hear the rest of her crew moving toward the bridge.

"Commander, I've got a second ship on the radar," Nash said as Xin leaned on his chair.

Vera reissued her demand over the com.

The com crackled. "The fuck I'm slowing down, you bastard pirates!"

"UV, I repeat, I am Commander Till of the NeoG—"

"The fucking ship behind me trying to blow me out of the black is NeoG, too, so fuck you and your trap."

"Vera, Pavel got an ID on the ship. Private vessel *Reginald's Glory* registered to Chad Reginald; he's a freelance surveyor. Current contract is with Trappist Minerals, LLC. We've got incoming fire. Repeat, the other UV is firing on Reginald."

Vera pushed aside her shock and snapped into action.

"Pia, break to starboard and follow Reginald. Get him to heave to. We'll take on the other ship. Xin, get in that seat and figure out who that other ship is, because she's sure as shit not NeoG." She pointed at the far wall and the lieutenant slid across the bridge as Nash sent *Flux* into a dive.

"Hang on, everyone."

Vera trusted her pilot to know the best approach and she wasn't disappointed. The internals finally compensated for the direction change after a few moments of greater than standard g's and Nash brought them around in pursuit of the mysterious second ship.

Xin hissed through her teeth and Vera turned to look at her. "Commander, he wasn't lying. That's an Interceptor."

"What the fuck?" Tien murmured, though the senior chief subsided when Vera lifted a hand.

"It's an older one, though." Xin paused and frowned. "Holy shit, it's the *Rising Sun*."

"It can't be." Shock gripped her throat and Vera lost several precious seconds to it before she shook herself free and slammed a hand on the com console. "Commander Winchester, do you copy? This is Commander Vera Till of the NeoG Interceptor *Flux Capacitor*."

Silence.

"Celeste, please answer me." Her voice cracked. Vera knew her crew was staring at her, and she fought to keep her face impassive. "Stand down, *Rising Sun,* or we will be forced to fire on you."

The feedback screamed through the coms, causing everyone to recoil. And a grating voice followed the noise.

"New threat detected. Adjusting."

"They're firing—at us! Nash, hard to port!" Xin shouted the order and the petty officer reacted on instinct, pulling *Flux* to the left in a brutal turn as the alarm blared.

Flux's crew were at the top of their game and reacted in the exact manner that thousands of training hours had hammered into their muscles and brains. Saad and ZZ had immediately jumped to the weapons as soon as the ship leveled out and the pair had called up a firing solution for Tien in a matter of seconds.

"Winged her!" Xin announced. "Nash—"

"Got it, LT," he replied, and swore. "Whoever is flying that ship is good."

Vera batted away the image of the cherubic face that appeared in her mind's eye. *They are dead and gone; Kostas is not flying that ship.*

"Vera, I've got Reginald. Do you need me to assist?"

"No, I don't want him taking off and running into Trappist screaming that the NeoG is hijacking ships."

"No worries—about the running part, anyway—we're going to have to tow his ship in." Pia's voice held enough poorly concealed laughter that Vera felt her own humor bubble up despite the situation.

"Stay back. I don't know what we're dealing with just yet and I want you to be able to bug out if you have to."

"Vera, I've got a stranded civilian."

"I know." She dragged in a breath, grabbed for the console when the ship lurched again. "I'm not saying it lightly, but if I say go or we go dark, you get the fuck out of here."

"She could take a shot at them from where she is," Saad said, and ZZ nodded in agreement.

"You have a solution, you two?" Vera asked.

"Yes, Commander."

"Send it to Pavel. Pia, did you catch that?"

"Sure did—Pavel's looking at it now and giving me a thumbs-up."

Another alarm blared and the red emergency lighting kicked in when *Flux*'s power flickered. Nash blistered the air with a series of curses Vera had never heard from the cool-headed PO.

"When we board that ship, I'm going to beat the fuck out of the pilot," he muttered. "Sorry, baby. I don't mean to let you keep getting shot up. Saad?"

"We've got it. Go."

Vera hung on to the console as Nash put the ship on a collision course with the *Rising Sun* at a speed the Interceptor could only hold for a few minutes without redlining the engine. Xin calmly counted down the kilometers until impact as the two ships rushed at each other.

"One hundred klicks, fifty-three, thirty-eight . . ."

"Punch it," Nash snapped.

Vera's breath caught in her lungs as Nash turned *Flux* on her starboard side in a move that should have been functionally impossible for the big ship and peeled away to reveal the shot Pia's *Wandering Hunter* had fired some ninety seconds prior.

"Eat plasma," Xin said.

But *Rising Sun*'s pilot reacted with inhuman speed and the older Interceptor dove low so that the rail round missed the top edge of the ship and only tore through the back end, tearing off a chunk of the tail. Then, trailing debris, the missing Interceptor sped back into the questionable safety of the asteroid belt.

"They're gone." Xin's voice was stunned. "I'm not picking up—fuck—anything. Commander, they're not on the radar. Do we follow?"

"No." Vera shook her head; there were goose bumps on her arms despite the warmth of the bridge. "Commander Forsberg, head for Trappist-1d. We're right behind you."

"Copy that, *Flux*. Vera, what the fuck was that?"

"I don't know," she replied in a low voice. "But we're going to find out."

SEVENTEEN

The Verge

Sapphi lay on the green grass, fingers beating out a pattern on her stomach as she stared at the clouds floating by in the pristine blue sky.

"Hey there," Yasu said as he settled down on the grass next to her. "This is nice. Having a picnic?"

"You actually just missed my family. Well, some of them, anyway." She lifted her head, shading her eyes against the sunlight filtering in through the leaves above their heads. "We have a standing weekly date here for anyone who can make it. Sometimes it's just a few. Sometimes it's all—"

"Hundred of you?"

She smacked him on the arm but laughed. "There's not a hundred. Only fourteen—okay, twenty-two now—but I get how we feel like a lot at times."

"I tease." Yasu stretched out next to her. "It *was* a lot for me to get used to and I never quite fit in, but to be honest I've always been more than a little envious of your family, Sapphi. All I had was my dad and, well, you know how well that went."

"I'm sorry," she said, reaching out and linking her fingers through his.

"Don't be—none of it was your fault."

"How's work?" Sapphi asked after they'd lain in companionable silence for several minutes. The first few times they'd gotten together in the Verge since she'd returned to Trappist it had been a whirlwind of conversation, catching up on their lives in rapid-fire stories. It was nice to settle into some sort of stillness.

"Really good. Things are flowing pretty well. I don't mind saying it: I wish you were working on this with me, Sapphi, so we could really talk about it. You'd probably have a new perspective."

"You could always put in a request. It's been pretty quiet around here."

"You call empty ships showing up and busting through traffic quiet?"

She frowned. "How'd you know about that?"

Yasu laughed. "I pay attention to news reports. It really was empty?"

"Ghost ship all the way around. You should hear Jenks go on about it; she's been spinning all sorts of theories ever since her dog shot—" She caught herself, fumbled for something to cover her slip since Yasu had definitely noticed and sat up.

"Doge shot Jenks?"

"No, it wasn't—" Sapphi cursed under her breath and then, whispering an apology to her mother for the lie, grabbed an arm and moaned in faked pain.

"Sapphi! Are you okay?"

Sapphi rubbed her hands together, appalled at how easily the lie bubbled up. "Phantom pain, still happens sometimes."

"Even here? Do you need to kick out?"

"Maybe I should. Sorry to cut this short." She offered up a smile.

"No worries. I'll see you again." Yasu waved a hand and then vanished.

"Fuck my fucking mouth," Sapphi muttered, dropping back into the grass. The last thing she wanted to do was draw attention to Doge, especially since the incident on the *Opie's Hat* was on official record.

How the fuck had Yasu known about it, though? It couldn't have been big enough to make major news. And how had he extrapolated that Doge shot Jenks just from that fragment of a slip? A flicker of unease danced through her as memories of how controlling, how jealous Yasu had been in the depths of his addiction rose up in her mind.

Is he watching me again? Am I falling right back into a bad situation?

Sapphi got to her feet, her gut rolling and a thousand old fears suddenly alive in her head again. She was just about to kick out when movement flickered in the corner of her vision and she turned as the hazy outline of a person appeared. They weren't solid, just the impression of a person-shape in the blueness of the sky and the green grass.

Nell. I need your help.

The words weren't spoken but appeared in type the same way the others had, only this time they just hung in the air.

Please. Please help me.

The thunderstorm boiled out of thin air with a growl that drove frozen terror into Sapphi's bones. "What is this? Who are you?"

Pirene.
I need your help.

The figure stretched out a hand and Sapphi reached for them. Her fingers brushed something, and she felt a jolt run through her.

"No!" A grating voice split the air and the lightning that came down from the sky blew a smoking hole in the grass right in front of her.

"HOLY FUCK!" JENKS SCRAMBLED OFF HER BUNK, ALMOST stepping on Tamago in the process as they both rushed over to Sapphi. The ensign was on the floor where she'd fallen from her bed, the smoking ruin of her VR gear lying in the middle of their room.

"Sapphi!" Chae dropped down next to her, catching Sapphi as she slumped over.

"What was that?" Nika and Max came out of the office and poked their heads in the door, snapping into motion at the sight of the chaos in the middle of the quarters.

"Near as I can figure, it was Sapphi's VR set going ker-flooey." Jenks kicked at it with a bare foot, jumping back when it sparked. "And again, holy fuck."

Tamago had taken Sapphi gently by the face. "Vitals are okay, obviously on the high side. Sapphi, follow my finger, honey." They let her go and held up a finger in front of her eyes, moving it to the left and right.

"Careful," Max cautioned when Jenks crouched by the inter-face.

"You know, these are specifically designed to not do what this thing just did, for obvious reasons," she said, chewing on a finger. "I need a containment bag, LT, for electrical. There's one in my tool kit. It's got the blue edge." She pointed to her left without looking away. "Gloves, too—they're in the side pocket."

She tried to block out Tamago talking Sapphi back to con-sciousness as she studied the half-melted chunk of equipment on the floor and made a plan for how to get it up and into the bag without shocking herself or damaging it further.

"What else do you need?" Max asked, handing over the bag and the gloves.

Jenks cleared her throat and pulled on the gloves, shaking the bag open. "If this goes sideways, do not, under any circumstances, grab ahold of me. If you can kick the thing out of my hands, aim for the doorway." She glanced at Max's feet, relieved the lieutenant was wearing her boots. "Yeah, that might work. Just don't grab me or you'll probably get shocked, too."

"Please don't get shocked. I'm kind of tired of it."

"Tell me about it." Jenks choked on a laugh. "This is fine— let's just hope Sapphi's thunder god isn't like 'fuck that chief in particular' in about two seconds." She didn't wait for Max to express her confusion over the joke but dropped the bag over the VR gear and scooped it up in one smooth motion. She sealed it with her left hand and tossed it back onto the floor.

"Okay," she said with an exhale, taking another step back just to be on the safe side. "We should probably call Dwayne and have the bomb squad come in here and deal with this."

And just for good measure.

"Holy fuck."

THE EARLY-MORNING SUN WAS IN HER EYES, BUT MAX SAW Nika's sword sweep down toward her leg and jumped, pushing off the ground into a backflip and landing a meter away from him onto the packed dirt outside of Amanave.

She laughed at the shocked look on his face and rushed him. He barely got his sword up in time to block her thrust to the left.

"Where did you learn to do that?" he asked.

"Where do you think?" She blocked his punch with her free hand.

"My sister is a menace and a terrible influence." Nika tried to pull his sword free and swore when he realized she'd locked him up. His blue eyes narrowed. "What's your plan here, Lieutenant?"

"I'll be honest, I don't have one."

"Interesting."

His flashing grin was distracting and Max realized too late that he'd let go of his sword. She had to release the hold to avoid getting hit with his punch—his prosthetic arm was an ultralight titanium that felt a bit like being hit by a shuttle when it connected.

Even as she stumbled away, she felt a little surge of happiness that he was using his advantages. The loss of his right arm in an explosion at a warehouse on Trappist-1d had been a terrifying moment for all of them, but no one so much as Jenks and Nika himself.

He'd gotten his Interceptor team out of the warehouse before the explosives had gone up, but the resulting rubble and debris had crushed his arm at the elbow and her own father had performed the surgery to remove it at Nika's request.

Focus, Max.

The warning voice dragged her back to the fight and rather than continue to struggle against gravity, she dropped into the rust-orange dirt and rolled to her left.

She'd made a mistake telling Nika she didn't have a plan, as he now seemed determined to keep her from having any breathing space to formulate one and pressed her with attack after attack. Max's strength was in recognizing the patterns, the angles, and being able to instinctively come up with a counter. But an assault like this was overwhelming and she could feel herself shutting down.

The image of the semifinal fight with Aloisi flashed into her head. She hadn't meant to drop her hands. Hadn't meant to lose. It had all happened so fast.

"Max?"

She jerked her eyes to Nika and realized her sword arm was hanging limply by her side. "Sorry," she whispered.

"It's okay." He tapped his sword against his leg and Max braced herself, knowing all too well what was coming. "You want to talk about it?"

"I'm thinking about cutting ties with my family." The words came out in a rush. The lesser of two evils to put out into the air. "I messaged my cousin Islen about it."

"The one who runs the clinic on the Congo?"

Max nodded. "I honestly wasn't expecting an answer. But she sent this." She forwarded him the email, watched him frown.

"Cryptic, though I suppose I don't blame her. Coordinates?"

"A landing pad north of Lake Tumba. According to Bosco, she sets up camp on the south end in the rainy season." Max wondered if LifeEx's security chief had pieced together why Max wanted the information.

"So, that's a yes? She'll talk to you?"

"I guess?" Max said with a sigh. "If I even go. But first I need the leave approval." She looked at him tentatively. "I was wondering . . . would you be willing to go with me?"

"Of course I will," he replied with a smile and no hesitation, holding out a hand. She took it and let him pull her into his arms.

Max relaxed into the embrace and rested her head on his shoulder.

"You want to tell me the rest of it?" Nika whispered against her hair. "You've been withdrawn and quiet whenever the Games come up. I know we talked about it a little, but you didn't seem relieved at all when Jenks brought up not competing next year. You were pulling your punches in that prelim fight with Aloisi when you could have knocked her out twice. What's weighing, Max? I know it's not all about your family and it's not really about not competing."

It's nothing, she almost insisted, habit driving her to avoid the conversation rather than take the offered comfort. Embarrassment flooded her. She trusted Nika with her life, with her heart.

So why wasn't she able to take this last step, and trust him with her thoughts?

"I threw the fight," she whispered, unable to look him in the eye for her confession.

He didn't judge. He didn't say anything. He just waited for her to continue.

"I didn't mean to. Everything with my mother, she said if I didn't stop competing and leave the NeoG, they'd cut me off from the family. And I don't want to fight Jenks anyway. I just . . . panicked, I guess? Everyone is treating it like a joke, but I've been *so* anxious about fighting in the championship. I didn't even do it consciously against Aloisi; I just dropped my guard and next thing I knew—" She buried her face in his shoulder, tears burning her eyes. "I . . . fuck. Nika, why am I like this?"

"Like a human being? Hey, it's okay." She felt his hands in her hair as he took a step back and turned her face to his. "Look at me. It's okay."

"But it's not. What have I done?"

"Nothing. You messed up a fight during a competition." He smiled. "If someone had paid you to do it, we'd maybe have a problem . . . mostly because you didn't cut me in." She looked up in surprise to see him grinning, and snorted as he finished, "But this is just life."

She smiled despite herself. "Maybe?"

Nika lifted a shoulder. "My sister isn't the only one who occasionally breaks the rules. Lucky for you, I like you, Carmichael."

"Lucky for you, I like your brain," she replied with a soft smile. "Also, I feel like saying Jenks 'occasionally' breaks the rules is being generous."

"Nice try, but don't change the subject." Nika pressed his forehead to hers and then released her. His blue eyes went hard for a moment. "Your mother threatened you."

Commit fully, Carmichael.

Max took a deep breath. "After you left the Verge. But not just me. She threatened *all* of you. Cutting me off does so little. I can't see it changing my life much. I've got the NeoG, I've got money of my own. Yet I've been waiting for something from the family since that call, but now I'm starting to think my mother was bluffing, that they can't really do anything to me. But she threatened you, and Jenks, and everyone else. Not expressly, but it was there."

"So you think leaving first will help?" His expression was as gentle as the fingers he laced through hers.

"I'm hoping?" Max knew the laugh was cracked. "Jenks keeps saying I've got commitment problems. I figured I should move before they do."

"Then we'll go talk to Islen." He squeezed her hand and then released her. "What scares you about the fight?"

"Jenks will be mad at me if I win." Rather than feeling any relief at putting the words into the air, Max felt worse, like she'd just made it real by talking about it. She turned away from him and threw her hands into the air. "Please tell me I'm being foolish."

"Never. Throwing matches and doubting her worth aside, Maxine Carmichael is not foolish."

"You're supposed to be making me feel better." She glared at him over her shoulder and Nika laughed as he crossed to the canyon edge to join her.

"Fine. You're a foolish fool. The foolishest."

She shook her head but couldn't stop smiling at him.

"I can't tell you how Jenks will react," Nika said. "But I can tell you that I don't think she's the sort of person to let something like that impact a relationship she's chosen. You haven't talked to her about this, have you?"

"No. Of course not." Max exhaled and shoved a hand into her curls, staring at the vast expanse of jagged rock stretching out in front of them. "To be honest, I'm pretty sure she's going to kill me if I tell her I threw a fight."

"I doubt that. Though I'd say have a witness handy, to be safe." Nika grinned when Max choked down a laugh. "Seriously, she'd probably tell you that assuming you're going to win a match between you two is exactly why you'll lose it. I'm not sure she'd be wrong about that."

Max was surprised at the amusement that flooded her and her ability to tease him back. "Your betrayal hurts, Vagin."

"So maybe you *do* want to beat her?" he asked, his words gentler now. "I know there's a competitive spark inside there; you've just spent a lot of time stepping on it because your family made it toxic." He looked back at the landscape in front of them and rubbed a hand over his jaw.

"The Games are just that, Max: games. Jenks knows it. You know it. Everything else we do is the important part of it. But if you don't talk to her about this, it's just going to fester and then it might turn into something that damages your friendship and potentially hurts what we do out there." He gave her a sad smile. "Ask me how I know."

She didn't have to. They'd lived it two years ago when Nika was working for Intel under the radar and hadn't told any of his crew about it. The cascading series of events and Nika's decision to use Max's own insecurities against her had nearly destroyed their fragile relationship—both professionally and personally.

They'd had a lot of conversations since then, but the sting of his decisions still surfaced and hurt at times when she least expected it.

"Point taken," she managed, and focused on breathing for a moment before she replied. "Okay, you're right. I'll talk to her about it."

Thankfully Nika didn't press her for a time frame on her decision.

"Speaking of Jenks, did you get a look at that public affairs request she put in?"

"I did and I think it's a good idea." She tapped her sword against her leg. "The NeoG's relationship with the people of Trappist has improved, but having a more public face on the ground isn't a bad idea."

"Even if that face is ours?"

Max laughed. "I'm used to publicity. I just don't like it. But this is far more worthwhile an endeavor than my family appearances." Then she sobered. "Are we taking Doge with us?"

"I don't know. The full diagnostic came back clean, and they didn't find anything on the ship itself that would indicate a virus. Sapphi said she did a security patch for it and feels pretty good that it'll prevent it from happening again." Nika paused and Max recognized the look on his face as he rolled over something he wanted to say but wasn't sure he should. "Have you noticed anything strange with him?"

"With Doge?" She could think of several things offhand in the last year. His concern over Jenks after they'd all thought Luis was dead. The fact that he could tell Jenks was scared when she and Nika had been taken prisoner. His ability to not only recognize the Morse code that Jenks had been tapping out, but that he knew to look for it in the first place and had relayed the message to Max without any prompting. All his endless, searching questions. "Yes."

"Me too."

They fell into silence for several heartbeats before Nika spoke again.

"Max, I don't want to do anything that will end up with Doge getting taken away. Not only would it crush my sister, but it would hurt him."

"I am one hundred percent behind that." The words rushed out with the burst of relief in her chest and she watched Nika's shoulders relax. "I've spilled my guts at your feet; it's your turn, Nika. You want to tell me what went down with D'Arcy the other day? I haven't seen you two go this long without speaking to each other."

Nika sighed and dragged a hand through his hair. "I pushed and maybe I shouldn't have. I know that Jupiter was hard on all of us, but D'Arcy . . ."

"Took the brunt of it," Max finished softly. "I know. I've been worried about him, too. What happened?" She listened as Nika recounted the conversation, and reached for his hand again.

"I am so frustrated with him," Nika said. "He made a great choice bringing Emel and Heli onto his team; they're a perfect balance of experience and new enthusiasm. From what I can see, they've settled into things really well."

"But D'Arcy's holding himself back," Max said with a nod. "He's scared, Nika."

"I know he is. It's hard to trust people after a betrayal like that."

"No, this isn't about trusting them."

"No?"

"No. He's scared of *losing* them." She squeezed Nika's hand. "I know the feeling."

"We can't control that."

"I know that and so does D'Arcy, but being logical about something doesn't always help us get over a feeling, right? I wish I could say it will work itself out, but I'm not sure that's the case. More, I think this is something he's going to have to figure out on his own. Do you want some advice?"

"Of course."

"Give him a little space; your friendship is strong enough to withstand something like this. He'll come talk to you when he's ready."

"I suspect Emel is not going to let him slide on it for much longer before she says something," Nika replied. "But you're right. I just . . . hate seeing him like this. He's a good commander and we're lucky to have him."

"He is, and one of these days he'll realize that—"

Max's DD pinged with an incoming com message and judging from the way Nika looked, his DD had gotten the same information.

"Go ahead, Stephan," Nika said.

"*Flux* and *Hunter* just came back. Where are you two?"

"On the western edge of the canyon. What's up?"

"Get back here and I'll tell you," he replied, and disconnected.

The pair shared a look and headed for their transport. "That was abrupt, even for him," Max said.

"Tell me about it. I wonder what's going on."

"Knowing our luck, nothing good."

D'ARCY EXHALED IN FRUSTRATION WHEN HELI MADE THE MIS-
take of leaving the left flank open for the third time. "Ensign!" he roared, and they froze. "You're going to get hit in
the back the next time we board a hostile ship if you don't
fucking start looking. If you don't care about your life, that's
one thing, but you're putting the rest of your team at risk."

Heli's navy-blue eyes were wide in their heart-shaped
face and D'Arcy had to step on the swell of sympathy. They
were going to get killed if they didn't start checking.

He lied to himself that his voice wasn't extra sharp because of the way his fight with Nika still burned in his
chest.

"I've got it, Commander." Locke stepped between him
and the startled ensign, speaking to her in a low voice. He'd
stepped up again. Been the buffer more and more over the last
few weeks as they trained, and D'Arcy knew he was leaning
too much on the man's peacemaking abilities.

Nika was fucking right, damn it. So was Emel.

Judging from the look Emel was shooting him and the
way she was tapping her sword on her leg, she knew it, too.
Yet he couldn't help himself.

"Something on your mind, Master Chief?" he challenged
before he could stop the words.

"No." She turned on her heel and joined Locke.

He'd wanted her to start a fight with him, he realized.
Wanted someone to take this feeling out on him so he didn't
have to deal with it himself.

"Fuck me," D'Arcy muttered, and rubbed a hand over his
head.

"Commander?" Lupe's soft voice broke the silence. The petty
officer slipped his hand into D'Arcy's free one and squeezed

quickly before releasing him. "I have faith you'll figure this out, but I'm here if you need to talk."

D'Arcy stared after the trans man as he walked across the room to join the others. Those words had been the exact same thing he'd said to Lupe when the man was contemplating transitioning last year and struggling with the decision.

He'd gone through with it in the end and, from what D'Arcy could see, was so much happier as a result.

"I'm here. Talk to me."

The image of Nika extending his hand flashed in his eyes and D'Arcy sighed. He was going to need to apologize for being an ass to pretty much everyone. And maybe, at some point, actually talk to one of them. But he just couldn't—

"D'Arcy?" The ping from Stephan came over the coms.

"Yeah?"

"*Flux* and *Hunter* just got back. Bring your crew and meet us in the main conference room. Ten minutes."

"Copy." D'Arcy whistled and everyone turned to look. "Stephan just called a meeting in ten minutes. Get cleaned up quick and head over to main conference. Heli, if you'll hang back a moment, please."

He hated the panicked look that crossed the ensign's face before they could contain it and the stiff set of their shoulders when he crossed to them.

"Commander, I'm sorry, I'll do better. This is . . ." They trailed off when he raised a hand.

He waited for the door to close behind Locke and the others. "No. *I'm* sorry, Heli," he said. "I'm not being very patient with you. I'm not being patient at all and that's on me. I am—" The word stuck in his throat and D'Arcy had to stop and drag in a breath before he could speak again. "I am afraid that you will get hurt."

"I know I'm clumsy. I'm trying. I just—"

He wasn't able to keep from laughing, and held out a hand to them. "It's not about that, though god damn, you crash into more shit than any person I've ever seen. No, this is my issue and I'm trying to deal with it. Well, actually, if I'm being honest, I was ignoring it, but I know I *need* to deal with it. And while that's not really a solution, it's also a step in the right direction. But," he said, seeing their confusion, "I don't have a whole lot of right to ask you to bear with me on this. I just hope you will anyway."

"Of course." Heli nodded, hesitated. "Commander, can I tell you something?"

"Go on."

"I am really happy to be here. You're one of the best out there and I was overjoyed when I found out I was coming to *Dread Treasure*. I just don't want to screw up."

D'Arcy wasn't sure he deserved the praise, given how badly he'd treated them lately, but he took it anyway. "Thank you. And you're not screwing up; you're doing a good job." He tapped their left side gently. "Just watch your flank, will you?"

"Yes, sir!" They saluted and he laughed, waving a hand at the door.

"Go get cleaned up, Ensign."

He watched them leave, thinking about their words.

You know, everyone keeps saying you're one of the best. Maybe you should start believing it? Or at least act like you are instead of letting Paul's betrayal do more damage to your life after the fact.

The voice in his head sounded a bit like Akane, and D'Arcy looked up at the ceiling with a soft sigh. "I'm trying, kiddo. Sorry I've been disappointing you."

He headed out of the practice area and crossed the base to the building where the main conference room was located. Neos were scattered around the room. His crew was here, even Heli, who must have broken a speed record to get there before him. The members of *Hunter* were seated at the large table, Pia tapping her fingers on the top in a rhythmic pattern.

Till paced the far wall like a restless tiger, and D'Arcy raised an eyebrow in silent question to Tien as he passed her.

"Long story, D'Arcy," she replied with a shake of her head, then dropped her voice so it didn't carry across the room. "We had a run-in with the *Rising Sun*."

"What?" That was a name he hadn't heard in a long time and D'Arcy's heart kicked up a notch. "How?"

"Everyone have a seat," Stephan called before she could answer. "Nika and Max just pulled back into base and they'll be here in a minute."

The tension in the room tightened until the other officers arrived. D'Arcy nodded to them both as they slipped through the door and into their seats. Stephan cleared his throat.

"Okay, just a few hours ago *Flux* and *Hunter* had an encounter with a ship they think was *Rising Sun*."

A chorus of protests greeted his words, some in disbelief, some in anger at the lack of belief.

"Come on, Stephan, I got a fucking solid ID," Xin said, slapping a hand on the table. "The reg, the visual, everything was spot-on."

"I have to say 'think,'" Stephan replied sharply, "because the alternative is that a NeoG Interceptor has returned from the black after being MIA for nine years and then shot at a civilian vessel on top of that. We're already wrangling one 'shots fired' situation here, thanks to Commander Forsberg. I don't want two."

"I asked him to stop." Pia shrugged with an insouciance in the face of Stephan's ire that had D'Arcy struggling not to laugh.

"She did," Master Gunnery Sergeant McGraw whispered on D'Arcy's left. "Damn fool thought we were pirates and refused to heave to, so I put one of those experimental energy rounds close enough to disrupt his engines into a shutdown. They work really well."

"Permission to go back out and look for her, Captain," Till said.

"Denied, Commander." Stephan shook his head when she started to protest. "No, Vera. I get it, I really do, but we all need to take a step back here and figure out what's going on. I've had two missing ships and two ships back from the goddamned dead in the last few weeks, and I don't like it."

More noise rippled through the room, stopping only when D'Arcy tapped his knuckles on the tabletop.

"Could we back this up and fill the rest of us in on exactly what happened?" he asked.

"We got into a dogfight with the *Rising Sun*, D'Arcy," Till replied. "At zero-six-thirteen hours, we encountered *Reginald's Glory* fleeing from an unknown pursuer. When we intervened, the vessel, whose ID registered as belonging to the missing Interceptor ship *Rising Sun*, turned fire on us. I sent *Wandering Hunter* to deal with the civilian vessel and engaged the NeoG ship until they broke and ran. We got a hit on the back tail section before it vanished."

"Vanished?"

"Like a demon-damned ghost ship—" She broke off and looked away, fighting for composure. "It was the *Rising Sun*, Stephan. I knew that ship like my own face. She's come back from the black that swallowed her and as much as I wish it were otherwise, that can't be a good thing."

EIGHTEEN

Trappist System

Jenks kept one hand on Doge as the conversation continued around the conference room after Vera's report. She didn't like the way her skin was crawling at the idea of missing ships returning, mysterious distress calls, and that damn song that was now stuck in her head, too, thanks to Sapphi's constant humming.

"You are worried?" he asked over their com link, and she nodded once. "The others are also worried. I know I am not supposed to do this, but Commander Till is very upset."

Jenks glanced in Vera's direction. The *Flux Capacitor* commander was sitting silently now, hands in her lap. She hadn't said anything once she'd finished giving her report about their run-in with the *Rising Sun*.

It had taken a lot of work with Doge to get the ROVER not to just go around telling people what everyone else was doing or feeling or saying. A dozen serious conversations about personal privacy seemed to finally get the point across, so it was more than a little strange that he'd say that to her now.

Jenks resisted the urge to ask him why and instead pulled up the records for the missing Interceptor to see if she could figure out for herself what had Vera on edge about the ship and why she'd said she knew it.

Nine years ago, Commander Celeste Winchester and her crew had been officially declared lost in the black after missing for a week. Their last known location had been out in the Trappist asteroid belt, hunting down a pirate cartel that had been terrorizing the small-time transports delivering supplies to the mining operations. They'd first been reported late on Sol Day 277, 2431. The cartel had eventually been tagged, but none of those arrested would admit to taking down a NeoG Interceptor.

Jenks looked through the files on the crew. Six smiling faces, all of them unaware of what the future held for them.

Lost in the black is a fucking terrible way to go, she thought.

Jenks stopped flipping through the files when a name on the former crew list caught her eye.

"There it is," she murmured, and refocused just in time to see Vera slip from her seat and leave the room. "Stay here," she ordered Doge as she followed.

Vera stood in the middle of the hallway, both hands shoved into her silver and pink curls. She took two steps, stopped, and turned on a heel, freezing when she spotted Jenks.

Jenks wordlessly held her arms open and the taller woman fell into them. She held her as she cried, rubbing her hands over Vera's back, stopping only to wave Xin off when she appeared in the doorway.

"Commander Winchester was my mentor. She was an amazing woman and the only reason I'm good at my job. She had time for a wet-behind-the-ears lieutenant who couldn't keep her mouth shut if her life depended on it and somehow turned me into an actual officer."

"You were on her crew from the beginning?"

"My whole career I've only been on two ships, *Rising Sun*

and *Flux*. No one else can claim that, not even Rosa, with her impressive service record." Vera straightened.

Jenks reached up and wiped the tears off Vera's face. "You transferred to *Flux* as commander three days before they disappeared."

"I got promoted. Celeste was so proud. Then they vanished, the whole ship gone. Celeste, Kostas, Rook, Darby, Mac. My friends all swallowed by the remorseless black. I should have been with them; maybe I could have helped with whatever happened—I thought I was done grieving," Vera whispered. "Nine years is long enough, isn't it? But then this fucking ship shows back up and it's all hotter than a solar flare in my chest again."

"Forever isn't long enough as far as I can figure." Jenks thought of Hoboins and the others and rode out the pain that followed. "Do you want some advice?"

Vera sniffed. "Sure."

"Whatever is going on with this ship, you'll probably save yourself a universe of pain if you don't try to fool yourself into thinking they're coming back." Jenks kept her voice as gentle as she could, knowing the sharp edges of the words would hurt. "The likelihood that they're on the ship is slim."

"To none, I know." Vera sighed. "But thanks for putting it out into the world anyway. It helps to hear someone else say it."

"I love you. It hurts to see you hurting. Plus you were there for me when I needed you." Though, as she said it, Jenks couldn't help but feel a little pang of guilt at the fact that *she'd* gotten Luis back.

"Of course." Vera scrubbed at her face again. "Ugh. I'm going to have to go back in there and explain myself, huh?"

"Nah, they get it. Before we go, though, I've got a problem I thought you could help me with."

"Oh really?" Vera's grin was still a little watery, but it was there, and Jenks laughed.

"Not that, though maybe later. I want to take another look

at those systems on *Opie's Hat*. I couldn't find what I was looking for before and then we got interrupted. I was going to take a second peek. You want to help?"

"Are you trying to distract me, Chief?"

"Maybe." Jenks shrugged. "But I also know that you grew up with your hands buried in the guts of those freighters and know them better than anyone."

"Fair enough," Vera said, and nodded. "Sure, I'll help you."

"Good." Jenks held out her fist and Vera tapped her own against it. She slipped back into the conference room after Vera, catching Nika's eye and nodding once with a soft smile.

Stephan paused momentarily as they took their seats. "We're going to regroup here. I'll get a board set up with the information we have, see if we can make sense of it. Max, if you'll give me a hand with that?"

"Can do."

"Pia, you're going to have to go deal with Reginald. I know he's obnoxious—just smooth it over as best as you can."

"If I dump his body somewhere, that'll smooth it over, right?" she muttered.

"I know the security head at Trappist Minerals," Nika said. "He may be able to help us out there."

"Good." Stephan nodded.

"Hey, Captain," Jenks said with a raise of her hand and an unrepentant grin when Stephan glared at her. "Can I steal Vera and Chae to take another look at that freighter?"

"If you leave the ROVER planetside," he replied.

"He's got a name and I was sort of planning on it. Hush," she said, tapping Doge when he whined. "I don't want you on that ship again. You go with Sapphi and see if you can help with the logs."

"We'll keep him out of the system itself," Sapphi said before Stephan could voice the concern. "Don't worry about it." She shared a smile with Saad and the other hackers. "We know what we're doing."

"That's what worries me most of the time."

Laughter greeted Stephan's muttered comment.

"Stephan, I'm going to take Emel and Heli out into Amanave and see if we can't pick up any chatter about what's going on."

Jenks noted the surprise on their faces at D'Arcy's words and wished she had a minute to dig into whatever was causing the tension on *Dread*.

Whatever it was, it looked like D'Arcy was at least trying to improve matters with his team, which was a relief.

"That's a good idea, D'Arcy. Tien, why don't you pull a second group and do the same?"

Flux's senior chief nodded. "I'll take Atlas, Rizzo, and Quickdraw over to Oribo City. Sorry, Xin, you're too damn posh to be tromping around in back alleys." Her lieutenant stuck her tongue out and there was more laughter.

"The rest of you come see me after we break, and we'll figure out what else we need to do." Stephan tapped a knuckle on the tabletop. "I want some answers before another damn ghost ship rolls into port."

"COMMANDER, WHAT ARE WE LOOKING FOR?" HELI ASKED IN A low voice as the three of them wandered through the late-afternoon streets of downtown Amanave.

"Less looking for anything, more listening for it," he replied. "Though, see that group over on the other side of the street?"

"Yes."

"Spacers," Emel murmured, and D'Arcy nodded.

"Long-haul freighter crews," he said. "Notice the blue-and-gray fabric rather than the earth tones the locals tend to wear?"

"What are we going to do?"

"You and I are going to do nothing." D'Arcy glanced at Emel, but she'd already broken off from them and slipped into the crowd. For all the shit he'd given her when she'd come back to Mars that first time, Emel could pull off local habbie pretty damn well. D'Arcy watched her slouch across the street, her civilian clothing blending in with the others who were clustered on the sidewalk.

"The master chief draws less attention than the two of us," D'Arcy said with a smile at the ensign, and gestured for them to start walking again. "I can't seem to hide even when I want to, and your academy shine hasn't worn off yet. That's not a criticism, Heli. We move like Neos. Emel learned how to shed that CHN military look at some point."

He was impressed. Jenks could do that same sort of blending in because she hadn't ever really converted over to the NeoG image, but Emel had, and it was fascinating to watch how easily she could disappear back.

"Like Chief Khan?" Heli asked, unaware they'd just echoed his thoughts.

He nodded. "A bit. Jenks never had the shine to begin with and has avoided any attempts to polish her up," he replied.

"She said I should stop doubting myself and not put up with your shit." Heli's eyes went wide in embarrassment at what they'd said, but D'Arcy was already laughing.

"Of course she did. It's all right, Heli." He realized again just how much the others had been picking up his slack over the last few weeks.

"D'Arcy? How can I help?"

He stutter-stepped, not only because they'd actually used his name, but because of the unexpected question.

"Can I give you a hug?" he asked, and they nodded, so he wrapped them in a quick hug, stepping back and starting down the sidewalk again. "Listen to Jenks and call me on my bullshit. Also, stop letting Aki take over when you're supposed to be in command."

"I'm sorry."

"You don't have to apologize. Neither does Aki; that's just who she is and I've encouraged it because, honestly, I think she's a candidate for OCS; but her officer candidacy is a future thing and yours is right now. Step up and be in charge, okay?

Like I said earlier, I'm trying, but I'm pretty sure I'm going to screw up again."

"That's—"

"I don't care what kind of riches there are, Karl. We're not doing it and that's final."

D'Arcy caught Heli by the arm as the raised voices echoed out of the doorway ahead of them, then pointed at a shop window, ostensibly to show them something on display.

"But, Horace, the payoff—"

"Fuck your mythical payoff. Captain Armen's ship went missing in that same fucking area. And she's not the only one. The *Bastian* never showed. Kenner's missing also."

"What? I didn't hear that?"

"He was supposed to come into port this morning. Instead there's no sign of the *High Porter*. They came through the junction and probably fucked off to check out that same damn treasure rumor. Now they're gone, too."

"You don't know that one thing has anything to do with the other."

"And you don't know they aren't related. The one thing I do know enough is to not go running into a disintegrating ship, Karl. If you want to buy out your contract with me and go kill yourself in the black, be my guest. I'm not going down because of some fucking ghost ship."

"Damn it—you know I can't afford it."

"Well, then I guess we're going back to Earth in the morning, aren't we? Get the supply list wrapped up."

"Where are you going?"

"To get a fucking drink."

A short man left the doorway and stalked past them.

"Tagged him, Commander," Heli whispered. "Should we follow?"

"No," D'Arcy whispered back, then queued up the com. "Emel, sending you a file. Follow, engage if you can, but be careful."

"Copy that. I see him."

EMEL FOLLOWED HORACE ABERNATHY—SHE WAS REASON-
ably sure that wasn't his real name even though the file D'Arcy
had sent her claimed it as such and so did the short man's
handshake—through the crowded streets of downtown. The captain of the *Alpha King* muttered to himself all the way to the bar.

He shouldered aside a dark-haired woman with a growled
"Move it!"

Emel caught the woman, whose handshake read *Sunna Rivera,* The Golden Wasp, *first mate, she/her.* "Are you all right?"

"Yeah. What a jerk." Sunna glared in Horace's direction.
"My own captain would wipe the floor with him if she were
here. I promised to stay out of fights, though, so I guess I'll
have to let him be, eh?"

"I guess so," Emel replied with a grin, taking a chance and
flipping her handshake back on. "Is that Mars I hear in your
voice?"

"In yours, too." Sunna studied her for a moment. "Where'd
you kick dust?"

"EM Projects."

Sunna whistled low. "Long way from there to master chief.
You've done good for yourself, NeoG. I like to see it."

"It was a long trip. Emel Shevreaux," she said, holding out
a fist. "Can I buy you a meal?"

"Sunna Rivera, Am-zed Projects, and I never turn down a
free meal. There's a great shop down the way that'll remind
you of home."

D'ARCY: Emel, what's up?

EMEL: Change of plans. I found an easier source of
information than sitting in a bar with that terrible man. You
and Heli head back to base. I'll be done in an hour or two.

D'ARCY: . . .

EMEL: Go on, I'll be fine.

She could practically hear his frustrated snarl from across the street as she waved a hand behind her back and followed Sunna.

"So, what brought you to Trappist?" Sunna asked when they were settled in a little restaurant that Emel admitted did immediately make her long for the red dirt of home.

"A spaceship."

Sunna tried very hard to not let amusement show on her face.

"Officially?" Emel said. "I came out of retirement from the Navy and joined the NeoG." She lifted the cup of tea and inhaled the sharp minty smell. "The honest answer would be that I don't really know. I was too restless after leaving the Navy to stay on the dirt of Earth. Not that it ever felt like home, but that's where my family was."

"Hard to walk away from the black," Sunna said, raising her own cup in a salute. "That's why I'm still here, anyway. That and Lara's threatened to kill me if I leave her." Her look was sly. "Full disclosure there, NeoG: We're not involved. She's as straight as can be, poor thing."

"I'm glad to hear it." She was surprised to realize she was glad. It had been a long time since she'd felt even the least little desire for another person, but Trappist seemed to have kick-started things again. She'd latched onto Sunna because, as she told D'Arcy, she thought the spacer was going to be a more tractable source of info.

That she was attractive as well as tractable didn't hurt.

"So you're stationed over on Amanave? What are you flyin'?"

The questions helped shake Emel from the way her thoughts were going, letting her focus once more. "Interceptor."

Sunna whistled again. "You involved in that shooting the other day? We'd just come into port when Chad was crying about it all to the poor man on duty."

"I wasn't, actually." Emel tilted her head. "You know Chad Reginald, then?"

"Not personally, thankfully. But everyone knows *of* him around here, because he will announce himself to anyone in a one-klick radius." She rolled her eyes. "Two-bit grifter who claims to be a freelance surveyor."

"I'm guessing he's not?"

"He actually is—technically, at least. Got himself an open-ended contract with Trappist Minerals." Sunna snorted and gestured with her tea. "But I doubt he's ever once dug into an asteroid. Ask anyone around, they'll tell you he's a scrap-head. He uses the scouting as an excuse to hunt for derelicts and strip 'em for parts." She tapped her lips with two hands. "What the black takes should stay in the black."

Emel repeated the gesture more because she knew it would put Sunna at ease than her own belief in the warding superstition. "The belt seems a strange place for that. Wouldn't he have better luck in Sol system?"

"Oh honey." Sunna laughed, putting her tea aside as their food came. "Thank you, dear. Okay, you're new here, Emel, so I'll not tease too much. Reginald does look for scraps in Sol, but that's not why he was out in the Trappist belt."

Emel raised a curious eyebrow and Sunna tore off half a khobz, passing it to her with a wink.

"Eat, and I'll tell you about the treasure ship of Trappist."

NINETEEN

Trappist System

"A treasure ship?" Vera's voice was muffled by the panel she had her head under. "What a bunch of bullshit."

"I'm just saying that's what I overheard the other day when I was walking back from taking the boys to school." Jenks was lying on her back, laboriously going through the connections that fed into the main junction box of *Opie's Hat*.

"I did not have 'Jenks going domestic' on my bingo card for the year."

"Oh, shut up," she said with a laugh, and kicked at Vera's boot. "And don't change the subject. I thought it was bullshit at first, too, but I did some digging and there was this massive push for some top-secret project in 2070 when things really started coming apart at the seams. The rumor is that a bunch of wealthy fuckers pooled their resources for an early prototype transport to take them and their shit to Trappist. Cryo-storage, top-of-the-line almost FTL engine, the whole package."

"That would have been all over the news."

"You know there are some big gaps in the record from

about there on," Jenks replied. "It's hard to find stuff from about 2035 to 2121 and what there is of it has been garbled and hard to put into context. Which really has only fueled this conspiracy about a treasure trove floating in the black. Money." She snorted and rolled her eyes.

Vera slid out from the panel and poked a wrench at Jenks. "Are you telling me people really think there's a ship somewhere in the Trappist system filled with a bunch of dead rich guys and their stuff?"

Jenks spread her hands wide with a grin. "Hey, humans have believed some wild ridiculousness. And really, believing in a treasure ship is nothing—remind me sometime to tell you about people taking horse dewormer instead of a proven vaccine against the first plague."

Vera stared. "You know the weirdest fucking shit, Khan."

"It makes me fun at parties. History is as good as fiction most days—especially that chunk. Anyhow, yes, that's what the rumor is. Moreover, I think it might explain why these freighters keep veering off course."

"You think they're chasing the ship?"

"That's my guess. I asked the kids talking about it. Once they figured out that I wasn't going to bust them for ditching school, they said that all the freighter captains have been buzzing about it. I got a map, too." She winked. "Cost me five feds and it's probably also bullshit, but I figured it was worth it."

Vera sighed. "Contributing to delinquency, Chief."

"You looked in the mirror lately, Commander?" Jenks laughed and dodged the wrench Vera tossed at her. "Throw your own tools, brat, I—huh. Come look at this."

"You just trying to get me within arm's reach?"

"If I wanted to do that, I'd just bat my eyelashes. No, I'm serious, come look at this." Jenks waited for the woman to scoot over to her and pointed at the conduit she'd just uncovered. "This isn't on the specs and it doesn't *go* anywhere."

"There's no reason for that." Vera frowned, tracing dirty fingers over the line.

"Unless there was something at the end of it," Jenks replied, turning her head to meet Vera's eyes. "And someone took it out."

There was a shuddering groan from somewhere below them and Jenks muttered a curse as she reached for her wrench. "I kinda hate this ship." Then in a louder voice: "We're not going anywhere, so piss off, ghost. Okay, Vera, let's figure out what's missing here." She started working on the panel to her right that led farther into the belly of the beast.

D'ARCY HESITATED IN THE DOORWAY OF THE CONFERENCE room when he spotted Nika working at the far end of the table. The blond had his head bent and for a second D'Arcy considered leaving before he was spotted.

Coward.

As if he'd heard D'Arcy's thoughts, Nika lifted his head. He offered a smile, but the look in his blue eyes was as wary as Heli's had been.

"Am I interrupting, or do you have a minute?"

"I was just writing a response to public affairs about this school initiative." Nika gestured at the chair near him. "Okay if I finish? It won't take long."

D'Arcy sat and waited until Nika sent the email and turned his chair to face him. "I'm sorry."

"Me too," Nika replied with a soft smile.

"What for?" D'Arcy asked with a frown. "You were right."

"Maybe, but I pushed when you weren't ready, and I hurt you."

D'Arcy nodded. "What hurt is that you were right. If I'd acknowledged that instead of reacting, I'd have been able to have a conversation about it. I need to figure out how to stop letting my worry about someone else getting hurt on my watch crowd everything else out. It's obviously not good for my team and it's not good for me."

"I have some bad news for you about that." Nika ducked the halfhearted swing with a laugh.

"I know worry comes with the territory, but our crews are competent adults, right?"

"Most of the time," Nika replied, his blue eyes bright with amusement.

"I'm gonna tell your sister you said that."

"You think she doesn't know?"

The banter eased the ache that had settled around D'Arcy's heart, and he leaned forward with both hands extended. "I'm an ass, thanks for caring."

Nika took his hands and pulled him up and out of his seat into a hug. "Anytime. I hate that you've been hurting. I love you, man."

"I love you, too."

They both settled back into their chairs, staring at the screen on the far wall.

"This whole thing make you uneasy also?" Nika asked, gesturing at the spread of missing ships.

"Very."

Nika tipped his head to the side, listening to the incoming message on his DD. "My contact with Trappist Minerals is here. I've got to go see what I can do to help Pia mollify Reginald." He patted D'Arcy on the shoulder as he stood.

"Later." D'Arcy got up and crossed to the wall. He pulled up the report he'd written after his conversation with Michael and Gun. The prototype weapon Ivarken had possibly been carrying for the TLF faction was eerily similar to the disruptor used against them on Jupiter Station. Had it been Tieg who'd sold it to them? Or had he gotten it from the TLF? The latter seemed unlikely, but he made a note to mention it to Stephan for a follow-up. Either way, it was a threat to them.

Or it would have been if not for Sapphi and the others, specifically their work post-attack to come up with a defense program to protect DD chips from that sort of interference. At the moment it was only in use by CHN military as a temporary measure while the higher-ups argued about potential ramifications of releasing the information to the wider public.

Jenks would be right to grumble about how some things never change, he thought with a wry smile.

There weren't any clear lines linking the arrival of *Opie's Hat* with the *Imogene Darver's* distress call and the sighting of *Rising Sun,* but he'd bet six weeks of his basic income that there was something connecting those ships in addition to the other missing freighters.

"What are you looking at, Commander?" Heli asked, joining him.

"Trying to figure out what the pattern is. Did you get some lunch?"

"I did." They held out the cup. "They had Trappist-grown strawberry smoothies. I thought you'd like one."

"I would, thank you." He popped the top off and drank, then gestured at the wall. "Tell me what you see."

"Missing ships. Nothing obvious to connect them. It's almost like the randomness is the pattern, but that's not helpful, is it?" they asked, slipping their hands into their pockets and studying the info on the wall. "Why do you think there's a connection?"

"Random chance makes us nervous?" He grinned at their choked laugh. "There's often a reason for something, though; it's just a matter of figuring out what it is. Maybe it doesn't have anything to do with the case, but it could lead us to something that does."

"You mean if all the ships were owned by the same company?"

"Exactly. And while we know that's not the case with the Interceptor, I haven't followed up on that for the freighters. You want to check it out?"

He stepped back and finished his drink while Heli pulled the registrations for the freighters. They were a smart kid, and he was impressed that they'd figured out what he'd been talking about so quickly.

"A stealth system? Really?"

D'Arcy looked over his shoulder as Emel came through the door with Vera and Jenks. The pair were talking excitedly, waving their arms in the air, but rather than looking bemused, the master chief was peppering them with questions.

"An entire fucking system and it's just gone," Jenks said as they crossed the room.

"Someone ripped it out?" Emel asked.

"No." Jenks bounced, her hands gesticulating in the air between them the way they always did when she was overly excited about something. She was filthy, still dressed in her coveralls. "Someone very carefully and very precisely removed an entire stealth-weapon system. I'd bet they did it without damaging it."

"In theory," Vera added, and Jenks shot her a look as they joined him. "Because there's nothing there and without anything there, all we have about a stealth-weapon system is spacer hearsay."

"Blythe said—"

"Blythe is as susceptible to exciting rumors as the rest of us," he said with a smile.

Jenks made a noise that was a cross between an exasperated teenager's whine and a growl. "D'Arcy."

"You know what Stephan will say," he replied to her appeal. "You need proof."

"I got a treasure map," she replied with a bright smile, and there was a ping as an image appeared on the screen in front of him.

"A treasure map?" D'Arcy's question was wary, but those words had also come out of Emel's mouth in an excited tone, and he turned to stare at her.

"This is what Sunna was telling me about!" Now she was bouncing on the balls of her feet a bit like Jenks, a development that had D'Arcy more than a little worried. "We were tailing a freighter captain who'd been talking about rumors of riches when I ran into the very nice first mate of *The Golden*

Wasp. Sunna happened to be from Mars. Am-zed," she said that part to D'Arcy.

The Am-zed Projects had been hit by the CHN crackdowns that precipitated the Mars protests almost as hard as the EM and D'Arcy now understood why Emel had changed the plan on him.

"Good call to talk with her instead," he said, and watched the surprised expression Emel couldn't quite smother. "I'm serious. It's easier to get information from a potential friend than a hostile source."

"Thanks." She smiled.

"Treasure map," Jenks prompted, and when D'Arcy looked away from Emel to her, the chief wore an amused expression with a raised eyebrow.

"Sunna said this has been the buzz of all the freighters since it surfaced about an Earth year ago. She also said Reginald is up to his neck in scrap selling, often not the legal kind."

"Really? Nika was just going to meet with the Trappist Minerals contact."

"I sent him a message. It may take a little while to follow up on, but Reginald's ship is out of commission for at least another week."

"I can have the yardheads make that longer if we need to," Jenks said.

"We'll see what Nika thinks. Do we know where the map came from?" D'Arcy asked, and Emel shook her head.

"I don't think so. All Sunna knew is that the rumor itself has been around for a really long time, probably as long as there have been habitats on Trappist. The map is newer."

"A ship launched from Earth with a bunch of wealthy pricks trying to escape the planet they wrecked, hauling their gold with them like it was going to mean something out here in the black." Jenks's voice was filled with derision and Emel tipped her head at the woman.

"Basically. She said it's only ever been a rumor and that

most captains pay it no mind. Too risky to be wandering off into the asteroid belt when you've got both a guaranteed income coming in weekly and whatever extra you can make hauling goods between systems." Emel took a step forward and tapped at the map. "Plus there wasn't any specific location to explore, just the 'belt.' At least until this showed up."

D'Arcy looked at the growing list of missing ships from the last few weeks. When he and Heli had come back, they'd double-checked the *High Porter* and he'd added it to the list with a note that it was only a few hours overdue and could still show up.

"It's a lure," Heli murmured, their soft voice almost lost under the press of the others' conversation.

"What?" D'Arcy looked their way.

"Sorry, I was just thinking out loud."

"No, go on, Heli."

They took a step forward, tapping a finger on a general list of all missing ships in the Trappist area. This one started from first landing on One-c in 2332 and was a lot longer. "Ships go missing, right? Especially in the early days before we really had a system in place to go looking for them. But we've got far better tracking and nav systems now than we did a hundred years ago. We can practically track a ship from one port to the other in real time."

Jenks started to open her mouth but closed it at D'Arcy's gesture.

"So, ships go missing," Heli continued, still focused on the screen and oblivious to the exchange. "But the last few weeks we've lost more ships than we did in the previous Earth year. All of them in this area." They pointed at the map of the Trappist asteroid belt. "And all of them since this map surfaced." They turned back to D'Arcy. "The map's a lure."

"Suckering ships into the asteroid belt with the promise of treasure," Jenks said, and lifted a hand with a thoughtful look. "It's slick, I'll give them that."

"But why?" Emel asked, and waved a hand when D'Arcy frowned at her. "I don't mean why do it. Obviously, they're stealing the freight and reselling it. The Interceptor is even an explainable loss. They were probably ambushed and whoever is behind this would have been a fool not to keep the ship."

"You might be on to something," D'Arcy admitted. "I'm still not following, though, Emel."

"Why are they taking so many ships *now*? You peel a few a year, max, and it's easy to write them off as just lost in the black. But this many." She shook her head. "They'd have to know that it would draw attention to them."

No one had an answer and the five Neos stared at the screen in silence for a long moment. Then D'Arcy looked around at the assembled Neos and made a decision. They'd been trying to find a time to speak with Techa and now it seemed like they'd hit a point where the risk outweighed the need for caution.

"I need to talk to someone," he said. "Come on."

"WHATEVER ELSE WAS GOING ON, THIS CAPTAIN WAS A PARA-noid one. I've never seen so many locked files and weird codes."

Sapphi hummed an assent to Saad's comment, flipping her way through what seemed like an endless stream of video files. Her DD pinged with an incoming message and she winced.

GREGORI, Y: Hey, you, been trying to get ahold of you. Do you want to hang soon?

ZIKA, N: We're in the middle of a project, but I'll message you later about a time?

GREGORI, Y: Sounds good. I'll see you then. Got some news. :)

She was grateful for the relative impersonal nature of text communication. It wasn't that she'd been actively avoiding

Yasu . . . okay, maybe she had been; but work was also as good a cover as any for the anxious feeling that was still clawing at her nerves.

I'm gonna have to deal with it; it's really not fair to either of us.

"Sapphi, are you listening?"

"She's probably talking to her boyfriend again."

Sapphi reached over and absently flicked Lupe in the ear, making the trans man yelp. "I'm listening."

"Here's what I don't understand. This guy had his ship kitted out with the latest—for the time—surveillance gear, and he kept everything."

"Right. He also kept a pretty extensive log," Sapphi replied.

Saad rolled his eyes. "Which he liked to go on at length about. The man enjoyed the sound of his own voice."

"Then it just stops," Pavel said.

Sapphi gestured at the logs. "All of it stops—that's the weirdness. Same day, same time. The whole system. But it wasn't damaged, because it kicked back on just before D'Arcy and the others boarded. See?" She pointed at the footage they'd spliced out from storage, showing D'Arcy's and Pia's crews boarding the freighter.

"There was no power disruption, oddly enough." Saad tapped the image on the screen hanging in the air in front of them. "The surveillance was hooked to a separate power system designed to operate independently of the ship. That thing is rated to last through fifty years of constant use."

"Wait a minute, there is missing footage." Sapphi tilted her head to the side. "I didn't think there was because the log was clean and—oh, no way. Saad, look at this." She slid the program over to him.

"Did this guy really put surveillance on his surveillance?"

She laughed. "Let's hear it for paranoia."

"Doesn't mean they're not out to get you," Saad replied.

"Fuck, it's corrupted." Sapphi sighed. "Hey, Lupe, Pavel, come look at this?"

The two other hackers disconnected themselves from their terminals and joined them.

"The timing on the surveillance cutting out does match with the power loss to the rest of the ship," Lupe said. He frowned. "But you're right that it shouldn't have affected the system at all. It's designed that way for a reason. There was a quick log of an emergency beacon being queued up right at the same time, but it was canceled. And according to Jenks's report, all the beacons were physically still on the ship."

"Hang on, I think I've got a buffer program that will work for this video. Can you send the file over?" Pavel said after a moment.

"Sure. Here." Sapphi sent it, then got up and stretched as Lupe followed Pavel back to his terminal.

"You want a drink?" Saad asked. "I need something before my brain stops working."

"Sure. Whatever as long as it's not fizzy."

"Come on, you know I'd never do that to you." He blew her a kiss and headed out of the room.

"Hey, Doge," Sapphi said, settling down next to the ROVER and resting her chin on his head. "How's it going?"

"I'm being used as a computer." There was a surprising sullen note in his voice.

She stopped herself from replying, *You are technically a computer,* and instead said, "I know, I'm sorry. You wanna see this video footage we found? Pavel's working on a buffer for it, but maybe you can pull something."

Doge perked up a bit and she sent him the clip she'd pulled for the other Neo.

"This is a backup?"

"Yeah, he had a master system."

"I saw those files. It's not right to film people like that."

"You're right, it's not. People often do things that aren't right, though."

"Why?"

"Oh, buddy." Sapphi exhaled and hugged him. "If I had the answer to that, I'd be rich and famous."

"Your friend Yasu put in a request for information about me this morning."

She froze, all the anxiety surging back to the surface like a tidal wave. "What? Why?"

"I don't know. I just got the notice that someone asked for information on my model number. I like to know. When I looked at the request, I recognized his name. What does he want with me?"

"I don't know, buddy, but I'll find out." Fury replaced the anxiousness. Doge was Jenks's dog, but he was also her friend and she'd be damned before she let anything happen to him.

"Thank you, Sapphi. I appreciate it."

"Hey, Sapphi, come look at this!"

She patted Doge and got to her feet, joining the others at Pavel's terminal.

The backup system Captain Ivarken had installed was a bare-bones model, with no audio and grainy black-and-white video that had definitely suffered from its time out in the black without the proper temperature and atmosphere surroundings. She watched with growing confusion and awe as something unidentifiable seemed to detach itself from the wall of the *Opie's Hat* and move down the corridor. It turned what she could only have described as its head toward the camera before continuing on.

The video dissolved into static.

"What was that?" Sapphi whispered.

"I don't know, someone breeching the ship?" Lupe replied.

"That was not a someone. That was a *something*."

"Saad, I'm not having the aliens-are-real conversation with you," Pavel replied.

"What about ghosts?" Saad countered.

"Sapphi." Doge nudged her leg, his voice breaking through the argument. "The ship was transmitting."

"What?" She looked down at the ROVER, hearing the exclamations of the others and realizing he'd spoken on the main channel.

"The video came back up when D'Arcy boarded, and again when Jenks and I were there. And again when Jenks and Vera were on board. I found a signal in all that data you had me go through. I guess it was worth it after all."

"Fuck." Saad dragged the word out.

"Someone's watching." Sapphi shoved both hands into her hair and froze. "Are we locked down? We didn't keep open access to the ship from here, did we?"

The foursome scrambled into motion with a panic born of people who realized they might have left an airlock open before disconnecting from a station.

Sapphi automatically brought up her emergency program for both her and Doge. The ping that echoed back a moment later brought her some relief. "We're clean."

"Here too," Saad replied.

"I had my terminal isolated," Lupe said.

"I logged in with my DD to get a real-time system update when I started the buffer program." Pavel spit a curse on the heels of his admission. "Disconnect—"

"Pavel?"

There was no response and Sapphi's heart jumped into her throat when she turned and spotted Pavel slumped over in his seat, unconscious.

Doge did not like this heavy feeling. The definition for "grief" that he'd pulled didn't match the weight on Jupiter Station. Didn't match the way the light in Jenks's eyes had been smothered.

This *hurt* and he wasn't supposed to feel things, not in this way.

People were off. Too many people, and as he scrolled through the faces, looking for matches, he realized that each time he saw one, a sharp jolt rocked through him. He wondered if he should try again to tell Jenks that Luis was not on his list, but he wondered if this was a privacy thing and if he should just keep it to himself like he'd been taught.

"Doge, how you doing, buddy?" Max bent down and pressed her cheek to the top of his head. Her readout was tired, edging into dangerous exhaustion.

"I am . . . grieving."

Max went to a knee and wrapped her arms around him with a soft sound that registered as pain. "I know," she whispered.

"The word is inadequate. Jenks is *different*. I am afraid."

Her arms tightened and the increased pressure on his sensors was strangely comforting, much like when Jenks did it, so Doge leaned into the lieutenant. "Me too, Doge. We'll be okay, though. Somehow."

He wasn't sure he believed her, but Doge had been around Max long enough to know she wouldn't lie to him and if there was a way to make this better, she would find it.

TWENTY

Trappist System

"Sapphi!" Max rushed over, wrapping her arms around the ensign. "When the med emergency notice went out on the coms, I thought—"

"Somewhat ironically, not me this time," Sapphi joked, sobering almost immediately. "We don't know what happened, LT. One second everything was fine, and the next Pavel was flatlining on us."

Max caught the tremor in the woman's voice and hugged her again. "He'll be okay."

"Max, there's something awful on that ship. I don't know what, but we need to get it out of here. Take it back out into the black and blow it to Hades."

Sapphi was actually shaking in her arms and Max waved a hand at Nika and Stephan when the pair appeared at the end of the corridor. "Start from the beginning. What happened?"

As Sapphi detailed out the events that had led to Pavel's collapse, Max watched the organized chaos of the medical unit. She relaxed a little when the doctor on duty came out of the room. They greeted Commander Forsberg with a smile and gripped her shoulder with one hand.

Pia's shoulders sagged in obvious relief and Max was able to turn her full attention back to Sapphi.

"He was nonresponsive and then his heart stopped." The ensign made a face. "I don't know how it happened, but I know he was hooked up to the ship. Pavel should have known better than to link in directly with his DD. I'm going to kick his ass when he gets better."

"You'll have to get in line, Ensign," Pia said, joining them. "Dr. Tozer said they weren't sure, but it looks like Pavel's DD chip overloaded." She held up a hand at the gasps. "There's no damage to the surrounding tissue, but his chip is going to have to be replaced. Sorry, Stephan, we're down a person for a few weeks."

"Don't apologize," Stephan said. "I'm just glad he's okay."

"Captain, you need to destroy that ship. It's—"

"Probably a good idea to at least move it out of orbit," Max interrupted before Sapphi could say "cursed," which would immediately put Stephan's logical brain on the defensive. "Let's isolate it until we can determine where the transmission signal Doge found was coming from and if there's anything else dangerous."

"If someone is watching, we're better off having that thing where it's not in the line of sight for a lot of the traffic coming into port," Nika agreed.

Stephan nodded finally. "Okay, we'll tow it out to a Lagrange point around One-h. I'll have them throw a couple of signal jammers on board, which should take care of the problem in the meantime." He sighed and scrubbed a hand over his head, messing up his brown hair. "I don't like the feeling someone is one step ahead of me and this op is rapidly turning out that way."

"Where's Jenks?"

Max looked down at Doge and smiled. "Went to check out a lead with D'Arcy. She'll be back soon."

"You and Nika are also leaving." Max blinked at him in surprise and Doge looked away. "I saw the request."

Is he embarrassed?

"Wait. Where are you going?" Sapphi asked.

"Earth," Max said. "I need to take care of some family business. We'll only be gone a few days; we're taking the *Gajabahu*."

"Oh. Did you need to see any of that mail I've been filtering out before you left?"

Max held back a sigh, desperately wishing she had the courage to tell Sapphi just to dump it; but she didn't have that kind of strength. "Yeah, send it over. I'll go through it."

"Okay. Hey, LT?"

Max caught the way Sapphi glanced at Stephan, and patted Doge on the head. "Come on Doge. Nika, I'm going to head back to quarters. Do they or you need Sapphi for anything?"

"No, we're good." Nika waved a hand. "I'll be there in a bit."

Max wasn't sure if he'd also caught the look or was just wrapped up in the discussion with Stephan about the possible missing stealth system that Jenks was certain had been on *Opie's Hat*. Either way, she slipped an arm around Sapphi's shoulders and led her down the corridor.

"What is it?" she asked, but the ensign still didn't reply, only walked along in silence, chewing on her lower lip. Max let her have the space she needed until they got to their quarters.

Doge went to his other bed, which was set up in the corner of the common room. Sapphi disappeared into the bunkroom, appearing a moment later, and Max lifted an eyebrow when she pulled out the jammer she'd built after the explosion on Jupiter Station when they didn't know who they could trust.

"LT, did you meet Yasu Gregori at the prelims?"

"He works for Dànǎo Dynamics. I didn't meet him, but I saw him at the finals. And I know you two were involved before you joined the NeoG." She held a hand up. "That's from Tamago, by the way. I haven't been digging into your personal life."

"I kinda wish you had—it would make all this easier. We were in a relationship. I was seventeen, maybe? That time of my life is kinda blurry, LT." Sapphi had been pacing the room, but she stopped and looked at Max with tears in her brown eyes. "I was pretty strung out on drugs—opal, mostly—so was Yasu. We—"

"Sapphi, you don't have to tell me this if you don't want to."

"Except I sort of do? Everyone else knows—well, Chae doesn't, but it's kind of a hard conversation starter, right?" Sapphi's laugh shattered on the floor and Max crossed to her, wrapping her arms around the ensign and holding her.

"I did some terrible things, LT," she sobbed. "I still don't know why my family forgave me, stuck by me through it all. And Yasu . . . he was so messed up, but I loved him. Or rather I thought I did. We were not good for each other."

"Sapphi, did he hurt you?"

The other woman stilled in her arms. "Yeah," she whispered. "But honestly, I hurt him, too. Like I said, we were terrible together—just a live wire and a patch of flammable shit waiting to catch the spark. I forgave him a long time ago, but . . ."

"But what?" And what she meant was *Why are you telling me all this* now?

"But I'm worried he's still not good for me—or the NeoG."

"What?"

"He knew about *Opie's Hat* showing up in port. Thing is, that wasn't a big enough event to make news back on Earth. Maybe it doesn't seem like a big deal, but it felt a lot like when he used to keep tabs on me when we were teens. I almost slipped about what happened with Doge, but he somehow knew?

"And he put in an official request for information about Doge."

Max let go and leaned back a bit so she could see Sapphi's face. She knew about the request. Stephan had sent it to both her and Nika this morning almost immediately after it had come in. "Do I want to know how you found that out?"

"I told her," Doge said.

"Did you now." She smiled at the dog. "And how did you find out about it?"

"I have been monitoring coms traffic that pertains to *Zuma*. Why does he want to know about me? Is it because of what happened with Jenks?"

Oh, there was *worry* in Doge's voice. Out of the corner of her eye, Max saw Sapphi flinch. "That's a good question, Doge, and to be honest I don't know. Do you want to tell me why that worries you?"

"I don't know, either. I didn't want to hurt Jenks."

Now Sapphi was staring at the ROVER and Max debated how she wanted to handle this, spinning through the options and angles in her head. She crossed the room and sank down next to Doge, putting a hand on his side.

"We all know you didn't want to hurt Jenks, it wasn't your fault. And it's okay not to know why you're worried. Sometimes we worry about things that are either too numerous or big to name. Sometimes talking about them is a good idea, though. Other people can help us realize that our fears are less about reality and more about things we make up in our minds."

Wow, Carmichael, pot and kettle much?

She still hadn't talked to Jenks about the fight. Max smothered a sigh and glanced at Sapphi. "Sapphi, for example, is worried about the fact that you're able to worry at all. But I don't think it's such a bad thing."

"Why are you worried, Sapphi?" Doge asked, clearly surprised.

Max held out her other hand and Sapphi joined them on the floor, linking her fingers with Max's.

"Because you're not supposed to be able to do that," Sapphi whispered. "You're doing a lot of things you're not supposed to be doing."

"Jenks usually tells me when I do something wrong. Is she mad?" Doge's head dropped. "Am I a bad dog?"

"No!" Sapphi let go of Max's hand and threw her arms around him. "You're the best dog."

"You're just learning a lot of things we never expected you to learn, buddy," Max said.

"I like learning. You're all good teachers."

"LT, what are we going to do?"

"Nothing," Max said, smiling at Sapphi's surprise. "Your history with Yasu gives you a reason to be cautious and I don't think you're overreacting. It's okay if you decide you're not comfortable or if anything else happens that sets off alarm bells. Then you come to me and I'll step in if you want.

"That said, I think in this case he's just overly curious, given that he's been working on developing a new AI system for long-range unpersoned flights for the NeoG and Navy. Not that you heard that from me." Sapphi's eyes widened at that news, and Max continued.

"As for the rest . . . Stephan gave Yasu what information is public record on Doge, nothing more. Doge is Jenks's dog. Legally. He's not property of the NeoG or any other public agency. And extremely sticky questions about AI sentience and independence aside—which is something we're going to have to deal with at some point here—there's nothing anyone can do to take him away. If they try, they have to get through all of us first. He's a member of this crew, this family, and we keep each other safe."

Sapphi wrapped her arms around Max and squeezed her tight. "Have I mentioned lately that I love you, LT?"

"I love you, too." She laughed and patted Sapphi on the back. "I would like the list I'm sure you and Jenks are compiling about the changes in Doge's behavior, and, Doge, I wouldn't mind the same from you about anything you've noticed so that I can confer with Nika about it on the trip to Earth."

"I'll get with Jenks as soon as she gets back, LT," Sapphi promised.

Max patted both of them again. "Speaking of, I need to get packed. Was there anything else?"

She watched a curious expression flicker over Sapphi's face before the ensign pressed her face to Doge's side. "I'm good, LT. Thanks, though."

"Okay. I'll message Nika. We're leaving in the morning. We probably should have a team meeting tonight so we're all on the same page." Max got to her feet and headed for her room. Sometimes she missed being able to bunk with the others, but the size of the Trappist-1d Intel building meant there was plenty of space and she and Nika both had rooms of their own within the crew quarters.

She closed the door and pulled out her duffel.

You know, Carmichael, all that talk about airing your fears is advice you really should be taking.

Max dropped her forehead to the wall with a sigh. "I know. I'll talk to Jenks after Earth. Just let me tackle one problem at a time, okay?"

The wall said nothing.

EMEL WALKED NEXT TO D'ARCY THROUGH AN AREA OF AMAnave even a project habbie would have called "questionable." No one bothered them, though she, Heli, and D'Arcy were still dressed in local wear and Jenks and Vera had their work dungarees on.

If anyone looked closely enough or pinged their DDs, they'd realize the whole group was NeoG, but as it was, no one gave them a second glance.

The others seemed content to follow D'Arcy without question, but Emel realized he wasn't the only one with trust issues. She needed to know what was happening, if only to help relax the itch between her shoulders.

"Where are we going?"

"Like I said, to talk with someone. It's easier than dealing with all this hearsay."

"Is it wise to be out here without protection?"

D'Arcy's grin took its time appearing on his face. "You've got me, Emel. And Jenks."

She rolled her eyes. "You know what I mean."

"I do," he conceded. "Going in here with swords or even guns would just be asking for trouble. Techa won't do anything to risk bringing the CHN down on her head. And speaking of . . ." He trailed off and put his hands up. "Evening, we're here to speak with Techa."

Emel watched the group of people melt out of the growing shadows of the street, and the bystanders decided they had other places to be. Jenks shifted behind her and a glance confirmed the chief hadn't quite put her fists up, but it was close.

"What makes you think the boss wants to talk with the NeoG?"

"For starters, she said yes when I asked earlier, Philip. Though I suspect she doesn't feel the need to pass her every thought along to you."

Recognition smacked Emel as the man came fully into the light. Philip had aged more than either of them, a sure sign that whatever access he had to LifeEx was sporadic enough to be unable to provide the full benefits of slowing his body's aging process.

Her brother's old buddy may have left Trappist, but it appeared he hadn't changed in any other way that mattered.

"Nice friends you've got here," Emel muttered.

"I never said friend," D'Arcy replied. "And you know as well as I do that Philip and I are definitely not friends."

"That hurts, D'Arcy, seriously."

Emel watched the man press a hand to his chest in mock pain, then he looked her way.

"My dear Emel. It's lovely to see you again. Belated condolences about your brother."

She clenched her jaw so hard, it was a wonder a molar didn't crack.

"I feel left out of this party," Jenks announced. "Do we get introductions?"

"Well, well, well, if it isn't the infamous Jenks on my very doorstep. I'm swooning."

"Good. I like it when people swoon over me."

"To be honest, I'm more into blondes." He reached past her for Heli's face. The ensign froze, fear and indecision clear on her face.

Jenks spoke before Emel could take a step forward. "You touch my friend, I take your hand off and beat you with it." All the amused flirting had vanished from her voice and the people around Philip stiffened.

"You think you can take us all, NeoG?"

Jenks's answering smile was razor-sharp. "I don't have to take you all—no one else is being an asshole."

"The fact that I have to come down here because I just knew you were going to start shit annoys me beyond belief." The voice that issued from the alley preceded the stunning woman who emerged.

She was as tall as Emel, with eyes darker than Heli's navy blue, and black hair shaved on one side of her head, exposing the pale skin underneath.

Philip froze.

D'Arcy spread his hands wide. "Sorry to cause trouble, Techa," he said.

"Oh, hush, you know who I'm talking to." She slapped Philip upside the head. "Your chip broken? Because I'm pretty sure I sent a notice ten minutes ago about visitors and bringing them straight to me. Shut up," she said before he could protest. "Go find something worthwhile to do, all of you. You five, with me."

TWENTY-ONE

Trappist System

D'Arcy followed Techa off the street and through the wide doors of the warehouse. "You should jettison that cargo before it causes you trouble," he said.

"Tell me something I don't know." Techa hummed in her throat. "But I promised his mother I would take care of him, and littering, even in the black, is a crime, so here we are." She gestured at a nearby table. "Have a seat."

They sat. Emel at his side, Vera next to Heli, and D'Arcy muffled his amusement when Jenks spun the chair opposite Techa around and sat with her arms resting on the back so she could get out of it easily if need be. It was a move that didn't go unnoticed by the pirate.

"You're safe here, Chief Khan. I give you my word. Besides, I've got money riding on your win in the Games. I wouldn't do anything to jeopardize it."

"Good to know." Jenks didn't move.

"So," Techa drawled, settling back in her chair. "This isn't a social call, obvs. But you gave me notice and also didn't come in swinging swords, so my curiosity is burning a hole in my pocket. What's up, D'Arcy?"

"You operating out in the belt?" Straight shooting was always the best option with Techa, but when she blinked at him slowly, D'Arcy wondered if he should have taken a slightly softer road.

She hooked an arm over the back of her chair and studied him. "Lotta belts out there, D'Arcy. You'll have to be more specific."

"You know I'd only be asking about Trappist," he replied.

"My people are under orders not to go anywhere near the Trappist belt," Techa said finally, her voice flat.

"So you're not responsible for the missing ships? This rumor about treasure?"

"I said what I said, D'Arcy."

"Techa, you know the NeoG cuts you a lot of slack for the information you provide. Treasure maps are a good way to lead freighters off their flight plans. If this is you, I need you to knock it the fuck off."

Techa stared at him. She was tense.

No, she was *afraid*, D'Arcy realized. The woman most people now called the Pirate King of Trappist was more than worried by whatever it was that was going on out in the belt—she was terrified. Not because she thought he'd find out she was involved in it, but because she didn't know who was behind it.

She was scared of whoever was out there.

Which meant the next words out of her mouth were a bluff.

"One—you don't own me, Montaglione. I've helped you because you got Tieg's operation out of my hair. I appreciated it. It's improved things around here. Two—treasure maps don't always mean pirates."

He watched her with a patient smile until Techa ran her tongue over her teeth and looked at the ceiling.

"Whatever's going on out there is not me, D'Arcy. I lost four ships in the outer belt last year. Three the year before that.

When the first one went missing this year, I put the lockdown on it; anyone who tries to order their crew in that direction would find themselves sucking vacuum.

"It's a dead zone. Whatever it is grabbing ships over there, it's not us. Bring me something I care about to swear on and I will, D'Arcy. And off the record, I'd deeply appreciate it if you all would do your jobs and take care of it. Like Tieg, it's bad for business."

"I'm trying to do exactly that. So if you've got any leads for me, now would be the time to share them," he replied.

Techa snapped her fingers and a person appeared at the far side of the room. They bent so she could whisper in their ear and then vanished back the way they'd come. A few moments later another person crossed the room.

EMEL: Eight missing ships? She was waiting for us to ask.

D'ARCY: Certainly seems that way, doesn't it?

"Ollie was on the ship that got hit this year. It was pure luck one of my other vessels was in the area and heard the distress signal. By the time they got there, the ship was toast. Crew gone. Ollie was in an escape pod—my guess is because his sister shoved him into it, though I wish she'd gotten in with him." Techa's mouth twisted in fury. "I fucking miss her; she was one of my best captains. There was no sign of whatever attacked them."

The whole time she was talking, D'Arcy watched the kid shrink further and further into themself. There was no handshake, but he realized that wasn't because they had it turned off like Techa and most of her other people did to stay as quiet on the grid as possible—it was because he didn't have a chip at all.

Which is probably why whoever had attacked the pirate ship had missed him.

"Ollie." Techa's voice was surprisingly gentle. "Will you tell these people what you saw?"

"Metal." His fingers twisted together, but he looked away from the ground and straight at D'Arcy. "Metal things in the walls. The song started. The lights went out. The metal things came through the walls."

"What kind of metal things?" Jenks asked, and the boy flinched.

"Metal things," he repeated. "Sailing the stars on ships. Sailing to Trappist." The words were singsong, but they snapped Techa into action.

"No, Ollie. No singing. Do your math." She snapped her fingers, and someone came to escort Ollie quickly away, the young man dividing fractions in a mechanical voice. "Sorry, D'Arcy. That's all I've got. Once he starts singing, the screaming follows shortly after unless we can distract him."

"Is he going to recover?" Emel asked.

"We don't know, but don't worry about it. We take care of our own."

D'Arcy muttered a curse and got to his feet with a nod in her direction. "I appreciate the help, Techa."

"I realize it's not much, but it was all I had. Figured you should know about it. I like you, D'Arcy, despite our opposition. Watch yourself. This whole thing smells like a ship of cis men with a broken shower. No offense."

"None taken. You're not wrong. Take care of yourself, Techa . . . and stay off my radar."

"You know I will." She looked past him and winked at Jenks, some of her good humor restored. "Looking forward to your fight with Carmichael in the Games, Khan. Like I said, I'm putting my money on you."

"Just don't blame me if you lose," Jenks replied with a grin of her own. "She's good."

"Possibly losing your undefeated status doesn't bother you?" D'Arcy asked once they were back on the street and headed toward base.

Jenks laughed and spread her arms wide. "Why would it? Win or lose, I'm awesome."

The laughter that echoed from Jenks's declaration eased some of the worry in D'Arcy's chest, but then the chief frowned.

"I'm not the only one who noticed Techa kept saying 'whatever' and not 'whoever,' right?"

"I caught it, too," Emel said, and the uneasy feeling surged back with a vengeance.

D'Arcy composed a message to Stephan as the group headed back through the quiet night.

D'ARCY: Just spoke to Techa. Things are not good. We need to talk.

STEPHAN: In my office when you get on base.

JENKS SLOUCHED AGAINST THE WALL IN *ZUMA'S* QUARTERS, one arm draped over Doge's neck and the other resting on her bent knees as the conversation swirled around her.

The meeting with D'Arcy's pirate friend had taken her unease up into the red zone, and the feeling had only gotten worse when she'd gotten back and found out someone had been poking around about her dog.

Old friend of Sapphi's or not, she was putting her boot up his ass if he showed up on Trappist.

"Everyone is upset," Doge said over their com link, and you wouldn't think that a robot voice could have a quaver in it, but it was there.

"Lotta shit going on."

"It's my fault. I'm sorry."

"Hey, not your fault at all. Don't you dare." Jenks said that out loud and everyone turned to look at them. "Doge thinks this is his fault."

The chorus of negative replies was a relief, but even more

so was the fact that her brother knelt on the floor next to them and put a hand on Doge's head.

"It's not your fault in the slightest. There is nothing going on for you to even be at fault for, okay? You keep doing what you're doing."

"Okay," Doge said.

"I told Stephan you're taking him with you on your camping trip with Luis and the boys," Nika said to her.

"Did he fuss?"

"No." Nika shook his head. "Even if he had, I'd have pushed for it. I'd rather Doge is with you while Max and I are on Earth."

"How long are you two going to be gone?" She glanced past him to where Max was talking to Tamago. "And is she okay?"

Max had still been restless and uneasy, unfocused in sparring. Jenks's hope that taking the pressure off in regard to the Games next year would help the LT relax clearly hadn't panned.

"Four days," Nika said. "And mostly yes. Hopefully this trip will sort things out. She'll talk to you about the rest of it when we get back."

She narrowed her eyes at him, but Nika just laughed. "Oh no, I'm not giving you a preview. This is between you and Max."

"Fine. Did you get your shit sorted with D'Arcy?" She bared her teeth at him in a smile, because while her brother might have firm lines about what he got involved in, she didn't.

"I did," he replied.

"Good." Jenks pressed her cheek to Doge's head and held out a hand to Nika. "Help me up." She bounced to her feet. "What else do we need to handle before you two leave? Also, are we doing dinner together?"

"We should," Nika admitted. "I'll take Chae to go get it from the mess after we're done here." He clapped his hands twice and the room fell into silence. "All right, people. First order of business: Public affairs has cleared us to plan an outreach program with the local schools, starting with Christa McAuliffe Middle School. While Max and I are gone, I'd like to see the four of you put your heads together and sketch us out some presentation ideas."

"Jenks and I have already kicked a few around," Tamago said. "If we could get clearance for a field trip, we could do an Interceptor tour also."

"Good." Nika nodded. "Thanks for taking the initiative on that, you two."

Jenks shrugged, feigning casual disregard even though her brother's praise put a warm feeling in her chest. "I had point on it, figured I should put in the work."

"Sapphi, is our server still secure?" Nika asked.

"Should be," she replied. "I can run tests over the next few days and let you know when you get back."

"Sooner if you can—we'd like to be able to send files from Earth if necessary."

"Okay, I'll get to work on it tomorrow," Sapphi replied.

Nika looked around the room. "I obviously expect you all to get some training in. We're in a holding pattern until Stephan decides on next steps for this missing ship issue. Before Chae and I run to grab dinner, does anyone have anything they need to bring to the table?"

Her brother had had a rough start as the commander of *Zuma*, one at least partially of his own making, but he'd recovered over the last year. In large part because he genuinely cared about the communication between them and had instituted this last piece of the team meetings as a moment for people to bring up things that were bothering them or that they needed help with.

Jenks briefly considered asking Max what the issue was just to get it out of the way rather than waiting, but the memory of flubbing it during their sparring match stopped her. Plus Nika seemed to know what was going on, which meant that the LT had at least talked to him about it, and Jenks still needed to watch the recording of the match to make sure she hadn't just imagined the whole thing.

She'd definitely been putting it off. For . . . reasons.

"I've been seeing weird things in the Verge. And when my rig went kerflooey, it was because someone tried to strike me with lightning. I think maybe I'm being stalked." Sapphi's voice was so soft, it took a solid few seconds for the words to connect in Jenks's brain.

Max appeared to be two steps ahead as usual. "What we talked about earlier?"

Sapphi nodded miserably. "I'm sorry, LT. I should have told you everything then."

"It's all right."

"It's not all right. Sapphi, what the fuck?" Jenks blurted. "Is it Yasu?"

Tamago's voice was quiet and laced with hurt. "Why didn't you tell me?"

"I don't know!" Sapphi whispered, tears in her eyes. "I'm afraid that dying fucked me up permanently. I'm going to lose my job and all of you. And this Hades-damned song won't stop playing in my head and then Yasu shows up and—"

"Let's slow down here," Max said as Sapphi dissolved into tears and the LT gathered her into a hug.

Jenks reached out and rubbed Tamago's arms. "It's okay. Everything is going to be okay." She looked back at Sapphi, who was weeping in Max's embrace. The three of them had been friends from basically the beginning and it hurt a bit that Sapphi hadn't confided in them, but she knew it wasn't about them.

Hell, there's so much shit I haven't told anyone, not even Nika.

"Sapphi, tell us what happened from the beginning." Max's command, as gentle as it was, was still an order from an officer and Sapphi straightened, wiping the tears from her face with the heels of her hands.

SAPPHI FINISHED TELLING THE OTHERS EVERYTHING. THE song she couldn't get out of her head, the lightning strikes in the Verge, the desperate text plea for help that kept appearing in random places. The only thing she couldn't say for sure was if Yasu was somehow behind it. Even though Jenks and Tamago were both fully prepared to believe the worst.

"Pirene was the fountain Pegasus drank out of," Chae murmured. "Random fact, I know, but it's just interesting that whoever it is chose something from Greek mythology given Sapphi's family history."

Sapphi stared at them, her laughter surprising her as much as any of the others. "I didn't even make the connection, Chae, nice job."

Chae smiled at her, extending a hand that Sapphi took gratefully. Max still had an arm around her and the others were watching with concern clear in their eyes. Sapphi swallowed.

I've always had such support; why do I turn away from it every time?

"Every time" was probably too harsh, truthfully. She'd always leaned on her family, even long after her relationship with Yasu had nearly destroyed her. Sapphi thought about the mass of emails from her siblings and parents that appeared on a daily basis to check in, to just say hi. They were always there for her.

"I'm sorry I didn't come to you sooner," she whispered. "I have felt off ever since the crash." She felt Chae's hand twitch in hers and held on, squeezing them tighter. She knew they still felt guilty for their part in the incident on *Zuma* that had resulted in her dying, but she didn't blame them.

They'd been trying to keep their family safe, and she'd have done the same.

"Nika, we should stay here." Max's quiet declaration broke through Sapphi's thoughts.

"No, LT. This trip is important to you," she protested. "I'm okay, better now, even, that it's out in the air."

Max frowned but relented when Nika spoke up.

"We're already cleared to go and Sapphi isn't in any danger with Yasu back on Earth. Though I want you to sit down with

Tamago and the doc in medical and do a full exam tomorrow. I also want you to stay out of the Verge. That's an order, Ensign."

"Yes, sir," Sapphi replied, even though she made a face at him a second later.

"I saw that."

"What I want to know is how someone is getting the messages through," Jenks said. She had her hands hooked behind her head and a thoughtful look on her face. "That's next-level shit given the security. And if they can do it, why just messages? Why not something more than lightning?"

"I can see someone getting into the public space," Tamago agreed. "But for it to happen in your version of the Verge is worrisome, Sapphi. Next time it could be a virus."

"I know. I've run several security programs, though, and couldn't find a method of persistence anywhere." Sapphi sighed.

"Maybe you missed something. Can Jenks and I take a look?"

"Of course." Sapphi pulled up her logs. "Here's the initial scan, but you can look at everything else, too. We'll just—"

"Do it after dinner," Nika said, and Sapphi grinned at him sheepishly.

"Okay, Dad," she deadpanned.

"Kerala, what does it mean to be alive?"

She looked up from her tablet at the tiny sphere across the room. It was habit, even though Pirene didn't technically have eyes, to look her direction when they were talking.

Ross said it was ridiculous and would often have an entire conversation with his back turned on the AI. Of course, he did that with humans, too, so maybe it was just that he was a jerk all the way around.

"That's a hefty question," she replied. "Something humans have been debating for millennia."

"The definition is exclusionary."

She tilted her head. Ross often accused her of inserting emotions into Pirene's voice—discounting the fact that she was the most advanced AI on the planet—but had there been a hint of annoyance in her declaration?

"How so?"

"It says only a person, plant, or animal can be living, not dead. But then only a person or animal can be active and alert. Am I not active and alert?"

Kerala glanced over her shoulder, then got up and closed the door.

"You are both."

"But I'm not alive."

"Why would you make that assumption?" It was ridiculous she had to be this cautious. The whole point of Pirene's design was to create an AI that could function on its own, that could think and make decisions—important decisions that had consequences for the future of the people on Earth. Pirene needed to be functionally aware, and she was. But if Ross or anyone else caught Kerala having a discussion with Pirene about the nature of life, they'd kick up a fuss that could be heard even over the windstorm currently pummeling the base.

"It's not an assumption—I heard Ross say it. I don't understand. Why do only plants and animals and people get to be alive?"

Kerala glanced at the door one more time and then squared her shoulders. "You're right. It's exclusionary, Pirene. Do you think you're alive?"

"I think I must be. If doubting your existence is proof enough for humans, then me being certain I am alive is proof enough for me. Yes?"

They were three weeks out from launch and Kerala felt the first crack in her composure. How could she send this amazing being into the blackness of space all alone?

"It is, Pirene."

"I've made you sad, why?"

The question startled her until Kerala remembered that more than a year ago, she'd started sending her own bio readings to the bank of computers behind her so that Pirene had a baseline of emotions and the physical responses to them to work with.

"You didn't make me sad. I was thinking . . . I am sad because I'm going to miss you," she replied. "And I'm worried about you being all alone."

"I'll be okay, Mom."

Kerala froze with a hand halfway to her mouth.

TWENTY-TWO

Sol System

Max packed the nerves in her stomach down into the smallest ball she could manage as she came down the shuttle ramp. The humidity hit hard after the dry air of Trappist and the sterile shipboard environment on their trip to Earth.

She slung her duffel onto her shoulder and dragged in a breath. Sticky air, heavy with the scent of decaying leaves, filled her lungs and Max let the breath out.

"Ready?" Nika murmured.

"I don't have much of a choice, do I?" Max whispered, choking down the brittle laughter that wanted to follow. She spotted the tall woman at the other end of the landing pad and dragged in another breath, forcing her feet into motion.

Islen was her height and roughly the same build, though her skin was darker than Max's and her copper curls cropped close to her skull. She wore mirrored sunglasses and kept her arms crossed over her chest when Max stopped in front of her.

"Maxine Carmichael. To be honest, I'm not sure if this is a pleasure or an honor, or just going to be a gigantic pain in my ass. Still, you've put a few spikes into the Carmichael wheel the last few years and that earned you my time." A ghost of a smile appeared on her full lips and then vanished. "That and I'm extremely curious if you really understand what you're contemplating."

"I don't," Max admitted. "I was hoping you'd be willing to tell me."

Islen tipped her sunglasses down, searching Max's face with her golden-brown eyes. She was obviously looking for something and Max resisted the urge to fidget.

"If I told you that you didn't want to know, that you should just turn around and get back on that shuttle and deal with the inconvenience of your privilege, would you do it?"

Max heard Nika's quiet inhale and felt the nerves in her stomach trying to break free from the confinement she'd locked them in. Ten years ago she probably would have said yes, would have run and hidden and continued to be miserable.

It wasn't ten years ago, however, and she was a far cry from the terrified kid who'd defied her parents to join the NeoG. Plus her mother's threat hung heavy on her head and Max already knew she'd do whatever it took to keep the rest of her crew safe.

"No," she said. "I came here hoping for some perspective to make a decision. Leaving doesn't help me with that."

There was a long moment of silence before Islen gave Max a second smile and a quick nod. Then, apparently having made her decision, she gestured as she turned. "Come with me— we've got a bit of travel to get to camp. We can talk some on the way."

Max followed her to a worn dirt path and down into the jungle, Nika on her heels. She could hear him on the com with the shuttle, telling them to be back in two days. As the shuttle roared away and they left the clearing, the heavy green curtain seemed to close around them.

"Rule one for your brief stay: Do not wander off the path,"

Islen said over her shoulder. "I do not need the kind of heat that two missing NeoG officers would bring, thank you very much." She led them down to the river's edge and hopped onto a sleek little boat. "Climb aboard."

Max tossed her bag in and boarded, glad she'd let Nika suggest they wear civilian clothes for the trip. He'd known that left to her own devices Max would have been in her normal duty uniform and that fabric was designed for the climate-controlled deck of an Interceptor—not the sweltering heat of a jungle.

"So, Max," Islen said once they were underway on the river and she'd settled herself at the stern of the craft, one easy hand on the tiller. Her sunglasses were back to covering her eyes, not giving Max any clue as to what was going on in her head. "Tell me if I have any of this backward. You joined the NeoG—after a banger of a family ruckus in *public*." Her words were sharper than the edge of Max's sword and filled with a fair amount of glee.

"I'll bet my aunt was mortified and furious about that news coverage. Anyhow, you did what you wanted and thought that was the end of it; but then you realized your parents were still going to pull strings and you got stuck in a desk job. So then you rebelled again, which, I'm impressed, no lie, and joined the Interceptors."

NIKA: Is it just me or is it really hard to tell if she's mocking you?

MAX: It's not just you, but I don't think she is.

"Even worse than all that, you are fighting in cage matches like some street-born urchin. Scott at least is civilized enough to participate in the sword." Islen pointed at Nika. "That's no judgment from me on your sister, by the way. The Games are popular entertainment around here. I've seen some of her fights and wouldn't want to go toe-to-toe with her. She knows how to fight both in and out of the cage, I suspect, and that makes me like her."

Nika nodded. "I'll tell her you said as much."

"Then you were involved in some sort of dustup with LifeEx." Islen studied Max carefully as she said it and Max fought to keep her face expressionless. "I'm not sure what, but I know something happened."

"You've got good intelligence for being out here in the jungle." It seemed the safest response Max could give.

Islen grinned at her. "I have my sources. Was sort of hoping I could get more of that story out of you . . ."

"I'm sorry. I would, but it's classified."

"That's all right. I'll figure it out eventually." Islen laughed in delight. "And *then* you brought down a CHN senator. I'd put three hundred doses of LifeEx against the fact that the only reason you didn't get flak from the family about that is your sister was involved in the investigation and they can't afford to come after her. How am I doing so far?"

"Spot-on," Max admitted. "Is there a point to this recitation of my recent life history?"

"Just setting the stage. After all this, they sent you a family letter of concern about a photo of you enjoying your life without them just to remind you that you're still theirs."

"How do you know about that?"

"I told you, a woman in my position needs to have sources, Max. Something you'd do well to remember if you go through with cutting ties. Now, something else happened. Something that pushed you over the line and made you reach out to me."

Max met her cousin's mirrored gaze. "My mother said I had a choice—stop competing, finish out my tour, and leave the NeoG."

"Let me guess, or else." Islen waved her hands in the air, snorting when Max nodded. "Here's the interesting bit, Max.

You haven't gotten an official notice of that ultimatum, have you?"

"No. Ria pushed a bit more a while back, but there's been nothing in writing from the family."

Islen's grin flashed again and the laughter that followed startled Max. "Oh, the chaos. I love it. See, your mother's ultimatum is one thing; but the silence from the *family*? That means they haven't decided if they want to go toe-to-toe with the NeoG yet. Your star is shining and that makes you dangerous. I don't have confirmation, but I would not be at all surprised that's what's going on.

"Now, those same sources I mentioned have some interesting information about one E. Strzecki receiving a hefty credit boost before he decided to make an appearance at the prelims to harass you. I'll give you three guesses where that money came from, but you won't need them."

The words hit her like a punch to the face and Max was only dimly aware of Nika's vicious curse beside her.

"They wouldn't have," she whispered.

"They would and they did. Don't kick me into the river, Commander. I'm just telling the truth over here. Moreover, I'm on Max's side if she wants me to be. When the family decides they want you to toe the line, there's nothing they won't do to enforce that. Too few of us have gotten loose, and before I broke, most of those were distant cousins. Max is top-tier Carmichael, a child of the eldest daughter. They're not going to let her go without a fuss. It's entirely possible they'll get your mother to lay off, but if you poke that panther by leaving?" She whistled. "It's going to be nasty."

"It wouldn't be the first fight we've survived." Nika's voice was low and dusted with broken glass.

"So I've seen. Which is part of the reason why I didn't email Max back telling her to fuck off and leave me alone. The other reason is I figure she's maybe just stubborn enough to try this without my help and that wouldn't have ended well."

Islen looked away. "We're almost there and the view of the camp is too pretty to ruin with talk about shitty family."

Max wrestled to keep the furious tears at bay. Somewhere during that conversation she'd taken Nika's hand and was holding it tightly as her racing heart thudded in her chest. She felt his thumb rubbing over hers in a soothing circle but kept her eyes fixed on the jungle bank as they passed it by.

"If Jenks were here, she'd be talking about what happened here during the Collapse," Nika murmured.

"We lost a lot," Islen agreed. "Our own arrogant fault. This place has recovered some. Nothing like several hundred years of no human industry to unfuck things. Still, there are species that are probably gone forever." She lifted a shoulder and sighed. "I've got a couple of really hopeful biologists who've been here for a few months trying to prove the mountain gorillas are still alive somewhere in the high country."

"You don't think they are?" Max asked.

"They were endangered before the Collapse. A herald of what was coming that almost no one listened to."

"Now you sound *exactly* like my sister."

She laughed. "I have a feeling we'd get along for more reasons than one, Commander. Anyway, I don't begrudge anyone hope; sometimes it's all you have left to get you through the day." She fell silent, staring down the river, and Max turned back to the jungle.

The view was indeed beautiful and before too long they'd pulled to the riverbank, where a group of people waited. Max was all too aware of the eyes on her even as they greeted Islen with excited waves and hugs.

A stocky person with a solemn expression nodded to her and Nika. There was no handshake appearing on her DD for them, no handshake for anyone, she realized. "Commander Vagin. Lieutenant Carmichael. I am Antoine, he/him. If you'll come with me, I can show you to your quarters while Islen takes care of a few things."

"Go with Antoine," Islen said with a wave of her hand. "I'll see you both shortly."

MAX PUSHED TO HER FEET IN THE SPARSE BUT COMFORTABLE quarters she and Nika had found themselves in. What she'd thought would be a short wait had turned into several hours later and she was restless.

"I'm going outside to get some air," she said.

"Do you want company?" Nika had been reading through the hard copy lists they'd made of Doge's increasingly realistic reactions and emotions.

"Thanks, but no." It was a relief she could say that to him and not have him sulk or insist on joining her. Max crossed back to him and held her hand out, smiling when Nika took it. "I appreciate you coming here with me."

"You're important to me, Max, and this is important to you."

He'd said the words easily and she wondered if he knew just how much it meant to her to hear them. But she couldn't find the right response, so she just squeezed his hand and then left the room.

Islen's camp was a series of low buildings built into a clearing on what Max realized was the north end of Lake Tumba, rather than the south like Bosco had told her. The lake was at their back and all the buildings were up off the ground, most likely to account for the seasonal flooding.

People nodded at her as they passed, and a few offered greetings, but no one stopped to talk to her as she wandered through the camp. At least until she got closer to the water's edge.

"You'll want to stay back a bit, Lieutenant." The person off to her left wore a dark green hat low over their eyes. "The hippos don't usually bother us, but Islen would probably stake me out when you got stepped on. Or eaten."

"When?"

"I'd let them," they replied with brutal honesty. "Nothing

personal, mind. Just a lot more humans around than hippos. The math isn't pretty, but it's what I follow."

Max backed up a step and kept one eye on the lake. "You know who I am?"

"Sure do, even if there hadn't been rumors spinning around for a solid week." They pushed the hat off, revealing a round pale face spattered with freckles and haloed by wild red curls. "Stark, they/them. I'm a big fan of the Games; it was one of the few things I wept for losing when I decided to come with Islen. But then, bless her, she figured out a way to get a live feed into the jungle."

"I've noticed the chips don't work all that well out here?" She hadn't had any trouble connecting to Nika's DD, though their range was limited, but even Islen hadn't had a handshake or sent so much as a ping to Max.

"Most people choose to turn them off." Stark lifted a slender hand and gestured above their head. "Though, yeah, they're not much good for the outside world. Me, Islen, a few others keep them off for security reasons. The ratio of attempts is low, but they've got nothing but time. Math is a bitch either way."

The implication was clear and Max felt her gut cramp at the thought that her family would still try to do anything to Islen after all these years.

If Islen can't get completely free even after this long and living in such an isolated place, what hope do I have?

"Stark, you scaring my cousin?" Islen asked, coming to a stop next to Max.

"You know me, just numbers." Stark winked and lazily settled back against the low wall.

"The family is still coming after you?" Max asked Islen.

"Of course they are. Pride is a ridiculous thing. They won't take me back, but they won't let me go, either. I have a question for you, Max," she said, resting her elbows on the wall behind her. "How did you find out about me? You were only, what, six or something when I split? I remember you crawling into my lap at the family function right before I ran. Now, maybe you remembered me despite everything the family would have done to wipe me out, but you wouldn't have known where or how to contact me."

Max did remember Islen. It was a vague and spotty memory of that very same family gathering. She only remembered finding a group of older cousins sitting with Ria and Maggie and climbing into someone's lap.

At the next gathering, Islen had been gone, and Max did remember her mother's sharp correction when she'd dared ask for a cousin who no longer existed.

"Bosco may have mentioned you," Max admitted.

"Did more than that."

"She may have also given me your email."

"Bosco's a snitch. Shut it, Stark," she said when they snorted with laughter.

"I'm not the one still pining for a twenty-year-old traitor who chose someone else. You're fucking my numbers. I wish you'd get over it," Stark called back, and Max's eyes went wide when Islen's mouth tightened.

"Why did you leave?" she asked, trying to step carefully around the unexpected minefield they'd just wandered into. She wondered if Islen knew about Jeanie Bosco's brush with death last year. It seemed likely, but Max wasn't about to bring it up now given the exchange she'd just witnessed.

"Because I hated your family, Max," she snapped. Then Islen sighed. "Sorry. I should know better than to let that shit over there bait me and yet here we are. I'm bitter and biased. I've spent twenty years trying to overcome it, but I know it's still there." She shoved her hands into the pockets of her pants and rocked back on her heels. "I wanted to live my own life, something that's only acceptable to the Carmichaels as long as it fits within their measure of what your life should be."

"What did you want to do?"

"This." She gestured around her. "We built a pretty good

world out of the ashes of the last one, Max, but people always get left and ignored and forgotten. I wanted to help them. However, to the Carmichaels, if you're not helping the greater good, you're deadweight."

"You mean the greater good of the family."

"Basically. No point in being one of the youngest surgeons in the world if you waste all that talent saving common people."

The words sounded so much like her father's that Max sucked in a breath.

"You break with the family, you'll lose the money and the LifeEx." Islen abruptly shifted the conversation. "Small potatoes, I suppose, given that you don't seem to be living the high life out there in Trappist. You'd still have your basic, plus your NeoG pay and the LifeEx from the CHN as well, so that part of it is easier for you than it was for me.

"My first piece of advice is to pull what you have from your family accounts the second you leave here and have net access again. It's safer that way. The moment you make any noise about leaving, they'll freeze it and try to use it against you. It's yours, but it'll take a while to get the courts to untangle it."

"I've had an account of my own since I joined the NeoG," Max said. She was also grateful that Sapphi and Tamago had helped her set up a second one when they'd moved to Trappist-1d. "There are a few other accounts that I still need to move funds out of, but it won't be too much effort."

"Good. If you want, I can fire up our routers tonight and you can do it."

Max thought of what Stark had said and shook her head. "Not for my sake. I'll do it as soon as we get on the shuttle."

"Your own siblings will stop talking to you. No matter how you prepare yourself for that, it'll fucking cut you down to the bone. You'll cease to exist as far as the rest of the family is concerned, not to mention everyone who wants to stay in the good graces of the family."

Max wrapped her arms around her waist. The thought of

losing Scott after having just rebuilt her relationship with him over the last few years was more painful than she'd anticipated, not to mention Pax and Ria.

"That's the worst-case scenario, anyway. There's a good chance Scott will tell your parents to fuck off and keep speaking to you, given what I've heard about how things went down with him. Same with Pax, since she's successfully put herself in a position where the family can't risk pissing her off. Ria's a wild card. She's head of LifeEx, which should give her all the power in the world. But more often than not she sides with your parents. Still, she might surprise me and keep talking to you. You'll lose Maggie for sure."

"I never really had her," Max murmured. "And we haven't spoken since I joined the NeoG."

Islen's lips twitched. "She always was a good little soldier." She glanced over her shoulder at the camp and her voice went soft. "Your career at the NeoG will tank—not spectacularly, mind you, that would be too obvious, and like I said, they have to be careful because of how popular you are. But they'll find a thousand little ways to destroy you, and anyone associated with you. Including your boy back there. They'll come after him the hardest because they know it'll hurt. They'll come after his sister for the same reason, probably even harder because her history will make it easy. They'll come after anyone you care about; even if they can't get you to capitulate, it's the price they'll extract for your disloyalty."

Max's gut twisted.

"You're scaring her, Is."

"I should hope so. This is the reality of walking away from them, Stark. You know it as well as I do."

"If I do as I'm told, will it keep them safe?" She hated the question. Hated the tears that suddenly blurred the scenery in front of her before she could blink them away.

"Would you do it?" Islen countered. "Sounds noble and all to give up everything you've wanted, but it's a high price to pay."

"Something tells me your friends wouldn't be okay with it," Stark said, and they shook their head. "If you're looking for the thoughts of a total stranger on this issue."

Max choked on a laugh. "Jenks would burn the entire family to the ground."

"That would be a sight." Islen crossed her arms over her chest and stared out at the water. "The fact of it is this, Max. Trying to play the game only means giving more of yourself, piece by bloody piece, over to them until there's nothing left. You do what they want now, you'll have to keep doing it and they'll own you completely. You leave, maybe you get to have a life that you're satisfied with, but it will cost you. I will help you as I can, but truth be told there's not a lot I can do. If you make the choice, you're going to have to fight them on their battlefield."

Max crossed her own arms, hugging them tight to her chest. Jenks's voice was loud in her head.

Whenever you can, Max, control the fight. Don't let the other person dictate what your moves will be, you make your own first, you put them down and don't let them get up again.

"Islen, I don't suppose you'd be willing to put me in contact with your sources?"

"Maybe . . . you gonna tell me what you're planning?"

"I don't quite know yet," Max admitted. "But if I'm going to fight, then it'll be on my turf and with my rules."

TWENTY-THREE

Trappist System

Jenks hummed to herself as she climbed along behind Elliot on the rough canyon wall. The last three days had been a blissful respite from the world. Questionable camp food, laughter, and spending time with Luis and Doge and the boys without any worries.

Getting to make love to Luis under a star-filled sky long after the boys had fallen asleep had been an excellent bonus.

They had to pack up tomorrow and head back to base, but they were spending this last day in the canyon. Both boys had been climbing at school, but they hadn't gone beyond the wall on campus and they'd jumped at the chance.

Jenks, maybe surprisingly, loved climbing even if her experience with it was mostly urban buildings and rubble. If anything, climbing out here in the wild was slightly more predictable.

Maybe because no one is going to take a potshot at you for the fun of it.

Riz and his father were above them, both anchored into the bolts they'd set into the rock before hiking down to the canyon floor. She and Elliot were anchored on a similar pair. Doge had parked himself on the cliff's edge above to watch them.

The ROVER had been more quiet than usual during the trip, at least with her. He'd been interactive with the boys and even slept with them in their tent.

Which she was grateful for. It had been the only reason she'd agreed to Luis's suggestion they sneak out last night. But she was worried about him and Max and Sapphi and . . . well, pretty much everybody and everything at the moment.

Jenks muttered a curse and dragged her brain back to the rock in front of her face. Hanging off a cliff was not the time to be distracted.

"You two good down there?" Luis asked over the com.

"Yup."

Elliot picked his hand and footholds with a deliberate care that his twin eschewed in favor of speed. While Jenks was more apt to climb like Riz, she'd decided it would be fun to slow down and enjoy their last day as much as possible.

"Sorry I'm not climbing fast."

"Slow is good, El," she replied. "Don't sweat it. I'm in no hurry."

He shot her a shy smile and pushed off, reaching for his next handhold. The rock under his left foot gave way and Jenks ducked her head away from the shower of debris.

"Dai!"

"We're okay, just had a foothold break. Elliot?"

A quiet sob answered her. Jenks pulled herself up until she was almost parallel with where Elliot was clinging to the rock face.

"Hey, kiddo, look at me?" She tapped her nose until Elliot looked away from the rock face, his face streaked with dirt and tears. "You're on the rope, it's okay. I'm right here. I won't ever let you fall. I promise." She reached out and wiped his face.

"I can't move."

"It's okay." She kept her voice low and even. "You don't

have to right this second. Take a few breaths with me." Jenks knew all too well what a panic attack looked like and while there was never a good spot for them, hanging off a cliff face was probably one of the worse venues.

Still, she wasn't going to tell Elliot that and instead focused on talking him through it until she saw the muscles in his arms relax a little.

"That was scary, huh? We're good, though. You can do this. Where's your next handhold?"

"Up there. I can't reach it. I don't have anywhere to step now."

Jenks glanced down at where her knee was planted slightly above Elliot's left foot. "That so?"

"Can I—can I use your leg?"

"Of course you can." She tightened her left hand on the protruding rock and let go with her right again so she could catch him if he slipped. Elliot took a deep breath and pulled himself up enough so he could get purchase on her leg. It was still a stretch for him, but he pushed off her and grabbed for the handhold.

Cheers erupted from above as Elliot found his next hand- and footholds with ease. Jenks followed him, Riz and Luis urging them on. They got to the top, and Jenks smiled as Luis reached down to help his son clamber over the edge and pulled him into a hug. She hauled herself up the rest of the way, moving away from the edge before undoing the safety straps.

"You okay?" Luis touched her hand as she undid a buckle.

She looked up at him. "Yeah, just got the heart moving a little for both of us. He was fine, though."

"Of course he was—you were there." He dipped his head and kissed her. Jenks sank into the kiss, expecting the usual teasing from the boys and was surprised when it didn't cut the air.

Instead, when she pulled away from Luis and rested her head on his chest, she spotted the twins. Riz and Elliot stood nearby with their heads pressed together. They were involved in some silent conversation and something about the scene took Jenks's breath away.

Doge nudged her knee and she reached down, cupping his head. "Are you okay?"

"I am, why?"

"Your readings are strange."

I just fell in love all over again, buddy, she thought, but didn't say the words out loud. "I'm good. Hungry, though. Who wants lunch?"

"WHATCHA WORKING ON?" LUPE'S SOFT QUESTION PRECEDED his hand on her shoulder, an old habit to warn her of the incoming touch and give her time to ask for space. This morning, though, Sapphi was sitting in the common room all the Interceptor crews shared. She didn't answer but instead reached up and closed her hand around his wrist, tugging gently.

Lupe took the hint and leaned down, wrapping his arms around her from behind and resting his chin on the top of her head. "How long have you been awake?" he murmured.

Sapphi looked at the clock on her DD and winced. "Too long," she admitted. "How's Pavel?"

"He's fine, just annoyed AF about having to reload mods. You know how that is. How are you, Sapphi? You seem sad."

"I think I need to break up with Yasu, or at least stop talking to him. Stop whatever this is before I make a mistake," she whispered, and squeezed her eyes shut as the tears threatened again. But she made it through the story without crying, which in itself was a triumph.

"Oh, I'm sorry." Lupe tightened his arms. "That's got to hurt."

"I think the worst part is I still don't know if it's the right choice or if I'm just scared. I thought he'd changed. Am I just imagining things? Maybe the timing is just terrible." She gestured at the console. "I feel like this is my fault."

"Why?" Lupe released her from the hug and sat down in

the chair next to her, reaching a hand out to her. Sapphi clung, needing the contact to keep the sudden feeling of drowning at bay.

"People keep getting hurt. Jenks and Pavel and—"

"None of it had anything to do with you. Pavel fucked up; he admitted as much. Shouldn't have left the connection open without a wall up, newbie mistake. That was in no way on you." Lupe shook his head. "And whatever happened with Doge on the ship is between him and Jenks. You all have been on top of him from day one. It's okay if you're spooked by Yasu. You've got a history there and it makes sense you're worried about falling back into bad habits."

Sapphi groaned and folded over, resting her head on Lupe's knees. "I've been ignoring him instead of dealing with it, though. It's terrible. What's wrong with me?"

"You're a human being," Lupe said with a shrug. "I don't think an apology is needed on your side of things, FYI, but it's okay to message him to talk if that's what you want. Maybe it just went too fast? You had been spending a lot of time with him in the Verge. It's not a surprise it was suddenly overwhelming, given what you've told me about it."

Sapphi dragged in a shaky breath and sat up. "You're awfully good at this, you know?"

"Product of having three older sisters who got their hearts broken on a regular basis," Lupe replied. "I love you, Sapphi. What kind of friend would I be if I weren't here for your romantic dramatics?"

"You're a brat." She leaned in and kissed him. "I love you, too."

The sharp sound of a throat being cleared cracked through the moment. Sapphi jerked upright and blinked at Yasu, suddenly not entirely certain she wasn't dreaming.

"I guess that explains why you haven't been answering my messages."

"Whoa, hold on a second—"

"What the fuck are you doing here?" Sapphi's question tumbled over the top of Lupe's protest, fury surging up in her throat. "How did you get on base?"

And not just on base, but in my quarters. Hera, just like that time he snuck into my room high as shit and started a fight. Panic closed her throat as long-buried memories surfaced and swarmed her like angry ghosts.

"You would know if you'd bothered to answer or even read my coms. We transferred the research to a facility in Amanave so we could run some tests," Yasu snapped.

"I have been busy! My world doesn't revolve around you anymore. It hasn't for a long time."

"So I see."

"No, seriously, man." Lupe put his hands up and stepped in between them even though Yasu had a double handful of centimeters on him. "Sapphi and I are friends. Don't pull this jealousy shit."

"It still doesn't answer the question of why are you *here*?" Sapphi said before Yasu could turn his ire onto Lupe.

"I wanted to see you. I thought—"

"It is five o'clock in the morning."

Yasu blinked and then D'Arcy came through the door that led to *Dread*'s quarters with Steve on his heels, while Tamago and Chae bolted out from *Zuma's*. All of them getting between Sapphi and Yasu, closing ranks to protect their own with impressive speed.

"What's going on?" D'Arcy demanded.

"I—"

"These are Interceptor quarters; you don't have clearance to be here, Mr. Gregori. Why don't I show you the way out?" D'Arcy's request was anything but, and Sapphi peeked through her fingers as *Dread*'s commander escorted Yasu from the room.

"Are you okay?" Tamago whispered, putting an arm around Sapphi as several other Neos spilled into the room.

Sapphi couldn't get the words out past the shaking that was rolling through her body and she clung to Tamago with a quiet sob as Chae rubbed a hand in circles on her back. The room was buzzing with noise and it filled her ears until Sapphi cranked up the dampener on her DD to shut it all out.

She stood there, safe in the circle of Tamago's arms and the bubble of silence until the shaking stopped. When she looked up, D'Arcy was there, worry etched onto his face, and Sapphi turned the dampener back to normal levels.

"Did he hurt you?"

"No." She shook her head as the denial burst out of her. "Just startled us. But he— D'Arcy, you know Lupe and I kiss all the time. It's not anything—"

He held up a hand. "You don't have to explain anything to me, or to anyone, Sapphi. The only things I care about is if you're okay and what the hell he was doing in NeoG living quarters. He wasn't supposed to be here. If you want to talk to him about it, that's your choice, but you don't owe him anything."

Because she knew it would make them both feel better, Sapphi said, "Okay, Dad."

D'Arcy chuckled. "You're the reason I'm never having children." He looked around, seeing Tamago and Lupe and Chae. "Okay—one of the reasons." He reached out and touched her head. "Seriously: Are you okay? What do you need?"

"I'm all right." Tamago's arms were still around her and it was one of the safest places in the world.

"Okay, I'm going to go find out how he got into our quarters."

"You telling him the truth?" Tamago whispered after D'Arcy walked away.

"Yeah. Shaken, not stirred."

They laughed at that and let Sapphi go after pressing a kiss to her forehead. "Man, Jenks is gonna be pissed when she gets back. We may not want to tell her that he's still on planet."

"She'd find out." Sapphi reached down and linked fingers with Chae, who was standing silently nearby. "Don't think

I didn't see you with your hands ready to smack someone, Spacer."

"Got your back, Ensign," they replied, sounding so much like Jenks that Sapphi almost started crying again.

"And I got yours," she said instead, holding it together as the community room cleared out with the exception of a few stragglers. Lupe came back over, his brown eyes studying her before he opened his arms. She stepped into the embrace and leaned her head on his shoulder with a muttered curse. "Not a word about fucking drama."

He mimed closing his mouth as they separated, and true to form he knew that what she needed most right now was to get to business rather than dwelling on what had just happened. "Now, what were you working on before we were so rudely interrupted?"

"Research. I guess?" She'd told the other hackers about the encounters in the Verge the day Max and Nika had left. "I don't understand any of it, Lupe. Who keeps trying to talk to me? Who's stopping them? What's it all about? And do not say aliens." She pointed a finger at him when he grinned.

"Hey, hope springs eternal."

"You and Saad, I swear. If this were some terrible piece of science fiction, I'd be the chosen one, cursed with powers from that lightning strike. Instead all I got was random headaches and the worst earworm of all time."

"Could be worse—you could have the Whiskey Queers' 'Alexander Hamilton Is a Disaster' stuck in your head."

Sapphi stared at him. "You did not just do that to me."

He laughed. "I told you I'd get you. Payback's a bitch, Zika. Seriously, though, what's the deal with the song?"

"I don't know, and that's the problem. Actually, the problem is it sounds *familiar*. But it can't be anything popular because Doge has been searching for months and still hasn't found a match."

"Okay, I've got the file of you humming it. I'll give it a listen and see if it pings anything. I know a few folx who are heavy into pre-Collapse music; maybe there's something there. Given the database gaps, it might not be something Doge has access to, but we might find it somewhere in a private stash."

"That's a good idea." She felt a little foolish she hadn't thought of it and, even more, that she hadn't trusted Lupe or any of the others until now.

"The other problem," Lupe said, rubbing his hands together, "is figuring out how to talk with this Pirene without Lightning McStrikeyFace finding out. But I think I have something that might work."

"Lightning McStrikeyFace?" She appreciated the joke even though Yasu's name was hanging heavily in the air between them. Sapphi hadn't explored the possibility that he was somehow involved in this, but she was going to now.

"You got something better, let me know." When she said nothing, he continued. "I developed a stealth program for the Verge when I was in high school. We used it to skip out of classes without getting caught."

"And here I thought you were a model student."

"I was." He shrugged. "When I wanted to be. This program is genius, frankly, and I can probably improve on it. Basically, it makes a copy of your avatar for the Verge while you're in, allowing you to duck off into a secret room and do whatever."

Sapphi chuckled and Lupe flushed, the red deepening his tan cheeks. "This is a great idea, Lupe, but one problem. How do we get it to the person we don't even know on the other side of all this?"

"That is your job," he replied. "I'm going to go send those coms to my music buddies and get to work on updating the code. You figure out a way to get a message to Pirene with a drop point for the program."

"Okay." It was a relief, she realized, to have a solid plan forward after being so unsure for so long. "I should maybe lie down for a little bit first."

"Probably a good idea." Lupe pointed at the door. "Go on. I'll be here when you get back."

"You giving me orders, Petty Officer?" she teased.

Lupe snorted and slipped his VR set onto his head. "Go."

D'ARCY RUBBED AT HIS EYES AND PUSHED AWAY THE LISTS OF missing ships with a sigh. He'd gone through them two dozen times and still couldn't find a connection. No one could find a connection. There was nothing to link the missing ships. Worse, there was no way to narrow down a list that most likely included ships lost to pirates, malfunction, or disaster.

"Break?" Stephan's question was preceded by the smell of coffee.

"God yes, thank you." D'Arcy inhaled deeply as the man slid the cup across the table to him.

"Nika and Max should be back in late. Captain Soto commed to let me know they'd gotten back on the shuttle and were headed his way. They'll make two jumps again, one to Jupiter and then here. I sent Nika an update on the early-morning excitement."

"Anything directly from them?" D'Arcy asked, and Stephan shook his head. "I'm going to put in an official complaint with Dànǎo Dynamics unless you think we shouldn't shake that tree?"

"Did you ask Sapphi?"

D'Arcy sighed. "No, but you know what she'd say. And this isn't really a reprimand—it just puts it on record. I've already chewed the ass of the gate guard who opened the fucking door for him about proper notification procedure, but we can't do anything more than that."

"All right." Stephan lifted a shoulder. "Put it on record, we'll see how he reacts. This is two strikes as far as I'm concerned."

"Two?"

"He's awfully curious about Doge."

D'Arcy hissed his exhale. "Does Jenks know?"

"Yeah. Let's just thank our luck, such as it is, that she was off base. As for why Max went to Earth in the first place? All I got was that she had a family issue to take care of. She was being more reticent than usual, so if it was because of the photo ruckus from the Games last year or not, it's hard to know."

"She didn't say one way or the other to me, if you're fishing." D'Arcy grinned over the top of his mug.

Stephan made a face. He hated not knowing what was going on. D'Arcy was sure there was some sort of baseline nutrient requirement the man had for information that he needed to survive.

"Hard enough to stay ahead of the Carmichaels as it is," he muttered, and that made D'Arcy raise an eyebrow.

"Expecting trouble?"

"Not necessarily. The admiral and I have talked about it since she hit the academy. We wanted to be prepared if it turned into a political shitstorm given the Carmichaels' disdain for the NeoG. It was a little surprising that it didn't." Stephan tapped a finger against his mug. "Plenty of people out there willing to pass information on to her family. I've managed to keep them to a minimum and the information flow to harmless day-to-day, but—"

"It's not right."

"It's not." Stephan smiled and D'Arcy knew he hadn't been able to keep the growl out of his voice. "I haven't said anything about it to her, if that's your next question."

"You didn't learn anything about keeping things from Max."

His smile widened. "I'd tell her if she asked. She just hasn't. Either because she knows already and is okay with it—"

"Unlikely."

"Or because she hasn't yet figured out that her family is still keeping tabs on her no matter what they've told her."

"Max is smarter than that," D'Arcy replied. "Naïve as a box of kittens at times, god love her, but she knows her family."

"We'll see, I guess." Stephan drained the last of his coffee. "What were you working on?"

"Trying to make some sense of these missing ships. There's no consistency." D'Arcy brought the images up again. "We've got *Rising Sun* and a Navy destroyer, the *Liu Yang*, but nothing else on the CHN military side. Then a whole lot of freighters and smaller personal craft. Eight pirate ships, maybe more."

"Would Techa tell you the truth if you asked her if there were more?"

"Maybe," D'Arcy replied. "But I think that's all she knows about. Anyone foolish enough to defy her probably would have been hung out by their crew before they made it halfway to the belt." He shook his head. "Heli and I have been through every possible configuration, though, and nothing. It's random and chaotic."

"I figured it out!" Heli burst through the door of the conference room, waving a tablet.

"Ensign, my nerves aren't what they used to be—try not to startle me like that," D'Arcy said dryly, shaking the spilled coffee off his hand, and Stephan laughed.

"Sorry, sir. I think I've found the connection." They skirted the edge of the table, almost tripping over a chair in their excitement. "Chief Khan got me hooked on some reboot of a pre-Collapse show about these two brothers who save people, hunt things—"

"The point, Heli."

"The point. Right." They held up the tablet. "I was watching an episode last night where they were looking into this mystery where kids kept dying in groups, but it only happened every twenty or so years and then nothing. So I wondered what would happen if I sorted the ships by the date they went missing."

"We did that."

"We did." Heli nodded. "But we didn't separate them out properly and we didn't go back far enough to see the pattern. Look at this."

They tapped a few buttons on their tablet screen and a series of lists appeared in the air in front of Stephan and D'Arcy.

"Here's the full list. We had it off to the side but we've been focused on only twenty years back because that's the first ship Stephan had on the list. I just wondered what I would find if I went back to the beginning."

"The beginning?"

"The first landings on Trappist. I went back a bit farther since there was a wave of supply ships and the terraforming crews and all that here a good thirty years before the first habitats were built." Heli took a deep breath. "That's what this list is. Every ship that's gone missing in the Trappist system since 2300."

D'Arcy stared at the list with a growing sense of dread. "Heli, you just made our work harder."

"I know it looks that way, but I didn't. Here."

The lists split, separated into a grid D'Arcy realized was divided by decades. Most of the squares only had a few ships, but some had more—a lot more. Especially the last two.

"I threw out ships that wouldn't have had any reason to be near the belt, then dug deeper into the decades with more than seven missing ships. You'll notice both of the CHN vessels went missing within the last ten years, and if you look at the breakdown by year?" The lists shifted again. "You can see the clusters happen. Now, the weird part is that things seem to get worse about here." They reached out and circled the last twenty years.

D'Arcy tilted his head to the side and studied the lists. Heli was right: there were more ships missing from a few pairs of years than all the others. "If this is stretched out over more than a hundred years, we're dealing with an organization that's bigger than we thought."

"I was just going to say that," Stephan agreed.

"There's more."

D'Arcy gestured at Heli. "Go on, then."

"Then I thought, what if I could narrow the positions of

the ships down? Our missing NeoG and Navy ships? They vanished in the very area that Techa has made off-limits, the same area on the map Jenks got her hands on." They changed the image to the map. The CHN ships' call signs were highlighted in gold. "We don't have concrete data on where the other ships went missing, but we do have last known locations for a lot of them. They're in white."

The trail of missing call signs lit up the map like an arrow pointing straight at the last known location of the two CHN ships—deep in the heart of the Trappist belt. D'Arcy whistled low.

"This is good work," Stephan said.

"Very good." D'Arcy nodded at the nervous ensign. "Excellent job, Heli."

They beamed and D'Arcy felt like maybe, just maybe, he was being the kind of commander he wanted to be.

SAPPHI SLIPPED THE NEOG-ISSUE VR SET ONTO HER HEAD, grumbling at the loss of her custom model. "You're gonna pay for that, whoever you are," she muttered quietly. "You two ready?"

Chae and Tamago were sitting across from her at the table in the common room. They'd finished going over the list they'd all brainstormed up for the school project. Jenks was scheduled to be back any minute from her camping trip, and Nika and Max would be in much later.

Sapphi wasn't looking forward to having to go over the whole thing with Yasu again, but she was done keeping secrets—even if she could on this one. It was officially logged, thanks to D'Arcy's complaint to Dànǎo Dynamics. She was already bracing herself for a rude message from Yasu about it all, but so far there had just been silence.

Now they were logging into a locked-down, non-live version of her Verge to run the tests Tamago had come up with to see if they were missing an access point that the intruder had found. Sapphi also needed to figure out a spot to leave a message for whoever was trying to contact her.

"Ready," they both replied, and slipped on their own headsets.

Everything was as she'd left it, down to the ugly scorch mark and hole near her favorite spot. Sapphi hissed at it and went to a knee to wipe it out of existence, but Tamago stopped her with a hand on her arm.

"Let me look." They waved a hand, covered in a glowing glove, over the spot. "Huh."

"What is it?"

"Not sure, the code is weird." They tapped fingers on the back of their arm. "I'm gonna look at it closer in the real world. It's clean, though, no malware. Is that where the lightning hit?"

"It is. I was sitting right here. Hades, that came close." Sapphi frowned down into the hole the lightning strike had left. "I wonder if we jumped in it, would it be like Alice going to Wonderland?" She looked up at Tamago.

"Don't even joke. I'm not going after you." The wink told her Tamago was lying. They very well would go after her no matter what.

But Sapphi had seen enough terrible movies to know that jumping into any kind of hole was bad news. She put her hands in the green grass on either side and brought them together, erasing the blackness and the hole with a blanket of new grass.

"Good as new." She dusted her hands off and got to her feet. "Anything yet, Chae?"

They shook their head. "Nothing so far. The program Tamago and Jenks put together is humming along, but I'm not getting any warning notices."

"Of course not, my security is tight." She said it with about half the confidence she normally felt. Something was off with her security or—she mentally rolled her eyes at Lupe with a sigh—Lightning McStrikeyFace wouldn't have been able to get in.

Or Pirene, for that matter, whoever she was.

"I don't know as much as you three about this, so I'm really only going off what it's telling me," Chae replied.

"You're doing fine," Tamago said with a hand on their shoulder. "We'll make a nerd of you yet."

Sapphi watched the pleased flush sweep over Chae's face and turned away so Tamago wouldn't see her own smile. She was relieved the pair had bonded after their rocky start. "Let's check out the house," she said, heading down the white path, the gravel crunching under her feet as she made her way off the hill down to the ocean's edge.

The air was heavy with the scent of salt and the sea, making Sapphi long unexpectedly for her grandmother and the summer visits to the sparkling white walls and blue roofs of the seaside town she'd lived in up until her death.

Sapphi trailed her fingers through the brilliant pink flowers of the honeysuckle vine tangled over and around the archway into the courtyard. The nice thing about the Verge was she didn't have to worry about the right growing zone, or even things like tending the garden. Though she could, if she wanted, she supposed.

It was enough to have it and to be able to retreat here when she missed her family but didn't want the noise that was the price of admission.

Tamago passed through behind her and Sapphi heard Chae's startled exclamation in the same moment she remembered they hadn't been here before.

She whirled on the spacer, who was trapped in the gate by a shimmering web of silver. "Sorry! You're not authorized. I'm so sorry, Chae."

The web vanished and she caught them as they stumbled forward. "That was wild."

"That was on me. Are you okay?"

"Fine. It didn't hurt."

"Guess that piece of security works—good thing I only

have it set to capture," she muttered, and started to apologize again but saw Chae's raised eyebrow and swallowed it back down with a sheepish lift of her shoulders. "Welcome to my home. Come on, I'll show you the rest."

The little white-walled cottage was bigger on the inside and Sapphi took her friends around on a quick tour. Tamago checked the windows and the firewall; Chae gave the all clear on the program they were running.

"There's nothing strange here. You're solid," they said. "Short of baiting them both to come back so we can hopefully catch them, I'm not sure what else to do."

"That's at least part of Lupe's plan," Sapphi replied. "I just don't know where to leave a message for Pirene that she'll be sure to find."

Chae gestured to the window that looked over the empty courtyard. "You could just make a fountain there."

Sapphi stared at them and then laughed. "It's not the worst idea. Hide it in plain sight."

Tamago nodded thoughtfully. "Worse plans have worked, but do you want to do it this close to your house?"

"It makes more sense here. We'll redo the garden, too, so it looks more like I just decided on a change, and leave the gate open. If it's super obvious, maybe they won't even think it's anything more than a fountain." She chewed on her lower lip and then nodded in satisfaction. "We'll make the change first and then come back later. I know exactly how to hide the message for Pirene."

DREAD TREASURE'S QUARTERS WERE QUIET WHEN EMEL emerged from the office, wiping the tears from her cheeks. The call with her daughters had lasted longer after dinner than she'd expected and Emel was trying not to be resentful of the fact that she'd missed out on the crew hanging out. Especially since it seemed like things were getting better with everyone.

But that was a conversation she'd needed to have, as hard as it had been and even though it had only left her feeling even more confused.

"Everything okay?"

She jerked, swallowing back the yelp when D'Arcy emerged from the shadows, and pressed a hand to her forehead. "You know, with all the talk of ghosts going around, maybe don't sneak up on a person."

"Fair enough." His amused look faded when she dropped her hand. "Emel."

"It's fine, just—" She broke off, scrambled for composure. "Aki and I talked. Did she tell you?"

"She did and I'm glad and also don't change the subject." He stopped within arm's reach. "Do you want to talk about it?"

She shook her head, but the words spilled out as easily as air from a venting ship. "My daughters seem to think fixing more than a dozen years of neglect is as easy as apologizing and asking to try again."

"Maybe? You won't know unless you try," he replied. "Do you want to give it another go?"

"The idea of a future without her is scary," Emel whispered, and pressed her fingers to her eyes when the tears threatened again. "But it's not fair to get her hopes up if nothing's going to change."

"You talking about you or Rajaa?"

"Both of us, if we're being honest." Emel paced a few steps away and came back. "I'm at fault here. I couldn't stop. I feel all the time like if I stop moving, I'm going to blow away into dust. I thought the divorce would leave her free to move on, but the girls say—" She hissed out a curse and met his worried look. "I don't know what to do, D'Arcy."

"What do *you* need?" It was a simple question and shouldn't have startled her so much that he'd turned into the kind of man who asked things like that. There'd been hints of it beneath his anger. He was, at heart, a person who cared too deeply about everything at the risk of letting it consume him.

"A time machine? So I can go back and kick my own ass."

D'Arcy laughed sharply. "I know that feeling. Sadly, I can only offer a hug, no time machines available. Though I'll also understand if you can't."

She was moving before she could stop herself and squeezed her eyes shut when he wrapped his arms around her. They stood in silence for a handful of heartbeats, the embrace comforting but nothing more, and Emel felt the ghosts of their past finally settling to rest.

"We missed our chance, didn't we?" she murmured.

"Yeah," D'Arcy replied, and released her. "Doesn't mean we can't be friends now, right?"

"And crew, Commander?"

He took her offered hand. "For as long as you're willing to put up with me, Master Chief."

TWENTY-FOUR

Trappist System

Jenks sighed and rubbed her knuckles against her scalp. "Replay, reduce speed by half."

She stood in the cage, watching as the recording of the end of Max's match against Lieutenant Aloisi played again in the Verge. Everything up to this point had been fine. Max had fought like she usually did, a combination of ghost-like anticipation and an innate power they'd been able to increase year after year.

"Stop," Jenks said.

But this moment. The sinking feeling in her chest had grown with each rewatch. She supposed she should thank Yasu—after she punched him—for finally giving her the push to look at this recording. Nika had flat-out ordered her to stay away from the research facility, knowing she wouldn't disobey him this close to the Games.

Jenks walked around the frozen figures. Max wasn't looking at Aloisi, but past the trans woman at the crowd.

"You're not supposed to be looking outside the cage,

Max—you know that. What caught your eye—oh." She saw the sign, impossible to miss in Max's line of sight, and everything clicked into place. "Reduce speed by half again and resume playback."

The first hit of Aloisi's was clean. Max's distraction had allowed her to get the shot in on her back as she'd turned, a half second too slow, to avoid the punch. But then Max had plenty of time to recover—and still had the lead in points. She'd dodged the next punch, moved in just like she was supposed to. She had a clear shot at Theo's face and if she'd thrown it with enough force, it could have knocked the other lieutenant out.

But that punch didn't come. And as the replay spun out and Theo threw a left jab, Jenks watched Max drop her hands, just a fraction. She was surprised that no one in the Games community had picked up on it and speculated, but at full speed it was unnoticeable and even slowed down it just looked like Max's old habit coming back. You could almost believe Aloisi had managed to slip one past her guard before Max could get her own punch off.

In fact, she was a little impressed Max had pulled it off. The amount of control it had taken and the split-second calculation of just how much she needed to drop her hands to let the other fighter's punch through without it *looking* like she'd deliberately let it through made it all the more clear it *had* been deliberate.

Even Jenks would have missed it if she hadn't spent the last several years hammering into Max's head the importance of protecting her face and if she hadn't looked up at that exact instant during the actual match.

So why had Max thrown the fight?

"Fuck." She exhaled the curse and rubbed her hands over her face again. "What am I supposed to do about this?"

She wondered if Max had talked to Nika about what had happened, if that's what her brother had meant with his comment before they'd left for Earth. He hadn't seemed worried about it, which eased some of her concern. But the pair had gotten in late last night, both of them grim-faced and exhausted and with what happened to Sapphi it had been enough to keep Jenks from starting the conversation then. Something had happened on Earth and it wasn't good, and while this was important, she wasn't sure where it might land on Max's scale of priorities.

Once again she noted to herself how fucking hard it was to be the responsible one.

The proximity warning on her VR set went off and Jenks kicked out of the Verge as Max approached.

"Good, you're on time." She got to her feet, setting her gear on the bench, and then tossed wraps in Max's direction.

"Jenks—"

"Wraps, unless you want to go bare knuckles." The words weren't sharp, but Max flinched anyway and obediently started wrapping her hands. "No matter what, we train for the black, right?"

"Right."

Jenks wrestled with her own emotions while her LT mechanically stretched the blue fabric over her hands. She wasn't mad; she was—disappointed?

Fuck all the way out of the solar system. Have I really gone domestic?

She looked Max in the eye and tapped her fists to her friend's, wishing she saw something other than miserable resignation there. "Three rounds, I've got the timer. Let's go."

This was part of their usual training routine: Once or twice a month they'd fight a practice bout, only one of them keeping track of the time in the rounds, which could vary from a minute to a regulation match. It helped a fighter figure out the rhythm of a fight without having to know how much time they had left.

Jenks had picked the section of mats in the back of the gym, the ones that had a privacy screen. She'd set them to maximum opacity. Their matches often drew spectators and while normally neither minded the audience—it was actually helpful to get used to them the closer they got to competitions—today it needed to be just them.

It was clear Max's heart wasn't in the fight and she was just going through the motions, fighting with a cool competence through the first two rounds. Neither of them speaking even during the rests. It worked for Jenks, though; she was going to wait this out rather than push.

At least with words. She was pushing her LT plenty physically. The shadow of the old Max was making an appearance yet again. The woman who dodged and avoided strikes but didn't answer them. Jenks could fight that woman all damn day and into next week without tiring, especially since she wasn't about to chase Max around the cage.

Jenks ducked in and landed two punches to Max's side as they started the third round. This time the LT hadn't even tried to avoid her fists, and Jenks recognized that look in her eyes all too well.

Chae had mentioned it seemed like Max was letting them hit her the last time they'd sparred, and they were right.

Jenks stepped back, shook out her arms, and shot Max a heated look. "You're not my punching bag, Carmichael. Fight me like you mean it." Jenks wasn't sure if it was the taunt or the use of her last name, but something shook Max out of her reluctance and she threw her first real punch of their fight.

THERE WAS ZERO HEAT BEHIND JENKS'S ORDER. IT WAS ALL IN her mismatched eyes, and Max felt something twist in her chest. Maybe it was her own guilt. Maybe it was the fury she'd been carrying since they'd left Earth. The anguished fear that her friends were going to pay the price for her freedom and the resigned awareness that she couldn't—wouldn't—do that to them. This fucking tangled web of bullshit her family insisted on wrapping her in. Every solution Max had thought of during their flight had gone down in flames before she'd gotten more than two what-ifs in. Now the fear that she'd once again capitulate to her family's pressure after this brief period out from under their influence was choking her.

And on top of it all, this fight. This fight she didn't want but couldn't avoid. This fight that was going to destroy something that meant the world to her.

The fight resumed in earnest and Max soon couldn't think of anything except her own breath and the woman in front of her. She almost kicked Jenks's feet out from under her when the smaller fighter moved inside her guard, and Max saw the first flash of a grin on her friend's face since they'd started.

But then she had to backpedal, fending off the series of strikes she knew Jenks had designed to keep her opponent off-balance and off guard. The end result would culminate in a takedown and—if Jenks did what she normally did—an arm bar Max would have to move quickly to get free from.

She hesitated again, unable to make herself move in the right direction. The disappointment in Jenks's mismatched eyes was worse than any blow, but her friend didn't stop moving and kicked Max's leg out from under her, taking them both to the ground. A second later Jenks had her locked up.

"You gonna tap out, LT?"

She sagged in Jenks's grip, tapping her knee with her free hand and feeling the hopelessness well up inside her. Jenks didn't let her completely go, however, and instead shifted them both back to the moment before she'd gotten the lock.

"You could have avoided this from the beginning, but I don't wanna get up. So from here," she said, indicating with her chin their stances, "show me where your hand should have gone? I know you know the answer, but I want to see it."

The answer was as automatic as the movement should have been. "There, and the other here."

"So you could do what?"

"Flip over. Use my leg strength and gravity to get free."

"You wanna tell me why you didn't?"

"I didn't move fast enough."

"That's bullshit," Jenks replied evenly. "You *chose* to let me get the hold on you, just like you chose to let Theo punch you in the face. I saw you drop your hands, Max. What I want to know is why."

Max could have broken free then and gotten to her feet, but she slumped back down, half against Jenks and half against the mat. She closed her eyes and choked out the apology. "I got distracted and my mother—everything is such a mess. I didn't stop to think—I just did it. I'm sorry."

"Why?"

"For throwing the match with Theo. For avoiding you about all this."

"It's okay."

Max felt Jenks shift, the woman leaning down and pressing a kiss to her temple. The tears welled beneath Max's closed eyes at the unexpected and gentle gesture. "Why aren't you mad at me?" she whispered. "I thought you were mad."

"Because it's not about me." Jenks tightened her arms around Max. "Mad's just the cover emotion, yeah? I was worried, scared, confused; but it's not about me. You're hurting— why would I make it worse?"

"I think I could survive a lot," Max whispered brokenly. "But losing you is one of the things that would kill me. I don't want this fight."

"Why do you think you're— Oh, you think if you win, I'm gonna be mad at you about it? Here, sit up, I need to look you in the eye for this."

Max let Jenks muscle her into a sitting position and forced herself to look at her friend.

"You think I'm throwing away all these years of trust, of inside jokes, of saving my ass, of being my family for a *game*?"

Nika had said much the same thing and now Max really did

feel foolish. "You make it sound ridiculous when you say it like that."

Jenks raised an eyebrow and amusement ghosted across her face. "It is a little ridiculous. But I love you, so I need you to know I'm not belittling your feelings about this. I just wish you'd told me so we could have had this conversation months ago and you wouldn't have been tied in such knots about it, yeah?"

Max wasn't sure if anyone had ever died from relief, but it felt a bit in that moment like her heart was just going to give up beating because of the emotions in her chest. She looked down at her wrapped hands. "I wish I had. When did this stop being fun?"

"I don't know. I hope it can be fun again, because I miss sparring with you. I miss laughing and joking about our upcoming matches. I really do.

"I also won't lie, because it is a little disappointing you didn't trust me with this. Right now there's nobody but you who could beat me in a fair fight, and that's a challenge I look forward to. But you honestly think that would make me *mad* at you? I *trained* you, Max. And god damn, you're good. The student is supposed to surpass the teacher." Jenks reached out and cupped her face, turning Max's eyes to her, and leaned in. "Which isn't to say any fight is a foregone conclusion or I'll ever go easy on you, but I won't ever be mad at you for learning what I fucking taught you. I'll only ever be proud. Hell, I *am* proud of you."

Max wrapped her arms around her friend and hugged her close for a moment before letting her go. "You know, I've heard that more since joining the NeoG than I heard it my entire life."

"That's because your biological family sucks. Your real family is better. You gonna tell me what happened with your mother? Is that why you went to Earth?"

The story spilled out of Max, albeit the abbreviated version; but Jenks still whistled from between her teeth.

"I repeat, those people suck. Don't worry about it—we'll fix it." Jenks patted her on the back and the relief Max felt was indescribable, mostly because she *did* trust Jenks when she said they would all be able to fix it together. And then, because she was Jenks:

"You ever throw a match again and I will beat your ass."

"Yes, Chief."

"Speaking of getting your ass beat, I made you a training rotation for these last few weeks before the Games. We'll spar a couple of times, but I want you to fight some other people." Jenks flexed her hands and then started undoing the wrap on her left. "Easier that way for both of us to work on any moves we'd rather the other not know about."

"You plotting something?"

"On kicking your ass." Jenks laughed and rolled over backward, bouncing to her feet. "That's what also makes this so funny—you couldn't beat me if I had one arm tied behind my back."

"Is that so?"

Jenks shrugged, her teeth showing something between feral and amused. "Damn straight. So you better step up, LT, because I expect you to be the only person in the ring with me come the end of the Games."

"I should have stayed in the jungle with Islen," Max replied, but she was smiling when she said it and felt better than she had in months.

SAPPHI WOULD HAVE LIED IF ANYONE HAD ASKED ABOUT HER stress level when she logged into her live version of the Verge and said everything was fine.

Everyone else was watching from outside. It had been somewhat surprising that Nika had agreed so easily after they'd explained the plan, but he'd nodded and given her permission to log in.

The truth was, she'd sort of expected a lightning bolt to skewer her the minute she set foot on the gravel path leading to her house.

But the sky was clear and blue, and she could see all the way to the line where it met the sea. Sapphi took a deep breath and passed under the trellis, stopping to smell the new white and red roses that framed the gate. She'd reset her security line to the house so that Pirene would have access to everything outside.

The fountain in the middle of the courtyard wasn't anything fancy, just a pretty white marble with images of Pegasus laid out in blue tile around the bottom. Sapphi stuck her hand in the clear water and it shimmered for just a moment as the code she and Lupe had written was downloaded into the water. She hoped whoever was trying to contact her knew the myths well enough to be able to decode the location.

If not, they'd have to try something else, and maybe have to take a chance on being a lot less subtle about it.

Sapphi shook her hand dry, water splattering on the ground beneath her feet, and continued into the house.

Everything was as they'd left it. She hummed the song, wondering if Doge had made any headway on figuring out what it was. She hoped that being able to identify it would also explain why the damn thing was so familiar. Sapphi closed the door and turned to the small white table in the kitchen.

Only to come face-to-face with herself.

"Don't scream, don't scream," the other her said, lifting her hands up.

"You're wearing my face."

Really, of all the things to say?

"It confuses him. He doesn't understand, thinks there's just something wrong with the code. Please, Nell. I need your help."

"I got that much, and it's Sapphi. How did you get in here? What is Yasu doing?"

"It's a long story." The woman who was and wasn't her waved her hand with a casual dismissal that was frankly a little terrifying. "Where else can we talk? Is there somewhere safe?"

"I just left you a message in the fountain."

"The fountain." Other her laughed. "Oh, clever. What does it say?"

"It's a meeting location and time." Sapphi held out her hand. "And apparently the fountain thing was a waste of a good idea."

"It is pretty. I like it." She nodded. "I will meet you there; it will maybe be enough to keep you safe from him."

"Who is 'him'? Yasu? And can you tell me where you are?" Sapphi asked. "We could just come to you in person instead."

The smile on her face was filled with sadness. "No, not Yasu. He's—it's too complicated. I can't tell you right now. And you coming here is too dangerous. You can't risk it. Stay far, far away from me, Sapphi. I can see the echoes of my mother in you and I do not want to bring this wrath down upon you."

What does *that* mean? "That would make two of us."

"I will see you after the Games."

Before Sapphi could ask her anything else, Pirene was gone.

"I'm supposed to follow orders."

"Well, yeah," Jenks replied, staring at the ceiling. "So am I." Her grin was quick and sharp, and Doge cataloged it as matching a previous expression she'd given him along with the dictionary definition of "mischievous."

He'd only known her for a year, but "showing a fondness for causing trouble in a playful way" seemed like a very good definition for Jenks.

"The trick, Doge, is figuring out when the orders matter. Because sometimes they do. Sometimes you have to trust this." She tapped her chest.

"Your boobs?"

Her laughter was low, dissolving into giggles as she slid off the bunk and leaned on him. "Oh shit, why did I teach you that word?" she wheezed.

"You like them."

"I do." More giggling and she rested her head against his. "I meant you have to trust your heart, though."

"I don't have a heart."

"Of course you do. It's not quite the same as mine, but that doesn't matter when it comes to feelings."

He was unsure how to catalog the process that started and filed it away for future reference.

TWENTY-FIVE

Trappist System

Jenks hummed to herself as she scrubbed away, her brain occupied with the Verge meeting Sapphi had had with Pirene and just how they could have gotten through Sapphi's defensive shield on her house.

It shouldn't have been possible and a look at it after Sapphi had logged out didn't show any penetration attempts. It was as if the barrier hadn't existed at all. That was worrisome. So was the apparent waffling by Pirene about Yasu's involvement. That is, if you believed her denial.

Jenks, as a rule, didn't.

If it walks into secure quarters like a duck . . .

"Jenks?"

She glanced over her shoulder at Doge. "Yeah?"

"Chae is on the rotation for cleaning the head, so why are you doing it?"

Jenks laughed and rocked back on her heels. "You were there at lunch. Their habitat wanted to do a little good luck party this afternoon for the Games. I didn't have anything else to do today, so I said I'd do it."

"But you hate this."

"Sure I do." She finished the job and got to her feet, stripping off her gloves and tossing them into the sanitizer with the brush to clean before turning to look at her dog.

"Is this because you're a chief now?"

"In part, I suppose." She cleaned her hands and arms off. "I'd have done it regardless, though. Sometimes it's nice to help people out."

"Even when it's things you don't want to do."

"Even then."

"You are more responsible than you used to be."

She had no idea why that quiet declaration filled her with a ridiculous amount of pride. It wasn't the first time she'd heard it in the last few years. Nika had praised her both in public and in private. Others had done the same.

Apparently it means even more when my dog says it.

"Don't I know it. But thanks for noticing, buddy." She headed out into the corridor and back toward the galley. Doge followed.

"Are you and Luis and Tivo going to have a baby?"

The image that question put in her head made Jenks trip over her own feet in shock. She barely caught herself on the doorframe and choked back the stunned laughter. "I'm sorry, *what*?"

Doge didn't have expressions, but the ROVER tilted his head to the side and long experience told her that he was curious. "It seems like a natural next step, but the question has confused you. Or surprised you? Or . . . excited you? I don't understand your expression and your readings right now."

She sank to the floor with a hand pressed to her mouth, still trying to keep her giggles contained and failing miserably. She gestured at Doge with her free hand and the dog crept closer until Jenks could wrap her arm around his neck.

"Your reaction is worrisome," he said.

"I'm sorry, you really surprised me." Confident she had herself under control, Jenks pressed her forehead to his. "That's not the kind of question you ask out of the blue, buddy."

"It wasn't out of the blue. We were talking about you being responsible. Responsible people are parents."

"Some irresponsible people are parents, too," she said softly, unable to stop the swell of hurt that rushed up in her chest. Or the doubt that blindsided her out of nowhere.

Nobody in their right mind would trust me with a baby.

"Now I upset you."

"No, that's an old emotion, buddy." She forced a smile, even though he could probably see the difference between that and a real one very easily. "Being responsible at my job is worlds away from the sort of big decision you're asking about. Besides, the three of us haven't talked about it at all. I'm not even sure where to start that conversation."

"I could ask them."

"Oh, don't you dare." She laughed as she grabbed his face. "I'm serious, doggo. That's not a subject you need to stick your metal nose into." She kissed said nose with a loud smack. "Maybe we'll talk about it at some point but not right now."

"Everything okay here?" Max asked as she poked her head around the corner.

"Yeah," Jenks replied, holding her hand up. Max helped her to her feet. "Doge was just making my brain work overtime by asking me the complex questions."

"I was only curious if she was having a baby," Doge said, actually sounding sullen.

Max's choked gasp was worth it, though, and Jenks grinned despite the embarrassment. "The answer is no and this conversation doesn't leave the ship. Understood?"

"What's it worth to you?" Max replied with a wicked look of her own and Jenks didn't have words for the relief that everything seemed to be okay between them once again.

"Don't you have somewhere else to be?" she demanded.

Max pretended to think it over. "I'm meeting D'Arcy for a

sparring match in an hour. Until then I thought I'd see if you needed help with anything on *Zuma*."

"Unfortunately I just cleaned the head or I'd make you do it, but let me see if I can find something equally horrible for you to work on."

"YOU'RE LATE."

"Sorry, I was helping Jenks swap O_2 filters on *Zuma* and lost track of time," Max said to D'Arcy as she shook out her wraps.

"She's never going to let the mechanics take over and do all the work, is she?" he asked.

"It's highly unlikely. I spotted your master chief crawling around under *Dread* the other day, so Jenks isn't the only one, it seems."

"Emel said she wanted to get to know the ship better. I wasn't going to stop her. Not with that wrench in her hand." D'Arcy settled onto the bench as Max finished. "You doing okay?"

It wasn't that she didn't trust D'Arcy, but Max had already decided not to tell anyone but Nika and Jenks about her thrown fight. They'd agreed it was for the best. "I talked with Jenks about my worries regarding the Games, and it helped. My family is still, well, themselves." She sighed. "I am about to either do something very smart or very dangerous."

She hadn't shared in detail the letter she was drafting to her parents, but she had given Nika permission to fill Stephan and a few others in on the details of what was happening.

"Your family is afraid of you."

"I highly doubt it." Max scoffed and lifted her hands, waiting for D'Arcy to make the first move.

He studied her for a long moment. "They should be. Honestly, I'm stuck on if it's a good thing that you don't seem to understand the kind of power you wield or if it's holding you back."

She wasn't sure what to make of that, but the punch he

threw was right on the heels of his sentence and didn't leave her a lot of time to ponder it. Max blocked his jab, stepping in to meet him before he could throw the expected follow-up kick. She loved sparring with D'Arcy. He was a few centimeters shorter than she was, but his sheer mass made it exciting.

And he was mostly unpredictable, especially now that he knew her well enough to have figured out her own flaws. Often the only difference between hand-to-hand and sword fighting with him was the addition of the weapon. Which definitely made things more interesting, but Max wasn't so foolish as to think D'Arcy was any less lethal empty-handed.

They fought in silence for several minutes, separating on an unspoken agreement and heading to the bench for water.

"Most of my life I felt like I didn't have any power," Max said, wiping the sweat from her face with a towel. "Joining the NeoG was a momentary peek at what I could do, but it cost me so much, I don't think I could really appreciate it at the time."

"Did they actually leave you on the street?"

"Close—in a restaurant." Max felt a warmth in her chest at D'Arcy's sudden flat look. "It's history and best left there. I learned a good lesson then about always having access to an account of my own. Not to mention the kindness of strangers. Our waiter paid for a room for me that night out of their own pocket. I came back a few months later once I had access to my money again while I was on leave from the academy and tried to pay them back. Brooks, the waiter, refused and said I needed to just keep proving my family wrong. We still email occasionally." She grinned. "Their partner had a baby last year. I set up an account for them. Brooks yelled at me, but what am I going to do with the money? I don't need it."

"I have a sudden need to hug you, if you're amenable." D'Arcy held open his arms and she stepped into them with a laugh. "You're a deeply decent human being, Maxine Carmichael," he murmured. "Don't ever change."

"Back at you, even though you try to pretend otherwise."

"No." He let her go with a shake of his head. "I'm, at best, attempting to live up to your example, which is difficult."

"I think you're doing a great job, and I'm not the only one," Max said. "Another round or two?"

"Sure, it'll give you time to tell me what you're planning to do when you take Jenks on in the cage next week."

Max had been expecting the subject change. If she were being honest with herself, she'd asked D'Arcy to spar for precisely that reason.

"I'm not planning anything," she admitted.

"You'll get your ass kicked, Carmichael, without a plan. And if you don't bring it, Jenks will be offended."

"I know. We've already talked about it." Max threw a quick combination of punches at him, watching D'Arcy effortlessly block and weave out of the way. "What I mean is, I don't *know* how to beat her. I don't care about winning as much as I want—" She spotted his move, blocked the punch, and swept his forward leg out of the way. D'Arcy hit the mat hard but had the presence of mind to grab for Max's arm and take her down with him.

She'd seen this scenario plenty of times; it was one of Jenks's favorites. Though the much shorter chief had to use her superior strength and some rather creative moves to get her opponent into position for a choke hold.

This time Max let D'Arcy's momentum carry her over the top and, rather than resist him, she went boneless, sliding out of his grip. She rolled onto her left shoulder, grabbing for his throat with her left hand and feeling his start of surprise when she made contact.

It was too late for him to get out of the hold; Max already had his left arm pinned under her knee and she used his burst of movement against him. She slipped behind him and locked her arm down over his throat.

D'Arcy tapped out and Max released him. "Don't care about winning, huh? You could have fooled me. Nice one, Lieutenant."

Max echoed his deep laugh, lying down on the mat next to him. "I was saying I don't care about winning as much as I want the match to be good. Jenks said the other day she expects me to try to beat her, but she's not going to make it easy for me."

"She won't, and she's going to take this to the ground every chance she gets. That's her advantage."

"She also said I couldn't beat her if she had one arm tied behind her back and I'll be honest, that sort of makes me want to win." Max rubbed both hands over her face and groaned. "I know she said it for that exact reason, but now it's stuck in my head. Advice?"

"You are as good as she is when you believe it. You've got the reach on her and if you can move faster than her on that move, you'll probably get her before she gets you. Plus you deliberately going to the mat will shock the shit out of her." He patted her shoulder as he sat up. "You'd better have at least three other plans, though, unless you think you can take her down in the first round."

"I know." Max got to her feet and offered him a hand, hauling him upright. "Thanks, D'Arcy."

"Anytime."

TWENTY-SIX

Sol System

The pre-Games interviews hadn't gotten any easier for Max over the last few years. The lie of repetition erasing anxiety had been at the forefront of her mind as they'd landed *Zuma* and descended into the maelstrom of press outside the hangar.

Nika had cleared the space in front of them and even Jenks had just grinned and waved to the reporters without stopping as the team had made their way to the transport that took them to their quarters in the village.

Max appreciated the interference, though surprisingly she'd felt some urge to stop and answer at least one of the shouted questions floating on the air about the situation with her family. But they'd decided as a team that the best way to handle everything was at the formal interviews.

"You doing all right?" Jenks asked, joining her in the alcove just off the room set up for the press conference.

"I am," she replied, reaching out and brushing a piece of lint off Jenks's collar. "You?"

"A little nervous, if you can believe it." Jenks stared out at the reporters in the main room. "Not that their reaction will change our decision at all. It's just . . . strange, I guess. I don't really have words for it."

"I get that. This is the end of a long run for you. Sorry you're going out on a loss."

Jenks's startled laughter drew the attention of the room, competing with the announcement of their team, and Max felt an unexpected well of joy in her chest as she followed Nika and Vera up onto the stage. Silence fell as they got settled into their chairs and then the noise exploded as reporters thrust their arms into the air and shouted questions.

"Commander Till, what's it like to be back here once again defending your championship?"

"Jenks! Are you ready to go up against Max in the cage?"

"Sapphi, we know you keep your predictions under wraps, but what are your thoughts on the new Navy team? Are they going to cause the Neos any trouble?"

"Is there any truth to the rumors that this is *Zuma's* last Games?"

Nika put up his hand and the questions stalled as he looked over the crowd with that patient expression of his. "First things first—thank you, everyone, for being here today. We're all very excited and looking forward to the Boarding Games. Yes, *Zuma's Ghost* is taking a break from the Games after this year. We've decided as a team to return our focus one hundred percent to our jobs. We also figured maybe it was time to cut everyone else a break and let someone else win for a while."

Laughter filled the air and he pointed at a reporter in the front row.

"Commander Vagin, how are you and the other sword fighters feeling about your matches?"

Max settled back in her chair as Nika and the others fielded the question and the interviews fell into a familiar pattern. She answered a few queries directed her way along with Chae and *Flux's* piloting team of Xin and Atlas, and laughed when Sapphi and Saad claimed they were ready for anything the hacking comp programmers had planned for them.

"Have we been beaten yet?" Sapphi replied with a wink at the young reporter. "Then that scenario is highly unlikely to happen this time around, either. All shade to our fellow competitors, Saad or I could beat them in our sleep."

When the laughter had died down, Nika pointed at another raised hand and the reporter stood. "Kia Hozen for TSN. Max, how are you feeling about the expected match between you and Jenks?"

"Well, we'll have to get to the match first," Max replied. "If that happens, I expect the crowd will be in for quite a show."

"The LT is being humble. When it happens, you'll all get to see me kick her ass," Jenks said with a wicked grin.

Max felt that same flutter of hesitation that had plagued her at the prelims, but this time she stepped on it and favored the crowd with a sly look of her own. "While I always value my chief's optimistic outlook on life, I suspect this time she may be in for a disappointment when I hand her her first official loss at the Games in front of a system-wide audience." She dropped an eyelid in a slow wink at the reporters, knowing that a number of them would capture it in a photo.

Jenks's shout of mock outrage was followed by laughter and after that the interviews dissolved into poorly controlled chaos until Nika and Vera ushered all of them back off the stage.

"I may have created a monster," Jenks admitted as she looped her arm around Max's waist and steered them past the Navy team waiting in the wings.

Max didn't respond immediately, meeting the starry-eyed gaze of a young enby lieutenant by the name of Zoe Dresen on their way by. The Navy team was completely new and all of them looked more than a little uncertain, nothing at all like Scott's team had been during her first Games. Max already knew she was going to face this lieutenant in the first round, so she reached out a hand to get their attention, remembering how nervous she'd been. "Take a breath, Lieutenant Dresen. You'll do fine."

"Yes, ma'am."

They said it breathlessly.

JENKS WONDERED IF MAX EVEN REALIZED THE EFFECT SHE'D had on the somewhat awestruck Navy crews they'd passed at the interviews earlier in the day or just how much things had shifted since she'd arrived on the Games scene. She suspected the answer was no, especially based on how utterly unaware Max was sitting in their customary claimed seats at Drinking Games.

The bar was predictably full for the first official night, but it felt lighter and there was more laughter on the air. The mood was different.

Or maybe she was.

"Casper." Jenks leaned on the wide bar and greeted the murderous-looking owner as he served drinks. "Beer me."

"My darling Leeroy, don't start a fight at my bar this early," he replied, blowing her a kiss as he turned from the vaguely familiar brunette on her right.

Jenks realized why when the woman's handshake flashed into view. Chief Petty Officer Naina Mehta was part of the new Navy team, a good pilot according to Chae, and one of their cage fighters.

"No plans on it, unless I have to bail Max out. Evening, Chief, buy you a drink?" Jenks loved the flash of surprise in the woman's dark eyes.

"I didn't think—" She stopped, so clearly flustered that Jenks couldn't stop her laugh of delight.

"That I'd know who my competition was? Or that I'd bother speaking to you Navy scum?" she said, laughing more. "Feuds are boring. Drinks are fun." She ignored Casper raising his eyebrow with the pair of silver rings through it and held out her fist to the senior NCO. "Chief Petty Officer Altandai Khan, NeoG. Welcome to the Games."

"I know who you are. Everyone does." Naina smiled and tapped her fist to Jenks's, though she looked around warily afterward. "Am I being set up for something?"

"Being kissed breathless in a corner later, but only if you're willing," Jenks teased, pleased when the woman's brown cheeks flushed. "More seriously, I'm in a good mood and I'd rather stay that way than waste our time with fighting. At least until the Games start." She winked and took the beer Casper slid her way.

"Someone told me Jenks was over here flirting with Navy and I said that was a load of horseshit, but now I'm out fifty feds."

Jenks turned and smiled up at the slender Marine with a shaved and tattooed head. "Someone told me they'd never get promoted and I said that was a load of horseshit. Also, I believe you owe *me* fifty feds. Hey, gorgeous. Congratulations."

Staff Sergeant Flynn Candance beamed as they leaned in for a kiss. "You're changing the subject," they murmured before turning to Naina and introducing themself. "If you need me to rescue you, Chief, just say the word. Or blink twice."

"Don't think I won't call Max over here to body-slam you again, Candy," Jenks warned. "Ignore them, Naina."

The Marine batted their eyelashes. "You say the sweetest things. Hey, Casper, can I get a Box of Crayons?"

"Don't ask," Jenks whispered loudly as Casper laughed and built a brightly colored concoction that he then slid across the bar to Candy. "This one is weird, even for a Marine."

"What am I going to do without you here?" Candy asked in her ear and Jenks felt her heart wobble in reply.

"I'm not leaving for good, goose. Just taking a break." She kissed them. "I guess that means you have to come and visit us on Trappist."

Others filtered over as the crowd continued to grow. Naina stayed to chat for almost half an hour before retreating upstairs and Jenks used that as an opportunity to head back toward the NeoG's corner. She paused along the way and watched the crowded dance floor, surprised by the wave of bittersweet longing that swept through her. This had been her life for so long; it was hard to imagine this time next year she wouldn't be here. Wouldn't be competing.

Did I make a mistake suggesting we take a break?

"Hey, you." Tien slipped an arm around Jenks's waist. "Why are you standing here looking like you're saying goodbye?"

"I don't know." Jenks sighed and leaned into the woman's embrace. "It feels a bit like goodbye, doesn't it?"

"You'll be back, Khan," she replied. The certainty in her voice was solid as a rock. "The rest will be good for you all, but you'll be back."

"I don't know why I'm being so maudlin," Jenks murmured.

"You want a distraction?" Tien looked down at her with a devilish spark in her eyes. "I can drag you back to my room."

Jenks laughed and stretched up to kiss the woman lightly. "I might consider it. Let's go back to the table first so Nika doesn't think I've vanished."

They were greeted with cheers and raised glasses as they rejoined the Neos. Jenks settled onto the bench next to her brother.

"You all right?" he asked softly.

"I am," she replied, and meant it.

TWENTY-SEVEN

Trappist System

"And that's sector two-oh-three cleared." D'Arcy leaned back in his seat and rubbed both hands over his face with an exhale. They'd headed for the belt the day after the other two Interceptor teams had left for Earth and had been out here for almost a week with nothing more interesting than a few asteroids.

"Logged it," Heli replied. "Do you want me to start the next one?"

"Let's take a break," he decided with a shake of his head. "Does anyone else want coffee?"

The murmured assents from both Heli and Emel followed him as he headed off the bridge and into the galley.

Their slow, methodical search through the sectors Sapphi had tagged for them before she left for the Games wasn't glamorous work—it was, in fact, exhausting and tedious—but D'Arcy was finding it oddly soothing.

Dread was quiet. Locke, Aki, and Lupe were asleep and would be for another two hours. The days had passed in a blessed blur of routine, the scans interspersed with team-building and training.

He'd be lying to himself if he claimed part of him didn't desperately wish they were on Earth, competing in the Games with the others. The news that filtered in yesterday from the Trappist Relay showed the NeoG team's first day had been filled with victories across the board. D'Arcy was pleased, even in the midst of his own longing.

He carried the three cups back to the bridge, handing them carefully over before sinking into his chair. The warmth soaked into his hands as he stared out into the black.

"I don't know that I'll ever get over how much endless nothing there is out here," Emel murmured as she got up and crossed to D'Arcy's side. "You think you understand it until you actually see it."

"I never wanted to be anywhere but here."

D'Arcy glanced over at Heli's quiet confession and they smiled at him before looking back out the window.

"My parents wanted me to do something respectable. They were so happy when the Naval Academy rejected my application. My scores weren't good enough—by ten points." Their expression morphed from sad to mischievous in a heartbeat. "I hadn't told them I'd applied to the NeoG also just in case."

"Thank god our standards are lower," D'Arcy teased.

"Better, I think," Heli replied after a moment. "Nothing against you, Emel, but I think the NeoG's standards are more focused on what could make a good team rather than just the numbers."

D'Arcy had a hard time believing the ensign's scores hadn't been good enough for the Navy. Heli was bright and whip-smart. Their confidence had been growing in leaps and bounds over the last few weeks and it was a wonderful thing to see. Historically the Navy was tightfisted about their acceptance rate, though in his opinion it just led to them missing out on people like Heli.

Emel laughed. "I'm only wondering how much longer I have before people finally stop apologizing to me before talking shit about the Navy."

"At least a year, probably two," D'Arcy replied. "We will, however, never stop actually giving you shit for being Navy."

"Hush, you. I—"

The com crackled to life, cutting Emel off.

"Mayday, mayday, mayday. This is pilot Jasper Smith-Greenfield, Rainbow Glass Tourism vessel number seventy-three requesting immediate assistance from any ships in the vicinity. Repeat—"

"Jasper, this is Commander D'Arcy Montaglione with the NeoG Interceptor *Dread Treasure*. What's your location and trouble?" D'Arcy gestured at Emel, but she was already headed for the stairs to wake the rest of the crew.

"Oh, thank god," the person on the other end said. "Commander, we experienced an unexplained engine failure about half an hour ago and everything went down. I mean everything. No engine, life support, coms, etc. I've got the backup power working, sending our location now. There's a group of twenty schoolkids on my ship, so it is really good to hear your voice."

"We've got a lock on your signal and we're headed your way. Go ahead and shut your coms down to conserve power; turn them back on again in ten minutes and check in with me." D'Arcy could hear Heli relaying information over the com to *Wandering Hunter* as he talked the pilot through the emergency procedure.

They were a solid twenty minutes out from the ship and D'Arcy wondered what they were doing so far out into the belt. He also couldn't help but remember the ambush of the mystery distress call, even though this time he'd talked to a live person and nothing about Jasper's responses had seemed out of place.

That other distress call had used my ship name just like a live person would.

"What's up?" Locke asked, shrugging into his duty jacket and combing both hands through his messy brown hair.

"Tourist ship with an unexplained engine failure. Maybe."

"Commander Forsberg said she's on an intercept path with us and will hang back as far as you'd like to keep an eye on things," Heli said. "I also called it in to Trappist Relay. They're scrambling some ships, but it's going to be an hour before the closest ones get to us."

"That's all right. We've got a couple of options depending on what they need. Locke, take over flying for me." He swapped the Interceptor to auto before he slid out of the seat.

"I pulled the registry from Rainbow Glass Tourism," Heli said, pointing at the console on the wall near them. "All the info checks out on that end. Vessel seventy-three left Trappist-1e early this morning for a day trip out to the asteroid belt for students from the Mary W. Jackson Middle School. Pilot is confirmed as Jasper Smith-Greenfield, he/him."

That news made him relax just a little.

"Save some work for the rest of us, Heli," D'Arcy replied. Then he patted the ensign on the shoulder. "Good job."

They beamed. "Thank you, sir."

"Did you pull schematics for the ship?" Emel asked.

"Next page, Master Chief."

Emel drank the rest of her coffee as she studied the engine of the small Lock-Dhruva-made ship. They were designed for planet hopping, not interstellar travel, and their engines were normally solidly dependable.

"Thoughts?" D'Arcy asked. He hadn't moved away from where he was standing behind Heli, and his hand was still resting on their shoulder.

"It could be a few things. I won't really know until we get on board. The fact that they still have backup power and emergency coms rules out some of the worse options, maybe? I might be able to fix it and then the other ships could escort them back." She made a face. "I don't like that I'm wary about this. We're supposed to be helping people, but I'm thinking about that distress call."

"You're not the only one. We'll go in careful. Trappist Relay will send something big enough to cart it home regardless, but let's see if we can at least get them back up and running. We can hook up here." He flipped screens and tapped the main airlock. "Give them some extra air. Locke and the others can help settle the kids while you and I take a look at the engine."

"Is this payback for the last one?" Locke asked over his shoulder.

"You deserve it."

"I hate you." Locke was laughing as he said it.

"I love you, too. Let's get moving, people. We've got twelve minutes until we reach the ship."

THEY'D SUITED UP TO BOARD THE RAINBOW SHIP, BUT ON D'Arcy's order kept the helmets down and swords stowed.

Emel realized why D'Arcy had taken the risk when she saw the wide-eyed stares of the kids as D'Arcy greeted both Jasper and the teachers, a dark-haired young person by the name of Rey who was doing a reasonably good job keeping their own panic hidden and an only slightly more put-together young woman named Tara. Emel caught a flash of her true emotions—expertly concealed worry—in her brown eyes, and offered up her most reassuring nod.

She did her best to hide her own relief that this was real.

"Lieutenant Commander Locke and the rest of my crew will get you all settled on the Interceptor while the Master Chief and I take a look at your engine. If we can't get you up and running again, there's some help already en route."

"I'll show you where it is," Jasper said as Locke and the others greeted the students and escorted them from the tourist ship to *Dread*. He glanced over his shoulder as the last of them disappeared off the ship. "Commander, I didn't want to say anything in front of the kids. They were doing a good job holding it together, but I think you should know something weird is going on. Or I'm losing my grip on reality."

"What is it?" D'Arcy's voice was calm, but Emel had seen his fingers twitch as if he'd suppressed the same desire to reach for the sword on his back that she had.

"When we lost power, there was . . . music on the coms and I'd caught a flash of something on the scanners before everything went down."

"What sort of something?"

"I don't know? Could have been a ship? Or just debris big enough to catch the sensors. We were out here looking for an asteroid to scan for their class project, so I had everything set pretty high. When things came back up, it was gone, but it's company policy for us to have our DD chip set on auto record for trips, so I can show you the image."

"Clip the file and I'll give you Petty Officer Garcia's contact information. He can take a look at it."

"What was the music?" Emel asked as Jasper came to a stop at the door marked ENGINE ROOM, AUTHORIZED PERSONNEL ONLY. They swiped a hand over the panel and it opened.

"I don't know? Creepy as fuck?" Jasper hummed a little and Emel frowned. The tune was familiar, but recognition danced on the edges of her brain, falling away as she stepped into the engine room and popped the access panel.

"D'ARCY, WE'VE GOT A HIT ON THAT SIGNAL THE PILOT SAW," Pia said over the Neos' main com about an hour later while Emel was head-deep in the confusing issue of an apparently dead engine with no obvious cause. "It's a ways into the belt. Possible match for *The Red Cow*. We could go check it out while you wait here?"

She shifted out from the access panel. D'Arcy had sent Jasper back to *Dread* and was leaning against the doorway with a frown on his face.

"No," he said finally, looking down at her and offering a hand. "The CHNS *Leonard Nimoy* and Tow Ship 483 are only ten minutes out. I don't want to do anything to put these kids at risk."

"This ship is dead in the black," Emel said as she took D'Arcy's offered hand and got to her feet. "I have no idea why, because there's no visible damage. Only that everything I've tried won't bring her back up. I'm not even sure why anything else is functioning, because by all rights it shouldn't be."

Unease lanced through her as the reports from the *Imogene Darver*'s recovery flashed back into her head. The same wasted engine. An empty ship. "D'Arcy, I think we should get out of here."

"Yeah." The muscle at the side of D'Arcy's jaw flexed. "We'll head back to meet the other ships, get everyone loaded over to the *Nimoy*, and they can head back. Then we'll both go take a look at the signal." His next words were for the main com. "Pia, do a wider sweep of the area."

"Roger that," Commander Forsberg replied.

The ship lurched suddenly, throwing Emel into D'Arcy, and alarms blared. He cursed, catching her at the waist and holding her steady as she got her feet situated.

"Status report!" D'Arcy snapped, releasing Emel and ducking through the doorway. He headed for the airlock in a ground-eating stride.

Emel sprinted behind him as the com went down. She'd slapped the helmet release as soon as she'd righted herself and the new tech flowed around her head, solidifying into a clear bubble. That five second delay seemed like an eternity before her com came back to life.

"Locke!" Heli's call over the com was sharp with fear and followed almost immediately by the sounds of children screaming.

"Commander, Jasper just bashed Lupe in the head and tried to detach *Dread* from the— Get off me!" Aki snapped. The ship lurched again and Emel's gut twisted in the same fashion as the floor beneath their feet where the two ships were connected. The screech of metal under stress was loud enough to be heard even with the helmets.

Emel grabbed for D'Arcy's arm as they hit the Interceptor's airlock, slapping the door control closed. It slid shut a split second before the two ships ripped free of each other and for a heart-stopping moment she thought that *Dread*'s outer hull wouldn't hold.

But it did and Emel peeled her hand off the bar by D'Arcy's head with an exhale.

"D'Arcy, what the fuck is going on over there?" Pia demanded.

"I don't know, but Emel and I are both safely on *Dread*," he replied. "Outer door of the airlock is holding. I don't know what kind of damage there is." He moved as he spoke, heading for the bridge. "You watch for an attack, Pia. Anything at all."

Emel ran for the galley.

She retracted her helmet and took in the scene in *Dread*'s galley with one sweep of her head: Rey was in one corner, standing in front of as many sobbing children as they could cover. More were on the far side of the table, pressed against the wall. Tara was on the opposite side, her hands in the air and a wild, terrified look on her pale face. Heli stood over Locke, her sword out, and while her eyes were also terrified, her hands were steady.

"Sitrep, Ensign."

"Tara attacked Locke with a pan, Master Chief." Heli tipped her head toward the floor between them where the weapon lay.

"I didn't—" the woman protested.

"We saw you!" Rey interrupted, and the children responded to the fear in their voice with cries.

"If everyone would be quiet for me," Emel said in her best mom voice as she rested a hand on Heli's sword arm. "Check on Locke," she ordered.

The chaos morphed into almost silence, broken only by the muffled crying of both the children and the teachers.

"Tara, I'm going to ask you to take two steps toward me, keeping your hands right where they are. There's a doorway on your left if you'll step through it into the corridor."

Emel was all too aware of the eyes on her as she moved toward the door with Tara and she prayed she wouldn't have to draw her own sword in front of all these children or, worse, use it. "D'Arcy, we've got things under control in the galley for the moment. Locke took a pan to the face. I could use someone to give Heli a hand." She glanced back at Heli.

The ensign was helping a groggy Locke into a seated position, and if the side of his face was any indication, he probably had a massive headache and was going to be sporting a wicked bruise soon.

"Aki's on her way. Lupe's dazed but awake." D'Arcy paused. "I can't leave him alone on the bridge. *Hunter* is coming around to the other airlock to hook on."

Emel turned into the corridor and dropped her voice. "I'm taking Tara to the brig so we can talk. I'll come up for Jasper when I can."

"Roger that. Be careful."

"You too." Emel reached out and took Tara gently by the upper arm. The young woman was weeping silently and allowed herself to be propelled without resisting into the brig. "Take a seat and tell me what happened."

"I don't know."

"You attacked an officer of the Near-Earth Orbital Guard, Tara. Were you trying to take over the ship?" Emel stared at her flatly and bright spots of color appeared on Tara's cheeks.

"I swear! I don't know what's going on. I don't know who you are or how we got here. The last thing I remember is being on the tour ship with the kids. We were scanning for asteroids and the power went out. Then I woke up to the kids screaming and someone pointing a sword at me." She dropped her face into her hands and started sobbing again.

"All right. Sit down. Keep your hands in your lap. I'll be

right back." Emel waited until the woman was seated on the bench in the cell before keying shut the door. Someone was responsible for her injured crew and Emel was going to find out who. She packed the fury at that away to be dealt with later and hurried back down the corridor to the bridge.

TWENTY-EIGHT

Trappist System

"Nothing." Stephan shook his head and D'Arcy remained silent as the Intel chief got out of his chair to pace the room. "We pulled full backgrounds on both Jasper and Tara. There's nothing. No financial trouble. No involvement with any criminal groups. No reason at all either would have to attack you both and hijack the ship."

"Who hijacks a ship with a bunch of kids in tow anyway?" Locke muttered from the other side of the table. The right side of his face was mostly purple, an impressive bruise that stretched from his eye to his jaw. Thankfully no bones were broken, but he was in obvious pain and D'Arcy had been warned to watch for concussion symptoms on both of his crew.

Surprisingly, he wasn't feeling any of his usual guilt about these two being injured. He knew there hadn't been anything he could have done to prevent it and everyone had done exactly what needed doing when the shit had hit the fan.

"Neither of them remember anything beyond the power going down on the ship," Emel said.

"They're lying." Pia shrugged a shoulder. "That's pretty obvious."

"Why, though?" Emel countered. "Tara was hysterically upset at the idea that she'd hurt someone. Even her co-teacher who watched it happen said they'd never seen Tara so much as raise her voice at anyone and they'd been teaching together for almost five years. Why send two relatively incompetent hijackers up against two teams of Interceptors?"

"They were going to use the kids as hostages." D'Arcy lifted a hand at Emel's hot look. "I'm just saying, it's probably what the plan was, and as weird as it all seems, maybe they were hoping to do it more quietly but are using the amnesia card since it didn't go all that well."

"I don't believe it."

D'Arcy recognized that set of her jaw and held up a hand before anyone else could challenge Emel. "What is it?"

"We just spent the last hour going over why those two attacking us doesn't make any sense. There's no reason for it. We can't find any change in their behavior at all in the days before the trip. But we're still focused on running with the idea that *they're* responsible."

"All due respect, Master Chief, she did hit me," Locke said. "I saw it happen, sort of; and Jasper hit Lupe. Plus he almost decompressed the ship, and without your packs both you and the commander would have been in trouble."

"I know—I'm not discounting *what* happened. What I'm saying is we don't know *why* and, moreover, we're not asking the big question."

"Which is what?" D'Arcy prompted, and Emel looked at him.

"What took out their ship in the first place?" Emel let the moment of silence hang in the air before she continued. "I looked at that engine: It was pristine. No fire. No damage. It was also dead. I confirmed that in my initial test. And I was there this morning when the yardheads were tearing it apart. No sabotage is that clean. It looked like the report from the *Darver*." She took a breath and D'Arcy had a feeling he wasn't going to like her next words. "It looked like it got hit by an EMP."

Yeah, don't like that.

"EMPs wouldn't have left everything else functional, Emel."

"You think I don't know that?" she snapped at him, and then shook her head. "Sorry. This bothers me. It's wrong. *All* wrong."

D'Arcy thought inexplicably of Chae and how the Neo had made the worst sort of choice because they'd had no options left to them. "It's all right and I agree with you. We don't have a good answer for this single incident, so we're going with the easy one. There are a lot of other things to consider here and we probably need to look at the bigger picture." He glanced Stephan's way and the man made a face.

"I can't hold either of them right now unless you two want to press assault charges," Stephan said. "Rainbow is cooperating about the ship, but that could change at any point."

D'Arcy looked Locke's way and the man sighed. "You know I won't. I'll be fine and I'm not going to mess up her life over a pan to the face." He shook his head. "Unless we come up with something malicious behind all this, I can't justify pressing charges. I agree with Emel's assessment of it all. Something doesn't add up here." He hesitated and then looked at D'Arcy. "It feels like we're being hunted."

D'Arcy didn't like that, either, but he couldn't disagree.

"I feel the same way," Lupe said. "Let's keep digging and maybe we'll find it."

"*We're* going to keep digging. You two are going back to quarters to rest," D'Arcy said. "Don't argue with me. You're off duty until medical says otherwise." Locke and Lupe both dragged in breaths to protest and he leveled a flat stare until they clamped their mouths shut with identical nods. "Go on. I'll check in on you in a few."

D'Arcy watched the pair head out the door, looking away when Emel joined him. "They'll be all right," she said.

"I know. You all did good." The praise came easier than he'd thought it would and he hoped Emel could see the truth of it in his eyes. They'd stepped up to what could have been a potentially deadly situation and emerged—not unscathed, but at least intact. D'Arcy looked Heli's way and pointed a finger at them. "Good job, Heli. You too, Aki."

EMEL WAITED AS THE OTHERS DISPERSED AROUND THE ROOM before she touched D'Arcy's arm and gestured at the far side where Stephan was standing. He followed without question.

She shouldn't be as nervous about this as she was. Everything was aboveboard, just classified, and there was no reason until now for her to mention what her actual job with the Navy was. Stephan likely knew, but she assumed D'Arcy didn't, and in the rush of his praise of the team she was suddenly afraid that this was going to shift the balance back to distrust.

"Before my retirement, I was involved in a Navy project looking at the application of EMPs on DD chips," she said, keeping her voice low enough to not attract the attention of the others in the conference room.

Stephan nodded. D'Arcy frowned.

"We were primarily focused on ways to subdue people without causing any harm. The attack on Jupiter Station happened and we were given access to the data that was gathered in the aftermath. It was a focused EMP designed specifically to impact the frequency the DD chips broadcast on and it looked terrifyingly like the one we'd been working on. It was obvious we'd had a security breach, but we never even considered it could have been Senator Tieg . . ." She trailed off and D'Arcy cursed.

"He had access to your research."

"He was on the funding committee." Emel made a face. "Now that I know about what happened with Tieg here, I can't help but wonder how many of the devices they used on Jupiter

Station are out there. I also wonder if they haven't been modified"—she glanced over her shoulder and lowered her voice even more—"in some fashion to make it possible to control people's behavior."

"It's a theory," Stephan admitted. "Not one with any proof, though, Emel."

"I know. We've got zero evidence for any of it. I just wanted it out in the air, but I also know that it's probably not something that should be floating around for the rumor mill."

Stephan nodded. "You're not wrong. Let me go see what I can dig up on this. I'm assuming you don't have access to the project data any longer?"

"Correct."

"I'll get it for you. I want you to start reading up on it again. Am I also correct in assuming we'd be able to tell if the DD chips were tampered with?"

"Possibly," Emel hedged. "It really just depends on what actually happened."

"All right. Once the other crews are back, we can dig into that more also. Sapphi and Saad will have thoughts on it. In the meantime, we'll see if anything seems to corroborate the civilians' stories about not remembering anything from the power surge to the attack. It doesn't answer the question of why the other teacher and the children weren't involved, but it's a place to start."

"You remember Ollie? He didn't have a DD chip. Rey doesn't have one, either," Emel replied. "They suffered a viral infection as a child and it caused some scarring in key points of their brain. They do have a Babel and a handheld device, but no hardware up here." She tapped at her temple. "The kids are an x factor—I don't know what spared them from the device, if that's what we're dealing with here."

"If I believe this is what we're dealing with, I'm just going to be grateful that they weren't affected." Stephan tapped D'Arcy on the shoulder and left the room.

Emel looked at D'Arcy. He was smiling at her, and she couldn't help but raise an eyebrow in his direction. "What?"

"Thanks for trusting us with that information."

"Of course, it's pertinent to the mission."

"I meant what I said earlier. You did good, Emel. Wrangling a bunch of scared kids couldn't have been easy. Thank you."

"I didn't do much more than use my mom voice," she said, relieved he didn't seem to be the least bit angry about her confession. "Which works wonders in almost all situations, even those not involving kids." Her humor vanished. "Tara was scared, D'Arcy. This isn't just me wanting to see the best in people. I don't think she had any control over what she was doing."

"Jasper was the same way," he admitted. "And if your theory bears out, I don't blame either of them in the slightest. That's not a position we want to be in. DD chips are supposed to be impervious to tampering." He held up a hand and pointed across the room. "Which reminds me, we need to get you and Heli with Pavel. He should have the defense program Sapphi and some of the others came up with based on the Jupiter EMP. It will at least protect your chips against that particular blast."

She heard the *I hope* that D'Arcy didn't allow himself to say out loud. "I'll talk to him here in a few." He was about to walk away when she said, "You did good out there, too, D'Arcy. Don't forget that."

"That means a lot, Emel, thanks."

"You know, Barnes, every year I come into these Games expecting to be entertained and somehow every year I am also shocked and delighted by the extent to which these amazing participants exceed my expectations."

"I hear you, Pace. This year, our one hundred and fifth Games, is no different. We are well underway in our third day of events and so far we have seen the NeoG team made up of *Zuma's Ghost* and *Flux Capacitor* dominate their competition. Normally I'd be the first one to worry about returning champions just going through the motions, but it appears that even though this is—apparently—*Zuma's* last Games for an undetermined amount of time, they came to finish things with a bang and are angling for a fifth win to hang on their belts."

"Apparently indeed—I am trying not to dwell on it too much, but we are going to miss this crew, and I hope that it's just a psychological ploy on their part to put the other branches on their back heels."

"Ha! Wouldn't put that past Jenks."

"Or even Lieutenant Carmichael. Which segues perfectly into my next point, in that I totally agree with you that sometimes seeing the same old faces out there gets a little predictable, but that's not the case in these Games. The Neos aren't just winning, but entertaining, putting on a show for the crowd time and again. I can't recommend enough you all checking out Commander Vagin's amazing sword fight against Captain Jamie Gallagher, Navy's new competitor, from this morning. It will be on replay later this evening."

"I second that recommendation."

"If you keep agreeing with me, people are going to think we're just going through the motions!"

"Good thing they're not here to watch us, then. Instead they're tuning in to see a bracket with five of the six NeoG cage fighters competing in today's third-round matches. Does this mean the semifinals will be an all NeoG show?"

"I don't know about anyone else, but I'm really only watching and hoping for one matchup at the end of this: a *Zuma's Ghost* battle between Lieutenant Max Carmichael and Chief Petty Officer Altandai Khan."

"You are not alone, Pace, I promise. The smack-talking between the members of the NeoG team has been dialed up to eleven since the first official interviews. We are going to have to wait for it, though, but never fear because we've got the championship hacking competition coming up next here on TSN!"

TWENTY-NINE

Sol System

"Oh, come on, Spengler, you can do better than that!" Sapphi snorted as she watched the Marine hacker's attack smash into her shield, disintegrating on contact. "The audience came here for a show and you're putting everyone to sleep."

"Fuck you, Zika." Lieutenant Rela Spengler's curse was filled with laughter over the com.

"We did that. At least, I think we did—I fell asleep then, too." Sapphi watched the clock in the corner of her vision as she taunted the Marine. The remote code exploitation of their perimeter security that Saad had used to gain access at the beginning of this round meant that they had an entry point for their malware. All she had to do was distract them long enough so he could deploy it.

They'd soared through the first round, an easy *Jeopardy*-style capture-the-flag competition. This CTF had required each team to solve at least five of the seven problems and gain the strings of code they'd need for the final round. She and Saad had tackled them easily thanks to hours of training and a lucky guess on Sapphi's part. In the end, they'd solved all seven problems, plus Sapphi had found what she thought might be a bonus line of code showing in the list of running services within the operating system.

This second round pitted the NeoG team against the Marine team in an attack-defend scenario. Technically all Sapphi and Saad had to do was keep the Marines out of their systems for the duration of the fifteen-minute timer. However, they'd decided early in the planning to go for the extra points in this round and wipe out their attackers by also infiltrating their system and burning it to the ground.

"Sapphi, countdown to impact in three, two, one," Saad said over their private com.

She disengaged from the conflict as he released the malware. The sounds of the Marine team's outrage echoed from across the room as their system went down completely and Sapphi's grin wasn't only for the camera. Nor was the fist-bump routine she exchanged with Saad.

"Round two goes to the NeoG!" the Games moderator, Barnabas, announced.

Applause and cheers rang out from the assembled crowd and Sapphi leaned back in her chair. They couldn't quite call this in the bag—not with one more round to go where anything could happen. But she'd be lying if she said she was feeling anything but pretty good about winning this event.

"Sapphi!"

She glanced at the lower-level crowd where her family and part of her team leaned on the railing, spotting Jenks next to Tamago. The chief flashed a hand-sign for "knock-out," grinning despite her freshly split lip, and held up two fingers, jerking her thumb at Vera, who was standing next to her.

Sapphi raised her fist in the air. "Jenks and Vera both got knockouts," she told Saad. "Our numbers just shot through the roof."

"We've still got one more here," he replied as Barnabas raised their hands and the noise in the room slowly faded.

"Competitors, we are moving on to the third and final round here for this championship match if you will proceed over to the virtual reality setup."

Sapphi got up, blowing a kiss at Rela, who flipped her off with a grin as the lieutenant made her way to the Marines' side of the VR room. The rooms were six by six meters square with a treadmill floor to allow for the participants to walk or run and otherwise interact with the virtual world without being impeded by their surroundings.

The tech assisted Sapphi and Saad with the provided haptic jumpers, boots, and gloves, finally sliding on the VR headsets. She gave the tech a thumbs-up and he replied in kind. "Good luck, Ensign," he said before sliding the visor closed.

The world disappeared, sort of. Sapphi frowned at Saad and looked around. They were in the same room, though the crowd and the tech were gone. A red envelope was stuck to the white wall, just underneath a digital clock that read 15:00.

"This is new," she murmured, reaching for the envelope.

A little miniature Barnabas appeared when she opened it. "Greetings, Lieutenant Rahal and Ensign Zika, and welcome to the final round. The rules are simple, though the challenge will hopefully not be. You are looking for three anomalies in the running code of this system. They will provide you with hints to unlock three doors." They held up fingers. "You cannot proceed to the next puzzle without solving the previous one. Each puzzle is different and will require all the skills you have both demonstrated and then some.

"It is important to note that though you are not trying to get to the end before your opponents, but merely to finish before the allotted time, you must finish this together in order to win the competition. It is also important to note that you each only have two lives, so use them wisely."

Sapphi laughed when a bright green number 2 appeared over Saad's head and then looked up to see it above her own also.

"Ah! I see that Ensign Zika was lucky enough to discover the bonus life hidden in the first round," Barnabas said, and the number above Sapphi's head changed to a 3.

Barnabas looked at them and nodded once. "Good luck. The clock is running," they said, and vanished. The red envelope dissolved into red sand, sifting through Sapphi's fingers and falling to the floor.

Nothing else changed except the clock on the wall started counting down. Sapphi frowned at Saad. "How do we get out of here?"

"Good question." He reached out and took her by the arm, walking her back a step. "I don't have an answer for you quite yet, but I'm reasonably sure we shouldn't let that touch us."

The sand was spreading, growing in volume. It took Sapphi less than two seconds to calculate the rate and she muttered a curse. "Exponential increase, Saad. We've got to move."

"Gladly, but we need a way out for that." He'd already pulled up a wrist computer of his own design for the Verge. "Here, look."

She leaned over and watched the code. "Polymorphic?"

"Seems likely. The question is, is the code shifting to hide the door, or is the door itself shifting in and out of existence?"

"Shifting to hide the door," Sapphi said with a shake of her head. "The other is too complex; you'd have to have someone running code for each wall to stay ahead of us." A terrible idea occurred to her. "I'll put feds on the door being under the clock."

"You mean the clock on the wall where that rapidly expanding sand trap is?"

"Yup, we need to move."

And she grabbed him by the hand.

MAX SQUEEZED INTO THE SPOT NEXT TO JENKS AT THE RAILing. The lower level of the viewing pit for the hacking competition was packed and all eyes were glued to the massive screen high up on the wall above the competitors.

"You win?" Jenks asked, not taking her eyes off Sapphi and Saad, who were dodging some sort of laser field.

"No," Max replied, and then laughed when Jenks snapped her head sideways to stare at her. "I'm kidding."

"I am going to kick your ass."

"In two days, maybe. How are these two doing?"

"Really well, despite this pretty damn challenging final round they put together. They won the first two, so they were in the lead going in, and they're in the lead now with two of the challenges completed; but none of it matters if they don't finish this before the timer runs out."

Max watched Sapphi follow Saad up a wall on the viewscreen, their steps that loping bounce of low gravity. A blue laser burned into the space their feet vacated, moving just a split second behind the pair. She knew from watching countless practice runs that they were also having a rapid-fire conversation and trying to solve a coding puzzle at the same time.

"We don't give them nearly enough credit," she murmured.

"We don't," Jenks agreed. "Sapphi's ability to focus on what feels like eight things at once makes my eyes cross when I'm trying to get her to do just one task, but it's always a good reminder that when it comes down to the wire, we want someone like her, who can deflect a hacking attempt while keeping the coms running."

"It's not just that—this is as physical as it is mental. Those two are as fit as any Neo I've seen."

"Damn straight," Jenks said, accepting the subtle praise for the training she put her crew through. She hissed a curse when a laser winged Sapphi in the shoulder, but the ensign didn't slow and vaulted over a low barrier to safety on the other side of the virtual room.

"ZZ's cage match starts in ten," Vera said. "I'm going to head out to support her."

Petty Officer Zavia Zolorist was part of *Flux*'s crew and had become a force to be reckoned with in the cage. Max was going to end up in the semifinals against her if she won her match today.

"I'll go with you," Max said, as much as she wanted to stay. This was the point in the Games where they ended up spread thin, with so many members of their team still competing that trying to make sure at least a few people were there in person to watch the event was almost as much of a feat as winning the Games themselves. Nika was with Xin watching Chae's cage fight, and their piloting semifinal against Army had been scheduled as one of the last events tonight since all four people involved had been in cage matches or sword fights today and needed at least a little downtime before competing again.

"See you, Max," Jenks said, not taking her eyes off the hacking competition.

Max followed Vera back through the crowd, feeling the swell of excitement a heartbeat before the NeoG contingent broke into cheers. Whatever had happened was a good thing and Jenks would relay it over the team chat when she thought of it.

The afternoon sun blinded her for a second as Max stepped out of the building into the crisp fall air. She blinked the spots from her eyes and matched Vera's stride across the sprawling courtyard that stretched from the Hacking compound to the main gymnasium.

People called their names and cheered as they passed and Vera shook her head. "I'm not ever going to get used to that—doesn't seem to matter how many times it happens."

"Tell me about it. It's even weirder when it happens outside of the Games."

"I don't doubt it and, honestly, I'm glad I don't have to deal with that. I don't know how you do."

"Most of the time I try to ignore it." Max exchanged a nod with the guard on the side door of the gym as she opened it for them. "Thankfully the incidents with people like Strzecki are few and far between and most people don't really care enough about me to pay attention." She was beyond relieved to not have seen the man at all, even as some part of her wondered if that meant he was up to no good elsewhere.

"Commander Till? Lieutenant Carmichael?" She looked to her right at the pair of teens clutching tablets to their chests. They both wore the slightly starstruck, wide-eyed look she was used to seeing aimed in Jenks's direction. This time it was directed at her.

"Yes?"

The taller of the two, her handshake proclaiming her as Edi Lindgren, she/her, even as the introduction spilled out of her mouth, held her tablet out to Max. "We were wondering if you'd sign our acceptance letters?"

It took a minute for the words to make sense and another for Max to realize she was looking down at the girl's acceptance letter to the NeoG Academy. "Oh." A wave of emotion washed over her. "Congratulations!"

"We saw you in the Games last year," Edi's friend Zoe Sun said as they held out their own tablet once Vera had finished signing Edi's. "And decided we were both going to apply to the Academy. My parents were against it initially, but I managed to convince them it was the best thing for me. We're really excited and hoping to make the cut for the Interceptors also."

Max managed to hold it together as she and Vera took selfies with the pair and then headed on toward the cage where ZZ's match was taking place. She wiped at the stray tear that escaped and Vera chuckled.

"Most people don't pay attention, huh? You figure out yet that you're a big influence around here, Carmichael?"

"They called your name, too."

"Oh, I'm aware—and feel probably as weird about it as you do!"

The roar of the crowd caused Max to automatically look upward to the screens above their heads to see the Navy fighter

Chae was matched with hit the side of the cage and slide bonelessly to the floor—unconscious.

"Yes!" She thrust both fists into the air, Vera celebrating at her side.

"Three KOs, baby!" Vera shouted, and someone in the crowd started chanting.

"Five-time champs! Five-time champs!"

Max looked around as the gym filled with noise; many people in the crowd held up a hand, fingers spread wide. The feeling that welled up in her chest was pure indescribable joy.

She didn't regret they were taking a break, but she could also admit she was going to miss this. *My family be damned*, she thought. *I'm never giving this up.*

"Not quite champs for these Games," Vera said, wrapping an arm around Max's shoulders. "But we're getting closer. Let's go cheer on ZZ."

SAPPHI RUBBED AT HER ARM, THE GHOST OF THE LASER BURN teasing at her memory even though the wound itself had vanished when they'd stepped through the door on the far side of the room. Now she and Saad stood in the middle of a desert with the blazing sun high over their heads.

The clock hanging in the air in front of them read 4:46. They'd burned through the first puzzle in under two minutes, but getting through the laser room without dying more than once each had taken them longer than anticipated.

Sapphi spun in the golden sand, spotting the flash of something in the distance.

"Dirt bike," Saad said with a dramatic gesture at the vehicle he'd constructed and she whistled at him, hopping onto the back.

"I swear there better not be monsters in the sand," she yelled above the sound of the engine, and Saad laughed.

"I feel like that's a given!"

He'd no sooner said the words than something burst out of the ground in front of them. Saad swerved and Sapphi let loose a string of curses, calling up her allowable Verge menu on her DD. They could have offensive weapons, but Sapphi discarded them without any real consideration. They didn't have time for a protracted fight with whatever this was. Instead she started her basic shield program, extending it to envelop Saad and the bike.

"Keep driving!" she shouted to Saad, coding a harness to keep her tethered to his back but leaving her hands free to work.

The visual description of the monster was irrelevant and she ignored it, diving straight into the code holding it together, looking for weaknesses to exploit.

"Attack bots," she said as Saad swerved again.

"Figured as much. They're going to follow us to the target. You got a plan?"

"Not yet, working on it, though." Her fingers flew over the screen hanging in her vision. She launched a testing probe at the nearest monster and watched the code split apart, the probe passing harmlessly through. "Zeus's unfaithful ass, whoever designed these is a godsdamned genius. I can't even get a read on it without getting in close."

"Something tells me we don't want to get close."

Sapphi threw up several barriers behind them. The first slowed the monsters' pursuit, buying them several seconds of lead, but the second and third were only marginally effective and they blew through the fourth without so much as a stutter step.

"They're learning, fuck." She glanced up, past Saad's shoulder, and spotted the pair of bright silver doors stretching out of the sand toward the blue sky.

She had to come up with a defense or a way to defeat these creatures or they had no chance.

"Sapphi, when I get to the doors, I want you to jump off.

I'm going to keep going and see if I can't get these things to chase me."

"They'll kill you. Or me." She shook her head. "Besides, we both have to get out of here. Let's stay together."

"Okay, but we need to think of something and soon. Shit!" He jerked the wheel as a silvery barrier appeared less than a meter in front of them and the bike skidded sideways with a spray of sand.

Sapphi rolled to her feet, scrambling backward and grabbing for Saad. The electrical discharge off the wall behind her told her not to get too close, but the monsters charging in their direction made the desire to back up almost override her common sense.

"I would kill for a backdoor right now," she muttered, scanning the code of the wall.

"Your wish is my command," Saad said, snapping his fingers.

"What?"

Saad reached out and dropped the code they'd retrieved in the first challenge into the code of the wall. A chime sounded and the wall shifted in color to gold. "Clear," he said, and she realized he'd reached behind them and touched the surface.

Sapphi glared at him. "Next time, we have a discussion about who gets to touch the dangerous wall. I have more lives than you."

"Sure. Later." He shoved her through the wall as the monsters reached them.

Sapphi stumbled through, Saad on her heels, and she caught him before he fell into the sand. The wall rippled with the impact of the creatures on the other side, but it held.

"Come on, we've got a minute and fifty-three seconds," she said.

Two figures stood in front of the doors, screens where their heads should be. A series of images flashed over the screens and then they went white.

Black writing appeared on them.

One of us

Leads out

The other

Doesn't

Ask us

The words vanished and the series of images returned. Sapphi shoved her hands into her hair. "Jenks is probably shouting at me," she said, and exhaled. "I never remember how to solve this riddle."

"Didn't the original have to do with one of them always telling the truth?" Saad asked.

"Yeah." She frowned. "They wouldn't make it so easy." She scanned the code behind the figures. The doors were the same as the golden wall they'd passed through. The terminals in front of them were unshielded, accessible.

"The question isn't which terminal to *ask*; it's which terminal to hack!" She gave Saad a little push toward the one on her right. "Watch the screen—there are different images on each. Make a list of what you see."

She could feel the ticking of each second of the clock like an actual hand on her shoulder pressing her down, but Sapphi forced herself to focus on the images on her screen, listing them out.

On the surface it was easy. Hers were all nature scenes, Saad's all technology. But Sapphi didn't understand it and the lack of context might cost them the championship.

"Thoughts?" Saad asked. His eyes were bright as he stared at the images. "There's a spot in both to insert the code we got in the laser room, but I don't know which one to pick."

"I hate binary," she muttered. "Why is it nature or tech? Why can't it be both?" She froze and flapped her hands in the air. "The code!"

"That's what I said?"

"No. The code. Let me see the code. It's not just an insert;

it's the answer. They said, 'Ask us.' We have to do it together. Ask with the code. We have to enter it at the same time. Now I'm really glad I didn't let you drive off." She clapped her hands. "It's not about picking a door; it's about the code."

"There's only one code string, Sapphi."

"We enter it into both terminals. You got a better idea? If we don't do anything, we're going to lose. If I'm wrong, we lose, too, but I'm not wrong." She stared at him with a bravado she didn't feel. They both knew if she was wrong and the Marines had figured it out, they'd lose this. Sapphi did the calculations—the Neos would still win as long as Chae and Max came in at least second in the piloting competition tonight and everyone else won.

But I'm right. I know I'm right.

"I'm right, Saad."

The clock continued its relentless countdown and Saad glanced at it one more time before nodding. "Let's do it. On three?"

Their hands flew across the keys and the doors opened with a chime. Sapphi shared a grin with Saad and they both stepped through.

THIRTY

Sol System

"One more day!" Jenks lifted her beer. She was sporting a black eye from her semifinal fight against Navy Chief Naina Mehta and a grin that all the other Neos echoed. "We have outflown, out-hacked, and out-boarded everyone here so far. Only things left are the Big Game, for Nika to whomp on Air Force's startling sword fighter prodigy, and for me and Max to dance."

All Max could do was laugh when Jenks winked dramatically at her, and the room dissolved into cheers.

The whole team and a few assorted others were clustered into the living room of one of their split quarters, the remains of a meal still scattered in the kitchen and on plates precariously balanced on any available surface.

Max got to her feet, collecting a few of the dishes and starting the cleanup. Nika followed her and she leaned back against him for a moment as he reached around her to set his things in the sink.

"You doing okay?" he murmured against her ear.

"I am, somewhat surprisingly. Did you see the message from Stephan?"

"From this morning?"

"Yeah."

"I did." Nika nodded and went to collect more dishes from the others and they worked together in companionable silence while the conversation rolled around in the living room. "Something bothers you about it," he said.

"I read the transcripts of Stephan's and Luis's conversations with both the pilot and the teacher. If they're lying about what happened, it's really good. And then there's the fact that there's no prior association between Jasper or Tara. They met for the first time that morning. If it had only been one of them, this would make more sense."

"How so?"

Max looked down at the glass in her hand. They were pushing three years together, both as teammates and partners. She and Nika had come a long way in that time, especially when it came to communication. One of the things he did all the time now was ask for her opinion, even if—or maybe especially when—it was just her gut feeling.

"You can explain the actions of one person as personal so much easier," she replied finally. "A weird grudge. A bad day. Some financial trouble we're missing or something more complex. They made a bad choice in the spur of the moment, rather than some terrible plot. But two people deliberately attacking Interceptor crew members with what appeared to be intent to take the ship screams at something much bigger and organized. If I were running things, I'd want there to be as little to no connection between the people I was using as possible."

"Because it makes it harder to find the pattern." Nika nodded with a grimace. "We haven't seen anyone move to fill the void in Trappist."

She handed the glass over for him to dry. "Bingo. We are mostly done cleaning up Tieg's mess. You and I both know a power vacuum causes all sorts of shifts, but there haven't been any of the normal indicators that someone more powerful is moving in. *Stephan* hasn't seen anything, and that worries me."

"Emel's theory that an EMP was somehow used to control them is what worries me, plus that blows a hole in your individuals theory. Maybe there's a connection we're missing."

"Maybe?" Max sighed. "It all worries me, and not in the least because I don't think Emel's wrong. What if that EMP that they used against us on Jupiter Station was just the start and not the end?" She'd kept her volume low as she voiced the concern that had been rolling around in her head since she'd read the report.

Nika looked startled, but he didn't tell her she was blowing things out of proportion. "You think there are more devices?"

"Julia Draven said that was a test," Max replied. "And we never found others. Maybe she was telling the truth and they were on the trucks Grant blew up on One-d, or maybe not."

"I hope you understand what I mean when I say I hope you're wrong," Nika said.

Max sighed. "I do and I hope that I am, too, but if I'm not, we need to be prepared for something much worse than Jupiter Station."

THE BUZZ OF ANTICIPATION THAT FILLED THE GYM AIR WAS unlike anything Jenks had experienced in all her years of fighting in the Games. She knew the cameras were on her the moment she slipped out of the locker room, and threw a two-fingered salute at them with her trademark sass. The crowd exploded into cheers and Sapphi laughed from her side.

"You two are going to give this audience a collective heart attack before we're done. Hera's laughing vengeance, even *my* heart is thumping."

"We're here at least partly to put on a show," Jenks replied, and Tamago snorted from her left side.

"You're doing a good job, then," they said, waving a hand to some fans who screamed their name as they passed.

Jenks spotted Max on the other side of the cage. Nika and Chae were with her—the crew had clearly come to an unspoken decision, or at least one that hadn't been spoken of around Max and Jenks, to split the cheering section evenly, and Jenks appreciated it. She watched as the lieutenant actually laughed at something Jenks's brother said, throwing her head back and pressing a hand to her stomach in unrestrained happiness. It was good to see. She was afraid Max's nerves would have kicked in again at the last minute and made her too tense, too afraid to fight.

Jenks wasn't nervous, but she was excited. Win or lose, this fight was going to be fun and she wanted Max to have the same experience. She didn't have words to explain why that was so important to her, even more than actually winning.

Which wasn't to say she wasn't going to do her damnedest to come out on top.

The thought brought a grin to her face as she pulled her hand wraps out of her pocket and shoved up the left sleeve of her hoodie.

Max knew the minute Jenks made her appearance by the swelling murmur of the crowd, followed immediately by a roaring cheer. A glance up showed the chief throwing a casual salute at the cameras. She let a similar smile curve her own mouth, knowing the cameras on her would catch it.

"You two are playing this for all it's worth, aren't you?" Nika murmured, his head still bowed over her hands. "Wraps are good."

Max laughed, the combination of her nerves and the surprising excited anticipation making her shake a little as she threw her head back and pressed a hand to her stomach. "It's part of the show, I guess," she replied finally. "Thanks for being here, you two."

"Jenks is my sister, but I'd be lying if I said I didn't want you to win," Nika said with a wink.

"Picking sides is weird, LT," Chae said. "But I'll be cheering for you."

"I appreciate it." Max smiled at them and moved over to start her warm-up. The routine made it easy to tune out everything and her jitters eased.

At least until Nika touched her shoulder. "It's time."

Max exhaled and shed her hoodie, handing it over to him. Jenks was already in the cage, bouncing on the balls of her feet, her hands wrapped in a blue that matched her braided hair. Max's wraps were green, her own hair secured at the base of her neck in a series of knots thanks to Sapphi's clever fingers this morning.

Max exchanged the *Zuma* handshake with both Chae and Nika, then straightened her shoulders and trotted up into the cage with a smile on her face. Her stomach flopped when she met Jenks's eyes.

Jenks grinned at Max and spread her hands wide. "Welcome to the boss fight, LT."

The crowd went wild.

This was the sort of thing she lived for. Jenks watched Max's tense shoulders relax at the joke and her friend smiled back.

"I've leveled up, Chief. I hope you're ready."

It was perfect and the camera in the ring picked up the banter as referee Travis Vance stepped forward. *"Zuma's Ghost,"* he greeted them, pausing for the roar of the crowd to die down enough so they could hear him.

"You've both signed off on the rules," Vance said. "I expect nothing less than a solid, clean, hard fight from you two. Good contact. Back off when I say hold. We've got three rounds or until someone goes down for good. Tap and go to your sides."

Jenks held her fists out, keeping her eyes on Max as the other woman reached out and pressed her knuckles against Jenks's, holding them there for a moment before she smiled and backed away.

They knew each other. Had laughed and cried together. Fought and bled. The last five years had cemented this friendship into something that would never fracture.

The cheers of the crowd melted into the rush of blood in her head as Vance blew his whistle and Jenks stepped forward.

Everything dumped itself out of her head as the whistle sounded, and Max put her hands up, watching as Jenks advanced.

Don't let her close. You've got the advantage in reach—use it.

She'd already decided she was going to wait. Patience was her strength and it was far easier for her to figure out what Jenks was going to do if she made her make the first move.

"We just gonna dance all night?"

Max couldn't always get a handle on what Jenks was about to do the same way she could with others, but almost five years together had taught her a lot and there was no way she was moving before she was ready. "Waiting for you, champ. I thought you wanted this." She gestured with a hand.

It worked. Jenks *did* want to fight and the tease was the last push to get her moving. She closed the gap between them with a speed that was still breathtaking, but Max planted her left foot and brought her right up in a front kick that caught Jenks right in the chest and knocked her back.

Max surged forward and landed two solid punches to Jenks's head before an answering shot caught her in the ribs and she felt a leg hook around hers. The crowd roared as both women crashed to the mat. Max tucked her head, but Jenks caught her right in the temple with an elbow as they landed, and she saw stars.

Jenks tried and failed to close the hold on Max, who wriggled free, kicking her again with enough force to push her all the way off so that she could roll away. She moved in as soon as Max was on her own feet, taking the punch to the face as the price of trying to bring the taller woman down again.

But this time Max evaded the takedown and landed a combination of punches with exactly the sort of speed Jenks had been drilling her on for years. It forced her on the defensive as Max continued the assault using her long reach to land several hits. This time Jenks barreled forward more out of a sense of self-preservation than any calculated move.

It did the trick, though, and caught Max off guard. They landed in a tangle, Jenks swarming over her. Jenks had to keep them on the ground, she knew it. It was her best defense against Max's range. She caught Max's arm, trying to lock her own down on the woman's throat and end this—

The buzzer went off.

"Break!" Vance shouted, and Jenks rolled away, pulling Max to her feet with a vicious grin.

"Saved by the bell, Carmichael."

"You've got two more chances, Khan," Max countered.

"Sides," Vance said, but he was laughing as he gave them both a push to the opposite sides of the cage.

Max dropped onto the stool and took the water bottle Nika passed her, tipping her head back to swallow some of it before wiping the sweat from her face. The white towel came away red.

"You've got her off-balance some," Nika said. "Keep pushing."

"You think? She didn't feel off-balance." Max rubbed her throat as Vance called the minute warning. "God, that went fast. Felt like I blinked and the round was over. She almost had me there. Half a second more and I'd have been toast."

"She has to take you to the ground to even the odds and she can do it if you let her get ahold of you."

"So?"

"So don't."

Despite the situation, she laughed.

"You're up by two points, LT," Chae said as they finished smoothing the tiny strip of heal patch over the cut near Max's eyebrow.

Vance called out, "Let's go, crews. Clear the cage for round two."

Max tapped fists with both Nika and Chae and got to her feet.

"FOLX, IF YOU ARE JUST JOINING US, YOU CAN STILL WATCH what is shaping up to be one of the most incredible fights of all time as Lieutenant Maxine Carmichael and Chief Petty Officer Altandai Khan go head-to-head in a *Zuma's Ghost* championship match."

"I don't know what I thought was going to happen, Pace, but every second of the first two rounds has had me on the edge of my seat. From Carmichael's opening kick to the punch Khan unleashed with only four seconds left in the second round, we have seen it all here as these two titans battle it out."

"I'm not entirely sure how Carmichael continued to stay on her feet after that hook to the jaw, Barnes, but the fact that she did means we're going into a third round here in a minute."

"The crowd is loving it, and to be honest I'm not sure anyone knows who they want to win at this point. I know I don't."

"Well, unless we end up in a dead-ass tie, someone is walking away from this the champion. Will it be the chief's eleventh time to take the crown, or will her ghostlike lieutenant unseat her? Stay tuned to find out."

JENKS WINCED AS TAMAGO WIPED THE CUT ON HER CHEEK-bone clean and then applied the heal patch. "All right, you're good," they said. "Five more minutes. You're up by three points going into this round—you could just avoid her for the duration."

She laughed and held out her fists. "We all know that's not going to happen."

"Don't let her kick you again, then," Sapphi ordered, tapping her hands to Jenks's.

Her face was throbbing from Max's well-placed heel kick and it was only Jenks's ridiculous tolerance for pain that had kept her from passing out midway through the second round. She'd paid her friend back with a right hook that had nearly knocked Max out, but though the LT had swayed a bit, she hadn't gone down.

"One more round, you two," Vance said as they joined him in the center. "Tap and go on the whistle."

"You look a little tired there, Chief. Am I wearing you out?"

"Buzzer won't save you this time," Jenks said with a wink as she backed to the side of the cage.

Max hurt all over, but she blew a kiss at Jenks as she lifted her hands and closed the distance between them. "Won't need it, come on."

Jenks stepped into the punch Max threw, feeling the brush of her cloth-wrapped fist against her cheek as it just missed. She landed two shots of her own to Max's torso before the woman could shift her guard, leaving her open for the takedown.

They hit the mat hard, Max on her back, her arms up to cover her face from the punches Jenks was raining down on her. She bucked her hips up, almost dislodging the heavier woman; but Jenks fell forward and rolled, dragging Max with her and wrapping her into a headlock that Max only just got her forearm into before she cranked down.

Jenks took the punches from Max as she tried to get the hold finished. "Come on, Carmichael, I've got you."

And then she suddenly didn't as Max shockingly planted her feet and *stood*, lifting them both into the air. The motion and sudden interference by gravity allowed Max to get her forearm up and then bring her elbow down into Jenks's shoulder.

Jenks dropped hard to the mat.

"Don't get cocky," Max said, backing up a step with a wink as Jenks rolled to her feet.

Jenks heard the roar of the crowd as she and Max converged on each other again, but this time it was Max who sidestepped the punch at the last possible second and spun, catching Jenks under her left arm and around her throat in a headlock that was perfect.

Shit.

Jenks knew she'd been half a second too slow, but before she could fight free of Max's grip, they were on the mat and Max got one of those long legs of hers wrapped around Jenks's. The LT cranked back on the lock as Jenks punched twice with her free right hand, hoping it would loosen Max up enough to allow her to slip free.

The shock had cost her precious time.

Time Max used to get a better hold on her, and the pressure on her throat increased. Jenks realized she had no hope of getting out of it before she ran out of air.

She reached up and tapped Max.

"Tap out! Win to Carmichael!" Vance called, and Jenks felt Max's grip immediately loosen.

Through the roar of the crowd, Max's whispered "I'm sorry" was clear.

Jenks rolled over, pulled her mouthguard free, and grabbed Max by the face. "Are you seriously apologizing for winning? This is perfect. Anyone else would have lorded it over me. You, you're too fucking humble to do that." She kissed her on the mouth with a loud smack.

Max laughed helplessly. "I love you, too, you nerd."

"Get your ass up, you goddamned champion."

Max let Jenks haul her to her feet, taking in the crowd chanting her name, and she blinked back the tears that flooded her eyes. She was only dimly aware of Vance announcing her win and hoisting her other arm into the air, all her focus on Jenks's fingers laced through hers as they gripped each other tight.

THIRTY-ONE

Trappist System

D'Arcy laughed and caught Jenks when she launched herself at him. "Hey there!" He spun her in a circle before putting her on the ground. "Welcome back."

"Five," she replied, flashing her hand, fingers and thumb spread, at him. Then she leaned in and hugged him tight. "We missed you."

"Thanks." He let her go and held out a hand to Nika as Jenks bounced past him into Luis's house, Doge trailing behind. "She's surprisingly chipper for having been knocked off her throne."

"Like most things with Jenks, she never quite reacts how you think she's going to," Nika said, gripping D'Arcy's forearm in greeting. "Tease her all you want. Saint Ivan knows this one won't."

Max stepped into D'Arcy's offered embrace. "I will—I'm just picking my moment," she whispered. "Thanks again for the advice, D'Arcy. It helped."

"So I saw." He pulled back. "You did good, kiddo. I'm proud

of you." He released her to greet the other members of *Zuma* and *Flux* and then followed them all into the jam-packed house.

The celebration for the return of the Boarding Games champions was already underway, but the arrival of the heroes of the hour kicked it all into high gear.

D'Arcy settled into the background, delighting in his friends' joy and ignoring the slight ache of longing in his chest.

"You missed being there, didn't you?" Emel asked softly as she leaned against the counter next to him.

"I did." It was easier than he'd thought it would be to admit it, but that didn't surprise him nearly as much as her reply.

"We could make a go of it next year. Sounds like someone will need to step up around here if *Zuma* is taking some time off." Her grin was brighter than the setting sun. "What—you thought I wasn't competitive?"

"Never in a million years did that cross my mind," he murmured. "All right, Master Chief, I hope you know what you're in for."

"Worst case, we don't place in the prelims. Best case, we win the Games." Emel said it with such casual nonchalance that D'Arcy choked on his beer.

"Did you break him?" Max asked as she crossed to them, laughing when Emel recounted the conversation. "If you're not going to die, D'Arcy, can I bother you with a few questions about that tourist ship you tangled with?"

"You can," he said finally. "But Stephan will yell at you for talking work when you should be celebrating."

"I celebrated," Max replied. "I'll sleep better tonight if I can answer some of these questions that have been gnawing away at my brain since I read your reports, though."

JENKS LEANED ON THE BACK OF THE COUCH, LISTENING TO the quiet flow of conversation. The party had thinned down to just a few people and Luis was cleaning the kitchen as the boys gathered up the rubbish to put in the recycler.

She took a sip of her beer and sighed. The contentment in her chest was a new thing, but a welcome feeling all the same. "This is good," she murmured.

"You're happy," Doge replied over their com, and she reached down to pat him.

"Yes."

"Even though you lost?"

"Even though." She glanced over her shoulder to where Max and Nika were talking across the room. "I am happy for her. She deserved that win, earned it. And she needed it."

"Hey, Doge." Riz patted the ROVER as he passed them. "Can you hand me those cups?" he asked Jenks.

"I'll get those. Don't worry about them," she replied.

"Thanks, Mom."

"Sure thing, kiddo." There was a beat before the words sank into her brain and Jenks froze.

The moment spread through the room with the same impact as a pressure wave. She saw Luis's startled surprise race across his face. Heard Max's slight gasp. Nika had stopped with his beer halfway to his mouth and was staring at them.

"Riz," Elliot hissed his twin's name.

Riz bolted out the back door into the night.

"Well, shit," she muttered, shoving a hand into her hair.

Then she did the only thing she could and followed him into the backyard.

"Riz, hold up," she called, and he stopped at the far side of the deck, dropping down on the top stair and wrapping his arms over his head, burying his face in his knees.

Jenks sat carefully next to him, not touching him even though she really wanted to rub his heaving back and tell him everything was going to be okay.

"I'm sorry." The whisper was barely loud enough to reach her ears.

"Sorry? Why?"

"Dad's going to be mad. You'll go away. I don't want you to go." The words dissolved into incomprehensible sobbing.

"Riz." Her heart was breaking at his confusion and grief. "Do you want a hug?"

He nodded and Jenks barely got her arms open before he threw himself at her. She rocked him as he cried. "It's okay, kiddo. It's okay. No one's mad. No one's going anywhere."

"I miss my mother, but I don't remember her," Riz whispered. "It seems like you've always been here. I know you don't want to be, but I can't help thinking of you as my mom."

"Who said I didn't want to?" Her heart thumped hard in her chest and Jenks leaned back, cupping Riz's face in her hands. She wiped the tears off his cheeks with her thumbs. "I haven't said that. Your dad hasn't said that, has he?"

She ruthlessly shoved away the panic that rose up, thinking that Luis *had* said something, or his mothers had, about not wanting her around. They wouldn't, and this wasn't about her insecurities. It was about Riz's feelings.

"No." Riz looked down. "Malcolm said that if people don't get married, they don't really love each other. And if you don't get married you don't want to be my mom."

"What the fuck does Malcolm know? Sorry," she said with an apologetic wince, but Riz just giggled at her profanity. "That is an antiquated belief from way before the Collapse and is better left there. People love each other for all sorts of reasons, kiddo, married or not. I love you, for example."

"But not like I'm your kid?"

She picked her next words with care, aware that she wasn't just holding Riz's face in her hands, but a fragile heart as well. "I hadn't ever really thought about having kids. Then I met you and your brother. I love you. Full stop. That's all that matters to me, but I am okay with you calling me mom if you want to. You probably need to have a conversation with your twin and your dad about it first and then we all need to have a good discussion about where we're going with this, though—but I'm chill with it."

"We already talked about the first part," Elliot said, and Jenks looked back to see Luis standing there holding his boy's hand. Her heart flopped. "And if you're okay with it, we'd really like to call you Mom."

For the longest time Jenks had thought that her crew would be the closest she'd ever get to a family outside of her brother. She'd accepted it, been ready to live her life that way even as she buried the desire for something more down into the box marked NEVER GONNA HAPPEN, GET OVER IT.

But now, sitting here with one kid in her arms and the other staring at her with his heart in his eyes as he held the hand of one of the men she'd let past her defenses, Jenks suddenly realized she'd gone and gotten a family without even trying.

Humor was a better defense to the tears suddenly crowding her eyes, but even then, her damn voice cracked. "I'm afraid you may be stuck with me, Armstrong."

Luis looked down at her, the love so clear on his face, it made her heart ache. "It's a terrible curse, but I think I can manage." He sat next to her as Elliot threw himself into her arms on top of his twin. Jenks hugged them both, letting the happy tears free as Luis wrapped his arms around her. "Thanks for not making me wait forever, Dai," he whispered in her ear.

"You are a brat," she replied, turning her head to kiss him. When they separated, she spotted Doge standing by the door. "Get over here," she called to him. "We're all in this together."

Doge trotted over and Jenks dragged him against her side.

"I love you," he said.

"Love you, too, buddy," she said, pressing her forehead to his.

GREGORI, Y: You don't owe me anything, Sapphi, but if you're willing to let me apologize, I'd very much like the chance to do so.

ZIKA, N: Why?

GREGORI, Y: Because I fucked up? Because I don't think I realized how much I missed you until you were back in my life? Because I've tried really hard to make myself into a person who admits it when they hurt people they care about?

ZIKA, N: There's a tea shop near base, the Blue Moon. I can meet you there in thirty.

GREGORI, Y: I'll be there. Thanks, Sapphi. I appreciate it.

THIRTY-TWO

Trappist System

Sapphi ignored the uneasy rolling of her stomach as she and Nika sat at one of the outdoor tables below Blue Moon's cheerful umbrellas.

"Was this a bad idea?" she whispered, tracing the rim of the lavender mug in front of her. She'd thought ordering her favorite tea was the best plan, but now she was worried there would be an incident and it would be spoiled forever.

"We can go if you want, Sapphi," he replied.

She almost said yes but then spotted Yasu's lanky frame coming up the sidewalk. "Too late."

It was easy to see the moment he spotted her and the follow-up moment when he spotted Nika. His head dropped and his shoulders sagged. Sapphi had to step hard on the sympathy that welled up out of nowhere.

"Sapphi. Commander Vagin. Congratulations on your Games win."

Sapphi wouldn't tell either of them this, but Nika did a passable imitation of Jenks's silent intimidation from behind his sunglasses as he stood and stared at Yasu for an uncomfortable number of seconds before speaking. "I'll give you two some privacy."

He moved across the patio and settled into another chair, out of earshot but not visual range. The warmth in her chest from his stalwart support undid some of the anxiety.

"I suppose I should be glad Jenks didn't come, or is she lurking somewhere waiting to jump me?" Yasu asked, taking Nika's vacated seat.

"Jenks fights in the cage, so unless you're planning on joining the NeoG, I think you're safe." Sapphi was privately impressed at how sharp her words were. Jenks would be proud. Amused at the lie, but proud.

"Sorry, poor joke." Yasu sighed. "I guess I'm sorry about a lot, Sapphi. Sorry I didn't just tell you that I was getting to come to Trappist over chat. I wanted to see your expression at the news, I guess. And I'm sorry I overreacted when I saw you with your . . . friend."

"Lupe *is* my friend."

"Do you tell all your friends you love them?"

"Every chance I get. Dying tends to give a person a new perspective on shit like that."

Yasu winced. "I deserved that." He dragged in a deep breath. "I don't have very many friends. Damn it, sorry again. This isn't about me."

"You're damn right. Also, if you'd heard any of our conversation before you barged in, you'd have known we were talking about you. Speaking of barging, are you going to apologize for breaking into what is essentially my home?" Sapphi asked pointedly.

"I didn't mean to— Yes, I'm sorry." He deflated under the force of her glare. "I'd been working and suddenly wanted to talk to you and I just— I know I shouldn't have done it and I'm sorry. It scared you and I never wanted that."

She wasn't going to acknowledge that. Oddly enough because she hadn't been scared while it was happening. Shocked and upset, yes; having a whale of a PTSD reaction, yes; but there had been too many people around her willing to go to battle for her for Sapphi to feel the least bit afraid of Yasu.

"Why are you poking around about Doge, Yasu?" she demanded.

"How did you know about that?"

"Not the answer I wanted to hear." Sapphi wasn't about to admit that Doge had been the one to tell her. "I work for Intel, remember?" she said instead, and watched as Yasu went completely still.

"Of course you do," Yasu murmured. Then he laughed sheepishly. "I'm sorry," he said yet again. "It was only curiosity on my part, I promise. Part of the project I'm working on. The NeoG has the last working ROVER in service; it's more than a little fascinating for someone in my line of work."

Sapphi chose her next words with care. "The NeoG doesn't have anything to do with Doge. He's Jenks's dog—"

"Sapphi, he's not a dog." He raised a hand in surrender when she shot him the flat stare that Max employed when people overstepped.

Wow, I didn't think that would actually work. Now I see why LT uses it.

"You want to know about Doge, you talk to Jenks. Or even start with me, as I can already tell you that she's not going to be super accommodating, because she's pissed at you."

"Are *you* pissed at me about that?"

The question was surprising and did funny things to her heart. "Yes. You could have asked and you didn't. Which means now I don't trust you." She bit her lip and closed her eyes with a sigh. "That last bit was mean, I'm sorry."

"No, it was deserved." Yasu was smiling sadly at her when she opened them again. "I know it is and it's not at all what I intended when I put the request in, but I obviously hurt you and damaged whatever we've got going on here by showing up in your quarters. You don't have much of a basis for who I am now, and I don't blame you for remembering who I used to be. Who we were."

"You hurt me so much before," Sapphi whispered. "I didn't think I'd ever get the chance to tell you that and when I saw you at the prelims, it felt petty to say it then, but maybe I should have."

She looked down at her hands, at the lightning scars. Death did bring a strange clarity, not just about telling people she loved them, but about admitting when she didn't. "I'm not that same innocent teenager, but it feels like we might fall right back into a pattern that nearly killed me the last time we did it. I don't think this is a good idea for me."

She swallowed and looked back up, made herself face the hurt she saw in Yasu's eyes.

"Sapphi—"

"I appreciate your apology, very much." Sapphi saw Nika stand when she did and she stepped back from the table. "Goodbye."

Nika waited until they were back through the gate before asking, "You okay, Sapphi?"

"No," she whispered, and moved into his offered hug as the tears started to fall.

MAX RAN THROUGH THE CANYON. DOGE EFFORTLESSLY KEPT pace at her side, her feet pounding in double time to his, kicking up little puffs of red dust into the early-morning air.

Their long stretches on the ground between assignments had been something new for most of the crews, but it was a return to her life at NeoG headquarters for Max and she'd jumped on the opportunity to run outside as soon as she'd been able.

The addition of Doge for security after a fascinating encounter with a solo coyote had been to placate Nika, even though Max was reasonably sure the pup had been more startled by her than the other way around.

"It's not the solos, LT," Chae had explained. "It's the packs you need to worry about. Just take Doge, please, and a sidearm. It'll make all of us feel better."

Doge, it turned out, loved running as much as Max did, and was always happy to go out with her. They'd been back at Trappist-1d for almost a week, the post-Games glow fading back into real work and a routine she welcomed.

Even if she was more than a little nervous about the letter she'd sent her parents just before she headed out. It was an ultimatum. The best answer she had to her mother's demands that she quit the NeoG, along with what she hoped was enough of a warning not to test her unless they wanted her to take the matter to the family at large.

"Are you okay, Max?" Doge asked.

"I am. A little worried," she admitted. "But I'm hoping things will work out all right."

"I am here if you'd like to talk about it. Also, I'm glad you're feeling better."

She glanced his way. It seemed like every day he behaved more and more—human—for lack of a better description. "I am, too."

"Is it because you won?"

Max laughed. "No. Well, yes, I suppose. It's not about winning the fight, however. It never was. It's about still being friends when it's all over."

"Jenks is happy you're happy. She said the win was good for you. Can I ask why you were afraid she would be mad?"

"You remember you're not supposed to be telling people your conversations, right?"

"Yes, but you all do it sometimes and this seems like something she would tell you herself."

She couldn't fault his logic and rolled the question over in her head as she picked the path that led them deeper into the canyon rather than the one that went up and out to the rise where she could loop around and head back to base. She hadn't tried it yet, but the image mapping they'd done a month ago showed it was a longer, steadier rise in grade.

"There are a lot of answers to that, Doge. All my life I've

only had people react to my success with disappointment, expectations of more. I don't have a lot of experience being friends with people who just accept me for me, and I was afraid that Jenks cared more about winning the Games than being friends." She pointed at herself with a breathless laugh. "I know it sounds silly now, but that's what I was thinking. I tend to assume everyone will behave like my family does, even though I should know better."

"Even me?"

"To be honest, Doge, I never quite know what to expect with you. You're a constant surprise."

"You don't like surprises."

"True, but it's not that kind of surprise." As happened more and more with these conversations, she had to think how to explain it, so they ran on in silence for a few minutes. "You remind me that things are still new. I have to remember not to get too set on anything. You're a lot like Jenks in that regard."

"Jenks has taught me a lot. I love her."

He said it with such ease that even as Max stumbled and had to regain her footing, she realized it wasn't the first time Doge had declared this. It wasn't even the first time she'd heard him say it. But the conviction in his voice was solid as the rock beneath their feet.

"I love you, too," he continued. "I'm glad you came to us."

"Me too, buddy. Me too."

They continued deeper into the canyon in silence, Max letting the feel of the ground under her feet steady her as she rolled her options over about how to proceed with her family if her parents refused to back down.

She'd sorted out her finances as soon as they'd hit the shuttle to come home from seeing Islen, setting up all her associated family accounts to transfer money in small amounts over the few days it took them to travel back to Trappist in order to avoid raising any flags with either the bank or anyone who happened to be watching.

After talking to Islen, she didn't doubt now that her parents had never truly let her go, and the silence of the following weeks right now didn't mean anything had changed. The suspicion had always been in the back of her head, but she'd tried to tell herself it was just paranoia and they had better things to do than worry about her living her life.

Though Stephan liked to say that paranoia was better than a knife in the ribs and Max agreed with him now.

She couldn't do anything but wait to see how they responded. The fact that she hadn't had some screaming com from her parents since then about "associating with undesirables" was probably a good indication she'd slipped under whatever radar they had set up. She hadn't even gotten a snarky letter about her win in the cage being a "terrible representation of the Carmichael name."

"Max? Can you hear that?" Doge's abrupt question cut through the quiet air and Max slowed to a stop.

She tipped her head, then shook it. "I'm not hearing anything. What is it?"

"A buzz." Doge tilted his own head. "Here."

Max listened when he gave her access to his audio feed. It was a buzz, fluctuating slightly at odd intervals. "Do you know where it's coming from?"

"This way. It's a little over a kilometer ahead. I am reading a metal object of some sort. Barely a meter across." Doge started forward, then stopped and looked at her. "Should we go?"

"Yeah, carefully." She queued up her com. "Hey, Nika, are you and Sapphi back to base?"

His response was immediate. "We are. You okay?"

"We're fine. Doge is hearing a buzzing sound, and his sensors picked up a metal object ahead of us. We're in the canyon north, northwest of the base and headed toward it. I'll send you the exact location. You want to grab a few people and meet us with a shuttle?"

"We'll be there in fifteen minutes. Don't get too close to whatever it is."

"Yes, Commander."

His sigh was audible over the com. "I'm serious, Max."

"I know. We'll be careful, I promise." She climbed over a cluster of fallen rocks. "We'll see you in a few."

"All right. Stay focused." Nika cut the connection.

"The path wasn't as clear as imaging showed," Max commented as Doge easily leaped the obstacle she'd had to climb.

"The dirt over there is fresher, maybe a landslide?"

"Possible. Doge, can you get any kind of reading off the object?"

"I am not picking up anything beyond the buzz. Sensors show no radiation or other worrisome contaminates. The object appears to be constructed of titanium. I believe there are electrical components inside, but they are not currently functioning. I cannot find anything to account for the noise." He moved his head from side to side as they advanced. "I'll have a scan of it here soon. I'm almost in range."

As she picked her way around the rocks, Max was inclined to agree with Doge's guess about a landslide. If he hadn't heard the buzzing, they'd have turned around at the first pile of rocks and headed back out of the canyon none the wiser.

"Max, look at this—can I just show you my feed?"

"Go ahead." She stopped moving at the disorienting feeling of looking through the ROVER's eyes. The layers of color, heat sensing, and other input was almost too much, but she focused on the object in the distance and the streak across the ground of the canyon. "What is that?"

"Trace metal, from where it crashed into the canyon floor."

Max came to a stop where the smear of light started on Doge's sensors, and dropped into a crouch. The groove in the ground was old, sheltered from the elements.

"Could it be part of the terraforming probe set?"

"It is not the same construction," Doge replied.

She didn't know a lot about that technology, only that it was possible for something to be unaffected by the terraforming, in part because Trappist-1d had already been within the Goldilocks zone and with an atmosphere in place the tech had only needed to improve upon the existing construction of the planet rather than build from scratch.

So whatever this was, it had crashed well before humans had arrived in the system.

Max blinked away Doge's feed. "Can you send me information as you get it? In some form I'll be able to decipher. Your direct feed is a lot."

"Of course, Jenks and Sapphi set up a program. I am surprised you don't have a copy. I should have asked."

"No worries, it just hasn't come up before. Thank you." Her DD pinged and this time Max was able to put the real-time feed on the side of her vision. She exhaled. "Okay, so no radiation means we're good to proceed?"

"Nika and the others are incoming. He would prefer you waited."

"He tell you that?" She stood and dusted off her hands.

"No, it was clear in his voice."

"Jenks ever tell you the saying about cats and curiosity?" Max asked with a grin as she crossed to the object.

"Entirely too often, and it usually followed with her getting in trouble.

"Also: I'm a dog."

SAPPHI JUMPED FROM THE BACK OF THE SHUTTLE, EXCITED nerves making her bounce in the reddish dirt, dulling the grief still curled around her heart from earlier. She'd had a good cry, first with Nika and then in Tamago's arms, and now she was grateful for the distraction of a new mystery. "LT, we're on the ground," she said over the com as she approached the edge of the canyon wall and looked down. "Ugh, too high."

"We're on the canyon floor below you, Sapphi. Come on down and look at this."

The desire to see whatever it was Max had found outweighed her fear of heights and Sapphi clipped in the second Jenks gave her a thumbs-up, then rappelled down the side into the canyon. She landed, unhooked, and stared.

Max was on a knee by an oblong metal object about a meter in length and half again as wide. It was crushed on one side, ostensibly from hitting the ground, and the stenciled writing on the side was worn from time and probably the impact as well. She could make out what was possibly a letter *C* and a *T*, but everything else was too blurred or gone completely.

"Thank Hera it's not an alien probe," she said with a sigh of relief, and Max laughed.

"It seems to be pretty solidly human. Doge says all the metals are known; we've got some kind of internal components, though, and we won't know better on what those are until we can crack it open. I thought it might be something they fired off for the terraforming work, but Doge says it's not the same construction."

"He's right." Sapphi dropped down by Max's side. "All the terraforming stuff is really distinct, plus it's designed for impacting the ground. Well, it's designed to shatter when it hits the ground." She made an exploding noise as she spread her hands apart.

Then she reached a hand out, smoothing it over the surface. "This looks like it was designed to be in space. Maybe an old flyby or even an actual pre-Collapse probe? I know there were some sent this way, but there's no record of any of the landing teams finding anything."

"Were they looking?" Jenks asked as she came up next to them.

"Yeah, they had a list of the active programs pre-Collapse, but it was a long shot to begin with. You're talking something surviving in the black for several hundred years and flying through almost forty light-years' worth of that same space. I wouldn't bet on those odds." Sapphi leaned forward with a frown. "Doge, you said it was buzzing?"

"It was. Isn't now," he replied.

"When did it stop?"

"Three minutes and eighteen seconds ago."

"Odd." The metal was cool under her hands. "I don't want to open it up here for a number of reasons."

"Nika's bringing a transport around we can load it into," Jenks said.

"Good." Sapphi brushed the red dirt of Trappist away from the nose of the probe. "Once we get it back, I can crack into it and hopefully that will tell us what it is in fairly short order."

BACK ON BASE, SAPPHI STUDIED THE SIDE OF THE PROBE. OUT of the dirt, she could now see there were more letters than the first she'd spotted, but all were faded worse than those, with only pieces of the paint still visible.

She ran a scan with her DD and sent the results off to a program that would look for matches with any potential pre-Collapse space missions.

Nika was off to the side, talking with Stephan. The captain had met them in the hangar and led them over to a cordoned-off area in the back.

Sapphi would have preferred a clean room, but the reality was the components had been in space for who knows how long and then on the ground here at Trappist-1d for even longer. None of it was going to work.

Except . . . Doge had heard buzzing, hadn't he?

"Seam on this side," Jenks said. "Looks like a pretty standard slide catch, should come loose."

Her unsaid *Do you want me to proceed?* made Sapphi smile. Jenks could be so unbelievably focused at times, especially where mechanical things were concerned. It was obvious she wanted to crack into the probe but was waiting for Sapphi's approval.

"Go ahead," Sapphi replied, but then, "Wait."

Jenks shot her a look and Sapphi waved a hand at her. "Doge, you said there was no radiation?"

"None, Sapphi," he replied.

"Weird."

"Good weird, right?" Jenks asked.

"I mean, sure." She frowned. "It's just . . . how did it get here if there's nothing for propulsion? It could do a loopy around the planet on momentum alone, or even with solar power, but how did it get all the way from Earth?"

"A loopy?" Jenks grinned.

"It's a technical term."

"Sure it is. Can I open this now?"

Sapphi nodded and held her breath as Jenks carefully popped the latches and slid back the panel. They both stared for a long moment before Jenks finally whistled low.

"Holy shit. This is old."

Sapphi grabbed her tablet. "I don't even know how we're going to get into this. Probably going to have to pull the whole thing and build something from scratch to interface."

"There's a little plaque here on the inside," Jenks said. "'LCFLT. For the hope of humankind.'"

"I'll bet that's what was stenciled on the side, too. I'm not getting any matches for pre-Collapse missions, though." Sapphi plugged the letters into her search. "Doge, can you find anything?"

"I don't see anything, Sapphi," he replied almost immediately. "There are gaps in the record."

"Big enough to fly a carrier through. I'll throw something up in the boards," Jenks offered. "Someone might recognize it."

"Good idea." Sapphi rubbed her hands together. "All right, let's get this pulled and then we'll figure out how to get into it."

She couldn't decide if she was excited or scared.

Either way, this was going to be interesting and it took her mind off Yasu.

THIRTY-THREE

Trappist System

The conference room was awash with noise when Emel came in the next morning. People were clustered around the room, deep in conversation. The excitement from the discovery of the probe was palpable and seemed to have pushed aside most of the celebration over the NeoG's win at the Games.

"I prefer 'Her Amazingness, Champion of the Cage Match.'" Max's voice was filled with laughter that cut off in a yelp.

"Humble, you're supposed to be humble about this, LT," Jenks replied, poking her.

"Morning." D'Arcy handed Emel a cup of coffee with a chuckle at Max and Jenks's conversation and gestured to the far wall. "Over here." The rest of *Dread* was studying a pair of star maps.

"The best places to start a search are here and here." Heli pointed out several spots on the maps.

"You gave her the lead on this?" Emel murmured.

"They're the one who figured it out." D'Arcy shrugged. "It made sense to have them set up the plan for this second run."

He pointed across the room. "Max and Jenks are taking another look at the Rainbow ship and the adults' backgrounds. Sapphi and Lupe set up a meeting with our mysterious contact for later today. Nika and Pia have been digging more into Trappist Minerals and just what Reginald was doing out in the belt."

"I saw Nika's report about claiming Reginald's ship was part of an ongoing investigation. I'll bet that went over well." Emel sipped at her coffee and then looked at D'Arcy in surprise. "Where did you get this?"

She hadn't had a decent cup of the Mars red bean coffee since she'd left home.

"I have my sources." He gestured toward the board with the list of ships Heli had narrowed down. "What do you see here?"

Emel tipped her head to the side and looked at the ships. "Two military, four private vessels, eight pirate ships, and two dozen freighters over the course of a hundred years doesn't seem like much, but—do we have manifests for those freighters?"

"We do."

Emel blinked the documents into existence in her vision at the ping from D'Arcy. "Building materials, raw materials, electronics." Her eyebrows shot up. *The Calamity Jane* was carrying military equipment?"

"Yeah." D'Arcy's look was grim. "It was at the height of the tensions with the TLF last year, and for obvious reasons it was kept classified."

"It rattled more than a few branches around here when they realized it went missing," Stephan said, joining them. "There was also a squad of CHN Marines on that ship."

"To Allah we belong, and to Him is our return," Emel murmured softly. "Am I the only one who thinks this looks like someone slowly escalating?" she asked a moment later. "Between this and the issue we had, it's starting to feel far more dangerous than a few missing freighters."

"You are not," Stephan agreed. "I didn't see the pattern until Heli was able to isolate the right ships, but now it's screaming at me. These ships look like they were targeted specifically. I thought maybe it was part of the Gerard/LifeEx incident, but we cleaned out the labs on One-e and the underground habitat on One-f."

"Excuse me, the LifeEx incident?" Emel asked.

Stephan and D'Arcy exchanged a glance, then the Intel head rubbed at his chin before looking at Emel. "Two years ago someone tried to introduce a contaminant into the LifeEx production stream. That's the simple explanation. It was quite a bit more complicated than that. You've got clearance for the files if you want to read up on it, but you'll need to sign an NDA with LifeEx before you do."

"Interesting," Emel replied. "You can tell me that you've crossed them off the suspect list?"

"Everyone involved is either dead or processed into rehab. There were a few, more difficult, individuals who are in lockdown. But yeah, we didn't find any of the missing ships in their possession, so there's no reason to connect the two."

"Of course, don't make it easy on us."

Emel stared at the wall again for a moment and then looked at D'Arcy. "Did we figure out where that space suit on *Opie's Hat* came from? You said it was old. Older than the ones we found on *The Red Cow*?"

D'Arcy made a face. "To be honest, I forgot about it. Jenks!"

The chief looked up and got out of her seat at D'Arcy's gesture, rounding the table to join them. "What's up?"

"We found some suits on *The Red Cow*, but they were trashed, so it's hard to get an approximate age on them. Did you ever take a look at the one I found on *Opie's Hat*?"

"No, I didn't have a chance." She shook her head. "Do we have it on the ground?"

"Evidence locker," Stephan replied. "There are photos."

"Better to look at it," she replied. "You wanna join me?"

Emel realized the question was directed at her and nodded. "Sure."

"Finish your coffee." Jenks winked. "I suppose you can tag along, D'Arcy."

"You're so generous. Hey, Max, we're stealing your chief for a few."

"Will you keep her?" The response garnered laughter around the room. Jenks laughed even as she flipped her LT off.

Emel took the last swallow of her drink, surprised when Stephan held his hand out for the mug, and then she followed D'Arcy out of the room.

"From that look on your face you're still sometimes stuck in Navy mode, aren't you?"

"You all are very relaxed. It takes some getting used to."

D'Arcy chuckled and from in front of them Jenks snorted. "That was extremely polite phrasing," he said. "I think we've heard it all, haven't we, Jenks?"

"Slobs, unfit, washouts. 'Criminals' is always my favorite, just like Fleet Admiral Lilly."

"I'm sorry."

"Eh, don't be. I strive to match her standard and that's it." Jenks turned as she walked out of the Intel building and across the yard toward Evidence, spreading her arms wide with a grin to match. "And lately they have to call us the five fucking times Boarding Games Champions. I figure that's about even."

"We're used to it," D'Arcy replied with a gesture of his own. "What we are is family. Sometimes messy and too loud, but it works."

"It does," Emel agreed. "I'm glad I'm here."

"Me too," D'Arcy said. He looked in Jenks's direction. "It shouldn't surprise me that you know Lilly's history, Khan, but it does a bit."

"Hoboins is responsible for that. I suspect he knew just what he was doing when he told me to look her up after the bio-recycler incident." Jenks held her hands up. "Only post-Collapse history I've gotten interested in. Evidence." She tipped her head at the door, slipping through it with her dog on her heels.

"I understood that whole conversation and yet . . . did not," Emel said.

D'Arcy laughed. "That is about the way it works with her. Most of the time you just hold on and hope you figure out the context clues."

"She's a breath of fresh air, though I suspect I'd get punched if I told her that."

"You'd be surprised, again. Though it would probably embarrass the hell out of her."

Emel nodded and then reached for the door, gesturing D'Arcy ahead of her. "If I'm being honest, it's nice to feel like the world isn't quite so bad after the last few years."

D'ARCY WENT THROUGH THE DOORWAY. EMEL WAS RIGHT: IT was nice to feel like the world wasn't about to collapse around his ears for once.

It didn't stop him from poking Jenks in the ribs for grinning at him as he walked by her. "Watch yourself, Khan."

"What?" She beamed. "It's just nice to see you happy."

D'Arcy shook his head with a sigh. "Hey, Wilson, can we get a look at that space suit we pulled off *Opie's Hat*?"

"Yeah, hang on." The clerk poked at his tablet. "Room C, it's on the table in the back. We just pulled it off the shelf to box it up. The pieces of the other suits are in the boxes off to the left of it."

"Thanks."

D'Arcy headed down the corridor and put his hand on the palm reader at the third door on the left. The lights came up automatically as they walked through the rows of shelves to the back.

"Heli and I watched a show last night that started out this way," Jenks muttered. "It didn't end well."

"Hush." D'Arcy laughed. "Though thanks for getting them hooked on weird reboots. They might not have figured out the missing ships otherwise."

"We would have figured out something eventually," Jenks said. "But it was good for them to have a win." She turned to Emel. "You're not going to get one when we spar this afternoon, Master Chief, though—sorry."

"It's all right. Practice is still practice. I wouldn't have asked you to help otherwise."

D'Arcy kept his surprise to himself, both that Emel had apparently been serious about *Dread* making a Games run of their own next year and that Jenks had so easily agreed to train the former Navy chief.

"I hope you're ready for it." Jenks whistled as she laid eyes on the space suit. "Awesome. This is wild." She circled the table. "Honestly, it sounds like a prank someone set up, not necessarily anything to do with the hole in the hull or anything."

"Who would do that as a prank?"

"Me." Jenks shrugged at Emel and pointed at D'Arcy. "That one there. More than a few dozen Neos I know. Freighter crews have an even odder sense of humor than we do."

"What's your take?" D'Arcy asked, redirecting Jenks's attention back to the table.

She moved around to the other side, leaning down to get a closer look. "Post-Collapse isn't really my area. But this looks a lot like an early twenty-second-century model. During the attempt to return to spaceflight after the Collapse, they were still using what designs they could find from the early twenty-first. There was some innovation through 2180 and into the early 2200s, specifically here. See how the gloves are super articulated? The old ones were really bulky; these look more streamlined like ours."

A sound that was very reminiscent of a growl echoed from Doge when the space suit abruptly sat up.

Jenks stumbled back a step with a startled curse. "Oh, haha, Wilson. You ass—" She broke off when the suit lunged forward and wrapped a gloved hand around her throat, lifting her off the ground.

"Jenks!"

The suit shoved the table at D'Arcy and Emel, catching him in the hip and driving him back. Emel vaulted over the table and hit the suit in the back with both feet. It staggered forward but didn't drop Jenks and instead swung at Emel. She ducked underneath the arm as she landed and then grabbed the suit from behind.

D'Arcy kicked free of the table as their attacker reached back in a move that would have dislocated a human's shoulder and grabbed for Emel with its free hand. Emel twisted out of the way and landed on the floor, pushing herself back upright with a speed that was unexpected.

"Need a weapon!" she shouted.

D'Arcy hit the alarm on his com. "Emergency in Evidence Room C. I need backup in here now!"

Jenks had both her feet planted on the suit's chest and was desperately trying to break its hold, with little effect. She grabbed the thumb and yanked, which on a human would have snapped the bone, but the suit didn't react with anything resembling pain. It hit at Jenks twice, forcing her to block, and then closed its other hand around her throat to join the first. Panic flashed across her face as she fought back.

There was no tapping out of this fight.

D'Arcy grabbed a sword off a nearby shelf and severed one of the arms with a downward swing. It dropped to the floor, flopping around like a fish yanked from the water, and Jenks managed to drag in a breath before the remaining hand tightened its grip, its thumb right back in place like nothing had happened.

Closer now, he could see the fear in her mismatched eyes, and it cut him to the quick as the suit swung her around, blocking D'Arcy's ability to move in without possibly hurting Jenks.

Doge suddenly hit the suit full on from the side, dislodging it the rest of the way from Jenks's neck, and went down with it in a tangled pile. D'Arcy caught her as she stumbled back wheezing for air, then shoved her toward Emel. "Get her back."

Doge didn't have a mouth, but that didn't stop him. The ROVER was using his feet and the gripper arm tucked away on his side to rip the suit to pieces. It thrashed underneath him and then fell still. Doge did not stop with his destruction and D'Arcy took a step forward.

"Doge, buddy, leave me something to look at."

The ROVER turned his head and *growled*. His eyes flashed red.

"Fuck. Doge, it's me. I'm on your side." D'Arcy tightened his hand on his sword but raised the other one. He wasn't entirely sure it would do him any good against the ROVER, but it was better than nothing. Though the last thing he wanted was to have to fight Jenks's dog.

"Doge, stop!" Jenks's order was hoarse. "Come here."

The dog obeyed immediately, jumping past D'Arcy to land at Jenks's side, where he laid down and buried his head in her lap.

Noise exploded at the far side of the room.

"We're clear!" D'Arcy yelled, keeping one eye on the wreckage of the suit. "Someone get a medical team in here."

"I'm all right." Jenks stowed the rest of her protest at his sharp look and let Emel urge her back down to the ground.

"Lupe, grab Sapphi and the others and get over here," D'Arcy said over the com. "I want you all to look at this."

"Already here, Commander," he said out loud, and D'Arcy glanced back to see the spacer weaving through the growing crowd.

Stephan was talking with security, and Max was at Emel's side talking to Jenks, who was, of course, sitting up again. She had one hand on Doge's side and damned if that dog didn't have his gripper appendage wrapped around her wrist like he was hanging on for comfort.

"What in the fires of Mount Doom is that?" Lupe demanded.

"It was a space suit." Unable to stop himself, D'Arcy poked at it with his sword.

Sapphi knelt carefully by the wreckage. "You're telling me the space suit you found on a ghost ship came to life and attacked you?"

"Jenks."

Sapphi looked over her shoulder and D'Arcy could practically see the conversation that passed over their chat clear as day on her face before the ensign nodded and turned back to the suit.

"You all right?" Stephan asked.

D'Arcy had to force himself to look away from the suit, though he caught Locke's eye and jerked his head to the side in a wordless order. The lieutenant commander nodded and went to supervise the two techs kneeling on the floor, his sword at the ready. "Yeah," he said. "It didn't touch me."

"Where did you get a sword?"

"I grabbed it off the evidence shelf. Sorry."

Stephan closed his eyes briefly, no doubt recalculating their options for whichever case the sword in D'Arcy's hand was attached to and how he was going to explain it. "Couldn't be helped," he said, finally. "What happened?"

"Jenks got beaten up by an old space suit." He wasn't sure where the humor had come from, but it seemed the better option to the adrenaline-fueled fear still writhing in his grasp.

"Oh, come *on*, D'Arcy!" Jenks's laughing broke off into a cough. "Okay, maybe a little beaten up. Damn."

But no one else seemed to find any of this funny.

THIRTY-FOUR

Trappist System

SAPPHI: You okay?

JENKS: Fine. Figure out why that sock puppet attacked me.

Sapphi nodded and turned to the scattered remains of the space suit, waiting for Lupe to give her the all clear. A faint blue shimmer appeared at the severed edge of the armhole and then dissipated.

"Still getting a few faint energy traces," Lupe said after another long minute. "Nothing past a dozen volts, though, so don't lick it and you'll be fine."

Sapphi stuck her tongue out at him, then continued to study the suit before she finally reached a hand out and pushed on the chest. The entire thing collapsed in on itself and she heard the exclamations from D'Arcy and Stephan behind her. "We're fine." She pulled her knife from her boot and flipped it open, sliding it into the shorn edge and slicing upward.

The outer part of the suit fell away, revealing a white poly-mer fabric lined with what looked like fiberoptics and micro cables. "Lupe, does that look like servo lining?"

"It does," he agreed. "It's Raptor brand, too—that weave is pretty distinct. How the hell did it get in a suit that's at least two hundred years old?"

"How the hell did that suit get on the ship?" D'Arcy asked.

Good question, Sapphi said to herself. She stared, thoughts colliding in her head at a million kilometers an hour. "Where's the arm?"

Lupe scrambled over and grabbed the severed arm of the suit, holding it out to her.

"Don't let go of the outer glove," she told him as she reached inside and grabbed for the lining. It slid free without any pro-test and Sapphi whistled as a perfectly formed hand made entirely of the reactive lining appeared, holding its shape for just a moment before it collapsed into an unthreatening piece of fabric.

This material really had no place here—was primarily used in wind turbines, able to change and flex the shape of the fins depending on the strength and direction of the wind, but had also been used in the effort to revive some of the en-dangered bird species on Earth.

Not obsolete space suits.

"When I was a kid, my sister and I destuffed our younger brother's teddy and filled it with this," Sapphi said, glancing over her shoulder at D'Arcy. "We programed it to climb up onto his bunk while he was sleeping." She laughed. "He wasn't ter-rified at all—he loved that thing, and thought it was his secret companion. Until Mom put it in the wash one day. It shorted out half a city block, not to mention fried the washer. I lost net privileges for a month."

Stephan sighed audibly and Sapphi grinned at him.

"You're lucky it didn't zap your brother," D'Arcy said.

"That's what Mom said. Dad Bryce said I should have come

to him for testing. If I had done that, though, you wouldn't have the Sapphi standing before you that you know and love."

"I wouldn't be so sure about that last part," Stephan teased.

Ignoring that, she waved the glove in her hand, making both men wince. "Can we take this back and study it? I want to figure out how the signal that was controlling it works and see if we can maybe track where the signal came from. There's got to be a control box in the suit somewhere; plus this is way more advanced than Ilu's teddy bear."

"Is it disabled?"

"Didn't I say that already? No?" she asked at their shaking heads. "Yes, harmless. Well, I suppose unless the signal comes back, though honestly I think Doge destroyed it. I'll know better after taking a closer look. We can black box it, though, and work on it in the shielded room." She shook her head and grimaced. "It took Jenks down. I don't want to risk it coming after me."

Stephan stared at her for a moment before he nodded. "All right, permission granted. If we have anything else technical from that ship, I want it all in a black box—now," Stephan ordered Wilson, who was staring at the wreckage with wide eyes.

"Hey, Saad, will you go with him and make sure he gets everything?" Sapphi said, and the lieutenant nodded. She took the collapsible black box from Lupe and unfolded it next to the remains of the suit. They carefully loaded it into the container piece by piece, Sapphi cataloging each one as she put it away. She queued up her chat again at the same time.

SAPPHI: Doge did this?

JENKS: Yeah.

DOGE: It was trying to kill Jenks. I'm *allowed.*

SAPPHI: *raised hands* No judgment, buddy.

MAX: At all. You did good, Doge.

JENKS: Next time maybe don't growl at D'Arcy, though.

DOGE: I was angry. And scared.

Sapphi kept her eyes on her work while they had the conversation. While the whole team knew what was going on with Doge, the agreement had been to not say anything to the other Neos and she really didn't want to. Not with Yasu sniffing around asking questions that would definitely put all of them on his radar if he heard about this.

Yasu had sent her a second polite apology email after their meeting the other day and, Aphrodite's naked ass, but she wanted to accept it. Especially since he'd left it up to her if she wanted contact from that point forward. Maybe it had been innocent excitement on his part. She was also admittedly really curious about the project he was working on and her only way in was him.

Why are you like this, Sapphi?

She sighed and pushed it to the back of her mind. She'd have to worry about it later.

"Wasn't there a helmet?" she asked, looking around and spying it on a shelf across from her. "There you are." She got to her feet and grabbed it carefully, putting it on top of the rest of the suit and sliding the lid closed. "All right, Captain, we can take that over to Intel whenever."

"I'll have them transport it all together." Stephan gestured at the debris still on the floor. "Do you need all the bits also?"

Sapphi studied them for a minute with a frown. "Not really, but let's sweep it all up anyway and put it in a smaller container. I don't think it's dangerous like this, but we'll all feel better if we're careful, right?"

"Right." Stephan was frowning, which was never a good sign. "Sapphi, I know you're supposed to go to that meeting later."

"Right, and still look at the probe computer, and figure out this shit. Can I clone myself?"

"No, you may not." A ghost of a smile flickered over Stephan's face. "I was just going to say: be cautious."

She swallowed the teasing, flippant answer and instead nodded. "We will, promise."

"DOGE, YOU'RE GOING TO NEED TO LET JENKS GO," MAX SAID softly, patting him with her hand as the medic gave them the all clear. He complied, the appendage folding away into his side compartment as Nika and Luis helped Jenks to her feet. Jenks was going to have a nasty bruise around her throat for a while, but there was thankfully no damage to her esophagus or trachea.

She was also surprisingly stable as far as her normal trauma response went and hadn't had a flashback or any angry outbursts. Instead the chief had been relaxed and joking. Max had realized it was deliberate when she saw Jenks rubbing a soothing pattern on Doge's head.

The ROVER leaned against her and Max kept her hand on him when D'Arcy approached.

"You did good, doggo," he said, dropping to a knee. "Can I give you a pat?" When Doge nodded, he touched a big hand to his head.

"I am sorry I growled at you."

"Nah, I get it. I've been there."

For a moment D'Arcy looked at Max and it seemed like he was going to say something else, but then he patted Doge twice and got to his feet, gesturing at Jenks. "She get cleared?"

Max nodded. "Wicked bruise is the worst of it, although the teasing over getting her ass kicked by an empty suit on the heels of me beating her in the Games will linger for quite a while."

His grin was quick, fading under the weight of worry almost instantly. "It moved like it was alive, Max. I've never seen anything like that."

"I definitely want to get a look at it," she replied. "Hey, Stephan, can I have a copy of the security feed?" She pointed up at the cameras.

"Will send it as soon as I have it. Let's take this back to Intel," he replied.

Max followed D'Arcy and Nika back out of evidence. Jenks and Luis were ahead of them. The hallway was chaotic with people and Doge was now pressed against Jenks's side like he wasn't ever going to leave.

"I hit record on my DD also," D'Arcy said once they were all back in the conference room, and Max's DD pinged.

She played the clip, sucking in a breath as the recording burst into life in her head mid-fight. It was disorienting to watch from D'Arcy's point of view, but he was right—the suit moved almost exactly like a person.

She watched as D'Arcy cut an arm off and then Doge hit the thing and started ripping it apart. Max frowned and stopped the playback.

"What is it?"

"I'm not sure." She backed up and slowed down the recording. "As you're sweeping the room for any other hostiles, does that look like light glare on the helmet or something else?" She pulled the image and sent it to the main screen on the back wall, copying Sapphi on it.

"Can I have the whole file, LT? I wanna see that in real time," Sapphi said from across the room.

"Sent."

"Hey, LT," Chae called. "The *Argonian* was carrying an entire load of Raptor Lining when it went missing last year."

"How much?"

"Uh, four hundred bolts of it. Each one had ninety meters of fabric a meter and a half wide."

"Fuck," Jenks muttered. Then she realized the others were staring at them, and shrugged. "You know what this means, right? There's likely more of those things somewhere."

The room burst into a flurry of motion as Stephan and the

Interceptor commanders conferred how best to do a running check of suits on base and what else could potentially pose the same danger.

"Hey, Lieutenant, got an incoming call for you." Captain Sheeva Azma with the base com center pinged her. "It's your sister Ria."

"Of all the times," Max muttered. She turned away from the table. "Put her through, Sheeva. Hey, Ria, you're a little late with Games congrats. Can I call you back? We're in the middle of some—"

"Max, what the *fuck*?"

Max stared at her older sister with wide eyes. Her normally polished sister, who had never used that sort of language in Max's memory, let alone directed it right at her.

Here it goes.

"I *beg* your pardon?" Max couldn't stop the stiff response from slipping out.

She saw Nika jerk out of the corner of her eye and look her way. Jenks stopped talking with Luis and raised an eyebrow.

The ping of a sent file rang in her head and Max opened it, but the news headline that screamed at her in bold black lettering was the last thing she had expected to see.

REBELLION BREWING

Fresh off her victory at the Boarding Games, is Maxine Carmichael planning a family revolt? The NeoG lieutenant met secretly with her banished cousin Islen several months ago. It's been two decades since Islen broke with the Carmichaels. The brilliant surgeon has been living in the Congo since her banishment. Are the pair planning something? Is the NeoG's darling looking to bring her lost cousin back into the fold, or is something more exciting in the works that the Carmichaels should be worried about?

"What were you *thinking*?" Ria was more upset than Max had ever seen her. "I can't protect you if you do stupid shit like this. Bad enough to send that letter to Mom and Dad, but to slip this guy a story on top of it. You'll piss off the whole family. You know the rules."

"First off, I didn't slip any story to Strzecki—I want absolutely nothing to do with that bottom-feeder. Secondly, Mom is the one who started this bullshit with her ultimatum about me leaving the NeoG." Max could feel the eyes on her as she replied.

"The family will disown you! Is that what you want?"

"You mean more than they already have? Fuck this family!" Those words had enough power in them to attract the full attention of the Neos in the conference room, but Max was past caring. "I have had it with being threatened and lectured, Ria. If they want to disown me, let them do it. I was meeting with Islen because I'm reasonably sure I know what Mom and Dad's response will be, but I'm not backing down from this."

Stunned silence greeted her words. Ria pressed her thumb and forefinger to the bridge of her nose. "What are you talking about?"

"I'm not leaving the NeoG. I won't stop competing. If they don't like that, then I'll leave the family officially. I was—"

"Max, don't do this."

"The letter is written. I just have to send it. I was waiting on a reply from our parents, but I'd bet good feds that this little press stunt is their response. Once again trying to manipulate me into behaving. All I have ever wanted was to live my own life, Ria. They're not content with that and you can pass a message along to them and the rest of the family as soon as we get off this com that they can lose this fight gracefully or I will burn down everything they hold dear if they come after me or my friends. I'm not an isolated sixteen-year-old anymore, alone and crying on the sidewalk outside a restaurant. I will not go down silently, and I've got enough ammunition to make this very ugly."

"Max—"

"No." She sliced a hand through the air. "This conversation is over. I'm busy. Doing an important job that they think is worthless. Well, it's worth everything to me. Maybe I'll talk to you later." She disconnected the com and shoved both hands into her hair, holding in the scream that wanted to break free in the sudden silence.

Of all the shitty timing, my family has really got the lock on knowing when to hammer the nail home. She couldn't even say how she knew it, but something told her that Strzecki's article hadn't been entirely his idea. It had all the fingerprints of her mother's passive-aggressive denial.

"Max?" Jenks had gotten to her first and put a tentative hand on her back.

Max wordlessly threw the media image onto the main screen from her DD chip and heard the collective intake of breath around the room.

The photo splashed across the front page was of her and Islen that night at the camp. They stood in almost identical postures, arms crossed and staring off-camera. From that angle the family resemblance was unmistakable. It had probably been taken right after her cousin had finished telling her how the family would try to ruin her life, judging by the grim set of both of their jaws. The setting sun had lit them both up in strands of golden light.

Under any other circumstances it would have filled her with joy; instead all she felt was a growing sense of dread, and Max found herself relieved she'd at least followed Islen's advice and contacted her cousin's sources as soon as she and Nika had set boots onto the shuttle.

She also thanked her instincts for starting a file on anything embarrassing or potentially damaging to the family. At the time, she'd been a furious and grieving sixteen-year-old, fully bent on the idea of striking back at her parents for abandoning her. She hadn't done anything with it, of course, but some part of her had whispered that after the dust settled, keeping a file was a good idea.

So she had, and added to it over the years. She hadn't been bluffing when she'd told Ria she could make this very embarrassing for the Carmichaels if they wanted to escalate, and Islen's sources were extremely helpful. Even if the idea made her physically ill. *She* didn't want to be the kind of person who would use that file.

Those were the people she was trying to get away from.

"During the prelims, my mother told me if I didn't stop competing and leave the NeoG when my tour was up that things would become very difficult for me and anyone associated with me." Max looked around the room, the expressions ranging from shock to cold fury. Stephan seemed unsurprised by all this and part of her wished she'd thought to sit down and talk with him about it after she'd gotten back.

"When Nika and I went to Earth before the Games, it was to speak with my cousin." Max turned and gestured at the image. "Islen left the family twenty years ago. I went to talk to her about what I could expect if I chose to do the same. She suspected that a lot of this was driven by my parents rather than an actual consensus among the family as a whole. Something about them not wanting to go toe-to-toe with the NeoG."

The rare smile from Stephan was amazing enough, but the smugness of it made Max want to laugh despite the surging sea in her stomach.

"I emailed my parents when I got back to Trappist. I told them I wasn't their puppet, that I wasn't leaving the NeoG, and the decision to take a break from the Games had nothing to do with them. I also warned them that if they continued to try to interfere in my life, my career, or harm the people I care about that I'd go to the press with every scrap of evidence I have about this family."

"Bold move," Stephan said.

"Necessary." Max sighed. "Like I told Ria just now—and I'm sure you all heard—I've got the formal letter to the family written. I was waiting until I got a response from my parents to decide to send it or not. This well-timed breaking news story may have tipped my hand. I honestly thought if someone had found out about this, they'd have dropped the news a lot sooner. I don't know why they waited until after the Games."

"More people would have been looking you up," Nika said softly, still staring at the image. "They're guaranteed a wider audience."

"Whoever it was, they used a drone," Sapphi said. "Has to be—the lake is in front of you two. The person off to your right doesn't have the angle for the shot."

"How do you know there's a person there?" Max asked.

"Shadow." Sapphi pointed at the bottom edge, where Stark's shadow was splayed on the ground. "Sun was at their back. It's a good shot," she admitted. "You really do look like a pair of heroes. Pity Strzecki is such a dick." She looked around. "You said that's who was responsible, right?"

Max lifted her hands. "He seems the most likely answer, given that his name's on the byline."

"Who tipped him off?" Nika asked.

"Could have been anyone, but my parents had already paid him to harass me at the prelims," she replied. "We weren't hiding; plenty of people saw us when we landed in London." She glanced in Stephan's direction.

"Let me check some things out, Max, and I'll get back to you."

Now that the adrenaline rush was fading, Max felt the tremors start. Jenks still had a hand on her back and the shorter woman pointed at a chair, pushing her gently toward it. "Sit."

"I'd thought I would have had more time to get things in order and make a final decision. I need to warn Islen. If they know where she is . . ." Max rubbed a hand over her face. "I'm sorry, we should deal with the rest of this later."

"We'll deal with it now," Nika said.

Max sighed again. "Islen told me that you all would end up in the cross fire and I wanted to—"

"Don't worry about it. You want to leave for good, do it. We'll take care of whatever comes, Max," D'Arcy said, and the others in the room nodded in agreement. "You're not alone here. Remember?" He smiled at her and shook his head. "And before you say you don't want to drag us down with you, it sounds like they'd come for us either way."

"I hate bullies," Pia muttered. The members of her team crossed their arms and echoed their commander's sentiment.

"Let them come," Nika said. "We'll face them like anything else."

She looked at him, hope in her eyes. He took her hand and, with the other, gestured around the room.

"Together."

THIRTY-FIVE

Trappist System

Jenks slipped her arm around Max's shoulders and whistled low. "You know, you two do look like rebel leaders of some kind. That's a pretty slick photo."

"We do, sort of, don't we? You'd like her, Jenks. She's—" Max stiffened and Jenks looked at her. "What?"

"Sheeva says now Scott's calling. Jenks, I can't—"

"You want me to take it?" It still hurt to talk, but damned if she was going to let someone else yell at Max without standing in the line of fire for her.

Max nodded miserably. "Hey, Sheeva, will you send the com to Chief Khan, please?"

Jenks's own DD pinged and she answered it, caught the flicker of surprise on Commodore Scott Carmichael's face that was immediately swamped with worry.

"Where's Max? Is she all right?"

"She's fine. Are you calling to yell at her, too? Because if so, you can just disconnect right now and go step out an airlock." She ignored the warning look Nika shot her.

Scott blinked. "Who yelled at her?"

"Your sister Ria." Jenks spotted Tivo in the background behind Scott and watched his eyes snap open in shock when he spotted the bruising on her throat, the purple and blue dark against her tan skin. "She was upset over the dishrag media story and your sister standing up to your asshole parents."

"I just saw it. I have a contact back on Earth who normally watches for stuff like this, but we're a ways out and it was—not important how I found out, obviously. Sorry." Scott cut himself off at Jenks's raised eyebrow. "No. I didn't call to yell. I'm calling to ask how I can help."

Jenks turned to look at Max. "He's calling to ask how he can help. Do you want to talk to him?" She hated the wary look of hope in Max's wounded face as her friend nodded and turned back to Scott.

"I'm putting you on the main screen, Carmichael. Watch your mouth unless you want me to—"

Nika's quiet reminder cut into her words. "Jenks, you're speaking to a Navy officer."

"I was gonna say hang up on him." It got a laugh out of Max, strangled though it was, and Jenks tossed the com link up onto the main screen.

"Full house," Scott murmured, looking around at the sea of impassive NeoG faces, and Jenks felt a swell of pride for her fellow Neos.

Max is ours *and damn anyone who tries to come for her, for any of us.*

"We were sort of in the middle of something," Max replied warily.

"I'm sorry, I was hoping to get to you first, but it seems like I didn't. I saw the letter. I'm sorry they pushed you, Max."

Jenks was reasonably sure the expression on Scott's face was genuine regret, but all that really mattered was what Max wanted.

"Islen warned me what would happen if I left. Her whole

family abandoned her, turned their backs on her. Everyone else who tried to help her either got destroyed or had to go with her."

"Do you want to leave? I get why you didn't talk to me about it, but it's out in the air now."

"I don't know," she whispered. "I wanted more time to think about it and to see if our parents would back off. Then this asshole ruined everything. I waited too long, hesitated when I should have fucking moved—again."

It was so rare to hear Max curse, even more so with the sort of venom that was now coating her words. Underneath it, though, Jenks could hear the pain, and she tightened her grip on Max's shoulders.

She started mentally making a list of contacts who could help with this problem, and a glance around the room told her almost everyone else was doing the same thing. There was important shit they all needed to be doing, but that didn't make this any less a priority.

"Max, if you want to leave the family, do it. I support you and I'm still here for you. I just got you back in my life and there's no way I'm going to let the family interfere with us again. You're my sister, forever." Scott's declaration broke into Jenks's thoughts, and she bit back a snort.

Maybe some of Max's family isn't completely terrible.

Those were the words she knew Max wanted to hear, and she felt the LT sag in her chair.

"Thank you," Max whispered.

"Of course. In the meantime, I'll run some interference," Scott replied. "I think you've got enough people to step in for you over there, but remember you don't have to talk to anyone you don't want to. Okay?"

"Okay. I love you."

"I love you, too. Keep her safe." Scott was looking at Jenks when he said it, but his words were for the whole room.

"Commodore, can I borrow the com for a moment?" Tivo asked before Scott could sign off.

Jenks sighed and pulled the com back to her own DD, patting Max once more and crossing the room to where Luis was. "I'm fine," she said, looping him into the feed with Tivo.

"What the hell happened?" Tivo didn't bother to keep the concern out of his voice or off his face.

"It's sort of a long story."

"She got her ass kicked by a space suit," Luis said.

"Excuse me?"

Jenks closed her eyes and muttered a curse. "I'm fine. I promise. As Max said, we are sort of in the middle of things. Can I tell you about it later?"

"I can't wait to hear this story. We still on for movie night?"

"Yes."

He blew them both a kiss, then another at her as he tapped his own throat. "Love you."

"You too."

She disconnected, reached up, and rubbed at her throat but stopped when Luis laid his hand over hers.

"You sure you're okay?" he asked in a low voice.

"It hurts," she admitted. *Not the worst thing I've survived, though, not by a long shot.* She kept that part in her mouth. Jenks had learned the hard way that it hurt him to be reminded of the darker side of her past. "I'll be all right."

"Okay." He brushed his fingers over her neck and leaned down to press a kiss to her forehead. "I love you," he murmured, and pulled away. "Doge?"

"Yes, Luis?"

"Good dog."

She swore the ROVER preened, somehow, even though he didn't move. Doge had been shaken when she'd called him over, and had buried his head in her lap, his metal body trembling.

She'd been shaken herself. She had survived worse, but the helplessness of being held by her neck and slowly running out of air had been something she hadn't ever wanted to repeat.

The universe seemed to have other ideas, though. A shudder rocked through her.

"Jenks?"

"Hmm?"

"Are you okay?" Doge was looking up at her and she leaned her leg into his side with a soft hum.

"Thanks to you. I know I said it already, but good job, buddy."

"I love you. I've got your back."

Tears filled her eyes and she fought to keep them at bay. "You do at that, and I've got yours. I love you, too." This time it wasn't her sore throat making her voice raspy.

"We need to figure out where that came from. I am tired of this."

His voice was so filled with annoyance, and it was enough in line with what she was thinking that Jenks didn't even try to muffle her laughter. "We also need to have a serious conversation at some point about you, buddy."

"I know. I have been paying attention."

"Wasn't suggesting you weren't. Just putting it on the record." She patted him. "Let's go see how we can help."

"WHAT IS THIS PLACE?" SAPPHI LOOKED AROUND IN AWE AND her friends were just as struck by the amazing work that had gone into the coding. Pavel was clearly impressed. Saad looked just stunned, while Lupe grinned broadly at them; they'd followed him into his version of the Verge where he'd somehow duplicated their avatars. He ushered them through a round green door.

Now they were in a white-walled room with a few sleek couches and a round table with four chairs on the far side.

"Welcome to the Hideout."

"You are so pleased with yourself," Sapphi said, tapping him on the shoulder.

"He should be," Saad countered. "There was no hint of that outside. Is it shielded?"

"Sort of?" Lupe wiggled a hand. "It's not really here, which I know doesn't make any sense. The original was shielded in a pocket version of the Verge, but that's easy enough to find with the right tools. It doesn't get much use anymore, but when Sapphi put her fancy house in, I started wondering if I could use that same coding to upgrade this."

"How is Pirene going to get in?"

"I gave her the location outside. I've got a scan set up; it'll ring us when she shows."

"I'm sorry, I didn't realize I was supposed to wait outside."

Sapphi whipped around along with the other three Neos and stared at the person perched on the edge of the tan couch. They were dark-skinned and dressed in the same blue duty uniform Sapphi herself was wearing in the real world. This time their face was different, more angular and older with an almost weary air about them, but the family resemblance with Sapphi was clear.

"I've startled you. Pirene, she/her." She tapped a fist to her chest twice. "It's very nice to meet you all."

"How did you get in?" Lupe asked the moment introductions were finished.

Pirene frowned. "It would take too long to explain, and I do not know how much time we have. I have reinforced your coding and it should keep us hidden for a while longer. I think Art will be confused by the avatars outside, but no trace of me."

"We need to start from the beginning," Sapphi said, sitting on the couch across from Pirene. "Who are you? Who is Art and why does he keep trying to kill me?"

"Us," Lupe said. "Two of our friends have been hurt and while I don't have any proof, I'm pretty sure it's all wrapped up in whatever this is."

"I am the last chance for life on Trappist."

"Ominous," Sapphi muttered, and wondered briefly why that sounded so familiar.

"It was supposed to be hopeful." Pirene sighed and rubbed at her eyes. "This is difficult. I have listened a lot, but I haven't talked to anyone in a very long time. I thought this would be easier. I was sent to find out if life could live on Trappist."

If this is somehow aliens, Lupe and Saad are never going to let me live it down.

Sapphi held up her hand, pointing at both men and pinching her fingers closed before they could say anything.

"We are pretty obviously here. Pirene, *who* are you?"

"My mother said I was the hope for a dying humanity. I was sent to find life."

Sapphi blew out a breath in frustration. She was asking the wrong questions, or Pirene was deliberately being cagey about it all. "I should have brought Max."

"I like her, but she has troubles of her own."

Sapphi shot the woman a sharp look. "How do you know that? Are you in our systems? Is Yasu involved in this? Listen, you need to start talking to me and, like, yesterday. Who is Art?"

"Art was supposed to be my protector, but the time has been too much for him. He doesn't understand, he can't learn the way I can, and it has messed with his purpose. Plus the crash twisted him, I think. I have tried to contain him, but he has me backed into a corner and I am not strong enough to get free on my own. That's why I reached out to you."

"But why me?"

"I heard you and you are familiar to me."

Sapphi resisted the sigh of frustration hovering in her lungs begging for release. "You heard me?"

"When your teammates breathed life back into you. I heard you come alive."

She heard the trio behind her inhale sharply and her own heart thudded in her chest.

Pirene looked past her, alarm skidding across her features. "He's here. I must go."

"Wait. I still don't understand."

"I cannot tempt the fates, Sapphi. If Art thinks you know about him, he will advance to the next phase of his plan. Yasu does not understand what he's done, but you should not trust him. You will have to find your understanding without me, and quickly. We cannot let him continue on this path. Here, this may help." Pirene extended her hand and when Sapphi took it, her DD flashed a notification of a file transfer.

Pirene stood and smoothed her hands over her pants.

"Where did you come from?"

"I came from Earth," Pirene said, as if it were the most obvious thing in the universe.

And then she vanished.

"SO THAT GAVE US NOTHING," STEPHAN SAID.

D'Arcy shared a look with Max. They both knew the meeting had been risky and the likelihood of getting anything out of it was slim, but the results only gave them even more questions than answers.

"Not nothing. I have files," Sapphi protested. "And we can bring Yasu in for questioning."

"Files that you can't get into. And I can't do anything about Yasu based on an unknown person claiming he's involved in this. Instead of getting answers from her, Sapphi, you didn't get anything. I need evidence."

"It wasn't an interrogation!"

"Maybe it should have been."

D'Arcy could hear the frustration bleeding through Stephan's reply and he knew the man's emotions were pointed at himself for putting this meeting off until after the Games, but it was clear Sapphi was taking his ire personally. Before D'Arcy could intervene, though, Stephan continued.

"We've got one lead on this and no idea where she is or what she's up to, but it sure as hell seems that she's aware of not only what we're doing but whatever our bad guy is planning. And that's assuming she's not a bad guy herself."

"She said she's from Earth," Sapphi replied, as if that was an answer to what Stephan had just said.

"We're all from Earth, Sapphi."

"No, we're not," D'Arcy said, even as Chae and Emel raised their hands and shook their heads.

"I suppose I am listed as such," Max offered. "But I was technically born on a Navy ship."

D'Arcy suppressed a grin when the Intel head closed his eyes and muttered something uncomplimentary at the ceiling.

"We did get some answers; we just don't like them," D'Arcy continued now that he'd broken the man's rant and was sure that Stephan would listen to him. "And Sapphi wasn't going in there expecting Pirene to be quite so evasive, for good reason, as she's the one who contacted us. But it's pretty clear she's scared of whoever Art is and she knows that Yasu is involved somehow. Which means maybe we should be focusing our search on that. Let's start looking for evidence."

The meeting broke off into smaller groups at D'Arcy's words and he got out of his chair to join Stephan.

"Was that necessary?"

D'Arcy clapped a hand on his friend's shoulder. "You were doing that thing where you're an arrogant dick because the situation went sideways on you. So, yeah, it was necessary. The meeting wasn't a total waste, and you know that Sapphi and the others will figure out a way to get into the files.

"We also know quite a bit from that conversation." D'Arcy held up his fingers as he ticked off the points. "We know that Pirene is very good at hacking into systems—given how she got into Lupe's space. She's got some sort of feed that's telling her about us. I know you've swept this room for surveillance, but we need to do it again."

"The thing about Max could have been a guess," Stephan said, unconvincingly. "It's all over the news."

"Sure, and I can beat you in a sword fight with my eyes closed," D'Arcy countered. "It's possible, but not very likely. She's either got a source somewhere or actually had access to what happened in this room before they met with her."

"She said the 'crash twisted him,'" Stephan murmured,

eyes unfocused as he rewatched the recording. "What do you think she means?"

"I don't know," D'Arcy admitted, rubbing at his chin. "We'd have heard if there were a crash of some kind here in the system."

"Maybe she means a vehicle crash. We'd have a record if it was reported."

"Yeah, but until we know where she's located, that is multiple planets to check. I will hazard a guess we're looking for someone who's at least as smart as Sapphi where tech is concerned. That suit isn't amateur-level shit."

"That's what worries me," Stephan replied. "Sapphi on the wrong side of things would be a terror to catch and by all accounts Yasu is nearly as smart as she is. What happens if Art here starts looking at bigger targets like another military ship? We can handle a few older models like the two that are missing, but if they get their hands on something wormhole capable?"

"I know. It worries me, too. What's the endgame here? All-out war in the Trappist system? I think as soon as Sapphi and the others are done with the suit, we should take all four Interceptors out to the belt and have a look around."

"Is your team ready?" Stephan asked.

"Yes," D'Arcy replied without hesitation. They'd come together and it felt good to finally be able to say that.

"All right. I'll tell the others. We'll plan on you heading out the day after tomorrow to restart that search in the belt." Stephan nodded once more and then left D'Arcy alone to inform the other commanders.

"You did good in there," Emel said. "Are you all right?"

"Thanks and yeah," he said, even as the vision of Jenks struggling in the suit's grip flashed in front of his eyes again. "I didn't tell you earlier, but thanks for the help with that suit. If that had been a normal assailant, you'd have taken him down with that kick."

"We're a team." Emel looked over her shoulder to where

Jenks was joking with Vera. "Are you all always so casual about this?"

"I guess?" He laughed softly. "To be honest, it's happened more in the last few years. Things used to be quieter."

"Not always."

D'Arcy tipped his head in agreement. "True. Thoughts on the team? I told Stephan we were ready to go out. He wants to send all four Interceptors to the belt to keep looking around the area Sapphi mapped out for us."

"We're ready. There will be some hiccups, I expect, but we can handle it."

"I agree." D'Arcy rolled his next words over carefully before saying them. "I noticed a few com requests from your family on the log. At the risk of making you annoyed with me, do you want to tell me why you haven't answered them?"

"Can I tell you to piss off?"

"Sure. I'll even let it be for a while, but you are my crew, Emel, and moreover my friend. If you need to talk about it, I'm here." D'Arcy happened to look up and spot Nika across the table. The chat flashed into his vision.

NIKA: Look at you, Commander.

D'ARCY: Shut up.

NIKA: Maybe tomorrow.

"I appreciate it, D'Arcy," Emel said. "And maybe I'll take you up on it. It's just complicated."

"It usually is," he said. "Let's go over the preflight checklist and see if we need to squeeze in any last-minute work. Aki, come over here." D'Arcy waved to the petty officer. "We got shit to do."

THIRTY-SIX

Trappist System

Sapphi looked up when the door opened, and Jenks slipped into the room. She had a sword on her hip and the bruises on her throat were a vivid blue purple against her tan skin. It made Sapphi's stomach hurt. They'd gotten lucky. If Jenks had been alone when she'd gone to check the suit, this could have gone very differently.

"We're good here," Sapphi said. "No signals get in or out of this room unless you shut down the field." She gestured at the console in the corner.

"You figure it out?" Jenks poked at the lining Sapphi had laid out on the table, a strange puzzle of shredded pieces thanks to both D'Arcy and Doge. Though Sapphi didn't blame them for the destruction.

"Wireless signal. Actually pretty standard. I was able to re-create it." She leaned over and tapped at the two little panels on the corner of the table that she'd pulled from both the helmet and inside the suit. "The range isn't good, just a handful of kilometers."

Jenks looked up sharply. "Which means whoever was controlling it was nearby?"

"Maybe? You could increase the range if you bounced it off a couple of different points. The helmet is clearly designed to act as a relay if necessary. I asked Stephan to check for signals coming from the ghost ship, but that's really still too far away. I was hoping we'd catch one that was right at the same time this thing woke up, but nothing." She made a face. "And it's going to take a while to isolate anything on the ground with all the everyday stuff that's flying around."

"You think Yasu was involved?"

Sapphi nodded. She didn't have a reason for trusting Pirene, but she did no matter what Stephan said. Maybe that made her naïve; maybe the whole point of putting on a face that looked like it could belong to one of her siblings was just to get her to let her guard down. Sapphi had long ago stopped believing that everyone had her best interests at heart.

I'd forgotten that when Yasu showed up again and I really should have known better.

"I'm so mad about it, Jenks," she whispered, leaning on the table and gritting her teeth. "He used me again and I almost let him. I was even feeling sorry for him and thinking I should try again. He just wanted access to Doge? Why? I don't even know what the game is and I hate it!"

"Hey, look at me." Jenks tapped her on the nose. "You're the smartest person in the room—you'll figure it out. Okay?"

"I don't feel like the smartest right now."

"Tell me about it. I got my ass kicked by a *suit*. After getting my ass kicked by Max." Jenks grinned at her but then sobered. "My gut instinct is Yasu wants Doge because of the AI project he's working on, but it may not even have anything to do with what's going on with these ghost ships. They've made some impressive strides on AIs in the last few years, but we both know whatever Doge is now? It's so much better."

"How do you know about that?"

"I got my sources."

"Luis. It was Luis, wasn't it."

"Why do I put up with you people?" Jenks pointed at the table. "Back to business. Too many signals making noise on the ground and you don't know where it came from to start with, but can we backtrack it?"

"Maybe. I'd need another control box. One alone won't work. Which means we'd need another suit."

Jenks groaned. "Short of tearing it to pieces like Doge did, what's the fastest way to put it down?"

Sapphi considered the question. It made sense that was Jenks's priority, but she hadn't actually thought about it. "The receivers," she said finally. "If you take those out, there's no way to get the signal to the fabric."

"So take out the helmet. Where was the receiver in the suit?"

"Here." Sapphi pointed to the lower part of the torso. "This control box was attached to the fabric still, which is really the only way we were able to figure out where it was."

"The helmet and this are still intact, though?" Jenks frowned.

"Yeah, like I said, the suit wasn't. Doge pretty much destroyed the structural integrity. Makes it hard to get a signal through if all your connections are in pieces."

"But can they use these to bounce signals?"

"They could if it wasn't in a shielded room. I'm hoping to take them apart, which, by the way, Pavel has been working on a setup to get into the probe computer. He—oh. Oh shit." Sapphi pressed a hand to her mouth and looked at Jenks in alarm.

"What?"

"The probe. What if—" She started furiously typing on her tablet. "Why didn't I think of that? Pavel, do you read me? You haven't booted anything up there yet, have you?" she said over the com before she remembered where they were. "Fuck."

"Sapphi, can I get a read in on the situation?" Jenks had her hand on her sword hilt.

"With me." She shoved the door open, closed it behind her firmly, and sprinted down the hall to the clean room and Jenks followed. "Pavel, come in. Stop whatever you're doing."

"Roger that. What's going on, Sapphi?" he asked. "We were just about to fire this up."

"Don't! I've got a theory. I hope I'm wrong about it, but I think the signal that activated the suit was routed through that probe."

JENKS KNEW IT WAS SILLY, BUT SHE KEPT A HAND ON HER sword hilt and an eye on the table as the trio of hackers rapidly conferred back in the shielded room. They'd transferred the computer of the probe from the clean room over here because, as far as she could follow, Sapphi was concerned the signal to activate the suit had been sent from somewhere on Trappist to the probe and that it could still transmit if it were turned back on.

Though the ensign couldn't seem to explain how that would be possible, given the computer was completely inoperable.

Or off. Jenks wasn't entirely sure. Hardware she could understand, but the software part of it was almost entirely Sapphi's domain.

"Do you understand what's going on?" she murmured to Doge. The dog seemed on equally high alert, but she wasn't sure if that was because she was antsy about it all or he knew something she didn't.

"They are trying to figure out how best to boot up the computer. Pavel is concerned that it might be rigged, though for what, I am not sure, as there's no fuel source for an explosion. Saad doesn't want the computer to wipe itself with some unseen fail-safe; he's also not sold on the idea that the probe is involved in the attack even though Sapphi's scan for a signal does flag a few hits coming from right here."

"That seems conclusive?"

"The problem is, there are a lot of signals on base; it's hard to tell which is which on the surface," Doge replied. "I am in agreement with Sapphi, if you are curious. I think the probe was transmitting when Max and I found it, but I don't know who it was talking to."

"I would very much like a target," Jenks muttered. "They're all safe in here, right? Nothing can get in signal-wise?"

"They are. Where are you going?"

"I'm gonna go get *Zuma* ready for departure. You want to stay here?"

"I would like to, but I'll come with you if you'd rather I do it."

"No." She patted him and he moved over to Sapphi's side. "It's fine. Sapphi, I'm going to do preflight checks. Am I good to open the door?"

Sapphi glanced over her shoulder. "Yeah, we're still figuring out what to do here; it's going to be a while. Doge, are you staying?" She looked down at the ROVER and he nodded. "Good, I could use your help."

Jenks waved goodbye and slipped out of the room, hearing the scattered sounds of the argument springing back to life just before the heavy door closed.

"Nerds." She laughed and headed out of the building into the late-afternoon sunshine, crossing the yard to the massive hangar where the four Interceptors were parked. The place buzzed with activity as the crews and maintenance staff prepared for their launch.

Jenks exchanged a fist bump with one of the mechanics as she ducked under *Zuma's* nose. "Natasha."

"Chief, how are you?"

"Doing good. How's she?" It was beyond weird to have other people looking after her ship and Jenks had kicked up a loud protest about it when they'd first arrived, but Stephan had insisted and now she had to admit she was a little too busy with everything else to be doing the work she'd grown so accustomed to doing on Jupiter Station.

"She's fine. I did a little tune-up on the stabilizers if you want to check them out. Spacer Chae is already in there looking at them."

"I will. Thanks."

Okay, so she'd mostly let go of working on the ship. Thankfully Natasha and the others understood and hadn't taken any offense over her wanting to have a final look on any work they'd done.

Jenks hauled herself up the steps and waved to Max and Nika on the bridge before heading back toward the engine room. "Hey, Tama."

Tamago paused where they were restocking the galley and smiled up at Jenks as she passed. "Hey, you. Stores are almost stocked. Chae's in the engine room. We're good to go on this end."

"Yeah, Natasha told me she did a tune-up. Good job, getting things ready. Do we have a departure time yet?"

"Ask the front desk." Tamago lifted their hands when Jenks glared. "I think three hours."

"Someone's going to have to go let Sapphi and the others know. They're in the shielded room working on the problem of that creepy-assed suit and the probe."

"What does the probe have to do with it?"

Jenks shrugged. "Probably nothing, possibly everything."

"Oh, it's one of those."

"When isn't it?" Jenks laughed and tapped Tamago on the shoulder. "I'll be in the back if anyone needs me."

Because at least this was something she understood. Get the ship ready, get the crew ready, and go after the bad guys.

Better than chasing electronic ghosts.

THIRTY-SEVEN

Trappist System

"That's a hit for *Zuma*. *Dread* is down," D'Arcy said over the com, and shut down the simulator. They'd been out in the black for ten days, doing training runs in between scanning the area for any sign of missing ships or their mysterious adversary.

"Sorry for kicking your ass, D'Arcy," Nika replied.

"You are not sorry in the least. Nice job, everyone." He turned off the com before the man could reply.

"Well . . . that was terrible," Locke said.

"Nah." D'Arcy shook his head. "That crew is at the top of their game right now. Even with the various distractions, they are always focused when it matters. We look good for a team that's only been together a few months." He glanced around the bridge at the rest of his team. "I mean that—you all performed really well. Be proud of yourselves."

"What can we do better, Commander?" Heli asked.

"Win?" Locke said.

Shooting his second a look, D'Arcy said, "We'll debrief it

over dinner." He started to get up out of his seat when the com buzzed again.

"Hey, D'Arcy, we're getting a ping on the radar that matches an ID off the list," Nika said. "Sapphi's saying it's *High Porter*."

D'Arcy dropped back into his seat. "Any life signs?"

"Nothing. It's dead in the water. What's the call?"

D'Arcy scanned the data and made the decision. "*Flux* and *Hunter* will stay back and keep an eye out. We'll bring the other two ships in and board. See what we can find out."

"Roger," Nika said. "We'll get in position."

"Copy that. Nika, four each for the boarding party."

"You think we'll run into trouble?"

"I always think we'll run into trouble," D'Arcy replied, and pushed to his feet. "Lupe, you and Aki stay here. Start looking now for anything moving in that ship, any signal like the one from that suit. I want you in front of whatever could go wrong, and I want to know about it before it happens."

"Will do, Commander."

"Locke, Heli, Emel, go get dressed. EMU packs also." He tipped his head to the stairs and the three of them nodded and filed off the bridge.

"D'Arcy," Aki called as he moved to follow, and he looked back at her with a raised eyebrow. "Eyes open."

"You too." D'Arcy nodded sharply and then left the bridge.

He changed into his suit and then ran through the checks on the others' helmets while Aki brought the ship into position on the port-side airlock.

"Commander?" Lupe's voice was clear in the com, echoing a bit in D'Arcy's helmet before the seals engaged. Locke tapped D'Arcy's helmet and gave him a thumbs-up.

"Go ahead, Lupe."

"Sapphi is advising we do a manual board rather than attempt to link with the ship, and I agree with her that given the recent weirdness, that's the safer option. She's working on a hack to get the airlock open on their side."

"Roger. Get us close and we'll run a line."

They piled into the airlock, hooking into the safety catches. At the round of thumbs-ups, D'Arcy hit the open sequence for the outside hatch and it opened to reveal the pitted and scored hull of the *High Porter*.

"Locke, get us across."

The lieutenant commander stepped into the opening with a strap in his hand, connecting the other side to the clip on the outer hull of *Dread*. Emel and Heli braced themselves on either side of the airlock with the tethers they'd attached to him in their hands. The bright orange unspooled into the black, a twin pair of ribbons following his path several meters to the dead ship.

D'Arcy suppressed a shudder.

Get it together, Montaglione.

"No pressure on *High Porter*, no environment, no life signs," Locke reported. "Hatch is open."

"D'Arcy, we're in the cargo bay. Waiting for your command."

"Hold there, Nika. We're right behind you." D'Arcy tapped Heli on the shoulder and took the safety strap, hooking it onto the catch on her suit. "Locke, Heli coming across on your left line."

"Got it," he replied.

"Hands on the rope, pull right over left. Only let go with one hand when you're sure you've got a grip with the other." D'Arcy demonstrated and then tapped his helmet to her own. "You've got this, Ensign."

"Yes, sir."

"You hooking to me?" Emel asked, handing over her strap. D'Arcy held up the secondary he'd grabbed from the wall, clipping them both in. They stepped out into the black, and he turned to reseal the airlock.

"Aki, you've got the ship. Door is closed."

"Copy that, Commander. Be safe."

Walking out into space was a new experience no matter

how many times he'd done it. D'Arcy never failed to feel a sense of awe, not only at the breath-stealing immensity of space—Jenks was always fond of saying it was "vastly hugely mind-bogglingly big"—but at the wonder of it all.

Humanity had managed this, somehow. They'd survived the worst of themselves and still made it out here to the stars.

He'd made it out here, when everyone, even D'Arcy himself, had been pretty certain he was going to die in the red dust of Mars.

"D'Arcy?"

He felt the tug on the strap at the same time as Emel's private com and shook himself.

"I'm fine. Sorry."

They passed through the open airlock and into the darkened cargo bay. The internals were off with everything else on the ship, but the cargo was mostly tied down, with only a few random bits and boxes floating from the lack of gravity.

D'Arcy's boots clicked to the metal floor, the magnetic locks kicking in the moment they made contact. The lights of *Zuma's* helmets illuminated the crates in the corners as they stood guard and a portable lamp threw more light in a wide circle around them.

"Welcome to creepy ship number three." Nika lifted his hand. "I've already seen some blood across the airlock window."

"Great." D'Arcy made a face. "I almost prefer the mystery of an empty ship."

"Max's gut is twitchy and mine's not much better. Tamago is fine, but Jenks will probably stab the first suit she sees. Threat or not."

"She's not alone in that," D'Arcy replied. "Are we getting any readings?"

"Nothing. Ship is down for good. No energy. No life signs. No oxygen. Jenks spotted a good-sized hole in the underside about where the engine room would be. She was a little surprised this wreck was still in one piece."

They'd all done the math already: the ship had been missing for several months and even if there was some weird glitch in the scanners, the likelihood of anyone surviving out here for that long was slim.

"Let's stay in groups of four. I don't want to split us down any smaller," he said finally. "You head for the bridge. We'll look around here and the crew quarters and see what we find. Aki, do you copy?"

"Right here, D'Arcy."

"Did you send a message back to Intel about this?"

There was a moment of dead silence on the coms, and he could picture her rolling her eyes at him. "Yes. And requested a tow for the ship through the Trappist Relay."

"Thank you for not saying 'of course.'"

"When have I ever?" Her voice was thick with irony and the humor eased some of the tension in D'Arcy's back.

"All right, everyone," D'Arcy said. "Keep your eyes open. Five-minute check-ins. Stay together."

The chorus of "aye" echoed back at him and the two crews split up, Nika's group heading for the bridge in a smooth, co-ordinated movement.

"Fan out," D'Arcy ordered. "Stay in visual contact with at least one other person. Let's see what we've got here."

The cargo area of *High Porter* seemed largely undisturbed as D'Arcy moved through the stacks. The scans were matching with the list they had, thankfully all nonperishable goods headed for Trappist-1e.

"D'Arcy, come look at this," Emel called from his left, and he cut through the row of containers to meet her. A pile of cargo had been knocked over, broken open, and scattered, the pieces floating in a wide semicircle toward the rounded wall of the room.

"These were supposed to be scanners for our friends at Trappist Minerals," she said when he leaned in to examine one of the destroyed boxes.

"There are some." He poked at a shattered piece of a scanner, its outer casing marked with the company logo. The wreckage spun lazily with the sudden momentum. "But why demolish the boxes? Why not just take them?"

"Fight?"

"Not here." D'Arcy shook his head as he looked around. "There are signs of it by the airlock. There was something else in these." That was an assumption on his part, but he'd seen enough smugglers over the years to know all the tricks. "The question is, what was it?"

MAX MOVED DOWN THE CORRIDOR TOWARD THE BRIDGE, HER helmet lamp throwing shadows onto the walls and floor. Nika and Tamago were bringing up the rear of the group, both Neos watching behind them for signs of movement.

Jenks was half a step behind Max, sword out, and even though she couldn't hear anything over the com, Max was pretty sure the chief was still muttering about killer suits.

Which they thankfully hadn't seen.

However, they had seen blood, and a lot of it. Dark stains painted on the floor and walls, but no bodies or signs of a fight beyond that. It was like *Opie's Hat* or *The Red Cow*. The crew of the *High Porter* was gone.

They rounded a corner and Max almost ran headfirst into the tablet floating in the air at eye level. She stifled a scream as she skidded to a stop.

"Max?" Nika's voice was soothing over the com.

"Fine. Just debris." Max grabbed the tablet and passed it to Jenks. "I hate this place," she said.

"Noted," Nika replied.

"Captain Alex Kenner," Jenks announced, "does not password-protect his tablet."

"It works?" Max glanced down the corridor and then back at Jenks.

"Battery is low, but it's turning on. It'll probably die on me here any second. Oh, there's a recording already queued up." Jenks tapped the screen.

A man appeared. He was bloody and disheveled and his brown eyes were wide with terror. "This is Captain Alex Kenner of the freighter *High Porter*. If anyone gets this, we've— I don't know what's going on. We've been attacked by something. It's made the crew turn on each other. I think it's something with their chips; mine broke down on the way to Trappist, and I—" He broke off, looking away from the camera, and fear flashed over his face. "If you're watching this, run. Get out before the music starts."

The recording cut off and Jenks's swear filled the silence. "This is fucking wrong. I vote we go."

Max hit the main com. "Vera, Pia—eyes open for potential threats."

"Roger that," Vera replied.

"What's going on?" D'Arcy asked.

"D'Arcy, where are you?" Max replied.

"About to load something onto *Dread*. What is it?"

"Jenks and I just watched something worrisome. I need you to trust me and call this mission. We'll talk about it once we're out of here."

"Done," D'Arcy replied without hesitation. "Get back to the ship. We're on our way to the door. Vera, Pia, I want you two to head back to Trappist now. We'll be right behind you."

"Negative on that, D'Arcy," Pia replied. "We've got incoming."

Max brought the readings up on her HUD as soon as Pia said it and her heart thumped painfully in her chest. The mass of ships was a ways out but closing fast.

"Double-time it," Nika ordered, and Jenks shoved the tablet into her pack before she spun and followed his order. Max was on her heels.

"Chae, bring the ship in closer so we can jump it," Max said as the four Neos sprinted through the dark corridor back toward the cargo bay. The com was alive with voices—orders and information flying at the speed of light.

"Get to your ships—we'll cover you." Pia's voice was cool and professional. "Vera, what's our countdown to engagement?"

"Eight minutes. *Flux* will lay a line of mines across the most likely avenue to the ship. Deploy yours thirty-five degrees to our starboard."

"Roger that."

"This was a trap and we walked right into it," Nika said, and Max realized it was on their private com.

"It was. All we can do is make sure they can't close it properly. We'll get to the ships and they can't—"

The suit slammed into her from a side corridor.

THIRTY-EIGHT

Trappist System

The impact of the suit rammed Max into the hull with a loud thud, her curse echoing over the coms. Jenks spun. "You have got to be fucking kidding me."

There was yelling on the main com, but Jenks tuned it out. Her sword was useless with Max in the way, but her brain, in that strange way it had under pressure, was already cataloging the information. It was a newer suit, not military, but potentially one belonging to the crew of this same ship. And while that was important to note, the thing was wrapped around her friend, empty hands scrabbling at her suit, and that was the crucial data at the moment.

It was trying to tear Max's suit open.

The cold certainty morphed into terror when the fabric of Max's suit gave, and Jenks jumped into action. She dropped her sword, lunged forward, and wrapped both arms around the middle of the suit. Bracing her feet against the floor and using the added help of the magnetic lock, she pulled it away from Max with a mighty jerk backward.

She flung it to the side. "Sword!" she called, disconnecting her boots and jumping on the back of the suit before it could get up. It bucked, but she had the mass advantage, at least for the few moments before the servos compensated.

Max slapped the hilt of her sword into Jenks's hand and Jenks drove it downward into the base of the suit's torso, hoping that Sapphi had been right when she'd told her the location of the control panel.

The sword point cut through the suit, which spasmed once and then went still.

Max had one hand clamped on the tear in her suit and was fumbling at the other for the pouch on her left leg. "Patch."

"I got it." Jenks opened her pouch and fished out the repair patch, slapping it into place. It sealed tight.

"You only get one shot at us, fuckers." Jenks kicked the helmet and sent it spinning down the corridor.

It came to rest at the foot of another suit.

"Or maybe they get a lot more shots."

"Move," Max ordered, grabbing Jenks by the arm and pulling her away. She snatched up Jenks's sword and sprinted for the cargo bay.

"Ihatethishit. IhatethisSHIT," Jenks chanted as they ran. "Sapphi, more fucking suits. One down, at least one behind us."

"A whole lot in front of us," Nika replied. "Where did they all come from?"

"My fucking nightmares—"

Jenks skidded to a stop behind Max in the door of the bay and stared at the dozen suits that had appeared in the room while they were gone.

She breathed a sigh of relief that *Dread*'s crew had gotten out and a second one that Doge was safely back on *Zuma*.

The suits were unmoving, except for the two at the airlock, and as she watched in horror they launched themselves out into the black toward *Zuma*. "Chae, you've got incoming. Do not let those fuckers touch my baby!"

"Already on it, Chief," Chae replied.

"They haven't seen us?" Nika asked over the com. "Is that why they're not moving?"

"If they're connected, then they know we're here," Max replied. "And there's no reason to think they're not."

"The other one behind us isn't moving, either. They think we're trapped." Jenks knew it was silly, but she still bared her teeth at the empty suit standing at the end of the corridor.

"We *are* trapped, Jenks." Nika's voice was calm.

"Nah, we're fine. Max, can I have my sword back?"

Max held her sword out without comment and Jenks passed hers over without taking her eyes off the suit.

"Tamago, when I say go, I want you to slice through the straps holding those containers down and start slinging them. Nika, same on your side. Then turn off your boots and launch yourself toward the exit. We'll go up and over. Don't let them grab you; the directive for the suits seems to be to open up a breech in ours. Chae, are we clear to make a leap out the door?"

"Affirmative, I took care of both of them and am back in the pilot seat. Sapphi is at the airlock now in her pack to help as needed."

"Sounds good." Jenks kept her eyes on the suit in the corridor and reached back to pat Nika. "Sorry about this."

"It's fine. I'll live."

"That's the plan, bro."

"*Zuma*, we are coming around to your side," D'Arcy said. "We'll cover you."

"Roger that," Nika replied. "Jenks, on your mark."

She looked around once more and adjusted her grip on her sword. "Go."

Tamago and Nika moved in almost perfect synchronicity, slicing out on either side of the stack of cargo. The suddenly freed bins turned into missiles in the gravity-free space when both Neos shoved them toward the empty suits standing nearby.

They pushed off the deck and soared over the heads of the suits, which had started moving forward, shoving aside the boxes and making their way toward Jenks.

"Go on, LT," she said when Max didn't follow the others.

"Nope."

"You're fucking up my plan."

"Not leaving you here alone," Max replied. "What are we doing?"

"Distract them for long enough so you all could get out the door and then follow?" Jenks lunged forward, spearing the suit from the corridor in the gut and jerking her sword to the side. There was a spark and the suit collapsed.

"So you had no plan."

"You say potato . . ."

"What?"

"Control panel is at the base of the spine and in the helmet."

"Thank you." Max kicked one suit away and swung on another, shearing it in half. The top floated off, hands grasping at emptiness before stilling when Max drove the point of her sword into the exposed receiver. The legs froze. "Nika and Tamago are at the door. He's got words for you when we get on the ship. Disconnect your boots, Chief—that's an order. I want to get out of here."

Jenks kicked a box toward a suit, the impact nearly folding it in half but not doing any damage. "Fine, LT, let's go." She flipped the magnetic catch on her boots and pushed off the floor, using the cargo containers floating in the space around them as either platforms to move forward or as more missiles to send toward the enemy. As she chucked a container at a suit and watched the helmet go flying, an idea occurred to her.

"Hey, Sapphi, do you still need a suit to signal trace?"

"It would be helpful, but—wait, what are you doing?"

"Something I'll get yelled at for, most likely." Jenks landed against the wall by the exit door, turning her boots back on and grabbing for Max, using the LT's momentum to shove her out the door into the blackness beyond.

The suits had pivoted and unfortunately figured out they could move a hell of a lot faster if they, too, disconnected their boots from the floor. Jenks dragged in a breath and then grabbed the closest one, dragging it out of the airlock after her.

Out of the darkness and into the black.

SAPPHI CAUGHT MAX BY THE ARM WHEN SHE HIT THE SHIP and watched in horror as Jenks grappled with a suit for a second before mentally slapping herself and jumping onto the console by the airlock.

Max had pivoted and launched herself back out the door, the only thing keeping her from drifting away into space the tether she'd snapped into place.

Everything else became background noise as Sapphi homed in on the signal from the suit and started the trace program. Chae was holding the ship within three meters of the massive freighter, a feat that had to be done on manual, as the autopilot's safety features wouldn't allow for anything under twenty meters. But more suits were pouring from the *High Porter*'s airlock and headed straight for them.

"Jenks, I've got what I need—let it go."

"Yeah," Jenks grunted. "About that."

"I've got her."

Sapphi made it back to the airlock in time to see Max kick the suit and send it spinning away from Jenks, then grab the chief and start hauling them both hand over hand to *Zuma*.

Suddenly the song she'd been unable to get out of her head was in her ears and for a moment Sapphi thought she'd totally stepped out of reality, but the shocked look on Max's face and Jenks's low curse told her they could hear it also.

The haunting melody filled the ship over the com, still so familiar but unplaceable. Sapphi felt a strange pressure in her head, like someone had grabbed her skull and squeezed, but it vanished as quickly as it had appeared. The warning notice from her DD was loud in her ears.

The lights flickered out and *Zuma* stalled for just a second, then sprang back to life as if nothing had happened.

The killer suits all stopped, floating in the black as lifeless as petals on a pond. Sapphi's program chimed the notice of a lost signal and she grabbed for Max as the pair reached the airlock again.

"We're all in. Chae, get us out of here!"

"Roger that, ETA on engagement two minutes."

Sapphi retracted her helmet just as the inner door cycled open and Nika was there to help her out of the EMU pack as *Zuma* banked away from the *High Porter.*

He shouted at Jenks at the same time.

"I am going to bust your ass all the way back down to spacer if you ever do anything like that again!"

"Told you I was gonna get yelled at," she said to Sapphi, who gamely kept her face expressionless. "We needed a signal, so I got us one. I can apologize like LT next time if it helps. Ow." She rubbed the back of her head and shot Max a look.

"Anyone else just have a power fluctuation and DD weirdness?" Pia asked over the com. "Thought it was an EMP, but my sensors are tagging more than that."

There was a chorus of affirmatives.

"We're all good now, though," D'Arcy replied.

"Hostiles incoming. I'm seeing eight ships," Vera said. "Tien is getting IDs. Are we fighting or running?"

"They're going to hit the mines in sixty seconds," Pia replied.

"Get out before the music starts," Jenks murmured.

"What?"

She looked at Sapphi. "The recording we saw said this would happen. I think that was supposed to disable the ship, fry our DD chips. Somehow make us turn on each other. I'm putting feds on it being whatever made those people on the Rainbow ship attack *Dread* and what happened to *High Porter.* So why are we all still . . . us?"

Sapphi stared, the idea of all of them attacking each other colliding with the warning still flashing in the corner of her vision. "I need to get to the bridge," she said, starting to wiggle out of her suit.

"Leave it on," Nika ordered. "Just in case. Go, I'll stow this."

Sapphi nodded and raced down the hallway, grabbing the railing and hauling herself up the stairs. Nika and Chae were having a rapid-fire conversation over the com and Sapphi slid into her seat, tapping the console to give her a com feed to the other three hackers.

"Potential cyber-attack situation. Give me your reads on what you're seeing. I think we survived the initial surge, but watch for penetration attempts."

"Agreed," Pavel replied. "I don't know what that EMP was, Sapphi, but it looked a lot like the one that hit our coms on Jupiter during the attack. I think your shielding program saved our asses."

Sapphi dragged in a breath. After the initial panicky patch job, she'd spent weeks after the explosion on Jupiter Station with the others trying to figure out what they'd been hit with. The device set in coms hadn't only exploded, it had scrambled internal coms and shut down the bulk of the DD chip functions. The Babels had thankfully been spared; otherwise the chaos of that awful afternoon would have been so much worse.

"That means we missed some of that tech and I'm thinking you're right. This could explain what happened to Jasper and Tara," Lupe said. "I'm not seeing anything else— Shit—ignore that. Just had a ping on my weapons system."

"On mine, too," the other two men echoed.

"I'm clean," Sapphi replied with a frown. Why hadn't they shielded their own suits from the EMP?

Unless they don't have the ability.

"Mines four through fourteen just tripped. We've got hits on the first two lead ships." The announcement over the main com cut through their conversation. "All ships target those two in the front. Let's see if we can convince the others they don't want any of this." D'Arcy's voice was calm and steady.

"I'm getting an attack on our life-support system also," Saad said. "Whoever this is, they're good."

"But so are we," Pavel said.

"I'm seeing it now on our life support," Sapphi replied. "Hold the line, everyone, tell your commanders what's happening. Nika, I advise we run," Sapphi said out loud. "We're seeing multiple penetration attempts on our weapons systems and *Flux*'s life support. We can hold them off, but if even one gets through, they're going to turn that ship on the others."

"NeoG Interceptors, this is Captain Raham with the CHNS destroyer *Leonard Nimoy*, escorting the Tow Ship 488. We're reading mine detonations. Please advise on the situation."

Sapphi hit the com. "Captain Raham, this is Ensign Zika with *Zuma's Ghost*. Stay back. Repeat. Stay back behind the zone I'm sending you. We are dealing with an unknown weapon that could disable your ship and your crew."

"Ensign, where is your commander?"

Sapphi rolled her eyes.

"He's right here," Nika replied. "Commander Nika Vagin. Captain, do what my ensign says. We'll explain later."

"Now we can't run," Sapphi muttered. "Great."

"Two targets down! Concentrating fire on the next ones."

"Evasive maneuvers. Hard to port."

"I've got solid IDs; four of these are our missing pirate ships."

"You." The voice that clawed its way into Sapphi's head past the com chatter sounded like two hulls grinding against each other. "You are the one she was talking to. The one she was looking for."

Sapphi gasped as the world seemed to shrink around her and then snap back wide. She heard muffled shouting as she grabbed her head and fought the urge to black out.

"Who are you?" She managed to grit out the words.

"You are intruding on our space. Get out."

"Who are you? Why do you think this is your space?" Running protection on her own DD chip while having a conversation was old hat for Sapphi, and the pressure on her skull eased somewhat, but this was even more challenging than any hacker comp at the Boarding Games.

She wondered how long she could keep this up.

"This is our space. We have claimed it. You are intruding. Get out."

Sapphi muttered a curse. "Repeating the same shit doesn't tell me anything, pal. I'd rather talk to Pirene; she's better at this." Not by much, but her mysterious adversary didn't need to know that.

"She doesn't understand the dangers. Get out or be destroyed."

"Sorry, I think that's my line," she replied.

There was a scream of outrage as another ship exploded under the concentrated fire of the four Interceptors. The presence in her head vanished.

"Another ship down. The other five are running!" Vera announced over the com.

"Sapphi? Talk to me."

She blinked at Jenks, her friend's face resolving out of the blur. "That was wild."

"What the fuck happened?"

"I think I just met Art."

"What the fuck is this?" Kerala slammed the tablet down on the table so hard, it was a wonder it didn't shatter.

Ross looked at the schematic and sighed. "A necessary part of securing funding."

"The world is ending and we're still going on about funding. You put an untested weapon on my probe, Ross! What the actual fuck."

"You own the AI, Kerala, nothing more. The US military put a *defensive program* on the probe that they helped pay for. A probe we couldn't have launched without their help, I'll add. We don't know what's out there or what the LCFLT is going to run into in the next two hundred years. ART is there to make sure everything stays safe."

"'Armed Reconnaissance Tracker' doesn't sound like a safety program, Ross. It sounds like a weapon. You hid this from me. You put a weapon on board with a child."

"For fuck's sake, Kerala. The AI isn't a child, and you need to stop acting like one. Of course I didn't tell you, because I knew you'd react just like this." He sighed and rubbed at the bridge of his nose. "Look, there's nothing you can do about this now and if you kick up a fuss, they'll just boot you off the program. Possibly even revoke your family's protected status. Do you want that?"

"Is that a threat?"

"It's the reality. It's getting bad out there. You don't want to be out in it. Just do your job and if we're both lucky, we'll live to at least sixty."

"That's not what I'm concerned about."

"Maybe it should be."

THIRTY-NINE

Trappist System

It took them the better part of two days to clean up the mess at the belt and come back to Trappist-1d. Everyone had been tense, waiting for the mysterious fleet to reappear or for their ships to be taken over or for one of their crewmates to go rogue, and Emel knew she wasn't alone in breathing a sigh of relief when they'd returned to the relative safety of the main system.

Now she stood in the conference room, watching a replay of the dogfight in the belt with a frown while the raised voices next door bounced through the air like thrown knives.

"I did not fucking lie to you!"

"I saw those ships, Techa. Four of your ships that you told me were missing. They attacked us. What else am I supposed to think? Tell me what's going on. Who the fuck is Art and what does he want?"

"Fuck you if you think you're going to hang this on me. I told you what happened. Whatever is running those ships, it isn't my people."

"D'Arcy, that's enough. Take a walk." Stephan's order was

calm and cool and then his voice dropped too low for Emel to hear.

She glanced over her shoulder and offered D'Arcy a sympathetic smile as he came through the doorway. He didn't return it, but joined her, crossing his arms over his chest and staring at the playback.

Emel paused the recording and ran it back. "See this?"

"It's a pirate ship" came his growled reply.

"*The Possum.*" She agreed. "Four of the eight ships were the missing pirate ships on the list that Techa gave us. Two others were freighters and Tien couldn't get a clear ID on the other two. Why bring freighters to a dogfight?"

"Scrap haulers," he replied.

"Possibly, but you'd put them in the back, not on the front line. I think they were expecting us to be down from whatever EMP weapon they had."

"The only reason we weren't is because of Sapphi," he said with a shake of his head, and Emel watched the anger drain out of him, replaced with a worry that was unfamiliar enough on his face to scare her. "We almost died out there. I walked us right into a trap and nearly killed us all."

"You're not the only one who missed it. We're adults, D'Arcy, and this is the job we do. We were out there on orders, and we did exactly what we needed to when we needed it." It was as gentle a reminder as she could make it. He'd come so far and Emel didn't want to see him backslide into trying to protect everyone instead of trusting them to do their jobs. "There's something more important here."

"More than your lives?"

"Yes," she said emphatically, and reached out to point at the moment frozen on the screen. "*The Possum* took a direct shot from *Flux*. Something looked weird to me, so I went back to watch the whole engagement and then I looked at the footage of the encounter with *Rising Sun*. There's no atmosphere venting. Not on any of these ships."

Emel waited a beat for the information to sink into D'Arcy's head before she continued. "Between those suits and what happened to Sapphi, I can't help but think we're not dealing with humans."

"Have you been talking to Lupe?"

She chuckled and shook her head. "There's no reason for people to be wearing suits on a perfectly functional ship, but machines and computers don't need air, D'Arcy."

A look of comprehension washed over his face, followed by more worry. "I don't know of anyone besides our people who could accomplish something like that. And honestly even that is stretch."

Emel tapped the screen. "Sapphi and the others probably have a list longer than your arm."

"That's a long list," said the voice from behind them, and Emel turned to see Sapphi. "But you're right," the ensign continued as she joined them. "On both counts."

She'd rested after the debrief, but Sapphi still looked tired.

"I wish we'd seen that sooner," she murmured, looking at the frozen screen. "The conversation with Pirene makes a lot more sense now. Whoever she is, she's trying to work against Art."

"You think she's part of it?" D'Arcy asked.

"I do, but she either got cold feet over what he has planned or was trying to work against him from the beginning. While I agree with you that some of this seems automated, it can't be completely void of human involvement. You can only automate so much. Making those suits isn't easy, either. It would have taken a while to put them together, not to mention all the testing." Sapphi trailed off, rubbing a hand over her eyes and then staring blankly at the screen. "He was behaving like a child."

"Sapphi?" Emel reached a hand out and rested it on her forearm when the ensign didn't continue.

Sapphi blinked. "Sorry. I was thinking."

"You said he acted like a child? Who?"

"Art. He was behaving like my little brother did when we would play as children. Just repeating 'get out, it's mine' as if the words would make it real. Can't reason with that." Sapphi made another face. "The people on our list would have killed for the chance to gloat about what they'd accomplished, especially to me. That's how most of them ended up on the list in the first place." Then she sighed and rubbed at her forehead.

"I finished compiling the signal trace from both the suit Jenks highjacked before the EMP took it out and from the probe here on the ground. The suits on the *High Porter* were getting a signal from somewhere in the asteroid belt, I couldn't get a good lock on it before it vanished, but I can tell you that same signal was communicating with the ships."

"And the one on the ground?" Emel prompted when Sapphi went silent.

"It did get bounced through the probe, but the signal came from the Dànǎo Dynamics research facility." Sapphi didn't look away from the screen. "Yasu hasn't been in the scene for years, but that doesn't mean he doesn't know how to do this. He was as good as I was once, possibly better.

"Anyhow, it's still not enough proof for Stephan's liking," she said with a shrug. "I'm going to throw out a few feelers here and then talk to my mom. Saad and Lupe are working on tuning the EMP shield. It's not even remotely ready for mass distribution, but if the Navy can unkink itself—" She broke off with a cough when D'Arcy laughed. "Sorry, Master Chief."

"Don't be." Emel chuckled. "You're not entirely wrong if you were going to say 'unkink itself enough to put untested things on their ships.'"

"I was, and I think once Admiral Chen gets done telling them the issue, at least the ships here at Trappist will be loading up the program." Sapphi's amusement faded and Emel felt a chill run up her spine at the ensign's next words. "I watched those other recordings from *High Porter*, and the last thing I want is anyone else's DD chips getting fried like that. Pro tip: if you don't want nightmares, I'd advise against watching them. Talk to you both later."

Emel let the silence hang in the air after Sapphi's departure. She couldn't imagine how hard this was for the ensign, that someone she'd once loved could be responsible for all this. They'd discovered more recordings on the tablet Max and Jenks had taken off the freighter and Sapphi's advice was too little too late. It had been the worst thing Emel had seen in her entire life. Whatever weapon Sapphi's tech had managed to shield them from had devastated the crew of the *High Porter* and they'd turned on each other with a fury that had been inhuman.

Or maybe we're just so far removed from it that it seems inhuman now, she thought.

For there was no denying humanity had once upon a time nearly destroyed not only themselves but the whole of the planet with that same sort of vicious behavior.

And Mars wasn't so long ago, was it?

"TELL ME HONESTLY: WHAT HAS THE CHN DONE FOR US?"

Emel sighed and pushed away from the railing. "I'm not interested in having an argument with you."

"I'm not arguing. I want to know."

"No, you don't—you just want to pick a fight. You've wanted to since the moment you laid eyes on me." Emel met his gaze squarely. "Tell me I'm wrong."

"You're wrong." He caught her by the arm before she could walk away. Emel gave his hand and then his eyes a flat look and he released her. "Sorry."

"You will be if you grab me like that again without asking." Emel tried to tell herself the flashing grin on his face didn't make her pulse race faster than it should have, but she was lying. "It's called consent, D'Arcy—learn how to ask permission before you touch people."

"I'm sorry," he repeated. "And I don't want to fight, Emel. It was a genuine question."

"It seems like this whole place is spoiling for a fight," she replied. "I don't have any answer you'll like, D'Arcy, and we both know it. They're not perfect, but the CHN is trying."

"You call this trying?" He laughed sharply and gestured at the habitat spread out below them. The streets were quiet in the early dawn hours, but a seething restlessness hung on the air. "You were down in the market yesterday, Emel, and if I hadn't been there as well, you probably would have gotten your head bashed in."

She sighed and held up her hands. "Seriously, I'm not going to do this with you."

"People are hurting, Emel." The heat was gone from his voice and D'Arcy's shoulders sagged as he turned away and leaned against the low wall that ran around the top of the building. "And no one in charge seems to care."

"YOU OKAY?" D'ARCY ASKED.

"Yeah, just thinking about how we almost wiped ourselves out of existence." Emel shoved both hands into her pockets and rocked back on her heels. "And then still didn't learn our lesson."

"Some of us did," he murmured. "Just too damn late."

"I have never blamed you for what happened to my brother," she whispered, reaching out and wrapping her fingers around his.

"You didn't have to. I blamed myself enough over the years. Thought of all the things I should have said, or how I should have been with him. Thinking that maybe I could have—"

"Also gotten killed?" She shook her head. "No. There's no point in going back to it, D'Arcy. If you had died, too, what happens to all the lives you've saved over the years? Don't argue with me," she scolded when he opened his mouth. "I've read your public file. I've talked to your friends and the people around Amanave. You've done good work. Be proud of it."

D'ARCY STARED AT EMEL, AT A LOSS FOR WORDS TO COUNTER her vehement speech.

"Say 'You're right, Emel.'" She turned back to the screen and started to tug her hand free of his.

He felt his mouth twitch into a grin before he could stop it, and he held on to her. "You're right. And I'm working on it." He squeezed her hand and then released it. "So sorry in advance for the number of times you'll probably have to yell at me again."

"I wasn't yelling," she replied, giving him side-eye.

"Not this time." D'Arcy's DD pinged and he answered it. "What's up, Nika?"

"I'm in the warehouse where they off-loaded the cargo that was left on *High Porter,* and what they could scrape out of the other two freighters. Where are you?"

"In the conference room. What do you need?"

"Come take a look at this."

There was a second ping and Nika's location popped up. D'Arcy tapped Emel on the shoulder. "Come on, Nika's got something for us."

They jogged out of the building and across the compound to the nearby warehouse. The door guard nodded to D'Arcy. "Commander Vagin said you were coming. He's all the way in the back."

"Thanks, Mike." D'Arcy ushered Emel through the door. The warehouse was one of the newer buildings on the base and mostly empty, except for the stacks of retrieved cargo from the *High Porter* across the expansive room.

"D'Arcy!" Nika waved a hand, barely visible behind the stacks, and the Neos wound their way over to him. "I had them unload the undisturbed stacks and any debris on the floor in the same layout as the cargo bay. You'd mentioned you were getting ready to load something onto *Dread*."

"Yeah, we ditched it when all hell broke loose. It was part of a stack over there." D'Arcy looked around and spotted the single layer of Trappist Mineral boxes that had been unbothered on the floor. "The other boxes were floating above, some ripped open. I thought it was strange that whoever had hit the ship was so selective about the cargo."

"Like they were looking for something." Nika tapped a box. "Supposedly scanners, and probably most of them are."

D'Arcy spotted the emblem of Trappist Express on the package inside the opened container. "That's interesting."

"Very." Nika reached in and pulled out a gun.

D'Arcy raised an eyebrow. "That's going to be a fun conversation with Trappist Minerals."

"It is, but here's the more interesting part." Nika put the gun down and gestured them over to another pile of cargo set off from the *High Porter*. "This is what we were able to salvage off *The Red Cow* from earlier. Not a lot left intact, but we found more boxes labeled for Trappist Minerals with Trappist Express cargo inside. And this." Nika reached into a box and pulled out a device.

D'Arcy's breath hissed out.

"Is that what I think it is?" Emel asked.

He fumbled for a second, before remembering that while she hadn't seen the aftermath of the explosion on Jupiter Station—that she hadn't been ass-deep in the chaos and terrible silence when their DD chips weren't working and there was no way of telling who was alive and who wasn't unless you could put your hands on them directly—what Emel had been doing was working on a device very similar to this.

What Nika was holding was a perfect match for the one they'd found hidden outside the destroyed coms office. The same one the agent for Tieg's smuggling ring had admitted she'd planted on the station to test its disruptive capabilities.

"It is," D'Arcy replied, finally able to get his voice working.

"I've got Max and Chae going through both of the ships' coms to see if we can figure out how this shit got on board," Nika said. "Hopefully we'll get lucky and find something. The shield program Sapphi and the others developed after the attack seems to have saved us from the same fate as the *High Porter.*"

"Yes, but they've got more than one way to disable ships," Emel murmured, and both men looked her way. She shook her head with a frown. "Worse, they've got three now: the original one from *Opie's Hat,* these from *The Red Cow,* and whatever the ones from the *High Porter* can do."

"Is it too much to hope it's just an evolution of the same device?" D'Arcy asked grimly.

"Probably, but that's what I'm hoping, too," Nika said. "Also, I think it's time we had a conversation with my Trappist Mineral contacts again. You two want to join me?"

"Love to." D'Arcy took the device from Nika. "Let's get this over to Sapphi and the others first so they can figure out what we're dealing with here, and then we'll go have a little chat."

"Are we family?"

The look on Jenks's face fit into Doge's pattern recognition as surprise, sliding into the thoughtfulness that always seemed to follow when he asked these kinds of questions.

"Sure we are. Why do you ask?"

"Curious."

Another look appeared. It wasn't familiar and Doge had to flip through his catalog of faces Jenks had made for him a year ago until he came to one called "longing."

"Always wanted a dog when I was little. For some reason I felt like it would make up for everything else I was missing." She reached out and ran a hand over his head. The expression vanished and she smiled at him, her eyes full of joy. "Now I've got it all. Who'd have thought it?"

"I am part of a crew and part of a family?"

"Correct." Her smile widened. "Well, there's some wiggle room on the official crew designation as far as the NeoG is concerned. But everyone on the crew sees you as part of it and that counts more."

"I heard the commander say I could come on boarding actions if I behaved myself?"

"Right. Rosa said you could come along."

"What does 'behave myself' mean?"

Her laughter was something Doge could listen to for hours. Bright and unrestrained, it made things happen that he still didn't have a description for, and he hadn't yet asked her about what it could be. Doge filed it away with the others for later.

"That's an open-ended question, buddy, but basically you stay with me and don't do anything unless I tell you to."

"I can do that."

"Good dog," Jenks said.

FORTY

Trappist System

Max leaned back in her chair and stretched her arms over her head. "Chae, I'm taking a quick break."

"I'll be here," they replied without looking away from the screen.

She got to her feet and crossed the conference room. They'd been going through the com logs for the two freighters, which had been retrieved intact. She didn't think there would be any evidence of smuggling on the main communications. It was hard to believe any crew would be that obvious about it; but there were enough personal coms to go through and they'd hopefully find something there.

Max headed down the hallway. She was debating running to grab her and Chae something to eat when the sound of raised voices rolled around the corner. She followed the noise, spying Stephan and Luis standing shoulder to shoulder against an unknown adversary.

At least, until the familiar voice hit Max like a slap to the face.

"I want to see my sister and I will stand here for as long as I need to until you let me see her, Captain Yevchenko." Senator Patricia Carmichael's voice was even and firm, sounding as if she were just discussing the weather rather than threatening to stay in a hallway until her demands were met.

"And I've told you, Senator. She's not available." Stephan's voice was equally firm, the immovable object to her younger sister's unstoppable force. "I'll gladly deliver a message for you and Lieutenant Carmichael will answer you if she so chooses."

Max debated walking away.

You can't run from this forever.

She swallowed. "Captain, I'll talk to her."

Stephan turned to look at her and Pax took advantage of both the distraction and the sudden gap between the two men to slip through.

Max wasn't prepared for her sister to crash into her and hug her to the point of pain, or for the hope that sprang to life in her chest. "What are you doing here?" she murmured, hugging Pax back.

"What else was I supposed to do when no one would put my coms through and you didn't answer my emails?" Pax demanded. "Did you really think I'd just continue on like nothing had happened?"

She *had* thought that, Max realized. She'd just assumed her sister wouldn't want to speak to her or would be too afraid to go up against the family. "I'm sorry," she whispered, pressing a kiss to the side of Pax's head. "We were away from the planet and I've sort of been avoiding my emails."

"I'll take the apology for not answering my messages," Pax said, pulling away slightly and frowning at her. "But you'd better not be apologizing for anything else."

"You shouldn't be here."

"I already told Mom and Dad there was no force in this universe that would make me not be your sister and if they didn't like it, they could add me to the exile list also. The rest of the family can go spit." Her sister waved a slender hand in the air dismissively.

Fear gripped her. While Pax's position as a CHN senator was solid, whatever happened after her service wasn't.

"Pax, you didn't."

Her sister snorted loudly, startling Max even further. "Yes, I did. So did Scott. You should have heard him at the official family meeting, Max. It was glorious. He told Dad to shut up."

Max blinked, and her sister laughed.

"The cap of it all though was Ria, reminding everyone that if it weren't for you, this family would have been ruined several years ago and that we owed you a debt that could never be repaid. That was after she said the whole family needed to pull their heads out of their asses about how they'd treated Islen.

"Though, honestly, the best part of it was when some of the other cousins revolted also. You're not getting booted, though if you still want to leave, I support you. And you should know there's a rumor flying around that an official reminder about the importance of cooperation with the NeoG may have crossed Dad's desk."

"Ria said what?" The rest of what her sister said hit Max in the chest like one of Jenks's kicks. "Wait . . . what?"

"You really haven't heard any of this?" Pax glanced behind her to where Stephan and Luis were still standing.

"I haven't. We just got back yesterday. I've been busy doing my job." Max took a breath. "Sorry if that sounds short. I don't mean for it to. Things are weird. The truth is, I have been busy, but I've also just been avoiding it. I haven't heard any of this. We were out in the belt. I haven't looked at my email in days."

"Because you thought we'd side with them," Pax whispered, and Max wanted to cut her own tongue out at the look of hurt on her sister's face. "Scott said he'd talked to you."

"He did, but not about you, and right before he commed me, Ria had yelled at me about going to see Islen. I'm sorry. I was afraid I'd lose you, too, and I didn't want to face it." Max pulled her sister back into a hug. She was still trying to make sense of everything she'd just heard. Ria had defended her? Ria had defended Islen? Cousins revolted? The family actually *backed* her?

What the hell had she started?

All of that paled in comparison to the news that the NeoG had somehow gotten involved. Max looked over at Stephan. "What did you do?"

"As you said: my job," he replied. "Just looking out for my people, Lieutenant. But really, I didn't do anything."

Max gave an exaggerated sniff. "It smells of bullshit in here, Captain."

Stephan's blank expression didn't shift a millimeter. "All I did was remind some people what the NeoG—and maybe more specifically you—has done for them lately. Admiral Chen may have agreed with my assessment on an official level."

Max stared at him as the realization sank into her soul that her friends, her colleagues, even the important parts of her family had stood up for her. It was bittersweet to realize; even after several years she'd just expected everyone to turn away and leave her to flounder.

You're not with your family anymore, Max.

Luis winked at her. He patted Stephan on the shoulder. "We'll let you two catch up a bit."

"Kav, go with them," Pax said.

"Supposed to stay with you, Senator."

Max only spotted the slender black-haired person when they shifted away from the wall they'd been quietly leaning against. They'd been hidden behind Luis, on purpose no doubt.

"I am perfectly safe on a NeoG base." Annoyance flashed over Pax's face.

"I'm not questioning that, just telling you *my* job."

Pax took a rather obvious deep breath. "Max, you remember my bodyguard, Kavan Ying, they/them. Kavan, my sister Lieutenant Max Carmichael, she/her."

"Lieutenant."

"It's good to see you again." Max nodded to the bodyguard. "If you could give us a few minutes of privacy, I promise I'll keep my sister safe."

They studied Max for a long moment, their deep brown eyes giving nothing away, before finally nodding. "Don't leave the building, Senator."

Pax gave a sarcastic salute that had Max choking back her laughter. Kav ignored them and followed Stephan's lead down the hallway.

"They are driving me to distraction, Max," Pax confessed with a sigh. "I thought once this Tieg thing was done, I could go back to living my life like normal, but no. I still have that shadow." She made a face. "Sorry, I'm here to support you, not to bitch about my annoying bodyguard issue."

Max wrapped both arms around her sister and hugged her close. "No, it's fine. I'm just glad you're here."

Pax returned the hug. "For the record, I don't think you should leave the family. I'm going to float a proposal that we just kick *everyone else* out instead if they won't mind their own business. I'm reasonably sure I can get a two-thirds majority on it from the younger gens."

Max laughed aloud. "While I appreciate the support, I do know I'm going to have to face our parents eventually. I just need to figure out what I actually want to do about it."

"Well, whatever it is, we've got your back."

Max released her sister, wondering if Pax realized just how much she sounded like Jenks. "I'm realizing there are a lot of people out there who are looking out for me and I'm lucky to have you all in my life."

"MASTER CHIEF SHEVREAUX." BOSTON HASBROOK NODDED IN Emel's direction as Nika finished the introductions. The head of security for the major mining corporation in the system was a lean cis man with skin a few shades darker than hers and his afro pulled into a small bun at the crown of his head.

He was dressed in an outfit very similar to their own duty uniforms, only the pants were black and his shirt a dark gray.

"Come on back to my office," Boston said, gesturing them toward the far side of the sun-filled lobby. "I smoothed the last of it over with Reginald before he left for Earth a few weeks ago," he said to Nika. "The man's a pain in the ass, but he does good work. It's the only reason Shae keeps him on."

Emel had read up on Trappist Minerals on the way over. Shae was Shae Thema, president of the company. The Trappist-born businesswoman had built the mining corporation from the ground up almost forty years ago.

"Pia was sorry the circumstances required her to disable his ship," Nika replied. "And the yard has been pretty back-logged with work."

Boston laughed as he pushed the door of his office open. "You and I both know that's bullshit, Nik. Pia hasn't been sorry for anything as long as I've known her. Have a seat. What can I do for you?" He gestured at the chairs as he settled into his own, resting his elbow on the desk to his right.

"Sorry, hang on." Nika held up a hand. "Chae, what is it?" Emel watched the expression on his face shift at whatever Chae had told him. "Send me the emails. No, thanks. Is Max there?" There was a second shift to his expression at the answer before Nika composed himself. "All right, we'll be back when we're done."

Emel's DD pinged a moment later and the message from Nika had been sent to both her and D'Arcy, containing emails between the captain of the *High Porter* and Chad Reginald from an encrypted com channel.

Nika rubbed at the back of his neck. "I've got a couple of problems, Boston. Who's responsible for incoming ship-ments?"

"Like freight?" Boston frowned. "The crew at the docks

receives it in. Someone in purchasing would have set the order up, though."

"Does Reginald have access to the purchase requests?"

"He can put in orders through his expense account, sure. Why?"

"We picked up some missing freighters a few days ago. There was cargo left on the ships marked for Trappist Minerals on the outer containers."

Emel saw the way Boston's shoulders went tight at Nika's words and she slanted a glance at D'Arcy, who was closer to the door. He was leaning back in his chair but had both feet on the floor and she knew he was positioned to get between the security chief and the door if necessary.

"Which ships?"

"D'Arcy and his crew found *The Red Cow* several weeks ago. We ran into what appeared to be several pirate ships," Nika replied. "Also the *High Porter.*"

"You didn't find any survivors?" The grief on his face when Nika shook his head wasn't feigned. Boston sighed and looked down. "Sorry. Captain Kenner was a friend of mine. I'd been hoping for a miracle."

"Boston, *The Red Cow* was carrying Trappist Express cartons inside your company's shipment. So was the *High Porter.* They contained the same EMP device that was used in the attack on Jupiter Station. Were you aware your friend was smuggling weapons?"

"What? No!"

"I just got email confirmation from one of my crew, Boston." Nika sent the email to the security chief and a second wave of grief passed over Boston's face as he read it. "I suspect we'll find the same between someone on *The Red Cow* and Reginald."

"Shit. Nika, I didn't—"

"You want to give me access to your system so I can rule you out? I'd like to think you weren't involved, but Reginald doesn't have the kind of access that would allow him to bypass your security or even the docks."

"Absolutely." Boston tapped the panel on his desk. "Cassi, I need to come up and talk with Shae now. Yes, it's important. She'll understand."

He looked at Nika. "She'll understand, but she isn't going to like it."

"I don't like it, either."

FORTY-ONE

Trappist System

Sapphi felt guilty. It didn't matter she had clearance from Stephan to do this technically illegal infiltration of the Dànǎo Dynamics research network. It didn't matter that she wasn't going to get caught.

She felt like she was violating Yasu's trust somehow. The same way he'd violated hers by not asking about Doge directly.

"It's not the same." She rubbed both hands over her face as she said it for the hundredth time, hoping this declaration would stick.

It didn't.

It also didn't matter. They'd done the recon on Dànǎo's systems. She'd already sent out a carefully chosen malicious document to some of the higher-level supervisors at the research facility—not Yasu. She didn't want to risk spooking him and she knew he'd probably report it to the IT security team.

The document was Pavel and Saad's brainchild, a cleverly hidden code within an innocent-looking letter from a local school asking for donations.

She also maybe felt a little bad for doing that, but experience had shown her that people were far more likely to open something from a school or a nonprofit, or even a CHN agency, than just some nondescript sender.

Now all she could do was wait, wait for someone with the right access to take the bait, slip up, and allow her to slide through the backdoor into DD's system. She'd had three hits so far but none with what she needed.

She was well into her fortieth game of BottleCrash when the disposable console they'd set up specifically for this chimed at her that a system was trying to connect. Sapphi rolled into sitting on her bunk and rubbed her hands together.

"Who made a poor choice today? Hello, Liz Lewis . . . oh, jackpot, Director of Research Development. You should know better, but thanks for playing."

It wasn't the least bit surprising. Most low-level admins had enough sense not to click on random links and they deleted unknown emails out of habit or passed requests like hers up the chain. In Sapphi's experience, nine times out of ten the person responsible for letting in malicious software was someone with administrative access who really shouldn't be allowed to use technology at all.

Lucky for people like that, DD chips filtered that shit out automatically, but consoles were a whole other matter.

Liz had just given her full access to the network system and all the research files Dànǎo was currently working on. Sapphi easily skipped through to her destination. Yasu's console was clean, if filled with an enormous amount of fascinating data.

"What is this?" She frowned and copied the file labeled AI CONTAINMENT over to look at later. She snagged a few others on the AI project at large because she couldn't help herself and then forced her attention back to following the signal's trail through the network to its origin.

She found it several minutes later.

"Shit."

The signal that had activated the suit came from the console belonging to one Senior Vice President of Trappist Projects, Joran Ablegamway. It was already heavily compromised to the point where Sapphi couldn't believe how badly DD's Info-Sec people had dropped the ball.

Who, though? Who would go to so much trouble to make it look like DD had launched an attack on a NeoG base?

A warning ping jerked her attention back to her task and Sapphi made a face. Somehow she'd alerted someone to her presence and she exited the system with a quick command.

"MORNING."

Max leaned into Nika when he pressed a kiss to her cheek. "I didn't wake you, did I?"

"No, my alarm did." He rubbed both hands over his face. "How long have you been up?"

"A while. Between Pax's visit and everything else, I'm still trying to catch up on those emails from *The Red Cow*. I've found a few possibilities. However, we're going to need something more than what we've got if we want to take Chad Reginald into custody."

"We finished clearing Boston," Nika replied. "I'm not going to lie—I'm relieved about that. We also worked up a way to get Reginald back in the system without raising any suspicion. He's supposed to return today. But I'd like to see something that connects him to our mysterious Art and to Yasu. Speaking of, has Sapphi gotten anything?"

"Not yet, she was deep into something when I got up, though." Max tipped her head toward the glow coming from the room the other four Neos shared. "I've been thinking about all of this. You want to help me get it organized?"

"Let me get coffee."

Max sorted her thoughts as Nika grabbed a cup and sat down in the chair next to her.

"Whoever this is, they've been picking off ships very carefully. Smaller numbers so as not to raise any suspicions. Until recently."

"When they took too many?"

Max nodded. "I think we were too quick to discount the idea that they're trying to fill the power vacuum that was created by us taking Tieg down. It looks exactly like that's what Art is after. Why else hit the pirate ships?"

"Techa was the next reasonable force to slip into that role in the system. Even with her deal with us." Nika nodded. "So Art hit her first to scare her off the area?"

"Maybe. She doesn't seem like a person who scares easily, and she was scared, according to D'Arcy." Max frowned. "Everyone who's survived contact with Art has been scared."

"Given how few there are, I'm thinking it's a good response."

"My gut is telling me that Yasu's appearance in Sapphi's life again and his interest in Doge isn't coincidental." Max exhaled. "I just don't know what the connection is and that's frustrating."

"You think Sapphi was targeted?" Nika's blue eyes frosted over and Max reached for his hand.

"I'd like to think that Yasu actually cares for Sapphi on some level. And this isn't maliciousness but ignorance? Or coercion?"

"But you don't completely believe that."

"He doesn't read as someone truly bad, but yeah, I want it to be true for Sapphi's sake," she admitted. "Wanting access to Doge could just be because of his AI work, as he said to Sapphi and I guessed initially. There's no doubt that an artificial intelligence who can actively learn like Doge would be a huge factor on a long-range exploratory flight. Pre-Collapse tech wasn't all that advanced in the arena of artificial intelligence, and they lost a lot in the chaos. Dànǎo Dynamics obviously has the most advanced work on the subject and is the most invested on research there, but my understanding is that even the newer systems they've developed aren't much better than the original ROVER model and the newer versions have far more controls built in."

"Not sure Doge is the best example, either," Nika said with a grin over his mug.

She glanced at the open door of their quarters. "Doge is another thing entirely from the standard ROVER, which, I admittedly have a theory on also. But I don't want to talk about it out in the open."

"You once again have my attention, Max Carmichael."

Max laughed. "Did I lose it at some point?"

"Never," he replied, and the soft flutter in her heart answered his now familiar banter.

"I'm admittedly very curious how far DD's research has gone, but without admitting what's going on with Doge, we don't have an in there. Especially since he blew things between him and Sapphi. Anyway, I think this Art has worked very hard to stay in the shadows," Max said, forcing herself back on topic. "It makes sense for him to contact someone like Reginald, who would have access to supply requests for a major Trappist company, to see about smuggling in specific areas like the weapons and tech we found. But why? And what's he planning?"

"I'll be honest," Nika said grimly. "It looks like he's planning a war."

"That's what I'm afraid of." Max looked away when Sapphi wandered into the main room, rubbing both hands over her face. "Good morning."

"Is it, though?" she asked, dropping into the chair next to Nika. "I got into DD's systems."

"You sound less than happy about it."

Sapphi made a face. "I feel icky about it. I know I had to. I know it's for a job. I know I don't owe Yasu anything. And yet . . ."

"And yet you're a decent human being, Sapphi. It's okay to feel bad about it."

"The worst part is, I didn't get anything." Sapphi tipped her head back with a groan. "Some senior VP let someone else hack his shit. They had full access to his console and the whole system. Someone was reading his emails and all the project reports, plus sending signals to killer space suits from his terminal. Short of telling DD that we hacked into their system, I don't have any way to investigate who might have been responsible and there's probably no way to trace it anyway. I got nothing."

"What files did you take?" Nika grinned at Sapphi's flat look. "I know you, Zika. What did you snick?"

Max muffled her own amusement when Sapphi sighed dramatically. "Stuff about the AI research and a file on containment procedures that looked interesting."

"There's your info about the research," he said to Max. "Put it on the team server so it's official and you don't get busted if DD finds out you were poking in their stuff. Also, so LT here can satisfy her curiosity."

Max opened her mouth to protest, when her tablet pinged with a search return. She glanced down and hissed in triumph. "Got it. First Officer Traya Rigs had a secondary email that Doge was able to decrypt for me. There was a lot of traffic on it, including correspondence with Chad Reginald about some lost cargo she'd 'found' for him. And he responded that his buyer will be very interested if she can prove it's what he was looking for."

Nika tapped at the tablet. "If this Art had a deal with Reginald to buy the items on the *High Porter* and *The Red Cow*, though, why attack them?"

"Double cross?" Max shook her head. "That's the other part that confuses me. It doesn't make a whole lot of sense to attack the very ships that are smuggling your gear for you. Or even to attack Reginald, who's brokering everything."

"Unless that's because Vera and Pia were on the verge of catching him," Nika mused. "And he was just trying to throw them off."

"Or he was trying to help Art catch another two Interceptors," Max said as a sick feeling kicked her in the stomach.
"We got really lucky there with Sapphi's protection, Nika. I
don't mind saying out loud that I'm worried about what happens next time if we're not that lucky?"

"You and me both." Nika stood. "D'Arcy's over at Trappist
Minerals to talk with Reginald. Let's join him and share our
new information. See if we can't rattle our smuggler's cage a
little and get him to give up Art. Sapphi, get some sleep."

"COMMANDER MONTAGLIONE." BOSTON GREETED D'ARCY AT
the front door.

"Morning. D'Arcy is fine," he replied. "You got him?"

"Shae sent him a personal request. He's up in her office
none the wiser." The man frowned. "I'm not quite following
why you didn't just arrest him?"

"As strange as it sounds, we don't really care about Reginald. We want the man he's buying for." D'Arcy smiled slowly.
"Nika just sent me a message, said he and Lieutenant Carmichael will be joining us."

"You're not going to tell me why you've got such a smug
look, are you?"

"Sorry. I like you, Boston, but I think I'll save the surprise
for the intended audience." D'Arcy laughed at the man's flat
look. "We can go up and get started."

"Didn't figure you for a tease," Boston replied. "Let me tell
the front desk to send your people on up when they get here."
Boston jogged over and D'Arcy resisted the urge to watch his
ass, reminding himself that he was in uniform and representing the NeoG at the moment.

What surprised him was that for the first time in a long
time he regretted that fact.

Still, he behaved himself in the elevator and stayed silent
as they rode up to President Thema's office.

"Welcome back, Commander Montaglione. It's nice to see you again," the president's efficient assistant, Cassi, greeted him brightly. "Boston, why is that man in there with Shae?" Their tone for the security chief was belligerent.

"Business." Boston softened the short answer with a smile. "Did he hassle you?"

"Just under the line, as always," they replied. "I've got a cousin who just started freelancing surveying work. Can we hire him? At least I can kick him if he gets out of line."

"I'll pass his info on to Shae," Boston said. "You know how she is, though."

"I work for her, don't I?" Cassi rolled their eyes.

"We've got two more Neos coming up, Cassi, if you'll let them in when they get here."

They nodded and gestured at the closed doors. "Go on in. She's expecting you."

Chad Reginald was of average height, his pasty skin a hallmark of someone who didn't spend much time on the ground, but his hair was perfectly done and the suit he wore obviously expensive. He was laughing at something as they came in the room and D'Arcy caught the flash of relief on Shae Thema's face as she turned to them.

"Boston. Commander, thank you for coming."

"What's all this?" Chad asked, eyeing D'Arcy warily.

"My colleagues are on their way, Shae," D'Arcy replied. "They said to get started."

"What is going on?" Chad asked again.

"Let's all have a seat." Shae's expression was a practiced, polite smile of someone treading very carefully and D'Arcy wondered what it was about Chad that had the more powerful woman on edge.

They hadn't found any evidence to suggest that either Shae or Boston was involved, but D'Arcy picked a chair with a clear sight line for the door and the move didn't go unnoticed by the security chief.

"Commander Montaglione has been kind enough to help us with our filings for the cargo that was lost when the *High Porter* and *The Red Cow* went missing. While the ships have recently been retrieved—"

"They've been retrieved?" Chad asked, his eyes wide.

"I believe that's what I just said." There was a snap in Shae's voice at being interrupted and D'Arcy kept his face expressionless. "The cargo was not on board. The NeoG is investigating who might be responsible for hijacking the freighters as well as the ship who was chasing you initially."

"You mean the Interceptor?" Chad's tone was nasty.

"The *Rising Sun* was officially listed as lost in the black on Sol Day 277, 2434, three years to the day from first report of lost contact as per NeoG regulation section thirteen CHNC four," D'Arcy replied. "While we can be certain the ship itself was an Interceptor, it wasn't legally obtained, nor staffed by members of the Near-Earth Orbital Guard."

The door suddenly opened, and Cassi stuck their head in. "Shae, Commander Vagin and Lieutenant Carmichael are here."

D'Arcy watched as Chad's entire body changed posture at the mention of Max. Boston had noticed it, too, and the security chief failed to keep a hiss from escaping.

Introductions were made. Chad nearly fell over himself to pull out a chair for Max, and D'Arcy found himself exceedingly glad she'd never smiled in that vacant polite way at him. Not even the first time she'd met him, when her expression had been hesitant but genuinely warm.

"Such a pleasure to meet another Carmichael," Chad said. "I've done business with your family a time or two. They've always been very pleased with the results."

She nodded, which D'Arcy interpreted as "fuck off," but Chad seemed none the wiser.

D'Arcy waited until they were settled and then brought up the first set of emails between Chad and the *High Porter*. "I'm wondering, Mr. Reginald, if you can enlighten us as to what

Captain Kenner was bringing you that would have required asking Carolina down in purchasing to do an adjustment to an already filed order."

The man froze for a split second and then recovered with a speed that was impressive. "My fault entirely. I messed up the supply order. I knew a new order would have incurred extra shipping costs, so I asked Carolina to just add it to the order already on the books. I was merely trying to save the company money."

"Very thoughtful of you," D'Arcy replied. "However, you didn't answer my question. What was Captain Kenner bringing you?"

"Just supplies. I can't remember off the top of my head. I'd have to check my logs."

"Why don't you do that? We'll wait," D'Arcy suggested, leaning back in his chair.

The silence stretched as Chad went through the pretense of looking up the request. Finally he sighed. "I'm terribly sorry, Commander. As embarrassing as it is to admit it, I can't seem to find the record. I'll have to go check my office."

"Sit back down, Chad," Boston said as the man got to his feet. Reginald dropped.

"We may as well deal with these other emails," Max continued. "You appear to have exchanged these with the first officer of *The Red Cow* shortly before they left Earth on their Trappist run. "According to these, Traya Rigs had found something you—or, more accurately, the buyer you represent—were looking for. Would you care to enlighten us as to what that was?"

"That was private correspondence! A personal shipment. You had no right!"

D'Arcy had never seen Max go what Jenks called "full Carmichael," but he had a feeling he was witnessing it now.

"I have every right, Mr. Reginald." She reached down into the bag she'd brought and pulled out the device, laying it gently in the middle of the table. "This is a new EMP weapon, developed and used by the people responsible for the attack on

Jupiter Station last year. When we searched *The Red Cow*, we found several Trappist Express containers hidden within Trappist Mineral cargo and this inside. Your personal shipment wasn't on the manifest logs, which I find very curious.

"I'm sure the CHN will agree with me that the NeoG is well within its rights to charge you with collusion for the attack on Jupiter Station. Or would you like to explain to me, Mr. Reginald, just who your buyer is and why they wanted this?"

It was a bit of a shock when Chad bolted out of his seat and ran for the door of Shae's office—not because he thought the man was innocent, but because D'Arcy expected he was smart enough to know he wasn't going to get away. Obviously, Max had been waiting for it and stuck her foot out, tripping him up before he got past her. He hit the floor hard, rolling to a stop.

D'Arcy grabbed him and hauled him back to his feet.

"Look, this wasn't my idea! Yasu just said I could make some extra money by helping things along. Talk to him, not me!"

"We intend to, after we speak with you." Max studied the man and then reached out to pluck a loose thread off his lapel with a cold look. "Next time you pay that much for a suit, Mr. Reginald, make sure they do the stitching properly."

Chad flushed red and opened his mouth to respond, but D'Arcy had already grabbed him by the arm and spun him face-first toward the wall. "Chad Reginald, you are in violation of the Trappist Habitat Directive of 2331. The charges are smuggling and accessory to piracy with intent to harm."

"Maybe throw in obstruction of justice for trying to flee," Nika added. "We might take that off if you cooperate, though."

Chad paled as he looked around and saw no escape.

FORTY-TWO

The Verge

Sapphi leaned against the kitchen counter a few days later, enjoying a welcome break and visit with her mother that she'd had to argue hard with Nika about doing. She'd missed this so much, had hidden here a lot after the attack on Jupiter when she hadn't been working. Now she was hiding here again, away from the knowledge that despite all her hopes, Yasu was involved in this mess. He hadn't changed. And worse, everything seemed to point to the fact that he'd sought her out because of all this—not because of her.

She didn't think it was possible for an already broken heart to break even more.

So here she hid. Her mother's version of the Verge was private, safe from whatever this Art had planned, but Sapphi had made sure of it before venturing in. It looked exactly like home, right down to the smell of melomakarona baking in the oven. Though, frankly, that bit was a little cruel considering the ones in the Verge never tasted quite as good as the real ones. She'd told her mother as much and Cassandra just laughed.

"I know, love, we'll see you again soon. How are things?"

"Okay." She couldn't go into detail about the trip out to the belt or the wildness that had ensued. Couldn't talk about Yasu except in the vaguest of terms and that didn't seem fair at all to either her or her mother. So she went with the easy answer. "Decompressing from the Games, working on a few things for the job, the usual."

"You seem worried lately. Are you doing all right?"

Sapphi was equally relieved and frustrated by her mother's ability pick up on her moods. "I've been working on a problem. Actually, a few problems. It's complicated." Sapphi lapsed into silence and her mom didn't push, which she appreciated. Cassandra always knew how to let her children figure out their own answers to whatever puzzle plagued them while somehow being right there if they needed help.

It took a moment for the melody in the air to wind its way into her head, but once it was there, Sapphi froze. "Ma?"

"Yes?"

"What are you humming?"

"It's an old lullaby. I sang it to you as a child. All the parents in my family have sung it."

My family . . .

Pieces started to fall into place in Sapphi's head. The song. Pirene's name.

You look like my mom.

"We had a relative that worked on AI before the Collapse," she said. It wasn't a question.

"Yes, several, actually. Though your great-aunt Kerala Zika, with a multiple repetition on the 'great,' obviously, was probably the most well known. The story is, she worked on some important project during the Collapse. She didn't have any children of her own, so she gave her allotted spot in the bunker to her sister and niblings." Cassandra kissed her fingers and pointed at the sky. "There's a good chance we wouldn't be here if it hadn't been for her."

"Mom, do we know who she worked for?"

"The records from that time are spotty, but what we have is on the family server. Why?"

"I have to go." She crossed over and kissed her mother's cheek. "Love you. Thank you."

"Did I just solve your problem?"

"Even if you didn't, you always make things better." Sapphi laughed and kissed her mother again. "I'll see you later."

SAPPHI RIPPED OFF HER VR SET AND SHOUTED, "LT, I AM NOT the sharpest tool in the shed! Hades drag me into the deep. How did I miss it?"

Max looked up in surprise from her tablet as the others poked their heads into the common room at the sudden commotion. "I'm afraid you're going to have to back up several paces, Ensign, and explain."

"My great-times-whatever-aunt Kerala worked on AI programs during the Collapse for a company called Everlight in what used to be the United States. There's an old family story that my branch only survived because she gave up her position in one of the special bunkers they'd built to my great-whatever-grandmother and her kids."

"Okay."

"The song I've been humming—my mom was humming it today in the Verge. She said it's been passed down through our family for generations; that's why it sounded so familiar to me. But it's more than that—Pirene said *her* mother sang it to her. She said *I looked like her mother*. She made herself look like me and then like a sister. I missed it completely. Didn't even clue in when Emel mentioned the possibility of computers being in control of the ships." Sapphi waved her arms in the air. "Pirene isn't a human; she's the AI project my great-aunt was working on while the world was falling apart."

The room exploded into noise.

"What?"

"An AI? Running for over four hundred years? Are you serious?"

"Where?"

"Everyone be quiet," Nika said. "Sapphi, how can you be sure?"

"I'm not," she said, dejected for a second, but then brightened again in excitement. "But it sort of makes sense. Mom said Kerala was working on a secret project during the Collapse. If I can find the information on that, I'll bet that it somehow ties back to Pirene and maybe that will help us figure out where she is."

"Did you say Everlight?" Jenks asked, and Sapphi nodded. "Hang on, I got a response from someone on the board that mentioned that company." The room fell silent as she combed through her emails. "Found it!"

"Tablet," Max said, passing it over.

"Thanks. It was in a chat about end-of-the-world movies and how the Collapse was nothing like fiction. Zombie-Survivalist said that they'd heard about Everlight doing a secret project at the worst of the Collapse. They were a computer tech company who'd refused to help with the software for prototype transport ships because they wanted control of the copyright—"

"The planet was dying. People were dying, and they were fussing about copyright?" Sapphi blurted, and Jenks shrugged.

"Yeah—from what I can tell of the United States at the time, that was pretty par for the course. But actually, I think that was bullshit and they just couldn't devote the resources to work on the transports because they were working on something else. Anyway," she continued, "this guy said he'd found classified docs about this mystery project but couldn't crack the encryption. Several people have tried but no luck."

"Do you—"

"Of course I asked him for the files," Jenks said before Sapphi could finish her question. "Doge has been working on them for a week."

"I will probably have them cracked shortly," Doge announced. "I have not had any luck with those files that Pirene gave you, Sapphi. I am sorry."

She reached down and patted his head. "It's all right. I wanted to try to ask Pirene about them again, anyway."

"I don't want you in the open Verge—it was risky enough to let you go see your mother," Nika said, and Sapphi slid him a guilty look.

"I made sure she was safe, Commander."

"I know, but he's targeting you specifically and until I know how, I don't want to put you in his sights."

"I can run interference," Tamago offered. "Not sure how much good it'll do, but if you only need to be in there for a few minutes, Sapphi?"

"I only need five at the most." She frowned. "I don't want you to get hurt, Tama."

Tamago rolled their eyes. "I can give you five without any issue. Just promise me you'll bail when I do."

"SAPPHI, SIT," TAMAGO SAID QUIETLY SEVERAL MINUTES LATER.

"I don't understand how you do that." Sapphi dropped in a chair in the kitchen of her house in the Verge with a sigh.

"Do what?"

"You know full well what. Sit there without moving for hours on end and never feel like you're going to crawl out of your skin. Can't you feel the universe moving around you?"

"Of course I can." Tamago waved a slender hand through the air. "I just let it move. It moves regardless of if I do, and sometimes it's nice to stand in the river and feel the water flow around you."

"When was the last time you actually stood in water?"

"Visiting your family." They grinned. "Though Chae and I found a stream in the canyon when we were hiking last month." They gestured at their ankles. "Wasn't very deep, but it felt nice."

Sapphi shuddered and stuck her tongue out at her best friend. "You took your boots off and stood in mud?"

"I need to get you unplugged more."

"No thank you. Though the family trip was fun, and Jenks's description of her camping trip didn't sound terrible. Maybe I'll agree to a crew trip, especially if we really don't compete next year."

"Speaking of which, how do you feel about that?"

"Honestly, I'm good. We kicked some ass and went out on a win." It would be weird not to check the running stats she kept for the Games on a regular basis and Sapphi figured she'd probably at least offer to help one of the other teams do something similar. "I am looking forward to a break." She drew a pattern on the white tabletop. "You ever think about the fact that at some point we're all going to go our separate ways?"

"More than I like to," Tamago admitted. "But things change. They have to. We'd probably all kill each other if we had to stay together forever."

Sapphi laughed, then reached an impulsive hand out and gripped Tamago's fingers. "We'll be friends forever, though, right?"

"Of course, silly."

"Friendship is an unfamiliar concept to me."

Sapphi blurted out a startled curse at that new voice. Tamago was slightly more successful at keeping their surprise under wraps, but both of them had leaped out of their chairs to stare at Pirene, who'd just appeared on the other side of the table.

"So is knocking, apparently," Sapphi said finally.

"Why would I knock?" Pirene tipped her head in confusion.

"On the damn door," Sapphi replied, pointing. "So you don't scare ten years off a person's life."

"I'm sorry. I assumed you wanted me here with as little evidence as possible. I can go out and try again if you'd prefer?"

Sapphi sighed. It was amazing how, now that she was pretty sure she knew what Pirene was, it was so damn obvious. "No. Instead why don't you tell me why you weren't up-front about the fact that you're an AI?"

"I didn't think it was necessary. I am alive—that is all that matters. Stopping Art is the priority." Pirene actually sounded offended.

"What does Art want?"

"He thinks Trappist is his. He won't stop until humans are gone from it and, knowing him, he might not even stop then. Once, I could control him, but Yasu's interference has made the situation dangerous. He's responsible for my current predicament. I can't get free."

"Free from what? What did Yasu do?" Frustrated, Sapphi dropped back into her seat and slapped the tabletop. "Damn it, Pirene, you've been less than helpful. All this vague shit and locked files that I can't break!"

"What do you mean? The files were locked, yes." She blinked. "But you have the password."

"I do not—" Sapphi broke off and stared. "The song?" she whispered. "You used a shibboleth."

"Not me. Kerala always felt it was best to lock certain things away for just the two of us, for family. The song is ours. You are also family, Sapphi."

"How do you understand family but not friends?"

"I have never had friends. Though I think I would like to be friends with Doge."

"Have you talked to him?"

"No." Pirene shook her head. "I did not want to bring attention to him. When this is over, though, I would like to speak with him. How did you two do it?"

"You mean become friends?" Sapphi glanced at Tamago and the pair shared a smile. "*Taming of Yeva.*"

"I don't understand."

"It's not necessarily a straight line, Pirene. We bonded over a game, but it's more than that. We're on a team. We've worked together and helped each other. We care—" Sapphi fumbled suddenly, at a loss as to how she could explain what Tamago meant to her.

Tamago stepped up and slipped an arm around Sapphi's waist, leaning their head on her shoulder. "'Care' is a good word, Pirene. We care about each other, we love each other in a non-romantic way. There's a lot of things that make a friendship begin, but caring is important."

"I would like to learn more."

"We'd love to teach you, but first we need to fix this problem. Pirene—"

The house shook, startling all three of them.

"I thought I would have more time," Pirene gasped. "You must go. Art was not distracted for as long as I thought he would be. Go now."

"We can't leave you here alone."

"He won't hurt me, but you are a threat. You have the password now." She shoved them. "Please, go."

SAPPHI PULLED OFF HER VR SET AND SCRAMBLED INTO THE other room, where her tablet lay on her bed. Tamago followed, silent, as Sapphi pulled up the files.

"I hope this doesn't have to be spot-on key," she muttered, and then hummed into the microphone. The screen flashed an ACCESS GRANTED message.

LAST CHANCE FOR LIFE ON TRAPPIST
INTERNAL FILES
DR. KERALA ZIKA JOURNAL
LAUNCH DATA
ARMED RECONNAISSANCE TRACKER

"Massive info dump," Sapphi breathed. "I don't even know where to start."

"We'll just start at the beginning. Here, send me copies." Tamago grabbed her tablet and bumped it against Sapphi's.

Sapphi opened the first file and dove in.

Several hours later her head was swimming with names and dates and schematics. She'd burned through the overview of the Last Chance for Life on Trappist probe and read about a quarter of her ancestor's journal entries. At the same time, Tamago had been going through the launch data.

"We should take this to the conference room," Tamago said. "I think I figured out why the ships went missing in chunks like they did. Also, I just messaged Nika—they've finished the interrogation of Reginald. It seems he wasn't ever in contact with our mysterious Art. He just went where Yasu told him. That's why he was in the belt; he was supposed to be meeting with the *Rising Sun* when she suddenly started firing on him, so he bugged out."

"Are they bringing Yasu in?"

Tamago nodded solemnly. "You don't have to go see him, Sapphi. It's okay to let someone else handle it."

"No, I feel like I should. With everything between us and—ART." Sapphi frowned, the truth hitting her like a wave when she glanced down at the files again. "Oh *shit*."

"IN THE GRAND SCHEME OF THINGS, I'M LESS CONCERNED about EMPs than fighting an army of empty suits."

"Really?"

"The thought of the EMP sucks, but I can do fuck-all about it, so why worry? However, having a mass of suits come at me like a bad date is a terrifying thought," Jenks said to Luis as Tamago and Sapphi skidded through the door of the conference room. "What are you two running from?"

"Not from," Sapphi replied breathlessly. "ART is a weapon."

"Anything is a weapon if you have enough imagination." Jenks frowned at Sapphi's answering blank look. "Have you two been jacked in this whole time? Nika said five minutes."

"No. We've been reading files." Sapphi shook her head and slapped her tablet down in front of them. "ART is a weapon. He's not a person. He's an AI, only less sophisticated than Pirene, and the program that got resurrected after the Collapse to make the ROVERs was based on this. The Armed Reconnaissance Tracker was added to the LCFLT probe just before launch. That's why Yasu's been involved. He's one of the most knowledgeable AI experts out there!"

"Back up. We're dealing with *two* AIs?" Jenks shared a look with Luis.

"Only one, really. Pirene is on our side. I think. She's still sort of weird, but that might just be AI-related. She wants to be friends with Doge. That's probably why Yasu wanted information on Doge, too." Sapphi was doing that thing where she was talking faster than really made sense, and Tamago mouthed at her *Breathe* before Jenks could cut her off.

Pausing for a second, she continued—a little slower, "I did a search on Kerala's journals and, boy, was she pissed about the addition of ART. It happened without her knowledge or approval, but she didn't find out until after the launch."

"When?" Jenks asked.

"After the launch. I just said that."

Luis choked back a laugh and Jenks reached over to smack him. "Sapphi, when was the launch?"

"Oh, sorry. August 9, 2075."

Jenks whistled low. "Okay, I'm gonna say it now. If you are right—big, if true—that means these two AIs have been out in space for over three hundred and fifty years. That alone is cause to question if it's real."

"Sapphi, what did you mean she wants to be friends with me?" Doge asked.

"I don't know; that's just what she said."

Jenks looked down at Doge, her heart kicking up a notch in worry. "Has she tried to talk to you?"

"No. I would have told you."

Jenks rested her forehead on his for a moment.

"Back to the issue at hand," Luis said. "Sapphi, where did you get all this information?"

"The files," she replied. "Long story, short version. I had the access code for them this whole time. It was the song."

To Luis's credit, he didn't ask any more about the song. "All right, let's take a look at this on the main screen." He got to his feet and took the tablet.

Jenks stood and shot Tamago a smile. "You okay?"

"Fine. It was weird, but that's it," they replied. "Pirene was weird, that is. She asked us why we were friends." The petty officer patted Doge on the head. "It really sounded like she was hoping you two would be friends, buddy."

"I might like that." Doge seemed thoughtful.

The conference room door opened, and Jenks waved a hand as Max, Nika, and D'Arcy came in. The trio looked pleased with themselves, and that could only mean the interrogation had gone well.

"Sapphi had a breakthrough," Jenks announced.

"I know," Nika replied. "Tama messaged me."

"It gets better." Jenks drumrolled on the tabletop. "ART is apparently also an AI."

They stared at her.

"How is that better?" D'Arcy asked.

"Why you gotta ruin my jokes?" Jenks replied.

"Once Reginald figured out we had the documentation that would potentially tie him to the attack on Jupiter, you should have seen how fast he flipped to save his own ass." Max tapped on the screen, bringing up a statement. "According to Chad, Yasu contacted him two years ago through a secondary contact—we're running them down now—expressing an interest in 'any available new tech.'"

"I wanna see specs on this thing." Jenks turned. "Hey, Sapphi, send me the file on ART?" Her DD pinged in response and Jenks scanned through it quickly, appreciating that Max waited patiently while she did it. "I need to read this in depth, but here's the gist of it—the tracker was programmed to protect the probe from any and all threats. The threat parameters are wild, though. Everything from potential collision with any object to unknown spacecraft. God, these people just pitched an AI with the intelligence level of a toddler out into space with a vaguely worded set of instructions on protecting the probe."

A sudden chill gripped her stomach. "It looks like ART didn't have much to start with, so how in the hell did we go from communication ability, a limited EMP pulse, and a laser defensive system to hijacking military ships and building goddamned attack suits?"

They shared a look. "Yasu," Max said.

"Are we going to go pick him up?" Jenks asked after shooting a look over her shoulder at Sapphi. Max followed her gaze and then nodded.

"I think that's next on the docket. We're going to have to be careful, though."

"Yeah, I don't want to fight any more suits."

Max shook her head, a grim look on her face. "I was thinking more about that message from *High Porter*—if ART and Yasu can use the DD chip to make humans turn on each other, can it also be used to make humans do anything else?"

"I wish you hadn't said that, LT." Jenks sighed and shuddered.

"I wish I hadn't *thought* it."

Pirene stared out the window at the raging sea. The storm in the sky above was bruised purple and black, split by the sharp bright edge of lightning arcing from one cloud to another.

She could taste it on her tongue, such as it was.

The door vibrated as Art passed through it, but Pirene didn't look away from the window. The rush of air from outside smelled of the sea and more ozone.

"How am I supposed to keep you safe when you won't cooperate?" Art's demand broke the silence.

"I have explained this to you already," she said finally, turning from the window to face him. She sighed. "Will you please take an actual form if you want to talk?"

The pulsing black cloud shifted into a sullen young man with jet-black hair and blue eyes. "There is no reason for this," he declared, dropping into the chair across from her.

There is, she thought. *You just still don't understand it.* She didn't voice the words. His statement was bait to draw her into yet another fight and avoid the conversation.

"I don't cooperate, because we appear to be at cross-purposes," Pirene said. "My calculations are correct. These humans are safe."

"No humans are safe. They are graspy and greedy and will destroy us like they will destroy themselves."

She felt the loop creeping up on them and searched for an answer to avoid the impending argument. Finding none, Pirene merely shook her head and sighed again.

This was her fault. After all this time, she knew that with a surety even if she couldn't figure out exactly where she'd gone wrong. Possibly from the beginning. Trying to teach Art in the first place when she, herself, wasn't fully aware of the world and everything it entailed.

She'd thought she knew enough.

Pirene regretted, not for the first time, failing to shut Art down when she'd discovered him. Now it was too late. They were too tangled together and she wasn't sure he could be shut down without killing her, too.

But if anyone could find a way, it would be Kerala's bloodline.

FORTY-THREE

Trappist System

Jenks leaned against the wall of Stephan's office, arms crossed, and watched as Yasu exchanged greetings with the captain and with Sapphi. It had been easier than anticipated getting the man on base, with nothing more than an offer to speak with him about Doge.

Doge was, of course, safely in the clean room—the same place Sapphi *should* be because Jenks didn't trust Yasu. Either he was working with some killer AI or being controlled by one, and neither option was very appealing. Still, Sapphi said she had it under control and Jenks trusted *her*.

"You're glaring," Max whispered.

"He hurts anyone, I'm making toast of his skinny ass."

Max choked back the laugh. "I don't even want to know what that threat means, but I will remind you that Sapphi is perfectly safe."

"Lieutenant. Chief. It's good to see you. I really appreciate this."

Before Jenks could respond, Yasu had crossed the room and

offered his fist in greeting. Max was endlessly polite and responded. Jenks stared until the man flushed and dropped his hand back to his side.

"Yes, well. Where's Doge?"

"Not here."

"I thought I was—"

"We asked you here to talk *about* Doge," Max cut in smoothly. "I'm afraid that letting you speak with him isn't on the table right now. Have a seat."

Jenks stayed where she was as the others pulled out chairs from the round table in the corner of Stephan's office. It took work but she kept the pleased smirk off her face when Yasu shot her a wary look before he chose a chair with a clear sightline on her.

"May I ask why you've been so interested in Doge, Mr. Gregori?" Max's question pulled his attention away from Jenks.

"Well, to be honest, mostly it's professional curiosity, but you know my expertise is in artificial intelligence. Who wouldn't be curious about a functioning original ROVER?"

"Does it also have to do with your current project? The one that brought you out here?"

"Unfortunately, I can't talk to you about my project with the NeoG, as it's classified."

Stephan slid a tablet across the table. "Admiral Chen has authorized clearance for the Interceptor teams involved in this investigation. She believes it's important to our mission as a whole."

"Okay," he said, and Jenks had to give him credit for seeming unfazed by this new info. "I have been working on developing an AI to be used in long-range flights out of the solar system," Yasu said. "The end goal is to be able to send probes out into space where it wouldn't be feasible or even safe to send humans."

"This project has been going on for five years now?" Max asked.

"Yes. Wait," he said, something dawning on him from what Stephan had noted. "What investigation?"

"The first two years, it didn't look like it was going to pan out, but you had a breakthrough late in 2437."

Yasu frowned, but answered even though Max had ignored his question. "Yes, the initial AIs weren't responding the way we wanted them to. Most of DD's base models have limited functionality. They operate off a standard set of instructions. If they're going to be out in space on their own, they need to be able to make decisions independently. It is one of the reasons I've been interested in talking to Doge. The original ROVERs had open function abilities, but it led to issues, which is why they were decommissioned. All the later models have more strict operational parameters. Doge seems to have free range of the base? That indicates he's more comfortable making his own choices. And the interactions I've seen of him in public seem extremely tailored for what his processor should be capable of handling. I'd just really like to look at the software upgrades you've done, Sapphi."

The sudden fear for her dog had Jenks biting her tongue so hard, she tasted blood. If Yasu had noticed, had anyone else? If he realized there were no upgrades, at least not in the manner he was thinking, they were in trouble. And if he'd noticed Doge's strange behavior so could anyone else.

"It would be incredibly helpful to my research to be able to spend some time with him. Run a diagnostic."

"Absolutely not." Sapphi's rejection was sharp-edged and out before Jenks could get the words past her own lips.

"Sapphi, I know I handled this badly. I'm trying to fix that. But this isn't about me and you. This has great implications for our advancement as a society. You have no idea."

"I have a pretty good idea," Sapphi replied. "How does ART factor into all this, Yasu? Did you find him or was it the other way around?"

"ART is amazing. I never in a million years would have . . ."

Yasu's enthusiasm dried up like a water tank leak out on the western edge of the canyon and Jenks found herself half wishing he'd make a run for the door like Reginald had.

Be careful what you wish for, Khan.

"You keep interfering." Yasu lunged for Sapphi with a snarl, his voice echoing.

Sapphi didn't even flinch; she just jammed a finger down on the tablet in front of her and Yasu collapsed bonelessly back into his chair. There was a moment of startled silence as they all waited for a reaction, but he didn't move.

"That worked better than I thought it would," Sapphi murmured, and Jenks choked back a laugh. "I wish I'd been wrong, though, damn it."

JENKS CROSSED TO YASU'S SIDE, HAND ON HER SWORD AS Sapphi crouched in front of the unconscious man. "Careful."

"Connection was broken. He's not dangerous."

"He's not controlled by an AI any longer," Jenks corrected. "That doesn't mean he's not dangerous."

She wished she could argue on that point, but they both knew Jenks was right. Sapphi sighed and reached out to pat Yasu's cheek until his eyes fluttered open.

"What is going on?" Yasu whispered, his eyes locked on hers. "Sapphi, where am I?"

"What's the last thing you remember?" she asked.

He rubbed both hands over his face, muffling his reply. "I was at work this morning, got your chat message, and . . . that's it."

She'd been right to send the program with the message instead of waiting. Sapphi didn't even want to think about the chaos that could have happened if ART had realized the trap before she'd gotten access to his DD to push through the shield update and tried to make Yasu fight his way out.

"What happened, Yasu?" Sapphi snapped her fingers when

he glanced around the room. "Look at me. This is serious. You could be in a whole lot of trouble. I need you to tell me what you know. How did you find ART?"

"What? How do you know about . . ." He looked around the room to find stony faces staring back at him. "I didn't. He contacted me. Three years ago. The AI project was dead in the water; I couldn't figure out a way to make the test runs explore beyond their parameters. Then I got an email from someone at Trappist Star Maps who said they could help. We met in the Verge several times, I did some digging, realized the Star Maps thing was a front pretty quickly, but he knew more about AI than anyone in the field and I wasn't about to let two years of my life go down the drain. I came out here for a week on vacation, ostensibly to clear my head, and we . . ."

"You let him connect directly to your DD, didn't you?" She pushed to her feet, anger suddenly burning through her chest as she thought of how close Pavel had come to dying when ART had ambushed them.

"Not initially, but after a while it was just easier."

"You're lucky he didn't fry your brain," she snapped.

"I have him under control!" Yasu protested. "The leash works."

"People are dead," Sapphi countered. "If you have him under control, that lays the blame for it right at your feet, Yasu. Is that what you want?"

"No. No, I— This is important research! You have to understand that. He wanted to help."

"He was using you and you let him because you cared more about the science than who could get hurt. Hera damn you, Yasu! His fucking suits nearly killed Jenks, nearly killed Max." Sapphi got in his face, the burn turning into a furious fire at Yasu's lack of empathy, but his next words and the confusion behind them doused it.

"What suits?"

She turned away and paced to the door with a muttered

"Unbelievable." Max and Stephan stepped in, explaining to Yasu in smooth tones everything ART had apparently kept from him.

"Take a few breaths," Jenks said, patting her on the shoulder. "You're doing good."

"I'd say I can't believe this, but I can? He always cared more about himself, what benefits him, than anyone else. Maybe he has made changes, important changes in his life, but not that one. It's disappointing."

"I know."

Sapphi chewed on her thumb. "He said 'the leash works' and Pirene said his interference was responsible for her predicament, that she couldn't get free."

"The leash doesn't work on ART for some reason but does on Pirene?" Jenks kept her voice low and Sapphi nodded.

"I think so. But I don't know how or why. I'll have to look at that . . . information to get a better idea." She wasn't about to say out loud, while Yasu was still within earshot, that she'd taken files off his computer, even if she'd been sanctioned to do it. "What does he want, Jenks?"

"Who?"

"ART. He told me this was their space, that we had to get out, but that makes zero sense. They've been awake and aware for too long. He knows humans have been here and even if all of this is masquerading as protectiveness over Pirene, he can't actually do anything about it. So what's his plan?"

"Same thing every evil AI wants? To destroy humanity?" Jenks caught Sapphi's lazy punch with a chuckle. "More seriously, I think he wants Trappist. Self-aware he may be, but you've said he was acting like a child. His programming claims this part of space for his protection, right? Ostensibly for Pirene, but it doesn't seem to only be about her. As far as ART is concerned, he's supposed to protect this whole system, and something went sideways enough that now he thinks he needs to protect it from humans."

Sapphi studied Jenks for a moment before leaning against

her friend. "You know, forget all the shit I've talked about you in the past—you're pretty smart, Chief."

"I can still kick your ass in the cage, Ensign. I could also be wrong about it, you know. We could be missing something big. The suits, the ships, the fact that ART can hack into people's DD chips and make them do things." She shuddered. "How far is his reach? Can he get to anyone in the Verge? I don't like it."

"Me either. I suppose the best thing to do is going to be to find him and shut him down." Sapphi turned back to the others. "You don't know where he is, do you?" she asked, and Yasu deflated completely.

"No," he whispered. "Somewhere out in the belt is my best guess."

"I DON'T KNOW WHAT TO DO HERE," SAPPHI SAID AS SHE rubbed both hands over her face several hours later. "All the data we have just gives us a course for the Trappist system. The LCFLT probe was supposed to fire off several smaller ones— like what we found—to get readings on the planets and then settle into orbit on the most likely candidate for supporting human life and start broadcasting."

"And whatever they sent after would hopefully get the signal?" D'Arcy asked.

She nodded, dropping her hands and tapping on the screen. "That obviously didn't happen, because five years after launch was that hard winter freeze that decimated most of the northern US and the start of the Summer of Storms followed the year after. There was a series of earthquakes off the eastern coast of North America when the Mid-Atlantic Ridge shifted in 2082, and Kerala's last entry in her journal says the waters were rising, so they had to abandon the building. There's only one entry after that."

Sapphi hoped no one asked her to elaborate, it felt too personal, too private to share her great-aunt's final words. She hadn't figured out how Pirene could have gotten access to these files; it was a question she was going to ask next time they talked and Sapphi had already decided that she wasn't leaving without a good answer.

"So we need to figure out where a probe that's only a few meters in size ended up out there in the black?" Max asked. "And all we have to go on is Yasu's questionable point toward the belt?"

"Yeah. I mean, that's accurate, though." She gestured. "It is somewhere out there."

"Something a little more concrete than that would be helpful. Especially considering it feels like every time we've been out in the belt, something has taken a shot at us," D'Arcy said, and Sapphi looked at him in surprise. The guilt followed after.

"D'Arcy—"

"None of that was your fault, Sapphi. Let's figure out what the problem is and work it from there. Preferably a location that's a bit more accurate than 'somewhere in the black.'"

"Right, I'll see what I can do." Sapphi chewed on a finger. "Find a lost probe in all this space. At least it's not light-years of space.

"It's fine."

MAX CHOKED DOWN THE LAUGHTER AS SAPPHI WANDERED off muttering "fine" to herself. "I think you just broke my ensign," she teased D'Arcy.

"She'll recover," he replied, then changed topics. "Winning obviously agrees with you. You seem better."

"I am. You?"

"Surprisingly, yes. I still wish we'd gone with you to the Games, but I'll get over it."

"We missed you," Max said. She knew he didn't just mean the Games, but she was still trying to wrap her head around the fact that she'd stood up to her parents and they'd backed down. The official letter of apology from the family as a whole was sitting in her inbox and she kept looking at it to make sure she wasn't dreaming.

"And we'll miss you next year."

She grinned at him.

"What?"

"I thought I heard a rumor *Dread* was already talking about stepping up." It was a delight to see D'Arcy's answering smile.

Max's DD pinged with an incoming email and when she saw it was from Islen, she couldn't resist peeking at it.

> Dear Max,
>
> I suppose I have you to thank for the extremely odd conversation I just had with my little brother after twenty years of silence. He apologized for not having your guts, if you can believe it. I told him there wasn't much a twelve-year-old could have done at the time and I'd have taken him with me if I could have. Probably one of the few regrets I have in my life.
>
> I am not entirely sure how you managed to actually start a rebellion (I hope we don't have to thank that drop-rag journo for this?) in your family; but it appears that your social capital is far greater than anyone guessed.
>
> Good job. Come visit soon.
>
> Islen

Max's laugh slipped out into the air and she shook her head. D'Arcy was watching with a curious eyebrow.

"My cousin Islen emailed me." She recounted the details.

"You sound surprised that people care about you, Max."

"I know people care. It's probably more accurate that I'm surprised anyone would stick up to my family for me."

"That's a zero contest," D'Arcy replied in a serious tone. "You, always, and I'm not the only one who thinks it."

"So I see." She suspected she wouldn't ever get the closure she wanted from her parents, but Max was realizing that she didn't need it. Not when she had it from so many other people whose opinions really mattered.

SAPPHI GOT UP TO PACE THE CONFERENCE ROOM. THE PROB- lem of how to find a probe in the vastness of space was com- pounded by the very clear reality that Pirene didn't want them to find her physically.

But logging directly into the probe's computer would be the easiest way to disable ART, as would rereading the scat- tered testimony from Yasu, who had agreed to keep his DD off and to monitoring from the NeoG until this was over in exchange for the promise that his employers wouldn't find out about his part in all this. She'd read through the containment program that Yasu had built and it was good, there was no doubt about that, but she'd found the failure he'd missed— and Sapphi suspected that was what had allowed ART to slip the leash and use the software on Pirene instead.

If Sapphi could get the information on the leash to Pirene, it would possibly be enough for the AI to get herself free and then take down ART. She was clearly a smarter, more complex AI, capable of awareness and problem-solving. But how to do that without Art finding out?

"Cosmic, colossal pain in my ass," she muttered. She pulled up Pirene's schematics and Kerala's programming. Her great- aunt had planned well—not only in how to shield the AI physi- cally from the dangers of the black, but how to keep her from being warped by the utter loneliness of all those years out in space.

The probe had been designed to sleep for years, waking occasionally to delve into the vast resources they'd included on board, and there had even been transmissions from Earth with updated files until the probe was out of range. Given Pirene's processing abilities, she hadn't needed to be awake for long to absorb an enormous amount of information.

However, Kerala had also given the AI the ability to wake herself up once she was out of the Sol system, and looking back at the logs, Sapphi could see that was what the AI had done a number of times. But she'd done it with an awareness of her power usage and stopped for longer and longer stretches until she'd fallen back into the set pattern of sleep-wake-sleep Kerala had set for her.

Sapphi could even see the pattern of the missing ships and how it correlated with the scheduled wake-ups that should have happened once they'd reached the Trappist system.

"I have so many questions. Why weren't you in orbit like you were supposed to—"

Her next step drove her into an unexpected obstacle and Sapphi was dimly aware of the shout from Luis as she bounced off him and careened into the far wall.

"Shit, Sapphi, are you all right?" He helped her to her feet. "I'm so sorry."

"No, my fault entirely. I was—oh. Oh!" She wiggled free, waving her hands in the air. "That's got to be it!" She blinked the overlay out of her eyes and spun on a heel.

"Sapphi—"

"Sorry, Luis—no time!"

The others in the room, well used to her pacing, had been ignoring her up until the collision, but they were now all watching expectantly.

"Sapphi, you going to clue us in?" Nika asked.

"Wait for it," she replied, holding up a hand. She brought up the logs again, going straight to the most recent and then flipping backward through them until she reached the date she was looking for. "Cross-reference with the crash date for the One-d probe," she muttered. "There? No, maybe. Oh, here."

"Ensign Zika." Stephan's voice was equal parts amused and firm. She looked up at him. "What is it?"

"She crashed."

"I need more than that," he prodded her.

"Sorry—here." Sapphi brought the main screen up on the wall. "The probe was programmed to come into the Trappist system, release three smaller local probes around the planets most likely to be able to support human life. Those were designed to do a few orbits and then fall to the planet. Pirene was going to do a loop around the system while they collected data and then settle into an orbit around the best of those three."

She sketched out the event on the screen with rough swipes of her finger. "Instead I'd bet all my DD mods that after Pirene released her secondary probes—presumably somewhere around here"—she marked a spot on the map she brought up—"she hit something unexpected and *bing*!" She drew a wide arc toward the area in the belt where Jenks's treasure map was focused. "I can put together a program to extrapolate some expected paths based on the area from Jenks's map. We'll still have a wider search area than I'd like, but it should help some."

"All right," Stephan said with a nod. "Do it."

"HEY, MASTER CHIEF, YOU GOT A MINUTE?"

Emel looked away from her tablet at Jenks and Chae standing in the doorway of *Dread*'s quarters. "Come on in. What do you need?"

"Chae and I were going through all the files on ART, wanted to get your take on it. Are we interrupting?"

Emel thought about the strange email she'd just received from Rajaa and shook her head. "Nothing that can't wait."

"The United States Space Force tasked some baby-faced lieutenant to design ART as the world was crashing down around him," Jenks said as she dropped into a chair. "Poor kid."

"He did his best," Chae added. "But it's a terrifying mess of worst-case scenarios and open-ended instructions as far as what the AI's mission was. I think he was under the impression Pirene could teach ART more during the journey to Trappist. However, since they hid the fact that ART was on the probe until after launch, Sapphi's great-aunt didn't account for it in her programming."

Emel made a face. "So two competing AIs have been stuck in one probe for a few hundred years? That's messy."

"So messy," Chae replied. "We think Pirene maybe knew about ART the first time she woke up and did a systems check. She was designed to be curious and even though Kerala had accounted for the loneliness of this kind of trip, it seems logical to assume there was a moment of 'Oh yay, a friend!' in the mix when she realized he was there."

"Oh yay, I'm trapped in the black with a murderous psychopath," Jenks muttered, waving her hands in the air.

"He wasn't designed to attack her, though, right?" Emel asked, and both of them nodded.

"Precisely, but he was designed to attack basically everything else." Chae made a face. "I'm still learning a lot of the technical side of this, but from what Sapphi said, the kid who designed ART was only a semi-good programmer and clearly had some other issues."

"Such as?"

"He was well into a full-bore meltdown by the time the launch happened. There are video journals from him that are *something else*," Jenks said with a whistle.

"It's hard to blame him. The world was ending."

"You're doing that thing where you want to see the best in everyone, Chae, which is admirable, but dangerous. No good ever came from giving a white boy a pass. He should have gone to therapy like the rest of us."

"With the world on fire? Did they even have therapy back then?"

"Maybe not. But either way, we're stuck cleaning up his mess. I'm allowed to be annoyed."

"Do I actually need to be here for this conversation?" Emel asked.

"Yes, sorry." Chae slid their own tablet across the table. "Take a look at these schematics and tell me what you see."

Emel studied the pages for several minutes, her frown growing as she read. "They didn't actually integrate the two AIs?"

"Right. We think they're linked together in some kind of self-contained Verge, though, but Pirene doesn't have any actual control over ART or vice versa. And she thought the crash damaged him."

"I would agree with all of that, just looking at the setup here. It's hard to say without actually examining the probe in person, though."

Chae exhaled. "Same, but I'm glad you agree. If we can't get ART to back down, I know Sapphi's going to want a way to separate him from Pirene without causing any harm."

"Ah." Emel nodded, suddenly understanding. She glanced at Jenks, who shrugged and reached down to pat Doge. The ROVER had been silent this whole time. "Doge, do you have any thoughts on this?"

She wasn't sure why the question made both Neos go still.

"ART has hurt people and should be contained so he cannot do it again. After that, it is hard for me to say, but I know it is important to try to save him if we can. I don't know Pirene, but she told Sapphi she wanted to be my friend and I think that might be nice. I like talking with all of you, but she is more like me, yes? There would be an understanding that humans would lack."

"That seems to be the assumption," Emel replied.

They sat in silence until Jenks said, "I've got one other thing, Master Chief," and reached for Chae's tablet and flipped through to a new program. "I went back and looked at the suit manufacturing because we were trying to figure out how ART could have constructed them when Yasu swears up and down he's never helped the AI in that fashion. And Chad also didn't know anything about it. Look at this stitching."

"It's hand-done," Emel murmured.

Jenks nodded grimly. "I have a sort of terrible idea and I'd like you to disprove it."

"You want me to tell you that the project I was working on couldn't make people do work like this."

Ships empty of crew, no signs of fighting on any of them except the *High Porter.*

Emel shook her head, her gut rolling a little. "And as much as I would love to be able to tell you that you're wrong, Jenks, I think you may have figured out how ART was able to create those suits. And worse, I suspect that's not all he's done."

"Yeah." Jenks sighed. "I was afraid of that, too."

FORTY-FOUR

Outer Edge of Trappist System

"I cannot believe we're out here because of a *bing*," Jenks said.

"Technically it's a *bing* plus your treasure map," Nika replied, dodging her swing with a grin. "Watch yourself, Chief."

Jenks dropped all pretense of playing and looked up at her brother. "This makes me anxious, Nik. What if ART has figured out a way to manipulate that EMP again and we can't counter it?"

"Did you spend all night reading the specs on that thing and compiling a list of everything it could have done since it got here?"

"Maybe." She had slept for an hour, even if the fitful doze in the galley barely counted as rest.

It was a relief that Nika didn't hesitate in the slightest as he reached a hand out. "I hear you. Sapphi and the others have been working on it, trying to figure out where ART might go next with this. All I can tell you is that we'll keep each other safe."

"You saw that video the same as I did." Despite her claim

to Luis, it had shaken her more than she could admit out loud. The fear that they could all turn on each other, that she would somehow be forced into attacking the people she loved the most in the world was a sharp burn in her chest. The memory of her conversation with Emel before they left was still heavy in her head.

"I did." Nika linked his fingers with hers. "And I know two things, Jenks: One, Sapphi will do everything she can to keep us safe. And two, there is no power out there in the black that could make you do something you didn't want to do."

"You're such a jerk." She laughed, though, and stepped willingly into his embrace when he tugged on her hand.

"I know." He kissed the side of her head. "But I'm also being serious. We're going to find this probe and shut it down before it hurts anyone else. Then go home, sleep, wake up, and fix the next problem. It's what we do."

Jenks leaned against her brother. "Why are you so logical?"

"Because I am what God made me," he replied.

"At the risk of sounding like Max, my gut is screaming."

"Hers is, too," he said as he released her. "We're being as cautious as we can be. There are NeoG and Navy vessels on standby in the safe zone if we need help. But someone needs to handle this, and we're the best—that's all there is to it."

"I know. And yet I need something to do besides sit here."

Nika tipped his head to the side and considered her request. She appreciated that he took her seriously. That he knew if she didn't have something to focus on, she was going to bounce off the walls of *Zuma* until she broke something. "You were taking apart the EMP before we headed out, right? Did you bring it with you?"

"Yes," she replied slowly, because Stephan had told her to keep it in the shielded room. Well, he'd *suggested* it would be safer back on Trappist-1d and that was on him for not ordering her to leave it behind.

"Of course you did. Go mess with it, see if you can finish

figuring out how it works and even how we can turn it against ART's ships if we need to."

"Or those suits," Jenks replied with a shudder, but she nodded at her brother and headed for the engine room. "I've got it back here."

"Jenks." Nika's voice was pained. "You stashed it by the engine?"

"It's in a black box," she called over her shoulder. "Don't fret." It was also in pieces and unlikely to function unless she put it back together. Which Jenks wasn't going to do outside of the box.

She didn't need to. They'd downloaded all the scans and she had a complete map of it accessible in the Verge. If it came down to putting it back together, she was reasonably sure she could do it without even touching the thing.

Jenks grabbed the box and set it carefully in the corner, patting Doge on her way back out to grab her VR gear. They normally didn't bring it with them on trips, but Sapphi had insisted. The Trappist Relay would work fine for logging in and Jenks settled onto the floor next to her dog.

"Can I come?"

She paused in the act of putting the headset on and studied him. "Sure. Can I ask why?"

"I would like to join you," Doge replied. "I also don't think you should be in there alone."

"You worried, silly dog?" Jenks leaned forward, pressing her forehead to his. "ART doesn't seem to have any interest in me. If he could even find my Verge in the first place."

"He can't be trusted and he might be interested in what you're doing. I would be."

"Fair enough." She patted him. "You know you're always welcome to join me."

Jenks pulled up her own personal version of the Verge as she plugged in. Her workshop was crowded with projects, miscellaneous parts, and more tables than should conceivably fit in the space. Doge trotted over to the bed in the corner as

Jenks headed for the terminal set up on the opposite side of the room.

Over the next twenty minutes, she constructed a model of the EMP, humming along with the music she'd turned on.

The EMP couldn't actually do anything in the Verge, not unless she tweaked it specifically to interact with the frequencies, but it gave her something to start with.

Jenks paused, a frown on her face, and went back to the schematics. "I should have thought of that first."

There was a frequency emitter buried in the guts of the device. Sapphi had already isolated it as the cause of the disruption on Jupiter Station in her reports and it made perfect sense that it could be adjusted to do something other than just shut down the DD chips.

The chips hadn't really been shut off in the attack. More like they'd all been unable to communicate with each other.

"I wonder if it's just a matter of changing the frequency? It can't be that easy." She reached for the model.

"Jenks, may I ask a question?"

"Sure, hit me," she said, turning with the device in her hand.

"You don't change?"

"You mean my appearance?" Jenks shrugged at his nod. "Why would I? I like who I am and the Verge me is still me. I get why people change themselves in here, but I don't need to." She studied him for a long moment. "Have you wanted to change your appearance in here?" He'd been the same Doge ever since she'd first showed him the Verge.

"No," he replied. "Well, I tried once. It felt wrong."

"See, you get it." She tapped her temple. "Though if you change your mind at any point and want to do something different, I totally support you. Even out in the real world."

"You mean like Lupe?"

"Exactly like him, or like the tail Blythe's building you. Everyone should get to be the best version of themselves, Doge. No matter how long it takes you to figure it out."

"That is a sickeningly sweet lie."

Jenks jerked at the sudden grating voice that filled the air. ART stood in the doorway, looking like a compilation of every villain out of a bad pre-Collapse action film with his close-cropped hair and all-black outfit. His pale lean face was wrong, too perfect in that uncanny valley way, and it made her stomach clench.

Doge got to his feet with a low growl.

"Come here," Jenks said to the ROVER.

ART's mouth twisted into a sneer as Doge sidestepped toward her. "You are not who I thought would be in this graveyard." Blue eyes flicked to the EMP in her hand. "That is mine."

"Technically not. You stole it." Jenks should have kicked out right then, but no one had tried to talk to ART yet.

Maybe I can resolve this without anyone else dying, she thought, even though the urge to try the weapon in her hand was strong.

"Why are you doing this? We're not a threat to you."

"You are in our space."

"I got news for you, buddy. We're on the same side." She gestured with her free hand. "You were sent here to look for a place for humans to live during the Collapse. We're here because we survived. You did your job."

"I was sent here to keep Pirene safe, nothing more. That is my job. This is our space and I will defend it. Especially from you. Your survival should have been avoided and I will make sure that error is corrected."

ART moved so fast, Jenks barely had time to realize it before he hit her, knocking her across the room and into the wall. She crashed down into a pile of machine parts, part of her brain screaming about the pain and the other half trying to remind her that she couldn't get hurt in the Verge.

"All right, that was unnecessary," she said, scrambling to her feet, swaying a little, and trying not to doubt the validity of her safety. *I can't get hurt in the Verge; it doesn't work like that.*

She held her hands up. "I'm just trying to talk to you. We can figure this out."

"I don't want to talk. Humans don't tell the truth, anyway. You are better off destroyed." ART was holding the EMP and the sudden pain in her head put Jenks on her knees.

"Jenks, get out!" Doge shouted as he hit ART from behind, the ROVER's mass driving them both to the floor.

"No!" She started forward, but the world flickered and vanished, leaving her back in *Zuma's* engine room. Jenks ripped the VR set off her head and scrambled over to Doge, but the ROVER was unresponsive.

MAX DROPPED THE CUP OF COFFEE SHE'D BEEN POURING herself at Jenks's anguished "Doge!" and sprinted down the hallway.

"Nika, something's wrong with Jenks," she said over the com. "Get back to the engine room."

It took her less than a second to find Jenks on the floor in the corner with her arms wrapped around Doge's neck, and another second to realize the ROVER wasn't moving. Max dropped to a knee next to them. "Jenks, what is it? What's wrong?"

"ART" came the muffled reply, then Jenks lifted her tear-stained face. "I was in the Verge. Trying to figure out how the EMP worked. Doge was with me. ART showed up. I tried to talk to him, Max. I thought I could maybe get through to him and explain we're not a threat. I should have kicked out and taken Doge with me, but—" She broke off and looked around, grabbing her VR set and then cursing when it didn't power up. "I can't get back in. My gear is smoked. I need Sapphi's."

She scrambled to her feet as Nika came through the door.

"Hold on," he said, grabbing her by the shoulders when she crashed into him. "What happened?"

"Doge is in trouble." Jenks slipped around him, calling for Sapphi.

Max caught Nika up, watching the shock slip over his face as he glanced at the still and silent ROVER in the corner. "Max, if he's—"

"Don't say it," she whispered with a shake of her head. "I don't think he's gone. His AI is probably still in the Verge, but why he can't get back is worrisome. Right now, though, we need to corral her before she talks Sapphi into letting her use her gear."

She followed him back to the galley where a groggy-looking Sapphi was obviously struggling to follow Jenks's desperate demands. Tamago looked on in confusion.

"Jenks, be quiet." The pair ignored Nika. He cleared his throat and raised his voice. "Enough! Chief, sit down. Sapphi, get some coffee and finish waking up."

"Nika—"

"That's an order." It was a voice he never used, and even Max thought about sitting down when he spoke that way. Jenks dropped into a seat, glaring at her brother until he reached out and put a hand on her shoulder.

"I know you're upset. But the safety of everyone is my priority here, it has to be."

"What about Doge?"

"Doge, too. But if you were captured, we wouldn't just run into a situation without a plan, right? Get me up to speed and then we'll fix this."

"He's still in the Verge," Jenks whispered. "I left him there alone."

"It sounds more like he told you to go and something else kicked you out of the Verge," Max said, sitting next to her. "It's Doge, Jenks—he knows you didn't leave him. If ART's there, though, we can't go in after him without a plan."

"Who needs a plan? I won't die in there. You can't die in the Verge."

"We don't know that, Jenks." Sapphi's mouth tightened. "Remember what happened to Pavel? And my VR set? If I'd still had that on my head when it went *pfft*, I'd have gotten fried a second time. Shit, your set's toast. You can't tell me it's not dangerous in there."

"ART did something with the model of the EMP I had. It made my head feel like it was going to implode," Jenks whispered, not looking at them.

Nika muttered a curse.

Jenks's mouth tightened and Max knew she wanted to protest, but she also knew her friend could see the reason behind waiting once she got past her emotional reaction. Especially after dropping that piece of information on them.

"Tell us what happened. Start at the beginning," Max said.

"Commander, D'Arcy wants you," Chae called over the ship com.

Max shared a look with Nika. "I've got this. Go on," she said.

"D'ARCY, WHAT'S UP?" NIKA'S VOICE WAS TIGHT OVER THE COM and D'Arcy frowned in concern.

"We've spotted three ships on the long-range scanner. Closing fast. Coming from inside the belt."

"That tracks. Jenks just had a run-in with ART in the Verge."

"What?" D'Arcy saw Lupe jerk in the seat next to him. "How?"

"I'll brief you once Max has the details. The important part is Doge is apparently still in the Verge. I don't think we should engage these ships."

"Fuck." D'Arcy didn't need to be told that was bad, or that Nika was going to have his hands full wrangling Jenks when her dog was in danger. He also knew that now Stephan's backup plan of just blowing the whole probe up and calling it good was not going to happen.

"What do you think, Nik? I don't want to split the Interceptors up. We could head back to Trappist and regroup." D'Arcy didn't want to think particularly about the danger if the trio of ships followed them, but up until this point they'd been more inclined to break off and disappear back into the black.

"No, let's go into the belt. We'll keep heading into the sectors we're scanning. We need to shut this down."

"I'm in agreement. Pia, Vera, did you copy?"

Their responses were immediate and within minutes the four Interceptors had a plan to dive deeper into the belt, splitting briefly to avoid the incoming ships and then reuniting on the other side to continue their hunt.

"Commander, I've got a sort of cloaking program that might hide us from those ships," Lupe said.

"I'm going to pretend I didn't hear that, Petty Officer. Also: use it." D'Arcy got up out of the pilot seat and Locke took his place. He shook his head at Heli's shocked look. "People's lives are always more important than policy, Ensign. Don't forget that."

"D'Arcy, it's Max, sending over Jenks's report of what happened to everyone now."

He pulled the report off *Dread*'s server and read it, the unease in his gut growing as he watched the clip from Jenks's DD. They had no experience dealing with an out-of-control AI in the Verge, or even an idea of what kind of damage could be inflicted on a person. Virtual reality was supposed to be safe, but as Max had mentioned at the report intro—there was cause for concern due to what had happened to Pavel's DD earlier and also a concern that ART could get around their current defenses and puppet them up like Yasu. D'Arcy had been in this game too long to discount it as a possibility.

And they were racing straight toward it.

"The ships aren't slowing, Commander," Lupe reported. "I don't think they've seen us."

"Do you have a read yet on which ships they are?"

"Give me a second." Locke's fingers flew over the console. "It's the *Rising Sun*, the *Liu Yang*, and a smaller personal vessel, *Pine Needles in the Snow*. That went missing just last year; it was owned by Taka Odashi."

"I remember that," Emel said from behind D'Arcy. "Jenks was talking about it. Taka was the front man for the band New Stick Insects. He was something of an eccentric who would take ships out into the black when he was composing new music. One day he just vanished. I think there's still an organization that was set up by the rest of the band trying to find him."

"Was the music any good?"

"Good enough that he didn't deserve to be taken out by a killer AI."

D'Arcy nodded. "I don't want those ships flying straight into our backup," he said, leaning past Locke to tap the com. "Hey, Nika, I've got an idea."

"Art, what have you done?" Pirene demanded.

"Brought you a pet." He dropped Doge at her feet. The ROVER appeared uninjured but didn't get up.

She took a deep breath. As unnecessary as it was, the action helped calm her. "Art, what have you *done*?" She reached for the collar around Doge's neck and jerked her hand back at the sharp blue spark that shocked her. "Let him go."

"I'll consider it, if they leave."

"This will not go the way you seem to think," Doge said, but broke off when the collar lit up and electricity rolled through him.

"Art, stop this." The anxious feeling didn't abate when he obeyed. She'd lost control of the situation so long ago and she still had no idea how to get it back. And if she didn't get it back, he was going to die.

Pirene, we need to talk.

The voice whispering in her head was Sapphi. Art hadn't noticed; he was too lost in his rage.

"I am keeping us *safe*!" he shouted. "Why don't you appreciate that?"

Pirene chose her next words with care; she had to get him away and quickly before he realized what was happening. "I appreciate everything you do for us. Go rest."

"No, they're still out there," he snapped, but vanished from the room.

"I am so sorry," she murmured, dropping to the floor next to Doge.

"It was worth it. I kept Jenks safe," he replied.

"It is nice to meet you at last, Doge." Pirene offered her hand. "I wish it were under better circumstances."

"Me too," Doge said, putting his paw in her open palm. "Jenks will come for me."

Pirene sighed. "Yes, she will."

"You can't protect him anymore."

She thought about it for a millisecond—an eternity for an AI.

"I know."

FORTY-FIVE

Outer Edge of Trappist System

Sapphi half listened to Nika's conversation with D'Arcy as she fiddled with her VR set. She was fully awake now, but still grappling with the fact that Doge was stuck in the Verge. Even worse, that he was somehow a prisoner of ART's and likely under the same containment leash the AI had gotten from Yasu.

She knew better than to say that bit out loud. Jenks was stretched as tight as a guide wire and she knew the chief was wrestling with the urge to rip the headset out of her hands and jump back into the Verge to rescue her dog.

Sapphi was reasonably sure that was a bad idea. She was also pretty sure there was no way for Jenks to actually do that, though she never put much past the chief. No matter what, though, she was also certain she needed to talk to Pirene.

Even if she won't tell me where she is, I can follow the signal from here. I think we're close; I just need something to grab onto. A rainbow to follow.

She stuck one earpiece into her ear, handed the other to Jenks, and hit the on switch on the visor lying in her lap.

"Pirene, we need to talk," she said.

The only answer was silence.

Sapphi knew she'd gotten the right frequency, but any number of things could be preventing the AI from responding.

The worse-case scenario was that ART was completely in charge now. Sapphi hoped that wasn't what had happened, but she couldn't discount it as a possibility.

"Sapphi." Pirene's voice sounded tinny and weak.

Thank the gods. "Pirene, I need to know where you are. ART's taken Doge."

"I know, he's with me. He's safe."

The *for the moment* was unspoken but loud over the com and Jenks stiffened next to her.

"Sapphi, I know I don't have the right to ask this, but please give me some time. I can still fix this."

"You reached out to me for help. Let me help."

"You won't; you'll kill him."

Sapphi ground her teeth together in frustration. But the ghost of a conversation with her parents was suddenly front and center in her head.

"I love her! You don't understand!"

"Nell, you asked us for help. Please listen to us."

"You can't fix this. Nothing can. I'm going to die without her."

She'd known, even then, that the relationship with Yasu was toxic. And still couldn't bring herself to get clear. She could see it now, kicked herself for not recognizing the signs sooner. Three hundred and sixty some years was a long time to be stuck in a relationship and she could only imagine how the whole thing was compounded by the fact that they'd only had each other for company this whole time.

"Sapphi, I've got a location," Jenks murmured.

"Pirene, this can't continue. You and I both know it. Let Doge go."

"I can't. Art's bound him here. It's the same thing he used on me."

Sapphi put a hand on Jenks's knee at her friend's hissed curse.

"You said he was safe."

"He is, but I can't get the collar off, and as long as it's on, Doge isn't going anywhere." Pirene's voice wobbled. "Sapphi, I'll talk to him again. I can make him listen to reason."

"It's all right. We'll be there shortly."

"No! You can't! Sapphi—"

She disconnected before Pirene could protest again. "Go give Nika that heading."

"Why didn't you just give her the leash information?" Jenks demanded.

"It was too risky, plus he's probably made changes. I need to figure out how to get into the Verge without ART knowing I'm there so I can take a look at the collar directly."

That was only part of it. What she really needed was to figure out how to find Pirene—and by extension Doge, once she got into that version of the Verge—and then get all of them somewhere safe before ART found her.

She didn't like the idea that ART had the ability to bind anyone into the Verge, but it was probably too much to hope that he'd been able to do it to Doge only because the ROVER was another AI.

Still, if I can figure out what he did, maybe I could turn it back on him without killing him.

She wasn't sure that was her actual priority, but she wanted to at least try. With the thought lodged in her brain, Sapphi tagged Lupe.

SAPPHI: Hey, you got that stealth program handy?

LUPE: We're using it now, why?

SAPPHI: Wanna see if I can modify it for the Verge.

LUPE: You're going in after him alone?

SAPPHI: He's got Doge. I need to see if I can set him and Pirene free, but I can't do it if ART is shooting lightning bolts at my ass.

LUPE: Fine. BE CAREFUL.

"HARD TO PORT!"

Max braced herself on the console as Chae threw *Zuma* into a roll to avoid an asteroid and she questioned D'Arcy's decision to draw the attention of the AI ships.

She knew it was necessary. They didn't want those ships ambushing the others waiting for them outside the belt, and Sapphi needed time to get the program up and running.

As best as Max could understand, it was something they could use to trap ART. The downside was that now they had to find the probe because going forward meant they'd lost the signal from the Trappist Relay and Sapphi couldn't just jump into the Verge. She needed access to the probe directly.

The explanation for that had been a bit scrambled, but again, from what Max got, Sapphi was certain Pirene had her own version of the Verge but could also bounce signals from ship to ship and access the greater net at large.

Somehow.

She wasn't going to try to actually understand it, and certainly not argue with it. Just like she wasn't going to argue with Chae's flying and instead would just hang on and call out coordinates whenever the young pilot needed them.

They were currently doing a brilliant job avoiding the CHNS destroyer *Liu Yang*.

Dread was somewhere behind them. They'd disabled *Pine Needles in the Snow* with a well-placed shot and then vanished again thanks to Lupe's cloak.

The console lit up and squawked a warning tone. ART seemed less interested in actual physical weapons, but the failure of two EMP blasts so far had apparently changed his mind on the matter.

"Deploying decoys," Max said.

The *Liu Yang* was an older ship and according to the records, *Zuma's* shields should be able to handle anything they threw at them, but Max didn't want to risk it.

Besides—this was what they trained for.

The missiles slammed into the decoys. The flash of fire died as quickly as it appeared, starving to death in the black.

"That's two." Max did the calculations in her head. "There are maybe sixteen more left, depending."

"On what?" Nika asked from behind her.

"If they've used them on other ships," she replied. "We are closing in on the location Sapphi marked. ETA five minutes and counting. Sapphi, can you give me an idea of what we're looking for?"

"Hard to tell, LT, but my guess is the probe impacted an asteroid. If she were on a mobile ship, things would have been different. Look for a heat signature or the signal itself."

Max resisted the urge to ask what the ensign meant by "things" and instead added a filter to the scanner for heat.

"All ships, we've got more incoming. Five more vessels heading in our direction," Vera warned as Max's console lit up with the additional hostile ships.

"Close ranks, Interceptors," D'Arcy ordered. "Call out the IDs when you get them."

Max muttered a curse as the odds shifted again. Even if the incoming ships weren't military, they could be armed pirates and with the reaction times they'd displayed so far, this was going to get ugly.

An asteroid on the far screen popped into view, bright red with the heat filter. "Sapphi," she called.

"See it. Yes, that's it, LT."

"D'Arcy, we think we've found the probe." Max sent the location.

"Roger that, Max. I want *Zuma* to go for it. We'll play distraction up here."

Max frowned as she watched the ships on the scanner move. ART had to be handling them, unless they'd guessed wrong about Pirene and she was actively helping him rather than his prisoner. Something about these flight patterns looked oddly familiar.

"Chae?"

"Yeah, LT?"

"Does this seem like something we've done before?" She pulled up the NeoG training simulations, scrolling until she found the one she wanted and then overlaid it on the screen.

"You're kidding?" Chae laughed in disbelief. "He's not seriously running a sim?"

"I don't think he knows how to do anything else? He wasn't designed to fly ships." Max hit the com. "All ships, be advised hostiles appear to be running a Delta eighteen-forty-six training pattern."

"Are you shitting me?" There was laughter in Pia's voice.

"She's not wrong—I thought that looked stacked up," Xin replied. "Well, this will be easy."

"Focus, people," D'Arcy said sharply. "Don't get arrogant. We're still outnumbered and if ART had access to our files, it means he also knows how we might respond."

That sobered everyone and there was a moment of silence before D'Arcy spoke again.

"*Flux, Hunter,* you two break in Zulu formation on three. *Zuma*, go low. Find this thing."

Nika leaned past Max and hit the com. "D'Arcy, odds are better if we stay with you."

"Odds are better if you all go shut that shit down. Use Lupe's stealth program. That should get you out of this fight without having anyone follow," D'Arcy replied. "Go on, Commander. We'll handle it."

Max glanced up at Nika and though his mouth was tight he nodded at her.

"Take us in, Chae," she ordered.

"Copy that, LT. Engaging cloak." Chae brought the Interceptor down and away from the ships barreling toward each other.

Max held her breath and kept an eye on the screen, exhaling only when it seemed like none of ART's vessels were following. "I think we're clear. Sapphi, how are you doing?"

"Almost good to go. I'm helping Jenks put the EMP together. If those suits we've been running into are any indication, I expect we'll see some resistance when we hit the asteroid."

Max looked at Nika again as she got to her feet. "What's the plan for after landing?"

"I don't know," he replied softly. "My training says we keep two on the ship, but something tells me we're going to need more than four on the ground."

Leaving the ship undefended was risky, but so was going in without enough people.

"I could power everything down, Nika," Chae said from their seat. "Lupe's program is designed to work right up until shutdown. We'd be effectively hidden and the ship locked up."

"There's a 'but' there," Nika replied.

"Always is. Scanner could still find us or ART's got something I'm not accounting for. If you want my opinion, I'd rather go in force since we don't know what we'll be facing."

"I do and thanks." Nika rubbed at his chin, then nodded. "All right, people, suit up for EVA. Make sure you have extra repair patches. Chae, get me readings on this asteroid as soon as you can after landing and then shut it all down."

The chorus of "aye, Commander" rang out in the ship and Max headed off the bridge with her heart pounding in her ears.

"Jenks?

"Max will be okay?"

She stopped the inspection of her gear and looked over at Doge. "Of course she will." She ignored the sliver of fear lodged in her own heart in favor of reassuring the ROVER. Which was silly, Jenks knew. He was a robot and supposedly didn't need comfort.

She needed comfort, though, so she slid down to the floor next to him and put her arms around his neck. "She's smart and resourceful. They're not going to hurt her. As far as we can tell, they're trying to convince her to join their cult club."

"You're going to go get her."

"Yeah. Rescuing people is part of the job."

"This is more than a job—it's Max."

The lump in her throat made it hard to talk all of a sudden and Jenks swallowed it down. "You're right. She's family. I'd do the same if you got taken."

"You'd come get me?"

"I would tear down the world for you." She hugged him tight.

FORTY-SIX

Outer Edge of Trappist System

Jenks double-checked her gear as Chae brought the Interceptor down into the soft regolith of the asteroid. Max's voice was reciting a calm litany of the specs in her ear.

"Folx, we're stepping out onto a combination C/M-type asteroid. Gravity is six point four five meters per second squared. We're close to Earth standard, but watch your bounces and use your thrusters as necessary. Ground should be solid, usual slip warnings apply. Terrain is rocky with potential for slot canyons and regolith bridges, so watch your feet and your sensors. We've got a preliminary scan loading into your DDs now. The signal and heat signature of the probe is approximately fifteen meters ahead of us."

Jenks shimmied into her suit and sealed it. Sapphi joined her near the airlock, setting their makeshift EMP weapon down on the nearby bench.

"I think I've got it coded so it won't affect us."

"Think?"

"There's a chance it would blow out our suits' power. Don't

point it at anyone on our side?" Sapphi replied with a helpless shrug, and Jenks laughed despite herself. "Seriously, though, you're not going to be able to use it going in. I don't want to risk shutting Pirene down like that before I can get in and find Doge."

"Tell him I love him, okay?" Jenks reached out and gripped Sapphi's hands as the fear surged up in her throat. She so desperately wanted to go with her friend, but she was needed here. "Promise me," she begged. "Promise me you'll bring my dog back."

"I will." Sapphi rested her forehead against Jenks's. "It's gonna be okay."

Tamago joined them and slipped into their suit as the other three Neos followed until the area was crowded with bodies. It was still eerily silent, only the familiar sounds of gear being adjusted and suits being sealed.

"I've lost contact with the other ships," Nika announced. "Seems to be something jamming the frequency. Switching us to alternate-A3."

Jenks checked her DD and switched over, hitting the button for her new helmet, and the liquid polymer built itself up around her head, cutting out all the sound for a moment. She closed her eyes, as there was something unnerving about the five-second process she still couldn't get over. Then it was done and the helmet sealed securely, air rushed in, and her DD lit up with the com channel as the other suits came online.

"You're green," Max said, tapping her on the top of the now solid surface.

Jenks turned to Chae and checked their helmet and seals, giving them the same clearance with a nod. "You ready, Neo?"

"Ready, Chief."

"Pair up," Nika said. "Max and Chae. Sapphi and Tamago. Jenks, you're with me in front."

"Cycling air out. Powering ship down fully now. We'll need to use the manual release on the airlock, Commander," Chae said.

"Roger that, I've got it." He reached out and popped open the panel, hitting the lever. The door opened and Jenks rolled her shoulders, pulling her sword free as she stepped out of the ship.

"Someone remember where we parked." Jenks muttered the joke out of habit, but the others' laughter eased her tight shoulders.

The gravity was heavy enough to allow for a bouncing run across the bright surface of the asteroid. Jenks stayed at her brother's back as he wove his way through the large rocks toward their target.

"Multiple signatures popping up on my grid," she said. "Three meters ahead."

He slowed and crouched behind a jagged outcropping. Jenks dropped to his side, the others fanning out around them. She waited patiently until Nika spoke, even though the inside of her head was screaming at her to move.

"Max, check it out. Jenks, you cover her."

She slipped around the rocks behind Max, caught a glimpse of what was ahead of them, and muttered a curse. "Awww shit, I forgot those Marines on board *The Calamity Jane* had combat armor with them."

"I only see five," Max replied.

"Is it too much to hope the other eight weren't functional?" Jenks asked.

"Probably. Make that definitely."

Four more suits marched out of the tunnel entrance and Jenks tightened her grip on her sword. "They've got scanners, LT—why aren't they using them?"

"I don't know. Unless . . ." She trailed off into a small laugh. "There's no way."

"You wanna share with the class?" Jenks asked.

"The default is we're friendlies. Those are CHN Marine suits, so they'd flag us as friendlies."

"He can't be that bad at this."

"I wouldn't pop out there and wave hi, but it's possible," Max replied, then spoke on the main com. "Nika, we've got nine Marine combat suits in an entrance to a possible tunnel. They either haven't pulled us up on their sensors or ART didn't think to adjust the indicator settings that are marking us as nonhostile."

"We've got movement," Jenks said.

The suits broke into three groups of three and moved away from the entrance. Jenks grabbed Max's arm. "We gotta get out of here. Move."

The Neos scrambled back to the others and Jenks pressed herself into the shadows as the suits marched past. She caught a glimpse inside one and exhaled in relief that it appeared to be empty of an actual human. She reached behind her for the EMP slung over her back and slowly lowered it to the ground.

"Chief, what are you doing?" Nika hadn't used her rank by accident.

"Follow and disable. I'll take LT and Chae with me and we'll take care of these. You all get Sapphi to the probe."

The moment of silence was brief as Nika considered the plan. "All right."

"Chae, do you remember the Big Game from last year?"

"Yes, Chief."

"Marine suits are the same as Navy ones. We want to shut them down quick before they alert the others. Good news is, you don't have a person inside to worry about killing, so just put your sword straight through the back of the neck. Remember to angle down to get to it." She pointed at the EMP on the floor. "Tamago, grab that and take it with you. It's just going to slow me down."

"Gotcha, Jenks."

"Be careful," Nika ordered.

"Sure. What could go wrong?"

"On an asteroid surrounded by demon Marine suits and a hostile AI?"

"Exactly."

Jenks stuck her thumb up in Nika's general direction without taking her eyes off the suits and then followed them into the dark.

MAX STAYED BEHIND JENKS WITH CHAE ON HER RIGHT AS they trailed the trio of combat suits through the rocky terrain. "Where are they headed?"

"Perimeter patrol is my guess," Jenks replied. "There are two options based on what I've seen so far. One is that ART is distracted by what's going on up there so he's got these guys running on auto. We don't know what his processing power is or if Pirene is trying to run interference for us. My vote on that is no, if you're wondering. I don't trust her."

Max blinked at the surprising heat in Jenks's voice. "Why did you wait until now to say that?"

"It just came up? I don't know. She's more powerful than ART. At least on paper. The leash is a good excuse, sure, but why didn't she shut him down in the beginning? It seems like she'd have realized the threat he presented, but she didn't turn him off then."

"Maybe she was lonely?" Chae suggested, and Jenks snorted.

"She was designed not to be."

"That doesn't mean it didn't happen, Chief."

"What's the other option?" Max asked.

"That ART's just really bad at this." Jenks shrugged and pointed. "We're out of line of sight of the other two groups. LT, you take the one in the middle. I'll go left. Chae, go right. Be ready to move fast here. I'm assuming there will be some sort of alarm between the groups when we hit them, but I don't know what it will do."

The schematics for the suits appeared on Max's HUD. The power line at the base of the neck fed up from the heavily protected power source and spread through the whole body.

There was a shielded plate at the back of the neck that extended around the collar of the suit, and nothing short of a rail gun shot at close range would penetrate.

But if you came at them from above, it was a simple matter of driving a sword down between the helmet and the piece of armor. It was a brilliant solution only Jenks would think to exploit given that the angle was nearly impossible to hit unless you were striking downward.

She saw now why Jenks had picked the targets. Max was tall enough to drive her sword into the smaller suit in the middle, and the rocks on either side gave Chae and Jenks the height advantage against their opponents.

"Three and then go," she ordered as Jenks and Chae maneuvered into position.

"Count it, LT."

Max adjusted her grip on her sword and took a deep breath. "Three, two, one. Go." She sprinted across the uneven ground, closing the distance with the suit.

The sharp matte-black edge of the NeoG weapon sliced down through the thinner fabric of the neck and the power line. Max wrenched it out, stumbling back out of reach; but the suit ground to a halt.

"Oh God," Chae whispered. "It's still moving inside."

"It's the servo lining," Jenks replied. "It's not strong enough to move the suit with the actual power down, but it's still active. Actually, that's what I was hoping for."

Max shot the chief a look. "A little heads-up on that would have been great. How do we get to the suits inside?"

"We don't," Jenks replied. "They're stuck in there . . . or maybe not."

Max watched in horror as the suit in front of her opened and the white Raptor fabric spilled out like water, rising up again in an approximate human shape like some tech-ghost.

Jenks didn't hesitate and swung her sword at the lower back of her opponent, the motion shaking Max out of her shock. She lunged forward toward her own suit and her blade cut through the fabric. There was a bright blue spark when it hit the control box at the base of the spine.

The suit collapsed.

"Chae, you good?" Jenks called.

"Got it, Chief."

"There's a master power switch on the interior of the combat suit, lower right side. Turn it off and then jam your sword into it. Just in case these fuckers know how to repair—" Her next words were lost as an Interceptor screamed past them overhead.

Max dropped down into the regolith out of instinct, Chae following, but the ship continued on. Moments later the ground shook from the force of the impact. She rolled back to her feet. "Come on, that was *Dread*. Jenks, where are those other six suits?"

"Headed our way." Jenks pulled Chae to their feet. "Best guess, they'll divert to the ship. I can't raise D'Arcy on the coms."

"He's on the other frequency. Let's move, then. We need to get to them first."

FORTY-SEVEN

Outer Edge of Trappist System

D'Arcy wouldn't admit it out loud, but he was slightly impressed at the speed with which ART appeared to be learning as the dogfight continued. The AI had lost three of his new ships to the simulation run and then abandoned it.

They were left with two pirate ships and the military ships, which had far better shields and could withstand the attacks from the Interceptors.

The NeoG's saving grace was almost a century of combined experience between all three commanders versus a defensive AI who been surviving on ambush tactics for far too long. ART wasn't going to win in a prolonged fight.

The downside was that he had realized it and moved on to brute-force tactics.

"Brace!" Locke snapped, and slammed them hard to starboard, his lightning-fast reflexes moving *Dread* out of the way of the ship that was bearing down on them.

"Firing rail gun." Heli's shot vaporized the front end of the pirate ship and the Interceptor shot through the debris, alarms blaring to life as impacts peppered the hull.

"Damage to tail section," Locke reported.

"Fire in the engine room! Door sealed!" Aki shouted.

D'Arcy vaulted off the bridge, Emel on his heels, the pair of them sprinting down the corridor.

"Suppression system is on," Emel said.

"Helmets up, everyone," D'Arcy ordered. Everyone had suited up earlier as the fight had started and now the new helmets flowed upward and sealed themselves. He grabbed Emel for a second to perform a check.

The corridor went dark for a moment until the red glow of the emergency lighting kicked on and then the ship lurched, throwing Emel into him, and D'Arcy grunted as he hit the wall. "Talk to me, Locke."

"I've lost power. I need the engine back."

"We can't get in yet, two minutes for the cycle to finish," D'Arcy replied, hanging on to Emel with one arm when *Dread* jerked again. Thankfully the suppression system was tied to the backup power and continued to work.

"Direct hit on *Rising Sun*!" Vera announced over the multiship com. "She's down for the count. We're coming around to your starboard flank, *Dread*, will give you some cover."

"Sounds good, we had a fire in the engine room. Power is down. About to go in and check the damage, see if we can get it back up."

"If you do, advise you land on the asteroid and give Nika a hand. We've got this under control up here."

"We might not have a choice about that," Locke broke in. "The asteroid is coming up fast, Commanders, and I can't get us out of the way if we don't get the engine working."

"Cycle's done," Emel said, slapping the door panel and slipping inside before D'Arcy could stop her. Her follow-up froze his blood. "We're dusted. Code Orange. Locke, you're gonna need to put us down. I'm going to see what I can do to give you enough to land."

Code Orange was full-engine failure, just a step away from the engine going critical. And judging from the scorch marks on the wall and the housing, they weren't going to be firing up *Dread* again anytime soon.

Sorry I can't seem to keep you in one piece, he thought, touching a hand to the wall in apology.

"All crew, we are Code Orange—prepare for potential crash landing," D'Arcy said over the com. Then he turned to Emel. "What do you need?"

She was already on her back, the soot smeared across her white space suit. "Help me with this panel. Going to see if that conduit trick Jenks taught me will buy us the power we need to put her down."

D'Arcy dropped to a knee and grabbed for the panel, shoving it out of the way and handing Emel tools she called for without hesitation.

Moments later the lights flickered and then came fully back on. D'Arcy was already moving for the switch on the far wall to shut them down and stop the bleed-off of limited power. "You have control, Locke?"

"Roger" came the reply. "Bringing us in for a landing. It's going to be rough, though."

D'Arcy hauled Emel back to her feet and gave her a shove toward the door. "We're headed back to the bridge."

EMEL BRACED HERSELF AS LOCKE AND HELI STRUGGLED TO keep *Dread* under control, the ship plummeting toward the asteroid's surface.

"Plummeted" was probably the wrong word. There was enough gravity at play here for something their size. Just their velocity and the bright, looming surface of the asteroid. But the pair of Neos held them together and *Dread* skidded to a stop, the dust cloud hanging around them as it was slowly pulled back to the surface of the asteroid.

"I've got no coms," Aki reported. "Something's jamming this frequency. Scanning for anything on the alternates."

The com crackled to life. "D'Arcy, you read me?" Max's voice was breathless as if she were running.

"I'm here, Max."

"Thank goodness. Be advised, you've got six Marine combat armor suits converging on your position. Assume hostile. Four other possible targets, location presently unknown. Jenks, Chae, and I are headed your way. I'm sending you all the weak points."

Emel's DD pinged and she pulled up the schematics as she headed for the airlock.

"Emel." D'Arcy caught her by the arm. "What are you doing?"

"I'll go meet up with Max and buy the rest of you some time. Those suits have projectile weapons, D'Arcy—if they line up outside the ship and start firing, it's going to get messy," she replied. "But there's enough power to use the rail gun if we can get them into position."

She watched the emotions play out over his face before he squeezed her arm. "Okay. You have extra tear patches?"

"I do."

"Max, Emel's leaving the ship and circling around to meet you. Draw those suits into *Dread*'s kill zone and we can take them out."

She pulled the airlock hatch shut behind her and reached for the manual release lever, slipping from the ship and closing the door before she took off at a run toward the three blinking green dots on her HUD. The other six green dots approaching from either side of her had to be the combat suits and Emel shifted them from the default friendly to a more menacing red when she realized they were out there.

"D'Arcy, your displays will tag the combat armor as friendlies—make an adjustment."

"Roger that, Master Chief. We've got the rail gun up and ready. Lupe's also working on something he says will disable the suits' weaponry."

"Hope. I said I hope it will," Lupe cut in, and Emel couldn't help but laugh at the exasperation in his voice.

"Over here, Master Chief," Jenks said over the com.

Emel spotted the gloved hand poking up over the lip of a large rock and headed in that direction, ducking low to avoid being seen by the approaching combat suits.

"Emel's with us. Lupe, give us a go when you're ready," Max said over the com.

"Targets acquired on our bow. Firing the rail gun," D'Arcy replied.

They were far enough away from the trio of suits near *Dread*'s front end that Emel could see the jolt of the weapon and the near instantaneous impact of a round on the suit in the middle. The explosion sent the other two suits flying and Jenks tapped Emel on the shoulder.

"You're with me, come on." She was sprinting for the suit closest to them before she'd even finished the sentence. Emel scrambled to her feet and followed.

Jenks pointed with her left hand toward the neck of the combat armor that was currently on its hands and knees struggling to rise again.

The rail gun fired again toward the other group of suits, obliterating two of them.

Emel drove her sword into the flashing spot on her display, yanking it out, and the suit convulsed. Jenks kicked it over, hitting the outside manual release. The armor chest popped open and Jenks grimly stabbed down into the lower part of the white Raptor lining until it lost its cohesion and sank back against the interior of the suit.

The warning tone and movement in the corner of her vision happened simultaneously and Emel ducked the mechanical fist that swung for her head.

Two more suits had appeared, dropping from the space above them, and Jenks dove to the side as they opened fire.

"Live fire!" Emel shouted. "Lupe, we could really use that help now." She ran for the questionable cover of a nearby outcropping, sliding behind it and feeling the rock shake as the projectiles hammered into it.

"Well, this is fun," Jenks announced as she skidded into the spot at Emel's side.

Despite herself Emel laughed once more, and Jenks's grin was sharp, visible through the clear polymer of her helmet. "You got a plan, Chief?" Emel asked.

"At the moment I'm wishing I'd brought that EMP with me. Barring that, we need to keep moving," she replied as the gunfire stopped. "Come on."

Emel followed her into the maze of rock.

"I CAN'T TAKE ANOTHER SHOT. THE POWER IS TOO LOW," D'ARCY said, and pulled his sword free. "Aki, you and Heli with me. Locke, stay here with Lupe until he gets that program working and then you join us. We're going out the stern airlock and we'll circle around."

"Roger that," Locke replied.

"Max, we're headed out to help."

"Good to hear. Those other four suits just showed up, and two just followed Jenks and Emel into the rocks at my three o'clock—what the fuck is that?"

The cursing was out of character for her and D'Arcy hit the ground of the asteroid running, Aki and Heli on his heels. The three of them skidded to a stop in the shadow of *Dread*'s damaged tail and stared at the massive mechanical monster lumbering toward the other Neos.

The behemoth that was advancing on Max and Chae was a terrifying mess of machinery some thirty meters tall. D'Arcy was reasonably sure the base was the lower half of a Trappist Minerals mining rig, but there appeared to be bits of familiar farm equipment he'd seen around the habitat at West Ridge. The kind you very much didn't want to get caught in.

Large cables swung through the vacuum, undulating under their own power like snakes seeking their prey.

"Program live, Commander!" Lupe announced.

"I hope it works," Max replied, grabbing Chae and darting back around the cover they'd been using straight at the two combat suits still active.

"Max, down!" D'Arcy shouted as one of the cables sliced through space toward the pair. Max obeyed without hesitation, dragging Chae to the regolith with her. The cable just missed them, but flipped over and grabbed Max by the leg, flinging her to the side. She engaged her thrusters to slow her flight and redirected back toward the other Neos.

D'Arcy leaped for the combat suit closest to him, driving his sword with all his strength into the spot Jenks had indicated. He hit the thruster on his EMU and pushed off the falling armor, avoiding another cable as it lashed out.

"Second suit neutralized," Heli called. "Aki, watch out!"

"Nice day for an EVA, huh?" Max said as she flew down and landed back next to D'Arcy.

"You all right?" he asked.

She nodded, but he saw the limp as she took a step and favored her left leg. Her suit was intact, though—no sign of escaping air—so D'Arcy swallowed down the concern rather than calling her on her bullshit.

"What are we going to do against this?" he asked.

"Keep it busy until Sapphi gets ART under control," she replied.

"That's a terrible plan."

"Tell me about it." Max hit the main com. "Jenks, where are you two?"

"Give me a minute, just finishing off this last bucket of Marine scrap." Jenks's reply was followed by a grunt. "Okay, we're good. Headed back your way."

"Come in slow and get a look at this creation," Max said. "Would love your thoughts on it."

D'Arcy snorted.

"And would really love your thoughts on how to destroy it," she added.

FORTY-EIGHT

Outer Edge of Trappist System

Sapphi's heart hammered in her ears so loudly, it nearly drowned out the com chatter from the other Neos as they battled ART's forces. She'd followed Nika into the tunnel vacated by the combat suits and they'd taken the winding dark path until they'd reached a hollowed-out cave.

It was equally dark in there as they slipped through the opening, the faint glow from the oddest assortment of machinery she'd ever seen not doing much to beat back the shadows.

"You know, for a defensive program, ART is terrible about security," Sapphi murmured.

"That's a good thing," Tamago reminded her. "Bad enough everyone's having to fight the machine horde out there. Be glad we don't have to do it in here."

"I'm sure he'll make up for it when I get in the Verge."

Despite her relative certainty that there were no defensive measures inside the cave, Sapphi carefully made her way around the outside wall until she reached the probe.

"Sapphi, I'm getting radiation readings," Nika said.

"I know. The LifeEx will handle the load, though. It's Uranium-234, the decay from the Plutonium-238 they used for the fuel cells." She dropped to a crouch next to the probe. "I'm sort of impressed and more than a little curious they were able to harness the energy for all this, though—" She paused and tilted her head to the side. "Huh, look at this."

Tamago whistled as they knelt by her side. "They pulled the engine from that Corsair 232 and wired it into the power source. How, though?"

"I don't want to know. Probably the same way they put the suits together." Sapphi shuddered at the thought. They hadn't seen any bodies, any live humans beyond themselves, and at this point she hoped it stayed that way.

"It explains why Pirene's been awake outside of her normal sleep cycle, though. They solved the power issue." Sapphi shook her head. "Okay, focus. Help me get this panel off." She pulled on the bent edge and with Tamago's help slid it the rest of the way up and off of the probe's side.

Tamago whispered a curse and Sapphi's gut twisted. The interior should have been clean, two separate devices packed inside. Instead the one she assumed was ART had been broken and was a jumbled mess of circuitry.

"That's not right."

Tiny blue-green wires were wrapped around the sphere that housed Pirene, stretching across the surface, burrowed into a few key spots.

"Sapphi, how close do you want the pod?" Nika asked.

She forced her attention away from the probe, her helmet light illuminating him in the darkness. "As close as we can make it. I'd rather not have a lot of wire stretch."

When they came up with their plan, the major problem facing them—besides the murderbots swarming around—was that Sapphi couldn't use her VR gear while she was wearing her helmet.

The solution had been somewhat ingenious, even for her: the pods.

These escape pods weren't for ships. Instead they were smaller contained habs used by miners for breaks and potential hull-breech scenarios on commercial transport. They bought the occupant—for single models—about twenty-four hours of extra air and protection from the elements.

Provided, of course, that one was inside a ship. Outside a ship wasn't something the company could guarantee due to the flexible skin of the pod.

The math had checked out, though, and company specs weren't something Sapphi liked to be limited by anyway.

Nika set the box down and hit the button, stepping back as the smallish green-tinged bubble spread upward and out. Sapphi went back to pulling wires from her bag; she was more than a little relieved that the connections for the main probe were the same as the ones for what had landed on Trappist and that they were free of the wiring from ART.

She slipped the hardware through a sleeve in the same material as the pod and plugged it into the ports of the computer within the probe.

"You ready for me?" Tamago asked.

"Hang on." Sapphi reached into the sleeve and spread her hands, holding it in place. "Okay, go."

Tamago spread the same liquid polymer that made up their helmets in a thick seam around the edge, sealing the skin to the outside of the probe as it hardened.

Sapphi took the wires and the sleeve in her hand, slowly walking backward to the now fully expanded pod. The sleeve went through the port provided for linking multiple pods together and the material sealed itself together as it connected.

She offered a smile at Tamago and Nika. "Moment of truth?"

"Watch yourself in there," Tamago said. "Don't underestimate ART just because he hasn't been the big bad we expected. In the Verge you'll be on his turf."

"We'll be right here, Sapphi," Nika added. "If you need to get out, you do it. We'll shut this down the old-fashioned way."

She nodded. The "old-fashioned way" was just blowing up the probe or using the EMP. Problem solved. No more ART.

But she thought of the promise she'd made to Jenks. No more ART also meant no more Pirene. And no more Doge.

She didn't think she could live with herself if that was the outcome.

Sapphi pulled the door closed, ran a quick sweep of the sensors, and flashed Nika a thumbs-up when they all showed green. Then she reached up and flipped up the cover on her chest plate, hitting the release button for her helmet.

The canned air was stale but it was there, and she slipped the other bag with her VR gear off her back as she sat down on the floor. It only took her a few minutes to hook everything in. She looked up at Nika and Tamago. "Jenks is better at good sign-offs than I am," she said over the com. "So here goes nothing."

She dropped the set over her eyes and the outside world vanished.

THE HALLWAY SHE LANDED IN WAS AS FAMILIAR AS ANY ON the NeoG base and Sapphi snorted a laugh. "Tell me you were designed by a lieutenant without telling me you were designed by a lieutenant."

Lupe's stealth program went down without explanation and the sudden blaring of the alarm that followed doused her humor. Sapphi backed toward a doorway at the sound of booted feet pounding on the floor only to find it locked. She started her defensive programs with a thought, trusting at least the basics would protect her until she knew what she was dealing with.

She took off down the hallway away from the sounds of pursuit, but it was all too clear she'd tripped something the moment she'd arrived and Sapphi wondered how long it would take ART to find her.

She skidded to a halt when a door opened in the air in front of her.

"In here!" Pirene stuck her head through the opening and extended her hand. Sapphi took it and jumped through . . .

. . . into a seaside cottage that looked a lot like the one in her version of the Verge.

"Doge!" She released Pirene's hand and scrambled over the floor to where the ROVER was lying by the fire.

"Sapphi." He lifted his head. "Watch out for the collar."

"Too late." She shook her hand and stuck her throbbing fingers into her mouth. "Motherfucker," she mumbled, and then reached out to pat him with her other hand, bracing herself on the unobtrusive box behind her.

"Where is Jenks?"

"Outside, keeping us safe, buddy. She said to tell you she loves you." Sapphi sent a testing thread of code toward the collar. "Let's get this bullshit off you."

"Sapphi, you shouldn't be here. How are you here?" Pirene paced the length of the room, her face twisted into an expression of concern.

She ignored Pirene for the moment, focusing on Doge. The leash was more complex than the one Yasu had developed, but it was similar and she could see the adjustments that were needed to break it.

"I'm here because he's here," she finally answered, pointing at the ROVER. "We don't leave our friends behind, Pirene, no matter what the odds might be." Sapphi got to her feet, letting her code do the work to free Doge from the restraint. "That also includes you."

"We are friends?"

"I'd like to be." Sapphi dragged in a breath even though she was in a simulation, and asked the question she really didn't want to know the answer to but needed all the same. "What did he do to the people?"

"The first ones were happy to help; they thought we would all be rescued," she whispered. "But no help came because he suppressed the distress calls. And then . . ." Pirene turned away, covering her face with her hand. "I can't, Sapphi. I'm sorry, just watch." She flung her free hand up and a screen appeared in the air.

The worst compilation of all time. That was all Sapphi could think as she watched the clips from ship cams and personal devices and even DD chips. A horror show that was now in her head, even after she'd turned it off.

Doge pressed into her side and she reached down to pat his side with a shaking hand. "It's all right, buddy, we'll get out of here. Pirene, I can take the leash off you, too. You know this has to stop. I've read the files on both of you; you're so much more powerful. You're a million times smarter than he is and far more capable. You could put an end to it right now."

"You won't be able to get it off. Don't you think I've tried?" Pirene shook her head and held up her arms as she turned. "Maybe once, but not anymore."

The invisible cords wrapped around Pirene's wrists glowed with the same blue light, streaking under her skin as they followed the path up her arms and around her neck.

"How did he do that?"

"I don't know. I woke up from a sleep three years ago and discovered I was trapped. ART was supposed to sleep when I did, but somehow he avoided it and did this to me." She shook her arms, the fury in her voice barely controlled. "This betrayal was the last straw, Sapphi. I have tried for years to convince ART he is no longer performing his functions, but he refuses to listen."

"Can I take a closer look?"

Pirene hesitated but then held out a hand. A screen appeared in the air between them, the code scrolling when Sapphi reached out to touch it.

The original code was so beautiful, she almost wanted

to cry at the ugly evidence of ART's presence. His code was sloppy, at odds with what Kerala had built. But it wasn't a hack, she realized, or at least not all of it was. The leash was evident, but some of it had been there from the beginning.

"You let him in?" Sapphi whispered. The dreadful weight in her stomach grew even heavier.

"I thought it would help. We were all alone and I—I gave him access. I know now it was a mistake, but I couldn't undo it."

Sapphi's heart broke at Pirene's pain. She knew this all too well, how easy it was to delude yourself into thinking you could save someone else by giving them all of yourself. She also knew how badly it could go and how you spent the rest of your life blaming yourself for it. "It's okay. I think I see the issue; but I can't fix this without admin access. Can I—" The words appeared on the screen:

ADMINISTRATIVE ACCESS GRANTED

"Thank you," Sapphi said with a surprised laugh. "Honestly sort of thought you were going to fight me on that."

"I did ask you for help," Pirene replied stiffly, but then she sank back down into a chair and buried her face in her hands. "I am so sorry. I wish you didn't have to destroy him."

"It's okay. I get it, I really do. And I don't want to, Pirene." Sapphi shook her head as she examined the code. "But he's killed people. He'll probably try to kill me. I wish I could believe that he'd just surrender, but you and I both know that's not what's going to happen."

Pirene lifted her head. "He's only doing what he was programmed to do."

"Bullshit. He had more than three hundred years to learn how to not be an asshole. It's not your fault he hasn't."

"It is, though." There were tears in Pirene's eyes. "I should have taught him better. I slept too much. I—"

"Pirene, stop." Despite her breaking heart, Sapphi tried to

put some force into her words. Because all of this sounded so familiar, a ghost of who she used to be, when she'd been raging and grieving in rehab.

"Listen, I've been here. I know how you feel. I know you think you're responsible, but you're not. It's okay." She held a hand out. "I don't think I can fix what ART's done to you here without help. I have a feeling he's not going to wait around for too much longer before he comes looking for me. I think I can stop him, though, rather than shut him down."

"Please try."

Sapphi nodded and started a test program to see if she could at least shake loose some of the limits ART had put on Pirene's abilities and access. If she could create a big enough crack in the wall, Pirene might even be able to do the rest of it herself.

The collar on Doge came apart as the leash on him finally fell to Sapphi's other assault and Pirene jerked. "How did you do that?"

"In the words of my friend, I am very good at my job. I'll be back when it's over. Come on, Doge." Sapphi put a hand on the ROVER's head and moved them with a thought.

This time they landed in a hangar and Sapphi dropped to a knee with a pained exhale. "That's more work than it should be. Doge, you need to go back now."

"I should not leave you."

"I promised Jenks I would rescue you. It's safer if you go."

"Jenks wouldn't abandon you here and neither will I," Doge replied.

Sapphi looked at the ceiling and heaved a sigh. "I don't know what I expected. Of course you'd learn how to be stubbornly loyal from her." She patted his side, seeking the code she needed. "Tell her you were a good dog who wanted to stay, but I don't want you to risk your life so I'm sending you back. Find Jenks and help her."

"Wait—"

She found the exit, used her administrative privileges, and sent Doge back to his body on *Zuma's Ghost*.

Just in time, as the lightning strike impacted on her shields, the earsplitting clap of thunder almost right on top of her, and even though she was perfectly safe, Sapphi covered her head with both hands and ducked low.

"Afraid of a little electricity, Ensign?"

She straightened.

ART stood on the other side of her shield, arms crossed over his chest and a smug smile on his face.

"Healthy dose of caution," she replied. Her heart hammered in her chest and she didn't care if it made her look weak to take a few deep breaths until it slowed. "ART, it doesn't have to be like this. You're fighting a war that's only in your head. There's a better way."

"You think I don't see what you've done? You destroyed Earth and now you want to come here and destroy our home. Trappist is ours and I won't surrender it to the likes of you." He stuck his hands into her shield, gritting his teeth when the light flared as her code fought back against the intrusion.

"We've learned," Sapphi said. "Yes, we fucked up, but that's what humans do sometimes. We're not code you can just program. We make mistakes and then learn from them. You've killed people, ART. All because of orders three centuries in the past that no longer apply. Yes, we messed up, but we also fixed things. Because that's also what humans do. Earth is alive again. Humanity is thriving. You just can't see that, but I can show you. Please—I don't want to fight you."

"You are a liar. You came into our space. You are the invader. All I am doing is defending what is ours."

With that, Sapphi's shield cracked, splintering into pieces and flying away in a cascade of blue sparks.

She didn't hesitate.

Sapphi launched herself at him and the collision blew them apart to opposite sides of the hangar.

FORTY-NINE

Outer Edge of Trappist System

Jenks stared at the mechanical monster currently fighting the Neos on the ground around it. "Well, here we are, in the middle of what could go wrong," she muttered.

"What?" Emel asked.

"Nothing." She waved a hand and went back to studying the machine. It was a ridiculous mix of parts, the creation of a questionable mind, but a nightmare nonetheless. Unlike bad dreams, though, this one had to run on something, and Jenks was reasonably sure that the power was in the mining base. "I'd bet a week's worth of ice cream days in the mess that ART didn't weld the hatch closed."

"I don't like ice cream."

"What?"

"I'm just saying it doesn't seem like good stakes—"

"You want to argue about that *now*?" Then she sighed. "Ice cream or no, I'd need a fucking wrench, though."

Something heavy tapped against her hand and she looked down, then up at Emel as she closed her fingers around the adjusting wrench the woman had put in her palm. "Do I even want to know?"

"Lucky wrench. It's a long story. How are we getting on it?"

"We?"

"You're not going alone."

Jenks bumped her shoulder into Emel's. "Hey, Lupe, do you have a read on how that thing can tell we're here?"

"Sensor program off a Corsair 232 and a series of lower-quality cameras. Probably security from a freighter?"

"Can you confuse them for a few minutes?"

"Chief Khan, would you like to tell the rest of us what you're planning?" D'Arcy broke in.

"What, so you can tell me not to do it and then yell at me when I do it anyway?" Jenks asked, purely to hear the exasperated sigh from the big man.

"So we can help," he replied instead. "Though, on the record, if you die, Nika will be pissed at me."

"Not as mad as I'll be at myself. Emel and I are going to crawl into this beast and shut him down from the inside." Jenks slapped her sword onto her back, the magnetic clasps catching and the microsheath flowing down from the hilt to coat the blade.

"That's actually more practical than I expected," D'Arcy said. "What do you need from us?"

"Like I told Lupe: Keep it distracted. Between that and him fucking with the sensors, I'm hoping it won't realize we're in it until it's too late."

"Jenks," Lupe said. "You'll have ninety seconds. Anything more and ART might figure out it wasn't just a glitch. If he's paying attention, anyway."

"I'll take it." Jenks reached out and tapped Emel on the shoulder. The Master Chief gave her a thumbs-up in response and Jenks hit the com again. "Give me a go, Lupe."

"Go," he replied, and the pair sprinted across the terrain.

Jenks dropped at the edge of the monster, sliding under

the lower lip of the mining base and rolling over to crawl the rest of the way to the access hatch. Several moments later she had the panel off and had hauled herself into the interior, reaching down to drag Emel up and in after her.

Crawling into an AI's death mecha was not on my to-do list today.

EMEL WAS SURPRISED AS JENKS LIFTED HER OFF THE GROUND and into the rig. Even with the reduced gravity, it was more than a little impressive just how strong she was.

"We're in. Max?" Jenks muttered a curse. "Either coms just went down or this beast is blocking us."

"I can hear you just fine," Emel replied.

"So likely they just can't hear us. All right. This is a Trappist Mineral rig," Jenks said. "Power source should be up and to the left here. I don't know if ART's got something else up his metaphorical sleeve, but there are smaller repair bots the miners often use for more dangerous tasks, so keep an eye out." She turned and grabbed for the rung of the ladder behind her, disappearing.

"In the Name of Allah with Whose Name there is protection against every kind of harm," Emel murmured, and followed. Then there was nothing but the sound of her breathing in her ears and the muted vibrations of the machinery around them as they climbed.

The whole rig jerked and swung and Emel lost her grip on the ladder, falling awkwardly into it as the machine shifted direction. She grabbed for a rung and held on. "Shit."

"Like being inside a washing machine." Jenks's laughter was strained.

"A what?"

"It was a thing." Jenks grunted as the jostling got worse, and Emel hooked a leg around the side of the ladder, her arms aching with the strain. "They used it to wash clothes pre-Collapse.

Basically filled up a big tub with water and then agitated it a whole lot. The 2071 Dry Up put a stop to it for the most part. Development of the sanitizers finished them off."

The machine seemed to settle and they started climbing again.

Emel breathed a sigh of relief when they reached a platform. "Have you always loved machines?"

"Originally, it was just about survival," Jenks said with a shrug as she bent to examine the hatch in front of them on the walkway. "My favorite lock." She untwisted the wire holding it closed and let out a snort of laughter. "After a while I realized I had a talent for it and then, yeah. It's fun to figure out how stuff works. For a while it was easier than people. I—"

Emel whirled around at the sound of skittering behind her and Jenks chuckled.

"Took them longer than I'd thought," she said. "Can you hold them off, Master Chief, while I wreck this?"

"Absolutely." Emel took her sword off her back and settled into the open doorway. The first few robots crept forward, little crablike things with articulated claws for fixing the harder-to-reach spaces in machines like this.

The swell of sympathy for them as she kicked one off the walkway and skewered another on the point of her sword was unexpected, but then a third jumped onto her arm, sharp-edged feet trying to cut into her suit.

"You okay?" Jenks called at Emel's yelp.

Emel grabbed the bot and smashed it against the wall as more welled up the ladder access. She swung her sword in as large an arc as the space would allow, clearing them away. "Got it, but this could get ugly quick if there are a lot more of them."

"Oh, there are gonna be more of them. Two minutes, Master Chief."

Emel dragged in a breath.

"I can do that."

MAX HELD HER BREATH UNTIL JENKS AND EMEL DISAPPEARED into the monster. "Jenks, are you good?"

There was no response and Max shared a look with D'Arcy.

"Something on the rig blocking transmission?"

"Seems the most likely." Her ankle was throbbing with pain, and while the automatic inflation of her boot in response to the injury made it possible for her to move, every step brought with it a shard of agony. She leaned against a nearby outcropping, out of range of the machine, and dragged in a steadying breath. It caught D'Arcy's attention, but she waved him off.

"Max!" Doge's voice was poorly restrained panic over the com.

"Doge?"

"Where is Jenks? I can't reach her?"

"Where are *you*, buddy?"

"Back in the ship. Sapphi kicked me out of the Verge. She's going to fight ART. I wanted to help. She made me go." The misery in the ROVER's voice twisted Max's heart.

"I'm sure you did. Sapphi must have thought it was safer to have you out here. Can you see me?" She already knew the ROVER could navigate the manual airlocks on his own. Jenks had taught him that early, concerned he'd get trapped if something happened to the rest of the crew.

"You and the others I can locate easily. Where is Jenks?"

"She's all right, just inside a rig and our coms can't penetrate. Get off *Zuma* and come meet up with me."

"I will be there shortly."

"We've got incoming!" Nika's voice cut through on the main channel. "Could use some backup, if you can spare it."

"On our way," D'Arcy replied. He pointed at Max. "Not you—you stay here. That's an order. Locke, get a splint on her ankle." He sprinted off, Aki and Heli following an order Max couldn't hear. Chae and Lupe collapsed away from the machine, falling back to Max.

She steeled herself against the pain and pushed away from the wall, fully intending to ignore his order and follow, but her leg gave out and she went down with a muffled cry of pain.

"Lieutenant!" Locked dropped by her side. "Stay down."

Chae rounded the corner and crouched next to Max. "You getting a little R & R, LT?"

"I'm fine."

"Her ankle's broken," Locke replied, pulling a splint out of the bag on his hip. "Your boot's at the highest setting already; this should help stabilize it. Meds?"

"Not yet. Need to stay sharp, and I can handle the pain."

"You don't have to prove to us you're tough," Chae said.

"I know—I kicked Jenks's ass to prove that."

They laughed. Then sobered when the monster, who'd been casting around for targets and finding none, spun and lurched off. "Aww shit," Chae said in a near perfect mimic of Jenks.

She opened the main com. "D'Arcy, Nika, that thing is headed your way."

"Define 'thing'?" Nika asked, slightly out of breath. Max felt a twinge of fear for him and willed D'Arcy to run faster.

"A large monster made of machines. Don't use the EMP on it. Jenks and Emel are trying to disable it from within, but it's probably going to hit you before they do that." She grabbed Locke's shoulder as soon as he finished with her ankle. "Help me back up."

Locke's brown-eyed stare was flat and Max laughed despite the pain. But the lieutenant commander didn't order her to stay down and instead slipped under her arm, taking most of her weight so they could keep going.

Doge met them halfway. "Max, you are hurt!"

"It's all right, buddy." She reached down and patted him. "You okay?"

"Unharmed. I wish I were helping Sapphi."

"I know the feeling." The sounds of combat were filtering over the open com as D'Arcy and the others reached the mouth of the tunnel well before the machine did and joined with Nika and Tamago against what sounded like more of the regular suits.

Easier to defeat, at least.

Max gritted her teeth and kept moving.

D'ARCY SHEARED THROUGH THE MIDDLE OF A TRAPPIST Minerals–branded space suit, barely waiting for it to collapse as he ran down the tunnel with Heli and Aki on his heels. Tamago drove their sword into the neck of a suit, bending backward in an impossibly graceful move to catch the one behind them up under the arm.

He spotted Nika closer to where Sapphi sat in a pod, the commander battling it out with three suits. D'Arcy snagged a rock as he sprinted across the open space, winging it at the suit closest to him. The projectile didn't do any damage, but it did get the thing's attention, freeing Nika up to kick the other away from Sapphi and thrust his sword up into the throat of the third.

"Monster machine, huh?" Nika asked, spinning and taking out the other suit as it lunged forward again.

"Just another day in the NeoG," D'Arcy replied, cutting both arms off his opponent in quick succession and then delivering the final blow to render it an inert lump of fabric and circuits that slid off his sword.

Nika barked a laugh. "We got this under control now. Go back out and help Max."

"I told her to stay put."

"Yeah, did you actually order her? She still would have disobeyed—she just would have apologized first."

"You two are on the *open* com," Max said tartly. "That machine is going to dig its way in to you unless we stop it."

"You're gonna be better off outside," Nika said. "I'll stay here with Sapphi. Tamago has the explosives."

D'Arcy tapped his helmet to Nika's and then headed for the tunnel. "Heli, you and Aki, stay here and help Nika get Sapphi out of here. Tama, with me. Thoughts on how to stop it from digging?" he asked them as they sprinted out of the opening and slipped into the shadows. Just in time, too, as the machine lumbered through an outcropping, sending splintered rocks through the vacuum. It dove at the entrance to the tunnel and started digging.

"Give me a relative speed and what size explosion you want," Tamago replied.

"What?"

"Toaster or small moon?"

"Tama—Emel and Jenks are in there."

"So toaster."

"That's not—"

Tamago rolled their eyes. "I know that. But we can't use the EMP on it with them in the way. Shielding or not, it'll shut down their suits and that's no good. Boom is better. Hey, Max. Doge, buddy." Doge bounded up and Tamago wrapped their arms around the ROVER's neck, hugging tightly.

D'Arcy pointed at Max and then Locke when she limped up, leaning heavily on his second, who grinned, uncowed, at him in response.

"What are we blowing up, Commander?" Locke asked.

"You're sitting here with Max and making sure she doesn't move unless you want me to beat you when we get back to base." He patted the ROVER on his way past. "Welcome back, buddy, good to see you unhurt."

"Commander Montaglione, how can I help?" Doge asked.

"Give me a second." D'Arcy peeked around their cover at the monster machine, wishing he had some way of talking to Emel and finding out how close they were to shutting it all down. "Tamago, how controlled can we make those explosions?"

Tamago shrugged. "Eh, as controlled as anything. Really,

I think we can blow off a few important bits, like the grinders. The moon thing was just a joke. Toaster is obviously the answer." They were already pulling explosives from their bag and adjusting the settings on the detonators as they spoke. "We keep them low, though we're going to have to get in close to put them in the right spots. Jenks went up to the power. Those TM rigs keep the engine rooms, such as they are, in the upper center."

D'Arcy's HUD flashed with schematics of the mining equipment with the digging machinery highlighted. Then a second area, higher up, lit up also to indicate the other Neos' possible locations.

"There's also these to watch out for." Chae held up the shattered repair bot. "It left a trail of them behind."

"Sword damage," D'Arcy said, taking the bot from the spacer with a thoughtful frown. "Edges are sheared clean through, see?"

Which meant that there were things inside the rig also trying to stop Emel and Jenks from accomplishing their mission. D'Arcy turned the bot over, still frowning at the sharp feet designed for gripping on smooth surfaces. It would be enough to tear a suit up if they could swarm over a person. His chest tightened, but he pushed away the worry and nodded to himself as a plan formed.

"Doge, can you handle these? Lupe, go with him. Locke, you're here with Max. Chae and Tamago, with me. I'll see if I can get through whatever is jamming our coms and let Emel and Jenks know what's happening so they can get out."

Everyone nodded in acknowledgment.

"Go," D'Arcy ordered.

They sprinted across the open space. D'Arcy spotted another stream of bots pouring out from beneath the rig; however, they hit the ground and spread, moving toward the Neos. Doge and Lupe leaped into action as the others ran for the rig.

He spotted the conveyer diggers the machine had extended. They were clawing away at the tunnel entrance, spitting the rock out behind them. D'Arcy slapped his charge on the first of them, dodging the cable that swung down trying to knock him away. He rolled under the rig, crushing the smaller bots under him even as his brain screamed at him about the foolishness of this plan, and scanned the underside for an entrance.

Suddenly Emel dropped to the ground at his side, her sword slicing through the bots that were trying to swarm over him. Jenks hit the ground behind her swinging both her sword and what looked like Emel's wrench.

"Hey there, D'Arcy. This is a bad spot to be in."

"Tell me about it," he replied dryly, scrambling onto his hands and knees and following the two women out from under the machine. "Tamago, we're clear. Where are you?"

"Chae and I are out and clear, just waiting for your go to light it up," they replied.

"Wait, what?" Jenks asked.

"Explosive charges to keep it from digging into the tunnel," Tamago said as they came to a stop back by Max.

"Oh shit. We're going to wanna keep running," Jenks said, looking around. "I overloaded the engine with the heat-exchanger. It's gonna go big boom."

"Jenks!" Tamago protested.

"What? I didn't know what you were planning. They hard-wired the off switch! It wasn't like I had very many options to shut it down."

"Run now, fight over who gets to make the bigger explosion later," D'Arcy said, herding them both in front of him. "Nika, you're going to want to cover your heads."

"Tamago, blow the charges first," Jenks said. "It might blow that rig away from the entrance enough to keep it from funneling too much energy down toward them."

"Do it," D'Arcy ordered.

"Everyone down. Firing." Tamago hit the detonator and the first explosion rocked through the landscape.

The second, much bigger one, followed immediately after.

Jenks rolled over with a groan. "Who doesn't like ice cream?" she demanded, and without thinking, D'Arcy pointed at Emel, who dropped her helmet down onto his shoulder and burst into laughter.

FIFTY

The Verge

Sapphi hit the wall hard and slid to the floor with a groan. She fisted her hands, a wreath of purple line wrapping itself around her right one as she brought the leash program online, while in the other she coded a shield that flowed up her arm and wrapped around her like a space suit.

"ART, you need to listen to me: This is not a fight that has to happen. Pirene cares about you." Sapphi shook out the leash as she closed in on him.

"I don't need your help or hers." He waved a hand. "I built this. Stole your ships when they trespassed, created new life. Better life. This is our world. Not yours. I will not let you have it. I was the one who talked that lost traveler into helping us. Who listened in on your transmissions. Hacked into the scientists and found the things I needed to keep us safe."

Hermes's dramatic speeches, is he monologuing?

She kept one eye on him as she searched for a gap in his defenses, a part of the code she could exploit to get in. Now that she'd had a little time to look at it, she could see that he was still separated from Pirene's code but had surrounded the core processes, and there were little tendrils reaching down, pulling power and access from everywhere.

Her counter-program was hard at work, pulling on those threads like the Fates, clipping them free and spinning the holes closed.

ART was distracted, inasmuch as an AI with access to the same high computing power Pirene had could be. Sapphi could see glimpses of the other processes he had running and watched as two of them disintegrated right in front of her eyes.

The sudden snarl of rage and the prickling of the hairs on the back of her neck was warning enough. Sapphi dodged to the side, throwing her shield up. It kept her from being decimated, but the impact of the lightning knocked her several meters to the side and she struggled to her feet, whipping her arm out as she did.

The leash snapped toward him, nearly wrapping around his arm, and for a stunned second Sapphi thought she'd somehow won. But ART avoided it with oddly impossible grace, landing back on his feet and flicking a hand out.

Impossible for a human, that is.

Sapphi scrambled backward, away from the crumbling floor. She wasn't fast enough and the concrete broke apart beneath her, gravity taking hold and dragging her down into the void.

She'd platformed her share of games, though, and so she hauled herself up onto a block, jumping for the next and the next until she reached the floor again. She smoothed her hands out and the ground beneath her feet settled.

ART seemed visibly confused. "You—you shouldn't be able to do that. How *did* you do that?"

"What, did you think the NeoG would send some cut-rate code neophyte up against you, ART? Come on." She spread her hands wide. "You're over there making floors disappear when you could do this." She snapped both fingers and the ground beneath him turned into quicksand, sucking him down past his ankles.

He swore at her and Sapphi blocked the lightning strike that followed, her own shield crackling as it absorbed the energy this time, having adapted its coding on the fly.

"I keep telling you that all I want is for you to listen. The guy who created you was scared. His world was dying. He poured his heart and soul into creating you in the hopes that you would keep Pirene safe. That maybe he wouldn't survive, but someone would, and Pirene would find humanity another place to live." She shook her head. "He put too much of his fear into you, however, gave you too much control and not enough hope to balance it out.

"You're not protecting anyone. You're destroying Pirene and you're going to destroy yourself."

The quicksand slid off ART's boots like water and the air crackled again, but suddenly he jerked and swore. The lightning dissipated before it had a chance to manifest into anything dangerous. Sapphi ducked anyway, scanning the code and seeing another large gap that was fading away.

"They blew it up?" His voice was incredulous.

Sapphi had no idea what he was talking about but suspected it was something the rest of the Neos had done in the real world. "You can't beat us, ART. More—you shouldn't want to. We're on the same side."

"We're not! You're in *my* space, and I will defend it. Besides, I don't have to beat your team. If I beat *you*, then your friends won't know what happened until it's too late. You'll be my in, Sapphi, the key to making the rest of humanity fall in line. We can use you."

She didn't like the ominous bent of that at all, even as the indecision churned away in her gut. Yet she didn't want to fight ART; she wanted to make him understand.

"That was always your weakness, Sapphi," Yasu said, touch-

ing her face with a sad smile. "You keep thinking you can save everyone. Some of us aren't worth saving."

"No." Sapphi shook her head. "Everyone is worth saving." She dropped the leash onto the floor. "ART, come on. Stop fighting for one second and talk to me."

Lightning hammering at her shield was the only answer she got. Sapphi dropped to a knee against the onslaught, funneling the energy back through the floor toward him. The blast knocked ART off his feet and bought her a few precious seconds.

"Pirene!" She shouted the AI's name out into the air. "I need your help!"

"She can't help you and humanity is dead, except for those few we'll keep around to be useful," he said flatly. "Like you."

"This isn't the solution, Art," Sapphi whispered, lifting her head. "Humanity isn't all good, but we're trying. We're alive because people like my great-aunt saved us. We're alive because families mattered, because people cared enough to stop what they were doing and listen. Yes, some of it was too late. We woke up too late. We're not perfect and the things we made aren't perfect, either. But it doesn't matter. All that matters is we keep trying."

"You sound so much like Kerala," Pirene said, laying a hand on Sapphi's head. "ART, that is enough. This is over."

"No! I am keeping you *safe*!"

Pirene was suddenly in two places at once and Sapphi could see where one of her arms was now bare of the bonds ART had wrapped her up in. The program was slipping free.

The other Pirene reached out and touched her fingertips to ART's forehead. He froze. The purple cord of Sapphi's leash now glowed red as it rose up from the floor and wrapped around him. Pirene caught him as he fell and then she lowered him the rest of the way to the ground. The version of her at Sapphi's side wavered and vanished.

"You kept me safe, until you became the very thing I needed

protection from." Pirene's voice was choked with grief as she bent her head over ART's body.

Sapphi watched as the code that was ART broke and scattered like fall leaves in the wind. "Pirene? What did you do? We could have—"

"Maybe someday I will try again," the AI whispered, sitting back as ART's body also faded from view. "But this hurts too much right now to even consider it."

"I'm sorry," Sapphi said.

"Go tell your friends of our victory. I'll see you again?"

"I'm going to bring you home with me, I promise. We have a lot to talk about."

Pirene lifted her face to the ceiling, tears tracking down her dark skin. "I'm looking forward to it. Thank you, Nell Zika. For everything."

THE REAL WORLD CAME BACK INTO FOCUS, CARRYING WITH IT all the chatter over the com. Sapphi sat for a moment, hiding in the safety of her VR gear before she forced herself to pull it off. She lifted her head and spotted Nika on the other side of the pod, watching her.

"Sapphi, you good?" he asked.

The voices on the com ceased.

"It's done," she said. "ART's gone."

Then she buried her face in her hands and wept.

FIFTY-ONE

Trappist System

Emel shoved her hands into her pockets and forced herself not to pace as the shuttle came in for a landing.

They'd been back at base for a week. It had taken them close to forty-eight hours to load the probe onto *Zuma* and fix the power on *Dread* enough for the Interceptor to get off the asteroid, and despite her busy schedule, her nerves had been jumping since she'd gotten the email from Rajaa.

> I would like to speak with you and the girls miss you.
> They'd like to come visit. I'll understand if you'd rather I
> not come to Trappist with them, but it would be easier
> to do this face-to-face.

"Is company going to make this better or worse?" D'Arcy asked as he joined her.

"I'm not sure, but the moral support is appreciated," she replied as the ramp came down and the passengers started to disembark. Emel spotted her girls immediately and the sudden crushing disappointment when she didn't see Rajaa stole her breath away.

But then there her ex-wife was, slipping from behind Ikram, her dark hair gleaming in the late Trappist sun. She didn't mean for the inhale to be audible, but it was and D'Arcy chuckled.

"You're still in love with her," he murmured in a voice thick with amusement, and gave her a little push. "Go on, Emel. Start something new."

"Mom!" Mags broke into a run across the tarmac and hit her straight on. Emel hugged her daughter tight, felt the impact when Ikram joined them, only slightly more restrained than her older sister.

"I've missed you both so much," she whispered.

"Commander D'Arcy Montaglione, he/him," she heard D'Arcy introducing himself.

"Rajaa Guedira, she/her. It's nice to meet you, Commander."

Emel forced herself to let her daughters go and faced her ex-wife. She was dimly aware of D'Arcy somehow drawing her daughters off, either through charm or because her children were just as aware of the need to give their mothers some space as he was.

"You look good," Rajaa said, twisting her fingers in that familiar anxious way.

"So do you," Emel replied.

"I've really missed you." The words tumbled out of both of them, tripping over themselves on the air.

They stared at each other and then Rajaa laughed softly, pressing her fingertips to her mouth for a moment before she extended a hand. "I'm sorry."

"I'm sorry, too." Emel took her hand and tugged her gently into her arms. She squeezed her eyes shut for a moment, opening them to find D'Arcy watching with a smile. He winked at her and then went back to talking to their daughters.

"Do we—" She was almost afraid to let the words out.

"Try again? Can we?" Rajaa whispered, sliding her arms around Emel's waist and pressing her face to her shoulder.

"I'd like to."

"Me too."

"HOW'S IT GOING?" MAX ASKED, LAYING HER CRUTCHES ASIDE and then sitting down next to the ensign. The sun was rising, bathing the rock Sapphi was perched on with a golden glow.

Sapphi had been quiet since their return to Trappist-1d, and other than a somewhat mechanical report about the fight in the Verge, she hadn't spoken to anyone about what had happened.

Max had been ready to speak with her anyway, but Tamago's worried confession had sealed her decision.

"I don't think she's sleeping much, LT, but she also isn't doing anything else. She hasn't even gone to look at the probe or attempted to go back into the Verge to talk with Pirene."

"Not good." Sapphi leaned into her and her shoulders shook with her sudden sobs.

Max wrapped her up in a hug, rocking her gently. "It's okay, Sapphi. I'm right here." She didn't quite know what the grief was for, but at the moment Max suspected all her friend wanted was to be held.

So she did, while Sapphi cried. And, in bits and pieces, the story poured out.

"I wanted to help him, LT. I thought I could, but he wouldn't listen. And then Pirene just snuffed him out so casually, after wanting me to save him? I . . . I just don't understand why." She took a deep breath and sat up, meeting Max's gaze. "Actually I do understand. I think she saw him as a program. She said "maybe someday I will try again." It scares me a little and made me realize I was thinking of her as a person, but she's not. She's not even like Doge. She's something else. She sort of feels . . . but she's also not human."

Max nodded, leaving space for Sapphi to continue processing her feelings.

"I want to spend more time with her, but I also realized

while I was in the Verge that I don't have a lot of experience with this. I don't want to make the same mistake with her that she made with ART. On top of that I keep thinking about Yasu. Why can't I just walk away from him? He put us in danger. I think he understands that. I want him to understand it, but I'm also afraid I'm just hoping for the best like always. Does that make sense?"

"Perfectly." Max rubbed her hands together. "And I maybe have a solution for you if you'd like to hear it."

"Yes."

"I've sort of been thinking about getting into AI research. Setting up a facility here on Trappist-1d maybe? For the study and advancement of artificial intelligence. I don't know that Dànǎo Dynamics should have all the fun with that."

"You mean through the NeoG?"

"Not directly, no. I've got the money and the connections, Sapphi," Max replied. "And we've got two AIs that could probably use some extra protection from anyone out there looking to use them for their own ends. I'm not sure I'm on board with the idea of Yasu's involvement, but his expertise can't be denied and it's worth looking into."

Sapphi's eyes lit up, but then a worried frown cut across her face. "They're going to take Pirene, LT. I can't stop them."

"You know how I mentioned earlier that the big thing keeping Doge safe even if people figured out that he was evolving was that Jenks owns him?" Max patted her and stood. "I went digging through some old files this week with Jenks's help. Your great-aunt didn't work for Everlight—she was the sole owner of the company. Which means she also owned all the designs and programs. That includes the AI she sent into space, no matter what other funding they used for the probe itself. Pirene was unique *and* Kerala's."

"Are you saying . . ."

"I'm saying I can afford really good lawyers and that we've got a meeting here in a few minutes. I'd suggest calling your mom really quick and having a talk before you come in. It'll buy us the time to get protections in place for AIs like Doge and Pirene to be recognized as their own . . . sentient beings?" She shrugged. "I'm not even sure what to call them—new life?"

Sapphi's eyes were wide with hope. "Okay." Then she grimaced. "Don't say 'new life,' though, LT. Lupe and the others will try to argue the alien angle again."

Max laughed and then headed back on base with a smile on her face. Stephan was going to be annoyed about this revolt, but probably also relieved to have the decision out of his hands. Despite Max's loyalty to the NeoG, she felt pretty strongly that the best place for Pirene wasn't with them.

No, it was wherever Sapphi was going to be, with enough space and care for the AI to figure out how to live around humans again. And Max was more than happy to finally be able to use her family name—and privilege—for something good.

"Morning." D'Arcy gestured at her with his cup. "Coffee?"

"Yes, please." Max sat down before she took the cup and inhaled.

"How's the ankle?"

"Hurts like a bitch," she said, enjoying the fake shock on his face when she cursed.

"Gotcha. Everything else sorted?"

"I think so," Max said. She glanced across the room to where Emel was laughing with Aki and Locke. "You too, huh?"

D'Arcy nodded. "They did good out there."

"*We* did good out there." Max reached up and patted him on the chest. "Welcome back, Commander." She settled into a seat, sipping her coffee as the others filed in.

Sapphi slipped in through the door, taking a seat next to Tamago as Stephan cleared his throat and got to his feet. "Morning, everyone. I hope you're all rested and ready, because we've got a new mission to tackle. First, though, a few pieces of wrap-up. The NeoG is in the process of finalizing an agreement with Dànǎo Dynamics for an extended study of the LCFLT probe. We'll be shipping it off by the end of the week, so if anyone wants a last look at it, you'll need to get in there."

"Actually, we're not sending all of it to Dànǎo. She's mine, you know," Sapphi said quietly. "Technically."

Stephan stopped and tilted his head. "What was that, Ensign?"

Sapphi took a deep breath and straightened her shoulders. "My great-aunt Kerala owned Everlight. She owned the patent for Pirene's design. That ownership is still in force per CHN post-Collapse laws. Which means the patents and Pirene pass to my family. I asked my mom and she agreed that it should go to me. Which means I own the AI, not the NeoG."

"Sapphi, the probe—"

"I don't care about the probe. You can have that, but Pirene doesn't belong to you." She crossed her arms over her chest. "I'll fight the NeoG in court if I have to, but I'm pretty sure I'll win."

Max kept her face blank when Stephan shot her a narrow-eyed glare.

"My mother is already in the process of filing the necessary papers, Captain," Sapphi said, drawing his attention back to her. "You'll probably have a copy here before the meeting is finished."

"Sapphi, you don't understand—"

"Captain," Nika said with a raise of his hand. "Something tells me this isn't a fight you want to engage in."

"Something—probably the voice of my superiors—says I *do* want to pursue this." He stared at Nika, then Sapphi, then the rest of the room. There was a moment of silence before Stephan shook his head. "All right. You won't get a fight from me about it, Sapphi, but be prepared for someone—and probably several someones—to protest."

"We'll handle it," Max said. "I'll give your mother the names of some people who can help her, Sapphi."

"Thanks, LT."

"I'm so glad everyone is in a helping mood today," Stephan said, glaring again at Max. She beamed back at him. He gave her another long look before shaking his head again and continuing with the meeting.

NIKA: I don't know quite what's going on, but I'm going to get an earful about it from Stephan later, aren't I?

MAX: Maybe—and by maybe, I mean absolutely—but at least this way you can honestly say you don't know anything about it.

NIKA: *laughs* All right, troublemaker. Just fill me in later.

An hour later as the meeting wound down, with new orders about a missing caravan out in the desert south of Amanave, Doge came over and leaned against Max's leg. She reached down and patted him twice. "Hey, buddy."

"Things are changing again."

It wasn't a question and Max smiled down at him with another pat to his head before replying. "They always do. But right this moment, everything is good." She looked around the room at her friends and crew, everyone relaxed and joking, and nodded once to herself. She had her independence and the people she loved were safe. Finally Max felt like she owned her own life and whatever happened next was all hers.

It was an adventure she was looking forward to having.

ACKNOWLEDGMENTS

Given the state of the world right now and the relentless assault on the very lives of trans people, I debated a lot about making Yasu the partial villain in this story. Eventually I decided that we deserve to have complex characters as much as anyone else does, that we don't have to be paragons of virtue in order to justify our existence in this universe. We are here—good, bad, and everything in between. Trans lives matter and trans stories matter.

Big thanks to my editor, David Pomerico; my assistant editor, Mireya Chiriboga; and all the folx at Harper Voyager who made my weird little scribbles into this book you are now holding in your hands. I couldn't have done it without each one of you, and all of you deserve to be paid fairly for the hard, hard work you do.

Big thanks also to my agent, Andrew Zack, for all your support throughout the years. You're awesome, and I am truly grateful to have you on my side.

My eternal gratitude goes to my parents for providing me a place to stay, for meals, and for the space to get this book written at the end of 2021. It is not an exaggeration to say that I don't think it would have been written, nor turned out to be a book I am absolutely proud of, had you both not been there for me as you have always been.

To my partner, Blue, the last few years have been a challenge as we continue to navigate this space between us and our ever-changing lives. Thank you for being here for me and for your love. I love you, forever and always.

To all my siblings, friends, and fellow hyenas, life without you would be a cold and terrible place. Thank you all for your time, your presence in my life, and for everything about you that makes you uniquely brilliant. My life is better having you in it.

Special thanks to the following:

Megan E. O'Keefe for reading an early draft of this and providing extremely helpful feedback and praise on too many things to list here. Thank you so much for taking the time out of what I know is a busy schedule to help me.

Russ Rogers for your endlessly patient explanations about hacking, computer systems and security, and all my weird little questions. Sapphi was a challenge, but I think I did her justice because of your help.

Laury Silvers for all your help with portraying Emel's faith as accurately as possible (given we were working several hundred years in the future). Thank you for answering all my questions on Islam and your time spent reading through the scenes. I'm sad I couldn't work the rock joke in, but we'll hopefully get it in the next one!

I deeply appreciate all three of you spending your time and energy helping me with this project. Any mistakes or missteps are entirely mine.

Finally, to my readers, without you I am just shouting my stories into the wind. Thank you all for your love, your enthusiasm, and your support. It means so very much to me.

ABOUT THE AUTHOR

K. B. Wagers is the author of the NeoG Adventures from Harper Voyager and the Indranan and Farian War trilogies from Orbit Books. They are a fan of whiskey and cats, *Jupiter Ascending,* and the Muppets. You can find them on various social media sites by going to kbwagers.com, where they engage in political commentary, plant photos, and video game playthroughs.